was born in Whitby, Yorkshire, on 8 January 1891. Her forebears had lived in Whitby, then a small fishing and shipbuilding port, for uncounted generations: her grandfather was a shipowner, her father a sea-captain. She was educated at a private school, followed by one year at the Municipal School in Scarborough. Awarded one of the only three County Scholarships available in the North Riding of Yorkshire at that time, she took an honours degree in English Language and Literature at Leeds University in 1912 and was given a one-year research scholarship, to be held at University College, London: she found University College dull, and transferred herself to King's College. Her thesis, on Modern Drama in Europe, finally approved by Leeds University, was rewarded by the Degree of Master of Arts; it was published in 1920, by the firm of William Collins. In the meantime she had married and had a son.

In 1919 she returned to London, becoming for a year a copywriter in a large advertising agency. She published her first novel, and began a two-year editorship of an obscure weekly magazine, *New Commonwealth*. From 1923 to 1925 she acted as the English representative of the American publisher Alfred A. Knopf, and later, for two and a half years, was co-manager, with her second husband, Guy Patterson Chapman, of the short-lived publishing house of Alfred A. Knopf in London. She married Guy Chapman in 1925, a deeply happy marriage, broken in 1972 by his death, after a distinguished career beginning with the publication in 1933 of *A Passionate Prodigality*, his classic account of trench warfare in France, and ending in a study of the politics and history of the Third Republic of France.

Between the years of 1919 and 1979 Storm Jameson published a total of forty-five novels. She has also written short stories, literary essays, criticism, and a two-volume autobiography. In 1939 she became the first woman president of the British section of International PEN, where she was an outspoken liberal and anti-Nazi, and a friend and helper of refugee writers. In 1952 she was a delegate to the UNESCO Congress of the Arts, held in Venice. She was awarded a D.Litt. from Leeds University in 1943, and is a member of the American Academy and Institute of Arts and Letters. With her husband, she has been an inveterate traveller, mostly in Europe. She now lives in Cambridge.

STORM JAMESON

WOMEN
AGAINST MEN

**With a New Introduction by
ELAINE FEINSTEIN**

PENGUIN BOOKS — VIRAGO PRESS

PENGUIN BOOKS
Viking Penguin Inc., 40 West 23rd Street,
New York, New York 10010, U.S.A.
Penguin Books Ltd, Harmondsworth,
Middlesex, England
Penguin Books Australia Ltd, Ringwood,
Victoria, Australia
Penguin Books Canada Limited, 2801 John Street,
Markham, Ontario, Canada L3R 1B4
Penguin Books (N.Z.) Ltd, 182–190 Wairau Road,
Auckland 10, New Zealand

The Single Heart first published in Great Britain by Ernest Benn Ltd. 1932
A Day Off first published in Great Britain by Nicholson and Watson 1933
Delicate Monster first published in Great Britain by
Nicholson and Watson 1937
First collected edition published in Leipzig by Bernhard Tauchnitz 1933
First collected edition published in the United States of America under the
title *Women Against Men* by Alfred A. Knopf, Inc., 1933
This edition first published in Great Britain by Virago Press Limited 1982
Published in Penguin Books 1985

LIBRARY OF CONGRESS CATALOGING IN PUBLICATION DATA
Jameson, Storm, 1891–1972.
Women against men.
(Virago modern classics)
Contents: Delicate monster—The single heart— A day off.
I. Title.   II. Series: Virago modern classics (London, England)
PR6019.A67W6   1985   823'.912   85-12137
ISBN 0 14 016.121 X

Printed in the United States of America by
R. R. Donnelley & Sons Company, Harrisonburg, Virginia

CONTENTS

INTRODUCTION

Margaret Storm Jameson was born in Whitby in 1891 and spent her childhood in the North Riding of Yorkshire. By then Whitby was no longer a shipbuilding or whaling town, but it remained a harbour, looking out across the North Sea. And her mother was a restless spirit; the daughter of a one-time shipowner who was no longer rich, but still fastidious and bookish. Storm's father was a seaman, who had not yet been given his first captaincy when he married. He was a brave, obstinate man; but his wife baffled and tormented him. She had a passion for china, rugs and furniture and, even though she bargained for everything she bought, he was made anxious by her expectations. Initially, he must have hoped she would rescue him from his own clumsiness and ignorance, but she had neither the patience nor the gentle disposition for it.

Early in their marriage, when Storm was their only child, the family accompanied him on his shorter voyages, and Storm's mother travelled as far afield as Vera Cruz and Odessa. After that, there were long separations and all family decisions came to be made by Storm's mother.

It was a fortunate arrangement for the children, since their welfare was her passion; she was determined to ensure they had an education in order to enter the world she felt she had been denied. In spite of the frequent thrashing she meted out to them, all four were filled with an overwhelming desire to do something in the world to fulfil ambitions they sensed had been disappointed in their mother.

From both parents, Storm drew courage and tenacity. And she was to need both; although her career opened easily enough with a county scholarship and in due course led to Leeds University where she took a first-class degree. Her first and strongest ambition was to be a don. When I met her for the first time in Cambridge in 1981, some sixty years later, she continued to insist that she had no comparable respect for the work of a novelist and had "only written novels for money because writing was the simplest way to earn money when you have a young child keeping you at home."

In the event, an altogether characteristic fecklessness put paid to her chances of a safe academic job. Awarded a research scholarship in University College to work under W. P. Ker, she chose instead to attach herself to King's College, London, and changed her research subject to a thesis on modern European drama without consulting the university authorities. It was not a shrewd move, but it did open the door into European literature; and in later years, her sensitive understanding of European tensions made her one of the most intelligently European novelists of the period *entre deux guerres*.

Storm Jameson's first successful work came, as so often, from the painful emotions of her own life. Of these, perhaps the most characteristic is that of guilt. In her autobiography *Journey from the North* she speaks of the five or six memories which still have the power to tear at her over the years and which are her idea of hell. All involve breaches of loyalty and failures of love.

When her brother was killed, after a short, distinguished career as a pilot, Storm Jameson learnt that for her, at least, what most women mean by love was a paltry emotion compared to the ties of the blood.

He had always been much less fortunate than herself. Not gifted at school, he had decided, against all his mother's opposition, to apprentice himself first to a Prince's Line ship and then on his father's. From that voyage the boy returned in a state of nervous collapse, and Storm Jameson was always to recall the cold implacable tones of her mother's voice pronouncing, "I don't know what his father did. But this finishes him with me."

After her brother's death Storm watched her mother's life seem to shrivel away. Storm had already disappointed her by making a disastrous marriage to a young man with little sense and a disparaging tongue. When war came, he found a safe job in England and a style of life that suited him; and for a time Storm, who by then had a son she loved deeply, returned to live in Whitby with her mother. She had finished her first "gloriously bad" novel in 1916, but what she needed was a job. When an offer came, however, to take a position on *The Egoist*, Storm rejected it because she could not bear to see her mother's loneliness. (The job went to Rebecca West.) It was a characteristically quixotic gesture, all the more foolish since Storm had soon enough to leave for London anyway to take a job in an advertising agency. It was for that necessary and altogether unglamorous job that Storm made the decision to leave her son behind in the care of a stranger. The pain of that separation was among the bitterest of all her memories.

It was not until some years after her first marriage had broken down, and she had begun to make forays into the English literary world as a talent spotter for Knopf, that Storm met Guy Chapman. At that time, he was working in publishing (he came from the publishing family that had published Dickens). Storm was not yet free and Guy was still psychologically cumbered by the treachery of his first wife. Yet their relationship was to be a source of enduring happiness to them both. Guy had a mind of great distinction. His own novel, *A Passionate Prodigality*, is one of the finest to come out of the First World War. When he became an academic historian he chose every word he wrote with severe honesty. Storm herself claimed that the plain style of her later work (so much a quality of *Women Against Men*) was learnt from Guy's criticism.

Always the least domestic of women, Storm Jameson rejoiced in sharing with Guy her own delight in travel. "My writing brain is at its easiest and most energetic abroad, or when I live in an hotel . . . My notion of perfect happiness as a writer is a foreign hotel of a decent, simple bourgeois sort—a wooden table in a window looking out at the sea, a garden, roof-tops, any expanse you like, coffee and croissants in bed, the morning and afternoon spent writing, the rest of the day sauntering, sitting in cafés, hearing music, seeing friends, reading, staring, making a few notes, while the next day's work ripens peacefully in the mind behind my eyes."

To achieve this happiness, she was, for all that "dour non-conformist" conscience she had inherited from her mother, often improvident and probably wrote more books than she should to pay for it.

But at the same time she learnt much about the tensions of post-war Europe. With Guy she cemented the deep love she felt for the simple peasant values of country France: good bread, coffee, peace and quiet. She was less drawn to Germany, though her compassion readily extended to the sufferings of its people after the war and she had no patience with those of her countrymen who cried out for revenge. Many of her best books came to be written from a deepening comprehension of the nightmare which was developing in Europe through the thirties. Among them, *Cousin Honoré*, draws a portrait of the province of Alsace as a microcosm of the forces undermining European civilisation as a whole.

Another late work of some prescience is *Europe to Let*; it is easy to see why Storm Jameson was to be such a gallant and humane President of the British section of Internation PEN. She loved and understood central Europe as few English writers have done; and she threw all her heart and energy into the struggle to help refugees, first from Nazi Germany, and then, after the war, to those who needed to find a place in the West after defecting from the Soviet Empire.

The three novellas which make up *Women Against Men* have a bitter clarity, which draws her close to the elegance of French writing at its coolest. The bleak vision of all three stories matches the dry manner in which they are written.

The first story contrasts two very different literary women, one a clever, awkward child, who finds social occasions an ordeal; the other an ebullient and promiscuous beauty, whose novels gush from her only too easily. The author is gentle to neither; we are never in any doubt that the straitlaced and less successful writer has a more fastidious regard for truth, but her rival wins a certain respect for the shrewdness and impudence that has carried her to success from an unpromising start in a dressmaker's family. The real contempt in this tale is reserved for members of the literary world who are afraid to say what they like in case it should turn out not to be to their advantage.

The purest and most chilling of these tales, *The Single Heart*, records how even the advantages of money and class are no defence against sexual need. Disappointed in her own marriage, Emily Lambton falls in love with an ill-paid clerk and determines to use all her worldly knowledge to launch him into the political career he desires. She can take the initiative, confident in her quick practical mind; and without concern for husband. In a characteristically cool sentence, Storm Jameson explains, 'Emily imagined that she was being too subtle for him.' But the cheated husband is one of the gentlest figures in the book, and Emily depends on him more than she knows. Emily's fine mind serves her lover well. No one has written more drily about sexual jealousy as an animal pain than Storm Jameson in this short book which charts the gradual death of the heart of women who have to learn to condone more than can be endured.

The last novella, *A Day Off*, Storm Jameson is surely right to call the "most imaginative" of her work. It involved her entering the mind of a kept woman, in middle age and without resources, who fears she is about to be abandoned. Storm Jameson calls up the stale scents and fading wallpaper of her room, and makes us share the anticipated joys of grilled food and cheap cups of tea. For all her varicose veins and sagging skin, the woman faces the world with a certain swagger. In the course of the day the surface of her life is ruthlessly split open, as Storm Jameson might have emptied clothes from a drawer. We gradually discover within her the sly, coarse millgirl she had once been and the shopgirl with sore feet, and understand how her life has been ravaged by war and its aftermath in England. Storm Jameson does not extenuate her (she must be the most casually cruel and uncomprehending of all the women in this sequence) but she does observe the one quality that she shares with the others. She faces her insecurities with courage.

Storm Jameson comes of that generation which had to confront in its own flesh the full mystery of human cruelty and human indifference.

"What I do not know and cannot even hope to understand before I die is why human beings are wilfully, coldly, matter-of-factly, cruel to each other . . . What nerve has atrophied in the torturer, or worse is sensually moved?"

Storm Jameson has always been a free-thinker both by temperament and conviction, yet she has nothing but scorn for those who have lost faith in humanist values, whatever scepticism she may have about humankind's right to the planet.

All her life, Storm knew herself tugged between contrary impulses. She joined no party, though she was anti-fascist to the core.

Remembering the human butchery of a whole generation in the First World War she was drawn to pacifism; it did not prevent her being among the first to perceive that no peace could be made with the evil of Nazism. Yorkshire to the bone, she "never felt separated from an exile by more than a thin membrane". All these contradictions made for a very special human resilience. At ninety-one, last week in Cambridge, admitting all the doubts she felt about the possible efficacy of any political protest, her blue eyes opened serenely to insist, "But of course you must *try*. You must fight."

Elaine Feinstein, Cambridge, 1982

DELICATE MONSTER

"A most delicate monster! His forward voice now is to speak well of his friend; his backward voice is to utter foul speeches, and to detract."

DELICATE MONSTER

MY MOTHER was a proud, angry woman, who had married a man less than herself in birth and intellect. Fortunately—since they never passed a day together without a quarrel, often of an insane bitterness—he was scarcely at home five weeks in the year. During his absence my mother ruled the house and me, her child, with a heavy hand. I think she loved me—but she was determined that I should grow up like herself and not like my father and his relations, and every childish fault became in her eyes a crime against decency. If I ran on Sunday, or scraped the toe of my boots on a stone, I was thrashed most unmercifully. When I knew that I was to be thrashed I would shut myself in the little earth closet at the end of our yard and stay there as long as a quarter of an hour, though I knew that my mother's anger grew by being kept. The walls were lime-washed and a little light came through a crack in the door. When she was happy we went on very well, I anxious to please her and she laughing and merry. The truth is—though I was too young then to understand it—her narrow, dull life fretted her past patience. She had in her what would have made her a fortune if she had been a man and her life was a long disappointment to her.

I was a clever, awkward child. I read all I found, but I had no natural taste and a four-and-sixpenny novel from the subscription library was as real to me as *Vanity Fair*. Early in my life I had taken up my stick to be rich and famous. I had no notion how to set about it and I thought I should be nothing unless I got myself to a university.

My mother had no friends, but she had an ally. You could be certain that if there were another woman in the town whose wits made her uncomfortable in her place my mother would take to her—and all the more readily if that woman were below the class into which my mother's marriage had forced her. There was a dressmaker called Mrs. Form who went from house to house sewing by the day. She and my mother were excellent friends. They had the same sharp ways of speech, the same natural cynicism, and even the same laugh. When I heard that loud jeering sound in the sewing-room I could never tell which of them had made it. Unless I were in the room and they were laughing at me. This happened.

Mrs. Form had a daughter, a year older than my mother's. At fourteen Victoria Form had everything that has since made her a reputation. She was as clever as I was and a beauty as well. Even then, she knew how to make the most of herself. She was small and well-made, her hair neat and silky, her skin white, her eyes large and brilliant, her mouth very red. She wore her clothes with an air, whereas I—who with careful dressing might have passed for a beauty—could not tie a hair-ribbon, my dresses were always too long and wide (to allow for growing), my hair hung in a lank bundle over my ears, and I hurled myself about, knocking into things as though my body did not belong to me.

I suppose I was more like my mother than I knew. Other girls did not like me at sight and since they were not asked to our house I had no chance of knowing them better. I was out of everything with them. So, because her mother went out by the day, was Victoria—but she was indifferent. There were always boys eager to know her. She would be at the street corner with three or four boys when I passed with my mother. I smiled at her consciously, and my mother would say drily, "That poor, silly girl." In the season she made friends among the town bandsmen, and could be seen walking along the old pier, between first and second violins, their voices carried away by the wind. In the winter the dancing-class started. I ran all the way, my ears tingling from the cold water, slippers and white silk gloves in a bag over my arm. Victoria and I sat together between the windows. We were friends. I was a little ashamed of her and she, I daresay, thought me simple. I disliked the classes. I was a bad, stiff dancer, and I would have given all my brains to be admired by boys. At the words, "Take your partners for a waltz," three or four of the older boys scurried to Victoria. She chose among them with great coolness, and of the others one perhaps would decline on me. More often, all rushed away and I was left sitting with that look of bright amusement stiffened to my face, my hands wet under my gloves—until a neglected girl asked me to stand up with her or the dancing mistress drew me to a swift competent turn of the draughty room. Between the dances little notes were passed to Victoria. "Walk home with me, Robert." "Don't forget Saturday. L. Collings." I hurried into my things, to be out of the house before any of the groups who would forget to cry, "Walk home with us." Before I slept I consoled myself with an interminable romance, in which two of the best-looking boys in the class disputed for my love. They quarrelled, wept, implored, I kept both on the hooks, and one I admitted to vague passionate intimacy. Do not suppose that the dreams of a girl of thirteen are pure. Mine were often impure and disgusting, though I was as ignorant as a stone and so remained. I had an imagination—which having nothing to go on was foolish, romantic, and indecent on nothing. I suppose Victoria was better informed, but she did not offer to tell me. One day we were "hearing" each other our scripture (one held the Bible while the other gabbled the passage learned) when I asked idly, "What does it mean when it says: 'And he went in unto her'?" Victoria gave me a clear, smiling look. "It means he—her. Do you know what that is?" "No," I said. "Then I certainly shall not tell you." Perhaps she waited for questions, but I—from some shame—held my tongue.

A girl told me that her brother had a photograph of Victoria naked. "She undresses to let them look at her," the girl whispered. So that, I said to myself, is "—", and before I fell asleep that night I went over a scene in which I granted one of my lovers to come in unto me and then, because he wept and fussed, the other.

To make Victoria respect me I told her that I was

writing a satirical story about the dancing-class. This was a lie. I had never written anything except the essays I wrote at school. Even these were marked lower than Victoria's, who lifted hers skilfully from books. I, on the other hand, was early infected by the modern disease. Nothing seemed worth saying. I would squeeze out a dozen cold lines on "A country Walk" or "Trees". While I scratched over my mind for others Victoria was adapting a passage from Charles Lamb or Hardy. It never occurred to me to look directly at a tree and try to describe that. I was convinced that the description existed already in my mind if I could drag it out. The more I read the drier I felt. I had the impulse of a Pope to flay those persons who without a tithe of my intelligence could dance, chatter, tie a hair-ribbon, and make themselves admired. I lived through scenes in which they cringed from my brutal wit. Alas, I was as witty as a post and brutal only in wish.

Victoria was not surprised to hear that I wrote. She had written poems and stories which I read with despair. I did not dare to admit to myself that she had the greater genius, but the fact was that she wrote and I pretended. The exquisite changes of light over the sea drove me wild with happiness. When I wanted to write about it the happiness vanished. Victoria wrote pages of description while I found six words and those inaccurate.

Although I was ashamed of being Victoria's friend I liked her. I disliked and envied her as much. I envied her fluency, her success with boys, and her fine, fair complexion, which she had just begun to powder. My own was rosy and transparent, and the least excitement or fatigue spoiled it—an inflamed spot broke out on my chin: to hide it I kept my head down, not even lifting it to speak. No one could be certain whether I was stupid or rude. I disliked Victoria's private manners, which were, to find a polite word, primitive. I liked her spirit. She received snubs with a cold smile and repaid a spiteful remark with interest. She was almost as much feared as disapproved of. When a girl spoke, so that she should hear, of "a down-at-heels dressmaker" she called out: "If your mother paid her bills mine could afford to buy boots." More than once she retorted sharply for me when I was attacked. She was more loyal than I was. When she was out of the way I would join the others in abusing her, glad to feel myself for once on the covert side of opinion. I don't think she knew.

Mrs. Form was a remarkable woman. Her husband was—had been, he was dead—a drunken journalist, ten years younger than herself. In later years Victoria spoke of "my clever father". Nevertheless, it was from her mother that she inherited her wit, courage and vitality. Mrs. Form's position in the town was one of absolute authority. She told her clients what they must wear and refused to make them anything else. A lady who brought her a length of crimson satin to make into a dress was told to use it for curtains. Another, who fancied herself still young, left Mrs. Form's—she lived in two rooms in the old part of the town, and to visit her you groped through a pitch-black yard called "Dark Entry Alley" and climbed fifty steps—in tears, with a roll of yellow muslin under her arm. My mother was the only person who gave her orders. On one occasion she had a green cloth coat made to a design of her own. Mrs. Form disliked it from the start but as always she obeyed my mother exactly. The coat was no sooner finished than my mother's eyes opened to the fact that it was ridiculous. She needed only breeches to become Robin Hood in a pantomime. She was the first to laugh. Then those two extraordinary women laughed until tears poured down their cheeks at the figure my mother cut in her new coat. Mrs. Form did not say: "I warned you." She offered to re-make the coat without charge. My mother refused.

Mrs. Form had, I feel sure, no idea that her daughter was "fast". There was an open antagonism between the two. Mrs. Form's most malicious remarks were directed at her daughter, who received them with a calm face. Deeper than her antagonism was Mrs. Form's almost mad pride in that daughter, whose genius seemed to her proved when Victoria had a poem printed in the local paper. After that event she would have supported Victoria in any project for bettering herself. She even spoke of sending her for a year to an expensive school, but Victoria had other, sounder plans.

Mrs. Form read into her daughter all her own virtues, but in fact Victoria had not inherited a trace of the scepticism which decided Mrs. Form's character. Mrs. Form saw every person, including herself, with the least possible illusion. It was not many years after this when she realised that her daughter had been born without modesty, but it was then too late to try to thrash it into her—as she would certainly have done if Victoria had not managed to deceive her for so long. This was the only thing she did not know about Victoria. She knew that in addition to being strong, healthy, intelligent, hard-working, and a genius, Victoria was incredibly conceited. It was against this conceit—in which she recognised her husband—that she sent her malice. It had no effect. Victoria's belief in herself was proof against any blow. Nothing touched it. Nothing can. In any circumstances Victoria sees herself as a romantic figure. She is, (you may say) fortunately, incapable of self-criticism. She writes in the full persuasion that she is a great genius. When she has a love-affair she takes care that the details shall be known to as many persons as possible, so that posterity can have no excuse for a mistake. When she reads a severe notice of her work she puts it down to envy. She does not understand that an envious critic may be telling the truth, since envy, hatred, and malice are among the motives that prompt critics to be honest.

Victoria often told me what she meant to do. I kept my plans a secret. When at last I told her, with a hypocritical smile, that I was going up to the university, she said: "What a waste of time!"

"What do you mean?"

Victoria looked at me coolly. "Tell me, Fanny. What do you mean to do with yourself?"

"I want to earn money," I answered.

"And you are going to a university! Now, if you had the sense to learn shorthand you could be earning in six months."

I kept to myself the feeling of superiority which filled me when I thought of my future and contrasted it with Victoria's. We travelled to London together, I to stay with my aunt and attend lectures at University College, she to spend nine months at what they call a commercial college. She lived in shabby rooms in Highgate and we met two or three times in the week. I had expected that our changed lives would mean the end of our friendship and perhaps I was not too sorry. But I found myself so much fonder of Victoria that I thought that an evening when she put me off was wasted. We had very little money to spend. We walked together about London and ventured into cheap cafés only when we were too exhausted to walk another step. Victoria, of course, had made other friends. One of these, a journalist, a man nearly middle-aged, had already taken her to bed. This was the phrase she used in telling me about it. She said it was the first time she had allowed this to happen and that she had enjoyed it. "I suppose you're still a virgin, Fanny. I was, until yesterday. Now I'm not and I'm very glad I'm not."

My ignorance was still too firm for me to know *precisely* what she meant. But I knew in effect—and added one more scene to the romance with which I filled idle moments and put myself to sleep at night. I daresay I gave as much time, emotion, and mental energy to these foolish and sensual day-dreams as Victoria to the novel she was writing, and the caresses I made my imaginary lover give me lacked only a detail to be complete, and made me weak with pleasure. The obsession I am describing will seem to some persons evidence of a coarse or unhealthy mind. Clever women who despise me will find in it an explanation of all they dislike in my books and my ideas—which certainly might have been expressed with more honesty. I am very timid, and mortally afraid of ridicule. For years I have never written a book in which characters, plot, and emotions were not purely imaginary and—what is not the same thing—unreal. All these years I have been telling lies not simply in order to get myself a reputation as a writer, but because it did not occur to me to tell the truth. That is to say, what

I wrote stopped where real truth and real honesty begin. Now that I am past the age when—with the exception of vain or pious or stupid persons—love is the constant pre-occupation of at least a half of every person's mind, when I no longer *imagine* what has ceased to be necessary to me, I shall perhaps begin to say what I think.

If I had had no imagination, and if I had not been in-telligent (as well as ignorant), I should not have fallen into the habit of dreaming about love. It is a habit which has all the effects of a drug. An early love-affair might have cured me of it. But I was not simple enough to let myself be seduced, from sensual curiosity, by a journalist of thirty-five. I should have had to be brought to the neces-sary emotional state by a long romantic courtship, and to have believed that I was passionately in love. Why? Is it simply that I lack courage? Let us admit that I had not the courage to be *natural*. But in order to be natural in this respect, I should have had to do violence to all the other sides of my nature.

A straitlaced or a fastidious woman always attaches a profound importance to the merely physical acts of love.

When Victoria wanted to take me to meet her friends I refused. I was afraid of becoming involved with persons and in a situation which I was forced to distrust.

I know very well why I like Victoria, and why, in spite of my contempt for her novels and the quarrel between us, which lasted for nearly ten years, I care for her more than for any other woman. She has a lively vulgar mind, which never fails to amuse me. What is important, she is the only person who liked me when I was young. After thirty, the friendships we make may be pleasant but they do not penetrate below the surface of our affections. No doubt I should suffer a little if Victoria died.

I still envy her, without in the least wishing to lead a similar life. She is everything I dislike—as well as every-thing I have not had the courage to be. I daresay there is a trollop in most women. I have never understood why clever women indignantly deny this—unless from an unconscious dishonesty. Only a very good, a very tired, or a very stupid woman can be believed when she says that she has never, never for a moment, imagined herself behaving like a loose (which is not the same thing as a passionate) woman. Victoria behaves as she does because she enjoys it—and because she believes that the only way to live a full life (I apologise for the stupid phrase, which is the technically correct one for the period) is to have as many love-affairs as possible and to yield to the most casual impulse rather than run the risk of being taken for a puritan.

This philosophy—which was coming into repute in 1910— might have been made for her. She listened carefully when the artist and his friends explained to her what she had already suspected, that to take a man into your bed is highly natural. They went on to say that to refrain is weakminded and nasty. Victoria was delighted to find that what she enjoyed doing was better than pleasant.

I do not object on moral grounds to this philosophy. Any system of thought which satisfies the minds of its disciples seems to me as good as any other, provided it does not lead to persecutions. What I dislike is the move to make a new religion of it. Victoria enjoys as many men as she can. Instead of accepting that she is one of the women to whom this form of pleasure is necessary, she wants to persuade us that no other life has value. Health, happiness, civilisation itself, depend on all able-bodied persons leading "full" or as it may be, "dark and sacral" lives. Nothing less, I assure you—and you may see that I am annoyed by the notion that my life is less full than Victoria's merely because I do not enjoy a blood awareness of the stable-boy.

It is a reformed phallic worship, with a different emblem and grace to Dr. Stopes. The ancient form, being strictly the worship of *fertility*, and the pleasure incidental, was both terrible and jolly—but what is there terrible or jolly about a lady novelist having a blood awareness of—say—a stockbroker?

Victoria regarded each new love affair as a fresh proof of her genius, to be exposed, with whatever else her lively imagination suggested, in the novel that followed it. She absorbed all the "startling" theories of love, sex, education, and what not, and used them to weight her books. There is a moment in the history of any new theory when it is just about to be assimilated to the collective knowledge of the race but is still—though only by a year—"advanced" beyond it. It is this moment when the so-called intellectual novelist finds it useful. Without falling into the mistake of mentioning a theory still too new or too hard for his readers to find themselves at home with it, he can give his novel a kind of glaze of culture which flatters them. This is a recipe for one type of popular novel, the popular-intellectual novel.

The extreme crudeness of Victoria's writing opens it to an even wider public than the one which understands Freud without having read him.

Victoria's first novel (and the third she wrote) was published when I had just left the university. A year later she met James Macgregor and married him in a month. This was in 1910.

She and I were together at a supper-party given by her publisher. Scarcely a soul spoke to us. We stood close to a table covered with dishes of sandwiches and Victoria pretended to be smiling as she made the grossest comments on the company. She was less hardened than I to seeming no one in particular. One man knocked her elbow and apologised, without ceasing to cram food into his mouth. He spoke like a Scotsman. I glanced at him. He had a shrewd conceited face and little black eyes, twinkling with health and good-humour. At this moment they were staring at a dish of tiny sausages just beyond his reach. "Will you have these?" I said, seizing the dish.

"I don't mind if I do." He gave us a condescending smile. "I'm Macgregor. I'm an art-critic."

"Really?" I said. "How interesting. I suppose you—ah—

attend the banquets at the Royal Academy and write them up afterwards."

He looked at me sharply. "I suppose you're another of these female novelists," he grumbled, "or you wouldn't be here. I'll tell you something I haven't told many people yet. I'm writing a novel now that will open a few eyes. It's pure Fielding and I'm the only man who can do it."

"I'm sure you can," Victoria said. I had noticed that in speaking to a man whom she wished to attract she kept her eyes on his face the whole time as she talked. This—which I am sure would irritate me—pleases all but a few men who find Victoria stupid or nasty.

"I *can*," Macgregor said, jerking his hand down flat on the table. A much younger man now came up to speak to him and gazed at Victoria. Macgregor pulled him by the sleeve. "This is Rodney Whimple. He tells me he's going to write a novel. I shouldn't wonder if he does, too."

Mr. Whimple was very young indeed, with wide-open dewy eyes. He was wearing a light suit and a waistcoat that buttoned up to his neck. He spoke on a high note, pleasantly tuned, like an extremely refined flute. The instant Macgregor pointed to him he sprang forward and held out his hand. The other was laid at his slender waist.

"I'm not really here at all," he said, in a confiding voice. "I *ought* to be in Oxford. But I felt I simply must see London before beginning my novel. *Do* say you agree. I should be *so* encouraged."

It would have been cruel not to oblige him. He repaid us with a bright glance. "I feel I must learn about life. Shall I read biographies? Or travel? *How* can I learn?"

He was forced to address these remarks to me, since Victoria had turned her back on us and was engaged in fascinating Mr. Macgregor. I suppose he concluded I was no use to him in his researches. He was *so* obliged to me for listening, and *so* encouraged, and he would without fail send me a copy of his novel, and off he went, leaving me alone. I sat in my corner for close on two hours. At the end of that time I found myself very ready to promise not to attend another literary party, except at my own charges. Mr. Macgregor was now so far gone with Victoria that he followed her across the room, stooping his great body in a suppliant attitude when she had the kindness to remember me. At this precise moment Mr. Whimple broke out into a sound like the screaming of a nervous young horse. Someone had been civil enough to make him a remark which he took for wit. He went on laughing, doubled up, until everyone in the room was looking at him with ashamed smiles. In France, south of Bordeaux, the smiles would have been friendly.

"You'd better take your thin friend away."

"I think I had," Macgregor said. "Here, young Whimple, come on, and stop laughing."

"Oh, I can't, I can't, really," Whimple gasped. Tears ran down his cheeks. He wiped them away with his wrists, still quivering. Macgregor stood beside him, quite unmoved, except for a faint twinkling *northern* sneer in the corners of his eyes. The paroxysms grew weaker and ceased, and Macgregor nodded to Victoria and went off, driving the boy in front of him. Whimple waved his hand to us. "Good-bye. *So* nice."

"I'll look," I said generously, "for your novel."

"*So* sweet of you," he cried. "I'll begin it at once."

"Do." We watched him go, with Macgregor louring behind. "Rodney Whimple, the dewy-eyed," I said.

Victoria did not answer. I think she was almost certain of Macgregor. But too much hung on it—the change for her from the office where she earned two pounds fifteen a week to be the wife of a safe five hundred a year with connections in literature—she was in a fever of anxiety. However, in a day or two she was out of her misery. Macgregor proposed to her—she told me afterwards that he said: "Well, I think we should do very well together." He was the colour of lard—and she thought he would have said more if he had not been afraid of breaking down. She gave notice at the office, wrote to her mother for a wedding-dress, and in three weeks they were married.

Macgregor was quite right about his *pure-Fielding*. It came out a year after this and sold eighty thousand copies in England and America.

Victoria's baby was given the name of the heroine—Camilla—and when I went to call on her I found a photographer in the room and Victoria as pretty and languid as you could want. When he had gone she asked me for a glass and was admiring her expression so that I saw she would use it again. She told me that she had never meant to have a child but now it was come she liked it better than James. "Poor Camilla," I thought. Then she asked me what I thought of James's book. I had not the courage to say I had found it dull.

No novelist was ever read by a million persons without having some merits. The merits of James Macgregor's novels are all obvious—bustle, colour, and that peculiar *commonness* which makes a reader exclaim: "Why, that's just like your John," or "My Aunt Clarkson to the life." To a reader like myself, who would run a mile rather than be jolly in company, such books are intolerable.

But Mr. Macgregor would be very ill-advised to write to please me. I do not read above three new novels a year and those on no better grounds than liking the style of their authors. Mr. Macgregor wisely lets his style take care of itself—which it is well able to do, being a robust, candid, no-nonsense sort of writing, very suited to a book that is to go much into company.

I see that I am showing a prejudice. The truth is I dislike extremely your *healthy* school of novel-writing. I like a novel to be sharp and bitter, or else so artificial that the manner is everything and the matter nothing. Mr. Macgregor's novels tire me by their excessive self-assurance. Surely, if this writer has a mind he must sometimes be uneasy in it?

My mind is too far past the age when it could be pleased with a sort of circus novels. I learn nothing from Mr. Macgregor's. They say out all they know, and that is no more than I knew before of myself. In all their mountain of words there is not one grain of pure gold, not one gleam of the peculiar *excitement* of literature.

There is a kind of young gentleman critic that talks about the "pure art" of the novel. I scarcely believe that the novel is an art at all. Certainly it is the most impure of the arts, and every rule that can be laid down for it may be broken by a master without shocking anyone but the foolish young schoolmen. Jane Austen and Stendhal are the only "pure" novelists worth reading. Stendhal I take to be *the* novelist, but I am not on his account shocked by the impurities of Fielding, Thackeray, and Proust. If Mr. Macgregor were really a new Fielding I should be delighted with him.

My first novel came out a week after *Camilla*—and was never heard of again.

James Macgregor is a very vain man. He inflicts the meanest punishments on persons who have hurt his vanity. He is mistrustful, grasping, and shrewd. But when Victoria left him, he forced himself to give up to her their year-old daughter. I doubt whether Victoria gave him enough credit for this triumph over his jealousy.

She left the house one evening and the next day gave a luncheon party to her friends. I could not help thinking, as I looked at her, that she deserved her success. She had started with nothing but her brains and a charming face and body. Thanks to Macgregor's money and her own wits she was now nearly as well known as he was. Her third novel to be published had sold forty thousand copies.

She had never felt the slightest doubt of her genius.

To tell the truth she has less genius than I, who have had one moment of genius in ten years. She has enormous vitality (Question: was her father really a Jew?), and a fluency that nothing can check. Words pour from her. Her emotions are always at white heat. She has no critical faculty and so is never in pain for the honesty of her writing. She is governed by her *enthusiasms*. The violent emotions she describes are only those she believes herself to have felt. She over-dramatises them without noticing it. Thus she would be startled if the nearness of an attractive man roused no emotion in her. With all this, she is never ashamed. She is shrewd, observant, with something of her mother's tart spirit in describing a roomful of fools.

This year she was twenty-four. She had saved a thousand pounds. There is nothing mercenary in Victoria's nature. Having been poor she knows the value of money but I am sure she never gave a thought to James's as soon as she saw she would earn two thousand a year without him.

Strangely enough, she had no reason for leaving him when she did, better than dislike of his person. Of course they quarrelled a great deal after she became known. That was less her fault than his. He disliked the rival and positively hated the independent woman. His notion of a wife was a good, pretty creature that enjoyed having children and looked up to her husband as the giver of good things. Angered and helpless, he saw Victoria becoming every week less dependent on him. His vanity suffered a great deal at this time. Once he caught hold of my arm as I was leaving their house and said roughly: "What d'you think of Victoria now?"

"Think of her?" I did not understand him.

"I suppose all you women think her a great writer?"

"Don't you?" I asked. I never liked him.

He made sly fun of Victoria's novels in her hearing. I don't think she minded much. No doubt she knew very well that he was hurt below his vanity, deep as it goes in him. At the same time she was not past making capital out of his spite. More than one of her friends who could have seen better for themselves went about saying that Macgregor was an impossible boor at home, not fit to be with a sensitive woman.

In the end she left him, after a quarrel she had brought on herself without knowing where it would lead. He refused her the divorce she wanted, but when he saw that she was not, whatever happened, coming back, he gave in. He was not one to overreach himself in anything. She did not marry again then. She bought and furnished a small house in Chelsea, and had it photographed for the press. Camilla had a nursery on the first floor, and a trained nurse, who had complete charge of her. Victoria had formed the habit of hard work and she wrote every day for five or six hours. Her fluency increased. Towards the end of the War she was earning five thousand a year and that by eight months' work. She was never without a lover. By saying every spiteful or coarse thing that came into her head she had got herself a reputation for wit. Nothing is easier than to be thought a wit among writers, since they are always afraid to talk freely for fear of dropping something that might be useful to them.

Victoria really believed in her philosophy. She believed that her love-affairs helped to make her a great writer. In the same way she believed that to be happy a woman must be constantly in love. (She used a grosser phrase.) One evening after a dance she was struck by the good looks of a young man selling papers. She invited him to spend the night with her, and told the story afterwards with half-concealed pride, seeing herself in it as a passionate woman or as a great lady indulging a whim.

She was determined to bring Camilla up in what she called "a free, natural manner". She talked coarsely in front of her and encouraged the little girl to use the homeliest words for the functions of her body. I don't know why she thought this would help Camilla to be free. It was occasionally embarrassing. When Camilla was almost three Victoria engaged a governess, who had the strictest orders not to put notions of religion or modesty into the child's head. Later she went away to one of those schools where they have a grand notion of respecting the child mind. In my childhood we were taught a great many facts which we accepted or rejected as we chose. Behind them our imaginations went free and secure. Now no child's imagination is safe from the prying minds of teachers with a little Freud and too much arrogance. I think we were the better taught.

I don't know how Camilla came on at school but I suppose she conformed, at least enough. There was never any trouble.

She was small and stolid, with jet black eyes under large black lashes that gave her an air of foreignness. Victoria promised herself delicious moments of intimacy in the future, when Camilla would confide her affairs to her mother. "I shall advise her to do exactly as she feels. If she wants to live with the man I shall give her my blessing...." Dramatising herself as a mother now, she envied Camilla the happiness of having in her a friend to whom *everything* could be told, and who would advise "sanely and cheerfully" in matters that less fortunate girls spend their days concealing. She gave out, and in time began to believe, a quite untruthful account of Mrs. Form. "My mother, being a respectable woman, had a mind full of the foulest suspicions. She would have made me as nasty-minded as herself if I had not got away young. Camilla, now...."

I think there was even a kind of anxiety in her mind not to seem jealous of Camilla. She had too much imagination not to foresee her eclipse. In those days, when she was old, there was still a part she could fill—of a Mme. du Deffand not blind and not jealous of her Julie de Lespinasse. She would sometimes look in the glass at her fine, brilliant eyes, and try to see them in an old face. During one of these moments she turned to me and said suddenly: "I often wish I could see myself waking up in the morning. I must look perfectly lovely." After a pause: "Camilla will never be a beauty, but she is very attractive. I can see my mother trying to marry her to the first man who offers."

"Camilla may want to marry him."

"My dear girl, what happens is this. At the age of fifteen you fall in love with the local draper and walk past his shop four or five times every day. In a month or so you see him out walking with his wife, both of them in their Sunday best, and for the first time you notice that he has a stomach and turns his feet in. Thereafter you loathe him—and begin to idealise a stupid lout of your own age. You read a great deal of bad poetry, underlining the passages that might have been written for your case. At eighteen you fall in love with a young clerk and go through all the stages of emotion until you reach the one where you suffer agonies in saying Good-night. No one explains to you what is the matter with you. You finish by marrying him, and settling down to a life of incredible boredom. When your daughter grows up you revenge your disappointment on her by teaching her to be ashamed of her body so that she will make the same bad bargain. The truth is that if you could have had the clerk without a license you would have discovered that he was a tiresome fellow, not worth a week. Camilla will have the advantage of you. She'll know, when she comes to it, what is the matter with her—and how to put it right. When she has made her trials she'll be fit to marry. And she won't plague her husband, if you know what I mean." She looked in the glass again. "I ought to have lived in the eighteenth century," she said in a pleased voice.

"You don't," I said as drily as I could, "write as plain as you talk. In your novels the young woman would have a blood awareness and a dozen other complications not in the least eighteenth-century."

"My novels sell and yours don't," Victoria answered pleasantly.

At this time Camilla was turned seven. I felt sorry for her—she could easily make some frightful blunder. I think I had a half-formed notion that I could help. Then I thought that perhaps Victoria was right. My own strict upbringing had nothing to commend it in the result. We shall see, I thought, what sort of human being this new "natural" education throws up.

She was very self-possessed for so young a child. She was always listening when you looked at her. Now and then I took her for walks and except when she called me a bloody fool we went on very well. She was surprisingly well-informed. At that age I was tongue-tied and knew nothing.

I saw Victoria three or four times a week for twelve years, the time after we came to London together until a day in 1919. I suppose we know each other as well as old friends can, having become friends before we were of an age to understand the need for caution. If you confide everything in your friend you will never have a moment's safety. At this moment, an impulse of which you know nothing may have loosened his tongue about your affairs. Since he knows everything about you he is infinitely more dangerous than an enemy. No other creature will ever do you such frightful harm as your friend can—and perhaps will. There is honour among thieves and politicians, but can there really be any among friends? Our sense of honour comes into play as soon as we feel ourselves in danger of appearing ridiculous, or mean, in the eyes of others—but those "others" do not include our friends, whom we expect to forgive us for being mean and ridiculous. "I knew you wouldn't mind" is the formula with which my friends begin the confession that they have made use of me in some indefensible way, or written a brutal criticism of my new novel. (The last "confession" is only made when the review has in any case to be signed.)

Victoria is the only person to whom I say what is in my mind. To others I try to seem what they are certain to like. I have a sharp tongue and the disgusting mind of a cynic, but I keep them to myself. Most people find me good-natured and sympathetic, though not especially intelligent. My friend Victoria knows better. She knows that I am envious, lazy, jealous, romantic, and a moral coward. I daresay she has noticed my good qualities, but they are naturally less obvious to her than the others. (Naturally, because what surprises us in an enemy is the discovery that he is sometimes kind, generous, and farseeing. We are surprised, or we pretend to be surprised, by a friend's *faults*—and so remember them.)

Here I should say that Victoria never shows off to me. All that faked naturalness of hers drops off and she is as natural as a girl of fifteen—that is, a little on the north side of nature. We talk spitefully about our friends and laugh like idiots, or schoolgirls. Perhaps we are laughing when her telephone rings. In a yearning voice Victoria says: "You haven't been kind to me lately. I'll forgive you when you commission a story. Oh, that's lovely of you. Oh, *good-bye*, my dear." To me, in the voice of the dressmaker's little girl: "Silly old beast. Wants his bottom smacked."

She has a naturally soft voice, spoiled for me by the harsh turn she gives to certain words—in which I detect Mrs. Form. For the moment I am back in our sewingroom at home, stuck between Mrs. Form and my mother, who are laughing at me.

My mother died this year, in June 1913. We were the last of our family except a cousin of my father's. This cousin did not come to the funeral, she said, because my mother had once insulted her.

After I began work in London I only saw my mother twice a year—but it never came into my head that one day she would die. For a time I was horribly lonely.

During this time I met and fell in love with a young man, Charles Blaikie. He had a little money of his own, two hundred a year, and what I thought sooner of, a very pleasant smile. He was tall, lazy, and good-natured. The day I saw him first I had just applied for a lectureship in a Scots University. This was a much better post than the one I had in London, but when it seemed that I might be successful I withdrew my name. I could not face the thought of leaving Charles. We met twice a week and went to concerts together. My passion for him sharpened my wits to such a point that he never knew how sunk I was. I made excuses to write to him. I write better than I talk. On the days when I did not see him I thought about him, sitting with my hands over my eyes, to have a clearer image of him. Often when we met I had looked forward to it so much that I was on edge and quarrelsome. One day we quarrelled with peculiar bitterness and in the middle of it he put his arms round me and began to stroke my hair. We were both trembling so violently that it did not seem absurd to say nothing. I was too much in love to be sure of him even then, and I waited in an agony for him to speak. At last he said: "Don't be angry with me, Fanny."

"Why?"

"I can't bear it."

"Why?"

"I love you."

All this was a long time ago, but I have not forgotten those words. I repeated them to myself too often.

I was twenty-four and he a year or two older. I thought we should marry at once but Charles's mother—his father was dead—begged him to wait a year. He gave in to her with an easiness that offended me, so that I thought I had the right to outwit her if I could. I worked on Charles's vanity until he began to see that she was a selfish old woman and one fine day we were married in a registry office, with Victoria and a friend of Charles's as our only witnesses. Old Mrs. Blaikie never forgave me. She was not a kind woman, but that is no excuse for the way I treated her at that time.

The War broke out when we had been married eight months. Charles did not enlist until 1916 and he managed things so that he did not go to France. During the last year he arrived at being adjutant of a training camp near Dover. My work kept me in London for two thirds of the year and the rest I spent with him. I was wretched away from him and not very content when I was with him. He had no ambition, and less intelligence than I had myself. I suppose that if he had gone to France I should have been considerably less critical of him—an inferior man who is in danger of his life has that advantage over the most intelligent of women.

We quarrelled a dozen times a week. All the irritation I felt against his want of spirit broke out over his use of a wrong word in telling a story. I forced him to admit that he was lazy and incompetent. His two hundred a year, I said, had been the ruin of him.

Worst of all (for me), I loved him more now than I did before we were married. This, while it embittered our

quarrels, made me blind to their effect. I thought that
my idiotic passion for him must be obvious to everybody,
and to him too. If I had been older or wiser, or only
kinder, I should perhaps have noticed that Charles was
happier when I let him talk freely about himself than
when I made love to him.

Immediately after the War I found him work in London,
in a publisher's office. We took a house, our first, and I
began to write another book.

During the War it had not seemed worth while to write
novels.

That summer I was ill, and when I began to be better
I took into my head to go to Dover for a week, to our old
lodging. I had lost my raincoat and, too listless to buy
another, I borrowed Charles's. He saw me off at Victoria,
very affectionate and careful of me. It was raining and I
wore his coat. As the train moved off I put my hands in
the pockets and felt a letter.

Victoria's writing was so familiar that I was scarcely
surprised to see it there. I began to read with only a vague
curiosity.

I think at first I did not take in what I read. I sat holding the letter. The first coherent thought I had was: "I
must take care of this." I put it into my pocket. That
was the first moment in which I realised that Charles and
Victoria were lovers.

I stood up. I was alone in the carriage. I don't know
what I meant doing, but I was hardly up before I was
flung violently to the other end of the carriage. There
was an extraordinary grinding screaming noise, then
silence, then a rain of glass, then groans and a few shouts.
I found that I was not hurt and pulled myself up by the
seat. The door into the corridor had jammed, so I climbed
out over the window.

The front carriage was in ruins. The next carriage was
a little better but I saw where a woman was hanging partly
out of a window in a most curious attitude. People began
to run along the embankment. I looked down and saw
a street of small shabby houses. More people came out of

these houses and scrambled up the embankment. I felt in my pocket to see that the letter was there and then I walked away from the train and got down into the street. "The train," I said to myself, "has stopped for good. It would be a waste of time to stay in it." I was pleased to find that I was still so logical. It seemed a proof that I was not overmuch hurt by what Charles had done to me.

I noticed that my hand was bleeding—I suppose I had cut it on the window. I stopped and fastened my handkerchief round it. By this time I was in a street of shops. I went into a café and ordered a cup of tea and biscuits. My mouth was dry. As soon as I was seated I began to tremble all over until I was afraid someone would notice it. When the tea came I drank it off but I could not swallow the biscuits. I filled my mouth with one but my throat closed against it, and when I saw no one was looking I put it out in my handkerchief.

I now decided to go and see Victoria. I forget how I came to decide this. All this time I seemed to myself to be perfectly reasonable, but it is one of the effects of an emotional shock to make you reason like an idiot, with perfect logic, and no sense. I left the café and walked along looking on all sides for a cab. One passed me but I had forgotten that I needed it and walked on. In a short time I found where I was, near Brockwell Park. I was two and a half hours reaching Waterloo Bridge from there, and then I was seized by a frenzy of impatience and ran to a cab-stand. The minutes my cab took to reach Chelsea were so long that I had time to see myself as I really was, a figure of fun.

Victoria knew what was wrong with me, I suppose. She looked into my face and said with her curious simplicity: "Sit down, poor Fanny."

"I've come about you and Charles," I said. That hurt me. I began again. "I've come about Charles."

"I knew you would take it the worst way," Victoria said.

I looked at her stupidly. "Is there another way?" For a moment I thought that I might have misread the letter.

"Charles is not in love with me. He thinks you despise him a little. It gave him a kind of advantage over you

to make love to me. That's all, I give you my word,
Fanny."

"But you've—been together?" I could not for my life use
a less ambiguous word.

"Oh, *that*," Victoria said.

I felt deadly tired.

After all this time, what? I remember but not as if it
had happened to me, that I cried every night for nearly a
year. The truth is that I behaved very badly. A great deal
of vanity was mixed in with my love, I suppose—or I
should have forgiven Charles. I never did forgive him. I
doubt whether jealousy is ever a curable disease. We don't
recover, we forget.

I trudged from Victoria's house to my own and silently
showed him the letter. To my surprise he seemed wretched,
but for his sake not mine. He was only anxious not to be
sent off and I after pretending to consider it agreed. To be
honest, the very thought of divorce wearied me. I knew
I should never have the strength of mind to carry it to an
end. I was afraid of loneliness. My heart failed me every
moment I imagined myself living alone, without Charles.

But I was eaten up with jealousy. Whether I had more
pride and vanity in me than love makes no difference to
the tortures I went through. I forced Charles to tell me
everything that had happened between him and Victoria,
where they had stayed together, what was the first time
he had been with her, what he felt then, had they spoken
of me at all, then what they said. I wanted to think that
everything in Charles's secret life with her had been given
up to me. When I had got a scene well in my mind I
brooded over it, looking for details that I might have missed,
and commonly finishing off in a fit of crying that might last
half the night. I tormented Charles with questions, even
when I saw that one more would send him out of the house.
I would hang on to his arm to keep him. "Only tell me
one thing," I implored him, "and I won't ask you anything
else." "What is it?" "Have you—did you kiss her exactly
in the same way as you kiss me, with the same smile?"

"I suppose so." This answer, the true one, makes me grin with anguish. "For God's sake, Fanny, try to let me alone about it now." "I will, I will. But just tell me one more thing. . . ."

From these memories, which I deliberately invented for myself, I could not help reaching to others. I recalled the first days after Charles had said he loved me, but in the place of that Charles, whom I could no longer think of without tears, I put the Charles who had for three years been deceiving me with Victoria. The memory of the pleasure I felt then made me wretched, as if he had deliberately planned it in order to humiliate me by the contrast with what I had now. Jealousy has the effect of destroying one's sense of reality almost completely. The very actions by which Charles tried to persuade me that he scarcely liked Victoria set me off again crying. "You don't care for Victoria, and you let her hurt me like this! What a lot you must think of me, then!"

I asked him why he had not told me about it, since the cruellest part of these affairs is always the deceit. You feel yourself a fool not to have seen what was going on under your nose. It may really be that the two who deceived you were ashamed to find themselves able to bring it off so easily because of your confidence in them. But to you it looks as though they must openly have despised the person they were deceiving. The frightful humiliation you feel is reflected back as their triumph. You grind your teeth over it, completely unable, such is the effect of jealousy, to understand that they did not look upon you as a fool, and that what they were doing never appeared to them in the least in the light of a triumph. It was simpler and more amusing than that.

When Charles told me that they had often stayed at such and such an hotel, without telling him I went and stood outside it for the best part of an hour. Then I hurried home, shut myself in my room, lay down on the bed with my face pressed into the pillow and pictured them crossing that hall of which I had caught a glimpse through the swing doors. I followed them upstairs to the room

Charles had engaged for Mr. and Mrs. Blaikie. This was as far as I could reach without crying. Scalding tears poured down my cheeks. I held my head, and even beat it against the wall.

I knew perfectly that if I were to go away for a year and not see Charles during that time I should be cured both of crying and of Charles. It was the seeing him every day, and with so many reminders of what had happened, that kept the cut open. The paradox of my case was this. If I went away I was certain to be cured, but I had not the strength of mind to go away because I was still in love with Charles. All the memories I had stirred up by turning this trouble in my mind put me back in the first weeks of our marriage, with the difference that now I was resentful and bitterly unhappy. I could only have summoned the courage to go away by ceasing to love him—and then I should not have needed to go.

All the time, too, I knew that I should come to an end of Charles. I had been coming to the end of him when this happened—and threw me back six years. But I felt that it would not take another six for me to reach the stage, of irritation and boredom, I had reached when I found Victoria's letter. Before I found the letter I was certain that Charles bored me. As soon as I had worn out the emotions revived in me by shock I should come up with my boredom again. It was a much younger Fanny who had charge of me now, who cried tears as bitter as gall, and struck her head on the wall. Yet I sometimes caught glimpses of another, waiting her time to take possession, to whom these agonies would mean nothing.

There were already days when I thought I had come to the end of my capacity for suffering. I would congratulate myself on it, as if I had just recovered from a painful illness. Indeed, the symptoms were much of that sort—I felt weak and happy, and very pleased with the look of a field of long grass, or sunlight creeping by an old wall. After a few hours or a day of immunity, some recollection would take me full in the heart and there in a moment I was crying and shaking, nearly mad. I would be in some restaurant with Charles, and ask him if he had brought Victoria there, and when. If I could pin him down to a day I would go back and try to remember what I had been doing on that day, and then I had the complete picture of all three of us, ridiculous deceived wife and gay lovers.

It is strange how little I blamed Victoria in all this. I think I felt that she was, after all, only going by her nature. She had no reason, beyond friendship, not to injure me. Where Charles had, or should have had, a dozen good reasons, as of loyalty, pity, knowing what I should suffer, and so on. So I blamed him the hotter of the two. And went on punishing myself and him for his not having had that carefulness of me that would have put it out of Victoria's reach to hurt me.

In the end I broke with her, but not until she had aggravated her offence in a very odd way. It was not odd but very natural—but I found it odd. I had forced a promise from Charles not to write to or see her again, but I was careful to make no difference in my own manner to her after the first day. I was miserably anxious to make her think that I scarcely minded what she had done to me. I thought I was managing this perfectly, until one time she took into her head to say she was sorry about Charles.

"My dear girl," I said, as carelessly as I could, "I don't mind Charles amusing himself. What annoyed me was the sum of money he must have spent on you."

"I always paid my share of any hotel bills," Victoria said quickly. "I know how much Charles has."

I felt this in the nerves of my chest, which seemed to nip me. The words "hotel bills" started a dozen frightful ideas, and for a moment I thought I was going to faint. I pulled myself up and said, smiling:

"If you could bring yourself to pay the whole in future. . . ."

"No, no, it's not worth it," Victoria exclaimed.

"Charles evidently thought that you were worth half an hotel bill," I suggested. I could feel the blood in my eyes. "He said you were quite amusing—but not so amusing as he had expected."

An extraordinary expression crossed Victoria's face. I realised suddenly that I had been a fool to trust Charles not to give me away. Of course he had written to her. She knew everything—as much as if I had wept all my tears where she could see me. In that case, I had just given her a fresh proof (if she had wanted it) of my excruciating jealousy.

"Poor Fanny," she said.

"You've had so many men. You might have left me mine," I said ridiculously.

Her maid came in and said that Mr. Crack, a journalist, was waiting downstairs to see her. She hurried out, and I knew that for half an hour at least she would be happy, showing herself off and posing for photographs. I went over to her desk and began to search it for Charles's letter. I opened every drawer and turned over all her papers. I daresay she had destroyed it—she was more careful than he was. I did not find it but I came instead on a note she had made under the head of "Jealousy. Extraordinary effects of it on F. Sense of humour shot to pieces by it. Imagination turned nasty—*e.g.*, yesterday when she was here she tried (clumsily) to trick me into telling her how often Charles had me. Another time I saw her look quickly at my bed and wonder if etc. Her emotions all over the place. A hurdy-gurdy stopped outside here and played *In the Shadows*, and tears jumped into her eyes— I suppose some memory of herself and Charles. *Use this for Flora in "The Faun's Progress".*"

Victoria came into the room quickly and saw me stooped over her desk, reading her notebook. I tore the page out and folded it carefully into my pocket, looking at her all the time. She did not say anything and I went out.

I hurried home and asked Charles why he had written to her, after his serious promise to me. He said: "You were in such a state I promised anything to get you quiet."

"Why did you write?"

"Well. Did you expect me simply to do nothing? I wrote to tell her that we must give up, because you were miserable about it. I didn't want her to think me a cad."

But that was exactly what I had wanted. I left him and went to bed, locking my door. What I went through that night numbed some part of my mind. I have felt nothing so acutely since. (Here I should add that nothing can be sillier than to compare agony of mind with severe physical agony. The worst of the former is easier to put up with than the second. A torn mind is pleasure to a torn stomach —even the after-pains of an abdominal operation are worse than being made a fool of, in the most humiliating manner in the world, by a husband or a lover.)

I continued for some months torturing myself with thoughts of an event *which I could not undo*. This—its irrevocableness—is the last twist of the knife. The phrase: "Whosoever looketh on a woman etc.", is mere Eastern psychology. A husband who has committed adultery "in his heart" has done nothing irrevocable. (We can none of us be held to account for our thoughts—they do not trouble to knock. You turn round with a start of horror —Good God, who came in just then?) A thought can be revoked, and no more about it. The act is irrevocable. It is done. I might cry until I was sick but I could not make it that Charles had never had Victoria. And I am the kind of fool who (if I may be allowed a phrase worthy of Victoria's novels) can think of no way of getting rid of a nail in my shoe except by treading it in with my flesh.

You will laugh to hear what put me in the way of being cured. Victoria wrote another novel, which I read—for no better reason than knowing it would give an account (romantic) of herself and Charles. Victoria never waits for an experience to cool before rushing it into print.

Charles was not the main of the novel. He was a chapter headed—you have guessed it—"Passionate Interlude". Early in the interlude Flora and Rudolf retire precipitately to a couch placed near a mirror (the original of the couch was as well known to me as my own face). Rudolf complains of being uncomfortable, and Flora sees in the glass that his legs—he is a fine figure of a man—are a foot beyond the end of the couch. (Realistic detail in the modern "passion novel".) When I read this, I began to laugh. The supreme ridiculousness of the image evoked in my mind was too much. I laughed with the tears rolling down my cheeks. I was not hysterical. The tears were wrung from me by my agony, while I laughed at the ridiculous figure Charles cut in the act.

Laughter of this kind is as strong an acid as thought itself. It dissolves everything—even, finally, its impulse. Once begun, the process cannot be stopped. I would look at Charles lying asleep, his face buried in the pillow, with untidy hair and softened features, and feel a stab of anguish at the thought that Victoria had seen him in the same attitude. Laughter, inextinguishable, overtook the agony in the moment when it sank its claws in my mind. I laughed longer than I cried. One day I laughed in Charles's face. I told him I was laughing at Voltaire's "adultery, a great sin which must be avoided as often as possible." At that moment I heard in my own laughter an exact echo of my mother's.

A little after this Charles took into his head to visit America. He was away six months, by which time I thought I had learned to do without him. I wrote to tell him. He took it noisily, came home, cried, which made me cry. I was almost weak enough to give in, but saved myself by asking for a three months' holiday. I went to Vienna. Lord, if there is a heartache Vienna cannot cure. I hope never to feel it.

I came home cured of everything except of Vienna.

About this time I left off my respectable way of life as a Reader to Kings College in the Strand and became a literary agent. I joined a firm with offices in Bloomsbury and earned in a year twice what I had earned as Reader, but the work harder and more disagreeable. I had to do with authors all the time, and in a few months I became and have ever since remained fast in the opinion that the bulk of authors is "the most pernicious race of little odious vermin that nature ever suffered to crawl upon the surface of the earth."

I should not like it to be thought that I am violent or

liable to *enthusiasm*—and if you object Mr. G— to me I shall agree at once that he is generous, charming, modest, and humane. But this is arguing from exceptions. Also to be taken into account—that Mr. G— has a large private income not dependent on his novels. In speaking of authors I mean the generality of the sect, which is very large, numbering, I believe, close on eight million, or a quarter of the adult population of England and Scotland without Wales. (The Welsh are fortunate in being highly intelligent and too poor to buy books. A private press has lately set up in Wales with the generous intention to sell finely-printed works in the language to its poor scholars. At least one of these works is being offered at the knock-down price of fifteen shillings.) It stands out of argument that more than a few of this eight millions will have the charm of Mr. H—gh W—lp—le, the intelligence of Mr. W—lls, the modesty of Mr. G—lsw—rthy, and the integrity of you know whom.

I had to do with every sort of author, except the great —of which we had two among our clients, but the head of the firm (a naturalised German, a little man, very old, a scholar—which made me curious why he had taken up such a profession) kept these in his own hands. The remaining five or six are divided among as many other agencies. Among the commoner sorts of author I suppose we had as wide a choice as any in London. One of my first clients was Mrs. West, wife of the editor of *The Critic*, whose work we in the office admired extremely, so much that if it had been a little more vigorous she ought to have come under the head of "great author", and the property of Mr. Spiegel-halter. At our first interview I thought her nearly too unworldly. Fixing me with her fine pale eyes she said she knew she was not an author for whom large profits could be hoped. Here I brought in the delicacy of her books, their extreme subtlety, wit, originality, and so forth. The largest sums, I said smiling, are paid for proportionately vulgar work. I thought her looks changed a little as I said this, but she continued very friendly and at last said she knew nothing of business and would leave all in my hands.

It was not long before I found that under cover of an unpractical manner—"dear Jane West is *so* vague" (she would forget to answer letters or answer ones I had not written)—she behaved in a completely unscrupulous way. She made the most inordinate demands, broke contracts, complained, scolded, and, in short, had been in the hands of five agents in as many years, none being able to come up with her notions of what was due to her.

I believe I shall scarcely be thought not to know my subject when I say that of all authors novelists are the least deserving of respect and the most arrogant, immodest, and grasping. I have heard of some very honest-minded poets and even of a dramatist or two not intolerable in company, while as for historians, philosophers, scientists (except those who write with one eye on the credulous layman), economists, and writers of books on mediæval Latin lyrics, they are as honest as persons of any other trade and only want a little less intelligence to be comfortable.

Novelists are rarely tolerable. I say nothing of their vanity ("*A little vanity does no harm in life*"), but novelists are almost alone in expecting to be paid highly for doing what they like. I have seen an author, whom everyone (including his publisher) had done all possible to discourage from writing another novel, come into my room ready to burst with rage and envy because no one would buy his books. In the same breath he would assure me that he wrote to please himself. "Then why," I thought, "complain that you have succeeded?" Why write to please yourself unless you are content that no one else need be?

"*My dear Fanny, the country which refuses to support its writers and artists is certain to be the poorer by it, etc.*" This is clearly nonsense. Our poor country was never in such a state as now, when we have eight million authors, of which five thousand are writers on serious subjects, ten thousand dramatics, fifty are practising poets, and the remnant (7,984,950) novelists.

A novelist hardened by his profession will take notes—of his feelings, exclamations and so on—at his child's death-bed. He will have convinced himself that it would be a grave pity if anything prevents his stories, with their imaginary situations, notes on character, witty speeches, and the rest, from being printed for posterity, which—if he had only the sense he was born with—he would expect to be far too busy with its own affairs to care what effects he produces by the nice placing of a semi-colon, or a fullstop in the middle of his sentences instead of at the ends.

Novelists are naturally spiteful. When you consider the great quantity of them in relation to the numbers of their readers this is not surprising, and they have a habit, when one of their number has been so far successful, of falling on him with the utmost contempt and hatred. Witness the treatment accorded to Mr. So-and-so's last two novels, which are no worse, certainly, than his earlier. Mr. So-and-so is accused of popularity, ambition, and self-admiration.

With all this, with their charges on posterity, malice, greed, self-importance, and believing themselves to be of more value to the community than an honest man, novelists are astonishingly ignorant. Scarcely one of them knows anything except how to turn a sentence, and that he often does clumsily. You can pick up this week a dozen new novels by as many best-selling novelists and, if you survive the trouble of reading them (they are longer and duller this year than ever), not raise the ghost of a thought or find one word to encourage the notion that the writer has ever been outside Chelsea or Devon or the Reading Room of the British Museum, or so much as suspects that the world, with England in its heart, is on the edge of disaster.

The critics are as good as our novelists deserve. Indeed many of them are drawn from among decayed or partially unemployed novelists, and can be relied on *to do justice to* the novels brought before them. A little education is of use to a critic, in enabling him to point his thrusts, quote a line of verse, and so on. Too much will be a vexation—a cultivated critic can scarcely avoid acquiring some standards of criticism, which in the nature of his task will prove a great nuisance to him. Briefly, an educated man can have only two reasons or excuses for becoming a critic of novels.

As having too much spite in his nature to rid himself of it in any other way. Or necessity. There are in London two critics of novels, men of taste and knowledge, who were not brought to it, certainly, by the first of these reasons (spleen) and must have been driven to it by need. I feel so much sympathy for them that I will never say a word more against critics. Beside that no critic has done me any harm except by bringing me his own novels to have them published. And I brought that on myself when I set up for a literary agent. And why did I? Driven to it by need, or so I thought.

I have run past the account of my life. Without wasting time on excuses let me say that never a day passes but I wish myself back in my first job. It was poorly paid, but the only authors I had to do with were dead or *in statu pupillari*.

As for the hopes with which I came to London—they take up very little room. I have never had any success. I have written nine novels to Victoria's twenty and now sell, of a new one, close on six thousand copies. "A very good sale," says my publisher, "considering. . . ." Considering what?

I have not even the reputation that might have consoled me. To be noticed, crossing the lower slopes of Parnassus, by Mrs. West, would console me.

With my seventh novel I shed my grossest faults and began to write tolerably well. It fetched me no nearer a reputation. I had the misfortune to be brought up in the belief that the first duty of a writer is to make himself clear. (That done, he may give himself the further trouble to be easy—and then, brief.) This was as ruinous for me as if I had been born with a squint. The climate of Parnassus changes five or six times in the century. During the present decade it has been fatal to plain speaking. The mark to be shot for at present is *subtlety*. To be subtle you must at all costs avoid saying anything in a plain manner. Above all you must never write down what was said or done in any event you may have arrived at describing. You may imply. If you are come to a divorce or a death or some other definite and inescapable fact in your hero's story you must immediately cease writing about it and describe instead a day in the country or a concerto for strings. If in doing so you cease to be intelligible so much the better. You will have avoided the meanness and shabbiness of a plain narrative. Even if you have a constitutional weakness for direct narrative you may disguise it by being very nasty or very arch in your employment of a fact.

In the end, though I am more anxious to be taken for a Parnassian than ever, I have given up all hopes of it.

I did not see Victoria again, except the once, until 1929—ten years. All this time—judged by her photographs, of which a new one was published every month—she remained unaltered. Her pure delicate face, the mouth fine and smiling, the eyes wide, looked directly at me from the latest of nine hundred newspaper articles written in a style no worse than the style of her books. The prudery of the English is incalculable. I am certain that the greater part of her readers are middle-aged women, unmarried or the wives of respectable men. The frightful boredom of their lives, without passion of imagination, finds relief in her fulsome novels. Reading them in the crushing security of their bedrooms, these poor women enjoy all the excitements of a seduction. I am sure, from remarks dropped to me, that this happens.

"But other writers have written novels of seduction and adultery, in a vulgar, romantic style, with no success." True.

In England a novelist can become famous in three ways. By merit, as Wells, Bennett, etc. By an excess of commonness (that is, good-fellowship), as James Macgregor—this is a form of genius, to be so common (friendly) that every chance reader sees himself reflected in your pages. By capturing, in your own person, the imagination of the vulgar. This is what Victoria has done. It is a triumph, the triumph of the dressmaker's little girl. Her only assets were looks, courage, impudence, vitality, shrewdness, and a coarse vigorous intellect. With these, in a few years, she has contrived to impress herself on the minds not only of the vulgar. You must be very much out of the world if you are where no one has heard of her.

Victoria is the first female novelist to have a public career equalling in interest the career of a Ziegfeld Follies girl.

During these years, when I was told anything about her, I had a curious sensation, as if I knew it already. Or as if it were the story of something I had done, in my own mind. I knew more about it than the teller—even when he had actually seen what he was relating.

She has been "news" for close on eighteen years. In 1924 a bundle of three hundred of her letters was sold at Sotheby's. They had been written to a young foreigner who sold them, thinking to annoy her, after she sent him packing. She pretended to be furious. She wrote an article —*The Most Humiliating Day of My Life*—and a daily paper printed it on the morning of the sale. In it occurred this remarkable sentence: "We were Paolo and Francesca together—but it is Francesca alone who has descended into hell: I shall rise again, as I have risen in the past—as for Paolo, I bear him no ill-will, and he may yet—*Quien sabe?*— come to regret the day he betrayed me with a kiss."

Sotheby's catalogued the letters in their stately way. "Form (Victoria). A very remarkable series of three hundred A.L.s, 1922–4, addressed to one recipient, M. Gustav Curt: they cover upwards of 1200 pp., 8vo., and are of particular interest as containing references to many persons and phases of modern literary life." A long extract, chosen with Sotheby's superb tact, followed.

In the week before the sale a number of persons took legal advice and were partially comforted by an assurance that though the letters could be sold they could be published only by Miss Form herself. The conversation at dinner-parties in Chelsea and Bloomsbury was less witty and more pointed than usual. Victoria took the occasion to weep publicly—under the eyes of thirty-five novelists, fifteen journalists, six waiters, two poets, and one dramatist—at

the reception given by a visiting American publisher. She
wept privately when the letters were found to be worth
only two pounds and five shillings. The two pounds was
bid by a lady who thought they might be nice to read
aloud at her parties.

I saw that in the same sale the same sum precisely was
paid for the estate of a scientist who had made some
noxious part of the world habitable by his researches and
having thus deserved the gratitude of his country died
and his estate coming to be sold was found to consist of
three letters to his wife, and one to a friend asking for the
loan of four pounds to pay a doctor's bill.

That year her novel *Green Passion* was banned by the
public prosecutor. The procedure was the usual one in these
cases. The editor of a Sunday newspaper printed—he may
even have written it—an article in which he showed the book
to be scabrous and indecent, and took the customary oath,
that he would rather see his daughter dead at his feet than
reading *Green Passion*. The next day the bookshops in
every town in England and Scotland were besieged by
young girls eager to buy copies of the book.

Victoria herself sent a copy to the public prosecutor,
with a letter which embarrassed the poor man worse than
the book. He had been hoping that the affair would pass
off without his having to notice it. He read the book and
was a little disgusted, being in his way a strict gram-
marian. Sighing, he told his wife that he supposed he
would have to stop it. "It's a disgrace to the English
language. If it *is* English," he said thoughtfully. "I have
counted fifty-nine inversions in one chapter."

"Inversions, dear?"

"Yes. *Blew the wind, Came the dog, Hung the bird*—you
know the sort of things. No—I'm sorry—the last one is all
right. It was a blackcock."

"A Nature book," his wife said, a little taken aback.
"But tell me, dear—is it indecent?"

"Eh? What d'you say? Indecent? Oh, yes—yes. Highly."

Victoria was surprised to find that *Green Passion* could
not be sold in England after the order. She had always

thought that a banned novel sells more copies than another. Furious with herself, with her publisher (who had warned her), and the public prosecutor (who had not), she made up her mind to appeal.

One morning I had a letter from her solicitors asking me if I would be willing to state on oath that *Green Passion* was not obscene and not likely to corrupt the morals of its readers.

My first impulse was to help Victoria. Then I began to be afraid for my reputation. Should I have to say publicly that *Green Passion* was a work of great literary merit? I shall lose all chance of being taken for a Parnassian if I do, I thought, sweating. I dropped my copy of the book behind the bookcase (to save it from the police) and waited for a wind.

I soon found that all the best-spoken-of writers were rallying to Victoria's defence, so hurried to add my name to the list. "After all," Mrs. West said, "they might seize a really good book next time." She went on gently, "We must take a doctor's view of *Green Passion*, as a *case*."

At the trial I stood at the back of the court, between a famous neurologist and a poet. I have never seen so many reputable writers gathered in one room. The sight was less depressing than you might think. A number of women novelists, implying by their glances and the angles at which they wore their hats the rigid classicism of their own novels, kept close together in one corner. I was intensely curious to see Victoria. For a moment, when she came in, I felt deadly ill. This was the last time the thought of Charles hurt me. I leaned against the dingy wall of the court and closed my eyes.

When I opened them a famous critic was in his place as the first witness for the defence. He leaned there wearily for an hour, head and profile of a dusty lion, while Victoria's counsel argued his right to call witnesses to the essential purity of her novel. In the course of the argument a passage from the book was read aloud again and again. "Came the dawn. Stark-naked her white body, Jenny turned in the grass and in the arms of her lover and said. . . ." What

Jenny said at this point is part of the evidence for the *prosecution* and I shall not risk copying it out.

At the first reading of the passage the great critic started violently. He forced himself to listen to the second and third without expression. At the fourth he threw an agonised glance at his friends, and his discomfort increased until he could be seen plainly, gripping his hands in a convulsed gesture. In the end he was dismissed without a hearing. We were all dismissed. Some legal shift put us out of court. A snub for Parnassus.

I was resigned not to be heard. On my way out I caught another glimpse of Victoria, very pale, appealing, and literary, in a black dress with orchids.

I had noticed at the trial a young man leaning against the wall, at the front of the court, close to Victoria. He kept his eyes turned to her the whole time and when it was finished she left the room with him and went away in a car he had there.

This was David Long, the son of a Colonial judge, whom she had known for three months. He was twelve years younger than Victoria and so much in love with her that for fear of offending her he had not yet dared to spend more than ten shillings on the flowers he gave her once a week. The first evening they met, Victoria had said casually that she hated ostentation. She was excusing herself for a miserly impulse but the young man took it as seriously as he took everything she said to him.

He was very good-looking, tall, with grey eyes, dark-yellow hair, and features of extraordinary beauty. Victoria was at the age now, thirty-six, when a little gratitude began to enter into the pleasure she felt in a love-affair. There was no need to help this young man to fall in love, but she took the trouble to protect some of his illusions. She wore simple dresses, had her hair dressed behind her ears like a little girl, and sacrificed wit to decency when he was in the room with her. She discouraged him from going to houses where he would meet others of her friends, but in spite of this he overheard gossip which drove him, shaking with fury, from the house. It never entered his head to repeat it to Victoria. She saw from his face that it had happened, got the story out of him, and then cried bitterly. "I should have been happier if I had never written a line," she said in a hurt voice, "at least I shouldn't have been lied about and slandered." David was in agony. Not knowing what he was doing he seized her hand. She threw herself into his arms.

His only thought was that he must not frighten her. He put her in a chair and dropped on his knees beside it. As she went on crying he began to comfort her, and I daresay it would have been all over with him then but Victoria suddenly changed her mind. She sat up and pushed him gently away, with a friendly smile. At least he had too much sense to apologise. It was after this scene that he asked her to marry him. He had a little money, and was earning another four or five hundred a year. He must, he said, have the right to protect her.

I think Victoria was now a little tired of the comedy. Certainly she had no intention to marry him. But her vanity was involved—she did not want to spoil the beautiful image of herself in his mind. The obvious thing was for her to say that she loved him too much to let him spoil his life by marriage with a woman years older than himself. A week of heart-breaking scenes followed. At last one day she managed to convince him that the only thing he could do for her was to go away. "For our beautiful love," she said. Half-distracted, he promised and left the house. An hour later, with a head of furious arguments, he walked in past a stupid servant and found Victoria with Stephen Lassalles. (Lassalles is the Jewish painter she was with that year.) I suppose there was no mistaking their situation, even by a romantic young man. He stood and looked at them for a moment. Lassalles began to bluster. David walked back to the door, opened it, took out the key, which was on the outside of the door, and put it in again on the inside. "I should always lock the door, if I were you," he said to Victoria. "This sort of thing is awkward for all of us."

I think that at this precise moment Victoria looked up

and caught sight of herself in the glass—the glass, you will remember, in which Charles-Rudolf's legs were reflected. She saw there what she had seen already in David's glance. It was cruelly unlike the portrait of a witty, shameless lady. When David walked out she ran after him into the hall, not even crying. He drew his arm gently away.

"You *do* look foolish," he said, smiling at her. "Fasten your dress, my dear." She went back into the room, raging at Lassalles, was very sorry for herself then, and cried. Lassalles watched her gloomily.

David had gone directly to his rooms. He destroyed a letter or two she had written him, asked if the water in the bathroom was hot, filled the bath, undressed, laying his clothes away as if for the morning, and shot himself, falling neatly half in and half out of the water.

Victoria was not involved in the inquiry. There was nothing to connect her with the dead young man, and his father—his mother was dead—had not heard of her. She told the story herself.

I think she was at first shocked—and then a little relieved that the young man was dead. After a time she began to speak of herself as a *femme fatale* (in a word—*famfatal*). This more than consoled her for the moment in which she had seen herself as a middle-aged woman.

She married again in 1929. She was forty-one. This year we became friends again and I suppose we shall not quarrel now.

A great many people were surprised that she married Rodney Whimple. They expected that she would have fastened on some rich man to marry her. But money means very little to her. Rodney Whimple satisfied her two dear ambitions, to know "good" people and to be taken for an intellectual. The Whimples are an old family related to other old families, and Rodney's career as a writer is the strangest possible. I forgot to say that in 1914 he enlisted in the I.C.O.T.C., was twice wounded, mentioned in despatches twice, and last, almost at the end of the War, he was given a D.S.O. Before this, when he was still at the university, he published a novel about the emotions of a middle-aged woman, the worst-written and silliest novel in the world. During the War nothing, of course. Three years after the War, *Sketch for a Portrait*, a short, grave, lucid story of an explorer, the writing as good as anything in its kind. Serious critics, at a loss to account for a novel written in what was undeniably *prose*, compared him to Defoe, Max Beerbohm, Dryden, and Jane Austen. He has written three since. There is really nothing to say about them except that they could not have been better done. His first novel is one of the mysteries of literature, as strange as if Mrs. Virginia Woolf were found to have written *The Sheik*.

After that uncomfortable party where we met him with James Macgregor, I did not see him until 1929. I expected that he would be changed for the better, but his hysterical laugh was the first sound I heard when I came into the Grotkopps' studio. This was before I had made up with Victoria. The room was crowded. I edged my way across until I was brought up by an eddy of people. Victoria said in my ear: "Well, Fanny?" I jumped round. The unexpectedness of it brought the blood into my face and after a moment I saw that Victoria was more nervous than I was.

"I didn't see you," I said.

Victoria had turned scarlet. "I thought you weren't going to speak."

I could scarcely keep from laughing. I was so happy as I never felt. It was as though I had wakened up to find myself ten years younger than I remembered.

"Is it all right?" Victoria asked. I was surprised that she spoke timidly.

"Isn't this a lovely room?" I said.

"I suppose so," Victoria said. She looked at me. "Yes, it is."

I burst out laughing. "Did you ever *see* such a fool as Rodney Whimple. He hasn't changed at all. He's a complete fool."

Victoria gave me one of her clear, cool glances. "He is, isn't he?" she said, smiling, "but I'm going to marry him, you know."

"I didn't," I said, taken aback. Victoria's mouth twitched. Seizing my arm, she pulled me through the crowd into a little room off the studio. It was empty, and we sat down on a couch and laughed until we *ached*. Then Victoria put her arms round me and we kissed, which we scarcely ever did. After a time it was as if we had never quarrelled.

"You're better-looking than you were, Fanny."

"You're more fashionable."

"The same sarcastic Fanny."

"The same Victoria," I said.

"Camilla's eighteen. You won't know her."

Rodney Whimple looked in at the door. When he saw us he minced across the room with both arms out. "*So* glad you're friends now," he cried. "I'm *sure* Victoria was naughty, but you won't punish her again, will you, dear Fanny? I must call you Fanny, mustn't I?"

I was afraid to look at Victoria but I felt her shaking. That did for me and in a moment we were laughing helplessly again. What Whimple thought of it I don't know. He stood over us smiling, while we rocked and croaked. Afterwards he walked us together round the studio, one on either arm, and told everybody that we were reconciled.

You can have no idea what a pleasure it was to me to talk to Victoria. It took me a little time to use myself to saying directly what I thought and then it was as though I had come home after being away.

One queer thing was that I forgot my mother had died and only remembered it, with a heart shock, when Victoria reminded me of a red glass vase that used to stand in our kitchen at home. I saw the kitchen and the vase, and my mother walking between the windows in the figured blue silk she wore that summer. A voice said quietly in my ear: "But she isn't there now." Why isn't she? I asked, between thinking and knowing. Then I remembered again that she was dead.

Victoria was quite mistaken about Camilla. I knew her much better than she supposed. And here is one item in reckoning up the new education which you will put on the credit side if you think extreme self-possession a virtue in a child. Camilla was eight when her mother and I quarrelled. In her first holiday, when I did not come to the house as always, she nosed around until she knew what had happened. Without saying a word to anyone she came to see me at my flat. She did not mention her mother's name. I was not certain at that time whether Victoria knew she came to see me.

After that she never failed to come several times during her holidays, sometimes telephoning to make sure I would be at home and always a little formal at coming and going. She might have been afraid I should not treat her as a caller.

At fourteen she was a queer, rough little girl, with shaggy hair and the tongue of a bargee. You never knew what she would say. She called a young writer who had come to consult me "a silly —" That it happened to be a bull's-eye made it no easier. Another time I had with me an important American editor (to himself important). He caught hold of her as she was slipping out of the room and said in a sickening voice: "Where are you going, little lady?" She told him at once, and you know how prudish an American can be.

She had read a great deal but of course without guidance, except where you would not look for it. (She had a book on Birth Control in her bedroom at home placed there by Victoria.)

When she was going back to school after her fourteenth birthday she put her hard little arm around my neck and kissed me. For a long time after she had gone I felt sorry I had no children. I began to cry and cried until I felt ill and empty. All the time I was thinking, "But what could I have done with them?"

I have never seen a child change so suddenly as Camilla. She grew three inches that year and from being a short, solid little girl became tall, pretty, and angular. She

brushed her hair and asked for a great many new clothes.
She was always very decided and would contradict anyone.
But she began smiling as she did it—to take off the curtness.
Even her gruff little voice altered. She became singularly
careful in speaking not to use an unpleasant word—much
carefuller than I am.

When she was seventeen she came home for good. She
began to read history at university college and spent a
great deal of her time in my flat. One day she took into
her head to go and see her father.

James Macgregor had married again, a year after the
divorce. You would think it obvious to anyone, with a
grain of intelligence, that there are far too many people
born in England. With half the number we should be
safe from starvation, even comfortable. James had given
rise to eight children. Lately his books had not been
especially successful. The Fielding strain was as rich in
him as ever, but—you know how it is—people were tired.
But he had saved a great deal of money. His vanity only
was pricked.

Success had made him coarse and arrogant (he was that
way inclined) and he now shrank a little. He did not like
failing, that man. When I saw him I used to feel sorry for
him, and said everything I could to make him feel that
he was still the greatest novelist in England. No flattery
is too gross for him to swallow, in which he is not unlike
other authors. As soon as I got away I forgot to be sorry
and began to feel glad that he had been taken down a peg
or two.

I don't know what Camilla thought of him. I fancy she
was disappointed. He was very kind to her, in a roughish
way, but she was sharp enough to know that he did not
care whether he ever saw her again. She was too sensible
to be surprised. After all, he had not seen her since she was
over the year, and he had so many children. She did not
go again.

She grew extremely pretty, with a look of fineness that
she had from neither parent. She was quick, rather than
intelligent. Her mother's friends thought her hard and

conceited, but she was not. She was proud, sensitive, and
quick-tempered. Her sharp ways made it difficult to know
her. I suppose I was the only person before whom she
would cry.

I asked her once if she had read her step-father's books.
She said, Yes, she had tried, but they were very dull.

"You're really wondering what I think of him," she
went on, laughing. "I like him. He's kind. And if you
notice, he's never idiotic when you are alone with him.
He has beautiful manners. I daresay you think him a
fool, and he's not that, I assure you, Fanny."

All this time Victoria was waiting for the girl to fall
in love, so that she could play her part of perceptive
mother. She complained to me that Camilla had no
friends, and I think I was the first to hear talk of "Fuller,"
who became "Richard Fuller," and then "Richard." One
afternoon she brought him to tea at my flat, a dark, sulky
boy, with an engaging smile. He was her age, eighteen,
and upon my word, they might both have been years
younger. They were like two children together.

The next week she took him off to Chelsea—but at this
stage everything went wrong. Richard did not like Victoria, and he showed it in every grim boyish effort he
made to please her. When he left us she mimicked his
stiff, slow voice and round stare. Fortunately Camilla had
gone with him. She was in arms always at the slightest
criticism of the young man. The day before, I had said
to her privately that I wished he would buy another coat
before going to Chelsea. She turned scarlet and cried: "I
won't let you laugh at him. It's not his fault if he's shabby,
poor boy."

His mother was a selfish, neurotic creature, the widow
of a lieutenant-colonel in the regular army, and she made
nothing of telling Richard that she could live in comfort
on her pension, if she had no great tiresome boy to bring
up. He had no pocket-money. He *walked* from Black-
heath to University College every day, and Camilla had
to be always on the watch to save his absurd pride. He
could be ridiculously haughty. They were talking in my

room of the books they wanted and Camilla without
thinking offered to lend him money. He pressed his lips
together and walked out. With a look at me she ran after
him and I could hear her talking, talking, on the outer
landing, until suddenly she gave a little cry. I suppose
he had kissed her. They came in then, looking young and
triumphant.

He had a singular charm, withdrawn in an instant if
he felt himself disliked. His peculiar childhood had made
him doubt the value of any kindness or gentleness done
him unless he could see an advantage in it for the doer.
With Camilla he was torn between worshipping her for her
falling in love with him and doubts whether it would last.
He was afraid to trust her very far. But you could see he
loved her with the whole of a warm, nervous and headstrong nature, which his mother's selfishness had not done
a great deal to spoil. Selfish mothers commonly have very
pleasant, generous sort of children.

He had an uncle, who was a manufacturing chemist.
This old fellow was supposed to be waiting until the boy
had his degree before he took him into the firm. Suddenly
all this was changed. The old man had a stroke, recovered,
but not until he had been so severely frightened that he
ordered Richard to give up his university course at once
and begin work. Richard and Camilla ran round to my flat
with the news.

They were extraordinary together, those two. I had
still to hear them use an endearment. They spoke to each
other as "Face", "Pup," "Dog." Sometimes they came to
the flat separately, and then the second to arrive would
rush into the hall and begin calling instantly for the other—
"Dog! Where are you?" They were very like puppies,
squabbling and tumbling together without a trace of
awkwardness or dignity.

This time they were too excited to speak soberly. They
interrupted each other, fought, argued—until at last Camilla
took Richard off his guard and rolled him face downwards
on the couch. She sat down on him heavily, knocking the
breath out of his short, muscular body.

"Fanny, dearest, listen to me, not to this fool. I want Richard to start with his uncle, so that we can be married at once—"

Richard had got his breath. He rolled quickly over, seizing her by the arms. "How can we be married?" he said furiously. "For the first four years I shall have three hundred a year. *You* couldn't live on that, you ass."

"I could, you ass."

"I won't let you try."

"You will. I want to be married."

"I won't marry you," Richard shouted.

In the end, unable to drag any sense out of them, I drove them out of the flat. I had work to do. Their voices, raised in the bitterest reproaches and fury, floated up to me from the street. I looked through the window. They were standing clear in the circle of light round the lamppost, their arms round each other's necks. "Dog, listen to me." "I won't listen." "You will, then." "You're a fool, Camilla."

The next day Camilla came to me alone, with a serious air. Richard had agreed, she said, with his uncle. They were to be married at once, if she would live on his three hundred a year and not take money from her mother. "We talked it out last night"—walking, if you believe me, from my flat to Chelsea, then about the Embankment until midnight, when he gave in.

"I was so tired then I cried—and Richard cried, then we laughed. I won, you see, Fanny."

The darkness, the stone parapet, the two leaning on it, sunk in the darkness and in each other—hurt me. I have nothing, I thought. Camilla was watching me with a smile. "May I think of this flat as my home for a time, Fanny?"

"If you want to," I said roughly, staring. "Have you told your mother you want to marry Richard?"

Camilla looked at me with an expressionless face, her eyes as round and stupid as marbles.

"I told her this morning."

"Well?"

"She laughed—and said, 'You needn't *marry* that stupid boy; *I* shan't mind you living with him, if that's what you're thinking of.'"

"Well?" I asked, trying not to smile.

"I told her that was not my idea at all, and hurried out. Fanny, I wish she wouldn't talk in that way. She doesn't understand. Poor mamma. . . . I'm only so afraid she may say things of the kind to Richard—who'd be furious, I can tell you. I thought—we shall have everything to arrange—if we could come here—"

I told her truthfully that nothing would please me better. She thanked me without showing any surprise or relief, and went off. Not until then I realised that she was desperately afraid of losing her hold on Richard. His ridiculous pride would seize any excuse to think that she was not *serious*. He had not given in last night until she was ready to drop with fatigue. The child—good God, neither of them was nineteen yet—saw her mother offending Richard, Richard shocked, furious, stubborn, and all her work to do again. I dropped my pen quickly and went to see Victoria.

She was really angry with Camilla—worse than angry, disappointed. She spoke of Richard as "the chemist's boy." "If she'd got into bed with him I should only have wondered what she saw in a stupid, clumsy *lout* of a boy —but to marry him. At eighteen. I could thrash her, Fanny." She began to laugh. "She calls him *Face. Come here, Face.* Don't tell me she knows what she's doing—she's been caught by the first boy to notice her. In a month she'll be sick of him."

I let her talk herself out. She promised me then to be civil to Richard. I went home—to find Camilla and Richard fighting in my kitchen. They had taken on themselves to set the supper-table and Richard had dropped a plate. As he stooped for the pieces Camilla began to hammer him with her fists.

"Fool and dog, you've spoiled Fanny's set. I hope she turns you out." He jumped up, almost angry, and was

shaking her when I walked in. I picked up the broken
plate myself, scolding them both—which set them nudging
each other like school-children. *Can* they be in love? I
thought. I went out into the hall. Taking my coat off in
front of the mirror I saw Richard's hand fall delicately
over hers. "Did I hurt you, my darling?" Camilla shook
her head. She leaned against him with a smile, and turning
her head brushed his coat with her lips. "My dear, *dear*
love." I made off as quickly as I could to my room, not
wanting them to look up and see themselves in the glass.
I could not help seeing as well the lines on my own face,
especially the line dragging down my mouth. I'm forty,
I thought. A tired, shabby woman.

Camilla had simply ceased to attend her classes at University College. It was the middle of her second term
there. She spent all her time looking at flats and small
houses in Stamford Hill, near the chemical works. Richard
was already working in the firm. They met at my flat for
supper and discussed endlessly every detail of their lives.
When at last Camilla had chosen a flat—for which they
were to pay thirty shillings a week—Richard hurried over
during his lunch hour to look at it.

The same evening he made a plan of the rooms to scale
and they began to compile lists of furniture they would
need. The list was complete down to two final items—3
dusters, 1 scrubbing-brush. Camilla had thought of everything, including a special pan for eggs. Someone had told
her that the water in which eggs are boiled grows warts.
I saw the pan later at the end of a shelf in her kitchen,
labelled Eggs Only.

With incredible trouble we persuaded Richard that his
dignity was uncracked if Camilla accepted a hundred
pounds from her mother to buy furniture. To this I added
fifty, and Camilla her several lists. She crawled over the
floors of the flat with a yard measure, and went from shop
to shop pricing curtain stuffs, rugs, and blankets. The lists
were brought out, before imposing frock-coated gentlemen,
while Camilla asked the price of everything on them, and

in the end bought a towel rail and some curtain-rings, marking them off on the list with a fortunate γ.

I asked her once: "Don't you think you'll grow tired of cooking and looking after a flat, and Richard out all day? Why not take your degree? A servant would do the work of that small flat and have a meal ready for you in the evening."

"And waste Richard's money for him, too," Camilla said. "No thank you, Fanny. Besides—I have no ambition. I shall enjoy keeping the flat clean and cooking for Richard."

"Have you really no ambition?" I was doubtful of her.

"Not a penn'orth," she said, laughing. "Except for Richard."

I could scarcely believe this. It still seems incredible to me that a young quick-witted woman can be satisfied by a life only superficially different from the life lived by her Victorian grandmother.

Richard could be very stubborn. Half their quarrels began there—Camilla as secretly pleased by his headstrong tempers as if he had been her son, and I believe provoked them, to have the pleasure of comforting him afterwards. First love is more disturbing than second, third, or even last. If it happens, for any reason, to become deep, it must be the most extraordinary and stimulating emotion in the world. Camilla's love was deepened by her knowledge of Richard's unhappy life until he knew her, and his, I suppose, by that life. They might have grown tired of each other as quickly as Charles and I did if she had not had to reassure Richard so often, or if he had been more certain of being loved.

One morning at eight o'clock Camilla walked into my flat and asked if I would mind telling Victoria that she had spent the night with me. I looked at her. I was ridiculously taken aback, but I controlled my voice and said: "Yes, of course. But what have you been doing?"

She sat down at the table and cut herself a slice of bread, which she spread thickly with honey and butter and ate like a hungry boy.

"I say, I'm starved," she said, with her mouth full. "Richard and I started for Epping Forest yesterday evening. When we were coming home I found I'd lost my purse and both our railway tickets. Richard was furious. You know, Fanny, he'd spent all his money on our supper and the tickets, and he hated telling me he had none left. He won't get his first salary until the end of the month and he had a pound at the beginning of it. I laughed—and that made it worse. We stood arguing in Chingford until the last train had gone and it was too late to get on to it without tickets, giving our names."

I poured her a cup of coffee. "What did you do?" I asked carelessly.

Camilla chuckled. "We went back to the Forest and rolled up side by side in a hollow, under beech trees, and went to sleep. My hair is still full of junk and Richard aches in every limb. Then this morning about four I shook five shillings out of a pocket. If you'd seen Richard's face. I thought he was going to beat me. In the end he didn't." She smiled without knowing it. "We made it up and caught the first train. Richard went straight to the works and I came here. You won't tell mamma about it, will you, Fanny? *You know what she'd think.*" She gave me a direct upward glance so like her mother's that I jumped.

"I don't think she'd mind," I muttered. "Even if you had."

"That's why," Camilla said gently. "I couldn't stand being understood by mamma. It's very prying—I've had some. You can't call a single nasty thought your own after mamma has gone through your mind. Psycho-analysis is seemly compared with it. And Richard would burst."

I had to leave her still stuffing herself. I turned with my hand on the door. "Come clean, Camilla," I said. "*Why didn't you?*"

She gave me another look. "If you must know. Because of Richard. If Richard once got into his head that I'm at all like mamma he'd be shockingly unhappy. See? Right." She ran after me to the stairs. "We shan't mind your going on the bat, Fanny dearest, if you want to," she cried. "Richard and I merely happen to prefer marriage. We're not pedantic about it."

I won't say what I thought.

In the evening they were crawling about the floor of my room round a new plan of their wonderful flat, half as wide as the floor, when Rodney Whimple came in. I think he had come to see them. He is not in the habit of calling on me. He examined the plan with little screams of ecstasy. I made coffee for them and Whimple held his cup with crooked fingers and gazed dewily across it. Torn from their plan, Richard and Camilla were arguing in loud voices.

"I tell you I won't have any nasty squalling brats," Camilla said.

"When I'm a rich man we'll have eight," Richard said. "Six boys and two girls."

"I won't be their mother."

"I'll get them somewhere else, and you can bring them up," Richard said calmly.

"Oh, I *don't* agree," Whimple said. "My dear, *too* immoral."

"They're both extremely moral," I said maliciously. "Almost Victorian."

Richard smiled. Camilla said rudely: "It's only you war wrecks who can afford to be immoral. We haven't the excuse of a war."

"Do you know, I never thought of that," Whimple fluted. "*So* sound. I must seize it at once. A pen, Fanny dear." In his fine sprawling hand he wrote: "Youngest generation turns from husks." He eyed Camilla archly. "*Do* tell me—shall you *beat* your children?"

"I certainly will, when they deserve it."

"Positively you'll *discipline* them? Fanny, my dear, *too* marvellous. That you and I should live to see it!"

Camilla rolled up the precious plan and stood it in a corner of the room. Richard moving to get up she helped him with a painful jerk at his ears. "Hurry up, Dog—time to go home." He hurried, and stretched her over his knee. There was a struggle, from which both came up panting and untidy. Outside in the hall he helped her with her coat, his hand touching her cheek. The blood came up into her face. She held his fingers and kissed them, turning her face to his hand, and he put the other on her hair, as gently as a leaf. You caught them off their guard so seldom that I thought I might watch.

Whimple looked up at me as the door slammed. "Victoria is simply livid about it," he sighed. "*So* unnecessary. I'm sure they're the backbone of the country. They never read, do they? I gave Camilla a copy of dear Jane West's novel and—believe me or not as you like—it *bored* her."

"So do yours," I said.

"And yours," Whimple said quickly.

A flame jumped in the fire and I saw that his hair was thin at the back. In the same bright second I saw my hand with its white, swollen knuckles and the torn rug where Charles caught his heel, striding about the room, the evening before he left.

"Why did you marry Victoria?"

"Vanity, I suppose," Whimple said, in a moment or two. "To be exact—it was an impulse left over from my youth. Do you remember our first meeting? Now, tell me why you can't do without her. You dislike her so much."

"An impulse left over from my youth," I answered. "No. My youth itself. And envy. She has so much *life*."

"But you wouldn't live Victoria's life, Fanny?"

"No, I wouldn't," I said swiftly. "Any more than I would write her dreadful vulgar novels."

He stood up, laughing, and went away. I was glad he had gone. I have grown very unsociable, and I am afraid, too, of not being able to interest people.

Victoria's anger sharpened when she saw the little flat in Stamford Hill. It had only three rooms, one of them looking on to a street, and the others into a yard with a plane tree. The flats above and below it were tenanted by Jews, and with one of them Camilla was already friendly, a fat, good-tempered woman, her breasts bigger than I have ever seen. Mrs. Rosenbaum had promised to show her German-Jewish cooking and hearing our voices

on the stairs she waddled out with a slice of *Apfelstrudel*
for her new young friend. Victoria was coldly rude to her.

From now on she never passed a chance of making fun
of Richard's poverty. "He must think a lot of his wife
to expect you to pig in with Jews and do his cooking.
What pleasant evenings you'll have, to be sure. Can the
chemist's boy play the harp?—I mean, the Jew's harp."

Camilla never failed to lose her temper when Richard
was laughed at. She answered her mother sharply, and
listening to her voice I understood why many people
thought her hard. She had scarcely a trace of imagination.
Her mind closed against any but her own and Richard's
thoughts, she had no conception, not the faintest, of her
mother's disappointment. But these scenes began to tell
on her. She spent the days in her flat, cleaning it, and then
decorating, making and putting up curtains and staining
floors. She was too angry to ask Victoria for any more
money and determined to have it perfect before the
wedding.

She put off the buying certain things until the last
moment, and on the very evening before the wedding her
linen had not come from the shop. She was ready to cry
with rage and fatigue. She screamed at Richard when he
tried to comfort her. He was pale with the strain of the
last weeks, and I thought both of them looked too young,
tired, and nervous to be married the next day.

Camilla walked up and down the room. "I came meaning to make our bed up for to-morrow—and now I can't.
Richard, if it hasn't come by ten in the morning you must
borrow some sheets for our bed from your mother."

Richard looked at her helplessly. "That he shall *not*," I
said. "I'll buy you enough myself and bring them in."

There was a knock on the door and Mrs. Rosenbaum's
face came slowly round it. She was dragging an immense
parcel by the string—the linen, delivered at her door.
Camilla jumped at the parcel and tore it open. Choosing
two of the "good" sheets, she hurried Richard into the
next room to help her to make up their bed. When they
called me I went in and found them standing hand-in-hand

admiring the fine big double bed with its useless posts and smooth, turned-down sheets.

Victoria looked magnificent at the wedding. The regis-trar was drawn to her by an irresistible, at least unresisted, instinct, as soon as he had done his business, no one taking any further notice of Camilla and Richard, who stood patiently near the door, one now and then looking at the other.

Mrs. Form was still alive. She was seventy-eight. All this time she had declined giving up her independent life and in spite of Victoria she went on with it, sewing for her living, until eyes, hands, and knees failed her together. This year she came to London to her daughter. She had once read one of her novels. It disgusted her, and she could see no merit in Victoria's successes. The day after she arrived she turned the sham modern furniture out of her room and replaced it by the solidly hideous mahogany she had lived with up to now. Victoria had refurnished her house this year, filling it with those glittering conic and cylindrical horrors, mechanically produced and repeated, which people buy now for the reason their grandmothers bought horsehair sofas—because others did and because they knew no better. The horsehair had a certain dignity.

Mrs. Form had not been in the house a week before she became Rodney Whimple's ally against the daughter she loved with a harsh, exasperated devotion. The malice she felt against Victoria had not begun until the little girl was four years old, in the moment when she looked up and saw on Victoria's round face the exact expression of supercilious conceit she had had so many good reasons to detest in her husband. In that moment she made up her mind to teach Victoria submission. Victoria easily defeated her. She knew that each spiteful stroke was followed in Mrs. Form's mind by an impulse of remorse and she made use of these impulses to get a new dress, a ticket to a concert, or the right to sit up until eleven o'clock.

For a long time after Victoria began to live in London she took pains to deceive her mother about certain things.

Now that Mrs. Form was dependent on her she gave herself no more trouble in this way. Mrs. Form soon knew exactly what was going on, if not under her nose, within a few yards of her locked door. Sometimes, waking suddenly in the night, and confused by the unfamiliar placing of a chest-of-drawers or of the window, she felt an impulse to light her candle and appear with it in Victoria's bedroom at the end of the landing. It was a few moments before she remembered that Victoria was forty-one and herself old and crippled, and for the rest of the night she would lie awake preparing malicious speeches at which Victoria only smiled.

Mrs. Form had quickly guessed the sharp mind behind Whimple's bright, pretty eyes. It took her some time to become reconciled to his voice and his bursts of hysterical laughter. She could not have understood that what mind he had was completely absorbed in the effort needed for his short novels. For the rest he was at the mercy of his impulses, one of which had led him to marry Victoria. Another—infinitely more subtle—was drawing him rapidly towards the Roman Catholic faith. Neither his wife nor Mrs. Form had wind of this. Victoria had declined all interest in her husband for some time past, but not, I think, before he left her bed of his own accord. And Mrs. Form, who knew a great deal about him, did not know that he was by way of receiving instruction—from a priest very well spoken of by Mrs. West, a showy, coaxing, literary sort of creature, with an affected voice, and I suppose clever enough to turn Whimple over his finger.

Mrs. Form was in Whimple's debt for more than the help he gave her against her daughter. He was very sentimental, and he suffered in watching Mrs. Form, tortured by idleness, the pains in her body, and a dry resentment against her life—she thought, now it was nearly over, that it had been wasted. He was infinitely kind to her. Sometimes, when she expected that he would certainly leave Victoria before long, she was fit to cry with rage, bitterness, and the injustice of being forced to live the last months of her life without seeing him every day.

Victoria had retained a certain respect for her second husband. (She had none for her first.) From this feeble root sprang moments of friendliness which Mrs. Form ought to have encouraged, since she dreaded above all the moment when Rodney would make an end of his uncomfortable marriage by walking out of the house. (To make it more uncomfortable Victoria had told all her friends that he was impotent.) But she could not resist the fun she got from setting the two of them at each other. One afternoon we were all at tea in Mrs. Form's room when the telephone rang downstairs and Victoria went to answer it. She came back yawning. "The editor of——. Eight hundred provocative words on *Can War Be Outlawed?* by to-morrow evening."

"It can't," Whimple said. His face changed, thinking of certain moments during the years 1914–1918. He had enjoyed the War, having enough sensibility to relish its intense contrasts and not enough to become blunted or sickened.

"I fear it can't," Victoria said with a complacent smile. "War and sex are natural functions of the male power instinct." She was thinking of her eight hundred provocative words and of Roger Stack, the explorer. Stack was, she knew, on the edge of asking her to leave her husband and she had already decided what to tell Rodney and the very words with which she would bring him to divorce her. The thought that in a few months she would be rid of him for good made her feel almost kindly towards him. "We don't often share an opinion," she said, smiling.

"You get your opinions from so *many* people, my dear."

"Do you mean that Victoria doesn't think for herself?" Mrs. Form asked.

"But of course she doesn't," Whimple said with a bright glance at her. "Women *don't* think. They imitate and repeat. Victoria is quite the best-informed parrot in Chelsea."

His gentle voice infuriated Victoria more than the words. She began a tart reply, but caught sight of her mother's pleased face and walked rudely out of the room instead, leaving the old woman pale with disappointment.

Victoria's anger against Camilla lasted until her vanity found her an excuse to drop it. She could not endure the notion that the girl was contented and happy. And I suppose she remembered all her talk to me about Camilla running to her for advice in her love-affairs. She must have felt the marriage a personal humiliation.

Anyone but Victoria would have left it at that—with or without forgiveness. But Victoria is something worse than a romantic. After a time her mind began to work on the fact of the marriage, and it worked in precisely the way you would expect. She imagined Camilla sickening of life in a small flat on small money, resenting it, resenting it on Richard then. She would come oftener and oftener to Chelsea in search of the excitements she missed. There would be another man, and a Camilla at first reluctant, then sunk, then (abandoned to passion) at last in need of advice and help. She would be particular not to smile or show at all that she was pleased. Make it seem easy and the common thing. And to avoid all possibility of reproaches she would send Camilla and the man to Italy until after the divorce.

She began to arrange parties for Camilla. She would ring her up and invite her to a first night or to dinner to meet a visiting genius from New York or Warsaw. Camilla's quick and invariable answer was: "Can I bring Richard?"

"Oh, my dear, I'm so sorry. It just happens I have enough men this time. Can't you *bear* to leave him for an hour? Or doesn't he let you out in the evening?"

Camilla laughed, and did not come. She would have enjoyed the first night, but not so much as she enjoyed Richard. Victoria would not let herself accept this simple fact. Instead, she pretended that Camilla was fighting temptation. She took to calling at the little flat with just a few of her friends. Camilla was quite pleased. She loved showing off her pretty rooms and the new teacups. She was less pleased if the party dragged on past the hour when she ought to be putting Richard's dinner in the oven.

More than once Richard came home to find two young

men handing Camilla's bread-and-butter to a roomful of
chattering, laughing strangers. He sat with his head down,
a sulky boy, until they had gone. Then Camilla jumped
into his arms. But they had to dine at the little, hot Jewish
restaurant at the end of the street.

The next day Victoria invited them both to dinner.
Seizing her moment when Camilla ran upstairs to Mrs.
Form, she told Richard gently that he must not try to
deprive his wife of the pleasures natural to a young girl.
Now that the novelty had worn off her days they would
seem very dull without some distraction. A young, lively
girl, etc.

This was the first Richard knew of the rejected invita-
tions. He glowered, and said that Camilla was free to do
as she liked with her time. "Then, try to make her go out
a little," Victoria said gently.

As soon as Camilla came into the room she saw that
something had been said to him. I don't know how she
put it right afterwards, but I suppose that if Richard began a quarrel it ended when they found themselves in the
big bed together and before very long they were sleepy
and reassured and it seemed foolish to have quarrelled.
The big bed was their ally against Victoria. It was not
their only one. There was Richard's absurd dislike of the
dark, and the way he ran upstairs calling, "Pup. I've
come," and his smile, and Camilla's rough little laugh, and
her pricked finger when she sewed. If you had asked
Richard why he loved Camilla it would have been of some
little thing like the pricked finger that he thought.

The excursions to Stamford Hill went on merrily. Victoria would call in to see me on her way home, to tell me
that Camilla had been pitifully grateful for the break.

"She finds life very dull with Richard all day at the
works and not a soul to speak to her but the Rosenbaum
creature."

"Did she tell you so?" I asked.

Victoria gave me a calm glance. "She won't admit yet
that she has made a fool of herself. But her looks give
her away."

"She looks well enough to me."

"You were always a sentimentalist, Fanny."

There were never less than five people with Victoria on these occasions. (To make it possible for Camilla to entertain three or four times a week Victoria took to making her little presents. Camilla was not her mother's daughter for nothing. She pocketed the money, saying nothing to Richard, and spent it on the flat.) The company changed, but there was a constant—a young man called Saint, a novelist, and a poor one. I suppose his novels are no worse than the novels of any other young man without experience of life, apprehensions, or any notion of writing—it never occurred to him that one word had any more value than another to convey what trifling meaning he had. Fortunately for himself he had inherited a considerable private income which was of great service to him in his career. In the first place it made the sales of his books of no material importance, and this in its turn becoming known brought about a great sweetening of critics' minds towards him. And this from no base motive—no reputable critic ever praises a novel because the writer of it is a wealthy man. But the mere fact that it scarcely mattered a toss to young Saint whether his new book sold ten copies or ten thousand had an admirable effect on his disposition. He was a gay, careless fellow, always merry in company, and thought no more of a critic than of an ordinary man. He had none of that anxiety inseparable from your tradesman-author who depends for his bread and cheese—which anxiety very naturally puts critics on their guard against him, with the effect that they look at his novels with a sharp eye.

In short, young Mr. Saint is a very cheerful good-natured fellow. I am not aware that he deserves any especial credit for it—since he has no reason to be anything else. Camilla was very friendly with him—chiefly, I think, because he made fewer pretensions to being a great novelist than Victoria's other friends, though I am sure he had as much right. He brought her a Siamese kitten—his mother bred them—and called sometimes of an afternoon in a big, fine-

looking car, an Isotta Fraschini, and rushed her fifty or a
hundred miles into the country and back.

All this was meat and drink to Victoria, who never lost
an opportunity of noticing their friendship, to me and to
everyone who knew them. I suppose Richard had heard
Saint spoken of four or five times and seen him once. I am
sure he did not know him from the rest—until Victoria
made her first cut.

Victoria's behaviour at this time looks ugly when you
put it down in writing. But it is to be understood by this
—she never saw anything she did in the light it appeared
in to ordinary persons. She behaved always as if she were
the principal character in a romance. From which it fol-
lows that everything she did, felt, and (I believe) thought,
appeared splendid and dramatic to her. Reality has never
yet broken in on Victoria without her finding some way to
be rid of it before it could finish her off. Her own love-
affairs were sordid enough in all conscience, but not to her
way of thinking. So with Camilla's marriage. She had
determined it should fail, through Camilla's falling in love
elsewhere, and from that she came to believe it *was* failing.
If I had told her she was responsible she would very
honestly have laughed at me. She had done nothing—
except wait for the inevitable to happen. The inevitable,
you understand, was that Camilla would sooner or later
have a blood awareness (or an equally violent affection) of
some young man, not her husband—and the rest.

Victoria's life is all of a piece with her dreadful noisy
books. She never wrote a book without getting herself
into it, with as many of her adventures as she could put
to a romantic use. This hindered her ever criticizing so
much as a scene in her novels. She could not criticize herself. To put it plainer—she never saw herself, except the
once or twice I know of. And then forgot it as quickly as
she could.

She saw sharply enough where she was not involved.
Where she was involved she saw everything swelled out
and distorted, men becoming fauns and what not, herself
a *famfatal*, and all larded with enough passion to baste

them. In this business, Camilla was the fatal girl, poor Richard the young dunce of a husband, and Victoria the witty, clear-sighted woman of the world.

I suppose she imagined any number of conversations for use when the time came. One of these was certainly for herself with Richard, and she was able to bring this on one afternoon in her own house—a piece of mere good fortune for her. She and I were at tea there when Richard came, expecting to find Camilla. It seemed he had left the works at three instead of six, but I forget why, and Mrs. Rosenbaum told him that his wife had run out past her an hour before, calling back something she did not catch but she believed it had been "Chelsea." So then Richard thought he knew where to fetch her.

He was for going back at once but Victoria made him stay to drink a cup of tea. I was tired enough, and sat sunk in myself. I came back to a vague feeling of uneasiness, the room full of sunshine, with some faint echo in it of Victoria's voice, and—as if it were the centre of a picture—Richard's dark glowing face.

"But do you know for certain that she was going out this afternoon with Saint?"

"It's quite likely she has gone," Victoria said. "I know he calls for her every afternoon."

This was a lie. "Where do they go?" Richard asked, looking at her.

"Nowhere you can follow by bus," Victoria said, with a smile.

I suppose Richard had been warmed up by what she said before. Ordinarily he would have gone all ends to avoid giving himself away. I frowned at him and said as roughly as I could that Camilla had tea with me four days out of five.

"Dear loyal Fanny," Victoria said.

Richard stood up.

"My dear boy. Camilla wouldn't be human if she sat moping at home when she would be enjoying herself outside."

"I don't want her to mope at home," Richard muttered.

"Then don't scold her. And don't, please, glower at her like that—you'll only precipitate things."

"What things?"

"Camilla is young and very charming," Victoria said delicately. "You mustn't expect to keep her for ever."

"Can't you say what you mean?" Richard said drily. "You've hinted enough."

"My dear Richard," I said, "I can't think what you are doing here when Camilla is at home cooking your dinner. I suppose she was out buying it."

He went off, looking very black. I suppose I should have told Victoria then what I thought of her sharp dealing—but my weakness has always been a dislike of censuring people to their faces. I like to be thought easy and sensible by whoever I am with. Beside that Victoria never minded what I said to her.

It was almost eight o'clock when Camilla rang up from Stamford Hill to tell me that Richard was not home yet. "He came in once, when I was out"—Mrs. Rosenbaum had told her that—"I've expected him since four, and now I don't know what to think. I don't want to do anything ridiculous, Fanny. But suppose Richard has been run over and killed?"

"Would you like me to come out?" I said. I was scarcely prepared to tell her over the telephone that she had her mother to thank.

"You sound as though you know something, Fanny."

And you sound at the end of everything, I thought. "I'll come out," I said.

I am sure I was *sorry* for her when she opened the door to me. I suppose she had had a moment's hope it was Richard. Her face had fallen into lines, and pale and drawn. You could see she had been up and down all evening, between the couch where her book and handkerchief were laid and the window looking on to the street. I have played that game myself, and I know how footsteps sound in a street, as they come and as they go.

I felt angry with Richard. It will not be the last time that she will pay, I said to myself, for his mother's training of him and his quick overbearing temper. To be honest, I wondered for a moment if she would not be better off with another sort of young man.

She held me so hard round the neck that I was reminded of the rough little girl. "Do you know something then, Fanny? Tell me. Tell me now."

"I only know that Richard was at Chelsea this afternoon, looking for you." I wondered how to tell her the rest without getting myself into serious trouble. "I think your mother may have upset him."

Camilla's face hardened. Just now she has a distinct look of Mrs. Form, I thought to myself. "I suppose mamma has said something again. Tell me every word she said to him."

"I can't remember that, Camilla," I said. "I was half asleep. But I think she had suggested to him that you might be in the country with Saint. I woke up just as he was asking her if she knew it for certain."

"Go on, Fanny."

"He went away after that."

"Can't you remember the exact words? If I know the exact words she used I can put it right. Try, Fanny."

"I've told you all I can remember," I said. I hope I did not look what I felt. Camilla gave me a queer absent glance, and rubbed her hand over her poor face.

"I think your mother doesn't understand Richard," I said slowly. "You can't, of course, say anything to her about it—but you might explain things to Richard."

"Explain mamma?" She smiled a little. "I've known all about mamma since I was five years old. She likes to be flattered, and Richard has never been better than polite to her—he doesn't like her. I don't suppose she meant to make mischief—but she will behave as though everything she does is exciting and dramatic. I suppose it *is* dramatic to be the reason why a man shoots himself, and I remember that happening, and mamma cried, lying across my bed and saying she would never forget it. But I could see she was excited and she never thought it might be her fault, as the servants said it was. It was just some-

thing horrible and dramatic that had happened to her.
She'd be the same over Richard and me. I'm not being
beastly about her, Fanny, but I should be a fool if I trusted
her beyond ordinary kindness—giving me clothes and money
and so on."

There was a tone in her voice, neither rough nor callous
but a little of both, that made me remember how long her
mother and I had been friends and were the same age (all
but a year) and so ought to hang together against younger
people. At the same time I was not sorry to know that
Camilla saw through her mother. It gave me a distinct
shock of pleasure. Camilla had gone back to the couch and
I saw that she was listening again to sounds outside in the
street. She looked at me the whole time in the hope I
would not notice what she was doing. I went over to the
window and tried to see down into the street. There was
the light click of the flat door and Camilla jumped up. She
had been so anxious that her first impulse must have been
anger, and instead of running out into the hall she stood
stock still, waiting.

I am sure, all my anger went when I saw Richard. He
looked fairly done. I suppose he had been walking about
London, thinking he might as well be dead as live without
Camilla. The dreadful thing about being young is that you
exaggerate everything—and are always sincere. You suffer
horribly and it is all stuff.

He came a few steps into the room, his eyes on Camilla's
face. She ran to him without a word, and there the silly
young creatures stood, more leaning on each other than
anything. They were as quiet as if their tongues had been
cut out.

In a few moments Camilla said: "Where have you been?"

"Walking about," Richard said, with an ashamed look
at me.

"I didn't know what had happened," Camilla said.

He looked at her. "I'm sorry, Camilla."

"You might have had an accident."

"I didn't think of that. I'm a beast to you."

"You ought to think of me sometimes."

"I've been thinking of you all the evening."

Camilla shook her head. "I put your dinner to keep warm on the stove over a pan of water, like Mrs. Rosenbaum said. It won't be fit to eat now, though."

"I don't want to eat anything," Richard said. He let go of her and sat down on the couch, with his head in his hands. "Oh, darling, I'm a fool, I'm no good to you. I can't afford anything but this flat and I haven't a car, I ought never to have married you."

"I don't want a car. I won't go out in Saint's again if it worries you," Camilla said.

"You must go. I don't want you to go without things because I'm a selfish ass."

"You're not an ass," Camilla said. She put her arms round him and rocked him against her breast. "My little child. Promise me you won't again."

After a while she said he must have some food or he would be ill, and he saying he would be ill if he ate anything she went out of the room to make coffee for him. I would have offered to get it for her but I saw she wanted to be doing something for him. She came back with the coffee and a piece or two of thin bread-and-butter, which she cut into fingers and fed them to him as if he had been too tired to take them up for himself. You could see how it pleased her to be feeding him. She watched every drink he took, making little encouraging movements with her lips. He finished, and she was taking the things away when her glance fell to his shoes.

"*Richard*. You had your best shoes on."

He looked down at them anxiously. "I put them on to fetch you from your mother's."

She was on her hands and knees examining them. "There's a great scratch across the top of one. It has cut into the leather," she said, frowning at him, vexed.

"I must have got it on that waste ground by the station," Richard said guiltily.

"You really are too bad," Camilla said angrily. "Your best pair, the only decent shoes you've got, and you must

put them on to tramp the streets in. Haven't you any
sense?"

"The last time I turned up at your mother's in my
ordinary brown pair you said everyone would be laughing
at me."

Camilla put her hand on him. "I don't care about your
shoes," she said quickly. "I don't care about anything but
you."

"I only care about you," Richard said. They looked at
each other, and then began crying on each other's necks.
They were both tired out. Their faces got all wet and
Camilla soon wanted to blow her nose. The sight of a
healthy young woman blowing her nose is not a romantic
one. It restored them to their senses. They sat side by side,
snuffling and wiping their eyes—too tired to be ashamed of
carrying like this in front of a third person.

"I'm sorry I cut my shoe," Richard said.

"It doesn't matter."

"It does. You'll see it every time I forget to keep that
foot behind the other."

"Perhaps I can smooth the edges over with something,"
Camilla said.

I had been afraid to go until now. I know how easy it
is to lose the thread of a mood and how difficult to draw
it up again—if you have had to break off for no longer than
it takes to say "Good-bye, Fanny. Thank you for coming."
I thought this a good moment to move to the door.

"I ought to be in my bed," I said drily.

"Dear Fanny." "It was awfully kind of you to come,
Fanny."

Dear Fanny. Kind Fanny. Neither one of them thought
to ask me how I should get myself home, at near midnight,
and I walked half way to Sadlers Wells before I came on
a cab.

For some little time after this I was doubtful how Victoria would look at my part in the affair, but I believe
Camilla avoided it altogether with her mother, not wanting to begin what would end badly. About this time, too
(the end of 1930) Victoria began to have other things on

her mind. She had just brought Roger Stack to the point of marriage. And now I think I had better say as little as possible about Stack. I never liked him and I knew one or two circumstances about him that I liked less—and there is a hypocritical prejudice in England against telling the truth about a man until he has been dead at least half a century. Then some young man, with a three-hatted style, or no style at all, may get a reputation on him.

I daresay Roger Stack was a very brave man—he often said he was—he was certainly a very stupid one. There was no reason on earth why he should marry Victoria. She was better to him without marriage than she would be with, and he had the shrewdness (that some very stupid stubborn men have) to know it. However, at the end of this year he did offer marriage, as soon as she could get rid of Whimple. And that she was in no pain for—she thought he might agree to let her divorce him: if not, she would let herself be divorced, for the second time.

There were a great many reasons why she should marry again. The marriage with Whimple had been as complete a failure as her worst friends wished at the time. I think they were scarcely on terms for a month. He was moody and delicate, and the fact of Victoria's expecting a great deal from him as a lover would put him quite past it, from resentment and his natural coldness. And the very reason she had married him—to better herself (as she thought) by marrying into an ancient family, one of whose ancestors had been kicked by George II—ceased to have any value in her eyes the moment she became herself a member of the family. So long as she was looking at them from outside, the distinguished connections of Rodney's mother and uncles and the position they occupied in the county were peculiarly attractive to Mrs. Form's daughter—from her memories of snubs offered to her by girls whose chances of being in the same room with a Whimple were wildly remote. But the moment the dressmaker's little girl found herself received, as one of themselves, by Rodney's stupid eccentric sisters, the whole family suffered a perfectly natural diminution in her eyes. She did not rise. They sank.

And it was for this—for the pleasure of speaking familiarly
of a number of persons who were not even amusing or intelligent—that she had saddled herself with a selfish, delicate
and penniless husband.

Apart from this, Rodney was not her style. Roger Stack
was. He had money, unbounded energy, and no particular
taste, except for exploring. But he liked good food and
noise, and to drive long distances, preferably at night, in
a brutal racing car he had. All this was quite in the line
with Victoria's novels.

But I think what most weighed with her was her new
feeling of insecurity. She was forty-two, and though she
looked ten years younger, she was beginning to feel a
faint chill on coming into a room full of very young girls.
So far she had held her own by being better company than
a young girl—but this was now not so much a matter of
course with her. She had now to think, and to arrange
her effects beforehand. If she married Roger Stack she
would have both less anxiety and less need to be amusing.
The conversation at the dinner-table of twenty thousand
a year need be little more than an accessory to the wines,
the comfortable bedroom, and the car in which your hostess
sends you to the station on Monday afternoon. And though,
no doubt, you do not write the better for being rich you
write more at your ease.

For the first time in her life Victoria had begun to feel
her success as an effort, and to long for something solider
under it than her own breath—which is what it comes to
with a popular novelist, once he is past his meridian.

I think, too, she was beginning to want the assurance
that she could attach a man when she chose.

She waited nearly a month for the right moment to speak
to Rodney either to divorce her, or take the blame himself.
But he was scarcely in the house all this time and often
slept at his mother's. So that the moment when she spoke
was not the one she would have chosen, but the best she
could get.

January the third (1931) was Mrs. Form's eightieth
birthday. She gave a tea-party in her room to celebrate

it, at which the only guests were Victoria, Whimple, and myself. Camilla should have been there but was in bed with a chill.

Victoria waited until after tea, when we had all laughed a great deal, and especially Mrs. Form, who was in pain that day with her gout. Whimple stood up to go and was nearly at the door when she said quickly: "I want to ask you something." He looked at her. "I want you to divorce me—or to let me divorce you. You don't want me, do you?"

"No," he said, "but—"

"Then it's all right," Victoria said, smiling. "We can settle it when you like. The only thing is, I want to marry Roger before he goes to South America. I might like to go with him."

I think I never saw anyone so taken aback as he was. He stared at her as if she had asked him something out of all sense. I thought at first this was a pose and that he must know what had been going on. Afterwards I came to believe that he was as surprised as if they had been the most loving pair in London. She was no more shocking an egoist than he was, and he had been so engrossed in himself and his conversion (as he would call it, his return) to the Roman Catholic faith that he had not paid the least attention to her for nearly a year. Surprise, bewilderment, and at last a kind of sympathy, showed in his face—which was still, at thirty-nine, that of a rather foolish young man; it had no lines except under his eyes and the cheeks not much fallen.

"I'm extraordinarily sorry for you, Victoria," he said. "But I'm afraid I can't do anything." He looked quickly at Mrs. Form and then at me. "The fact is—I ought to have told you—I was received into the Catholic Church last Friday. There was a paragraph in one of the evening papers. I thought you would have seen it."

"I never saw it," Victoria said slowly.

I had been looking at Whimple. I turned right round to her. She looks her age now, if never before, I said to myself. She was gazing in front of her without much expression. She must have been stunned by the collapse of her plans but she looked and spoke calmly.

Whimple hurried away. As soon as he had left the room Victoria began to shake with passion. She called him every name she could lay tongue to, from fool to cad. Her voice lost its polite modulations and became vulgar and shrewish. She clattered on the table beside her with her hands. Her thin delicate face seemed actually to swell with anger.

In the middle of it all she saw that Mrs. Form was laughing at her. Her head bent down, hands gripping the arms of her chair, the old woman was trying to speak without being able to get out one word. At last she managed to say: "That spikes you, my girl." She was in such pain, that the sweat ran over her face. Her breath came in groans. She had slipped half down in her chair, and was as unable to right herself as to stop groaning deeply and laughing.

Victoria stood and watched her. The strangest look crossed her face, as if she had remembered something from a long time before. Perhaps Mrs. Form used to laugh at her as my mother and she did sometimes at me.

"You'll break something if you go on like that," she said coldly.

I went over to the old woman. She was an alarming sight and I was relieved when she got the better of herself. Victoria had left us together. I helped her to undress and into her bed, thinking in a vague not very happy way as I did it of the sewing-room, and of Mrs. Form's big scissors lying in the sun on the window-ledge, and the room and my mother's face and myself standing in a petticoat and frilled skirt to be measured for some dress of which no sharper memory remains.

I got Mrs. Form to be as comfortable as I could. Looking back at her, my hand on the door, I saw her mouth still softened with smiles in the same moment as she had to put her hand over it to suppress the cries wrung from her by her pains.

I think that was the last time I saw her alive. She died before the end of that month.

Victoria showed her spirit in the way she took her severe disappointment. She pretended to believe that Rodney would tire of trying to be a good Catholic, and then she would find some way to manage him. She had too much sense ever to expect this. I suppose he had more reasons than one for turning Roman Catholic—as intellectual vanity, snobbishness (it was already becoming a fashion among Mrs. West's friends and disciples), a natural weakness in him to such things as ritual, submission to authority, and so on, and the emptiness in his mind after he left off being a soldier, which was the most satisfactory life he ever had. But apart from all these, and what made it certain that Victoria was done for, he was sincere. He is worse than sincere—bigoted, with bigotry of a vain, nervous, weak-minded and imaginative man. Victoria will never be able to marry again—unless he were to die before she is quite past it.

For the matter of that, her intended third husband was killed a few months later, in the Dolomites. Victoria had the pleasure of wearing black, which suits her, and of recalling the legend of the *famfatal*. I was mean enough to try to take away from it by reminding her that as an explorer puts himself in the way of dying oftener than other men so Roger Stack would very likely have died in a few years without her help. She was not in the least put out. After all, he had not died exploring—his foot had slipped and he had fallen down a crevasse. Perhaps he had been thinking of her when he ought to have been thinking of his foot.

I suggested that she ought not to claim him as a definite kill but as "last seen going down out of control."

I have often wondered what will happen to Victoria in ten years' time, "an age," as Lord Hervey said, "not proper to make conquests." What does happen to women of her sort when they reach fifty? I daresay she will have to choose between beginning (at that age) self-control and some shoddy and humiliating experiences.

It was once "poor Fanny." Perhaps then it will be "poor Victoria."

I suppose her novels will go on. I forget now whether I wrote anywhere before in this that Victoria has a lower boiling point—the point at which, in the mind, experience boils over into words—than any writer I know of. She dishes up her experience of life almost raw. By which means nothing of it is stored in her mind to mature for her old age. When her experiences fall off—as they will with age, since they all come to her by her senses—her novels will become thinner and less lively. (I doubt whether they can become more tawdry.) She will re-hash old stuff. And so, quickly or slowly, her swollen reputation will squeak out.

Or so I think. But there are times when I doubt this. Surely, with all the vitality and the kind of common *nature* she has even at her crudest and silliest, she will last better than I think. If, as I believe, her father was Jewish, she has all that vitality added to the shrewdness and soundness of her mother's Yorkshire peasant stock. However, we shall see how she does. She is forty-three this year, and (I suppose) her new novel sold as well as the others. It is the story of a woman's fatal love for an explorer and his despair, being hindered from marrying her by a Catholic wife. In the end he takes train to Switzerland, seeks out an unpopulated snow-field, buries himself up to the neck in it and so dies. *Famfatal.*

A much worse blow than Whimple's turning Catholic was in store for her and soon fell. But before this something happened to me which in a sense is part of her story. Charles wrote to me from America begging me to live with him again. "I am forty-three," he wrote, "and I have done nothing with my life. And I know now that I never shall do anything. You will be getting a poor futile creature if you have me again, Fanny. If you won't have me I shan't bear you any grudge—not that you would care if I did—you were always someone to yourself and I am no one, either to myself nor anyone. Yesterday the typewriter you gave me broke and is not worth mending. It is the only thing I have from those days. I felt like crying over it. Another memory gone."

It is very clever of him, I thought, to make himself out disappointed and useless. When we were together it was always because he knew how to make me sorry for him that our quarrels came to an end. And now, if I take him back, it will be because he needs me or pretends to need me and not because I have any feeling left for him.

My hands were trembling as I read the letter. It was not true that I had no feeling for him. When you have been married a long time, and when you have been faithful, if no better than physically faithful to your husband, all those ideas and emotions which centre in sensual love are attached to him at some point, even though at another stage in their growth they may have become a novel or a phrase used in a novel or a scheme for re-decorating your room or the particular adjective you have found to describe the colour of moor water at night. I had no longer any love for Charles but I was mortally involved with him. What I had broken before remained to break, and for a time I could not bring myself to do it.

I put the letter away, to think over it—if I could— quietly. A few days after this I was walking along the Strand and I saw that they had pulled down the old Golden Cross Hotel opposite the station. This was the hotel where Charles and Victoria "habitually committed adultery" (the dreadful legal phrase). I felt an unpleasant grin coming on my face. Another of Charles's old memories gone, I said to myself.

I was on my way to Chelsea. I found Victoria alone, trying to read a book she did not understand, and I told her about the letter. "No one but Charles," I said, "would draw a picture of himself crying over his last friend, an old typewriter."

Victoria looked at me. When she saw that I was trying not to laugh she put her hand over her mouth. But it was too much for her and in a moment we were both shaking with the hysterical laughter that used to seize us in class or at the tea-table with my mother's cold glance on us. As soon as I had recovered I felt mean and awkward—as if I had given Charles away to her. Another impulse made me say hurriedly:

"Did you—were you ever with Charles after I knew about it?"

"I can't remember," Victoria said, after a moment.

If I delayed another week writing to Charles to decline his offer it was because I am a fool. I thought of many things that have no reality now. I mean that it does not now matter what Charles said or did on one of those days of which I remember nothing except a glance or a phrase. None of the kind words we used have any meaning, nor none of the unkind either.

When I lived with Charles I had to arrange for his meals, order the food he liked, look over his clothes—I gave my mind to the Lord knows how many dull tiresome details every day, and my temper and writing were the worse for it. Since I have lived alone I have done exactly as I choose. With no person except myself to be considered by me my life is tranquil and easy. Here Victoria would interrupt to tell me that I lead a narrow, dry life. I tell her that it is the one I chose. More's the pity, Victoria answers, smiling. Don't you know, my poor Fanny, that you've missed all the fun and warmth of life. Perhaps the ridiculous phrases mean something.

All I know is that it suits me to live alone, to eat when I choose, to think constantly of the novel I am writing, and to sit down to my desk the moment I get up from my dinner-table. If I were living with Charles I should have to think instead what he could eat that night and a hundred other things in which I had not the lightest interest, only a duty.

There was a moment, or two moments, before I had answered Charles's letter, when I felt a pang at the thought of growing old. I should still be alone.

The moment passed. I went over to my desk and sat down to write to him. It is only when we are young that we fear loneliness. As we grow old a useful instinct reconciles us to it—unless we have been weakened by a happy

marriage or the too loving company of a friend. I suppose
that the farther we travel (in Time) from the enclosing
flesh of our human mother towards that of our mother the
grave the more independent and indifferent to anything outside ourselves we become. (I hope this is not fine writing.
I intend it in the barest sense.)

Another reason for living on alone. I now expect so
little of my friends that I am never shocked and rarely
hurt. This detachment—which costs me no effort—would
break down over Charles. With the best will in the world
to remain comfortably indifferent to him I should find
myself expecting from him sympathy, understanding,
kindness, delicacy, and an absolute loyalty—all qualities
of which he has no more than other people, and which
I should fail in myself, but without condemning myself.

I no longer expect anything splendid to happen to me
and so, though I am bored, I am tranquil. Perhaps Charles
would remove or at least change the nature of my boredom
—but at the cost of my happiness.

As soon as I had got off my letter to him I began to write
my tenth novel. I was seized by the desire to portray
Victoria, with complete coldness and honesty. I would
make her the central figure in my book and without ex-
aggerating a single detail I would pick down to the bones
of a successful vulgar writer, of loose morals and no taste.
The impulse was a spiteful one. But in a very short time
I forgot it entirely. I felt nothing but love—love of a purely
impersonal sort—for my subject. For the first time I understand how a writer can make use of his own most intimate
experiences and the experiences and emotions of a friend,
a wife, a lover, without the lightest feeling of guilt or
compunction. And be genuinely surprised when his book,
in which he has dealt cruelly with the life of the person
closest to him, gives rise to anger or tears.

The truth is that to a writer (other than a mere vul-
garian) his subject is, or at once becomes, completely impersonal. His state of mind resembles that of a surgeon
about to operate or of a painter considering, with his
painting eye, which is not the eye of a lover, the face of

the woman he loves. When I am writing about Victoria she ceases to be my friend. She is no longer anything but *a woman of a certain type*—a type which I am excessively anxious to convey alive.

Writing is, for me (since I realised my previous dishonesty and failures), a painful process. I write slowly and coldly, with innumerable corrections. Very often it seems that words mean nothing, and I spend a whole day searching through the words offered to me for one, only one, that has the reality of the skeleton. Very often, too, a kind of paralysis descends on my mind and I write nothing at all—for the simple reason that I cannot believe in the *utility* of words. As for their beauty, form, music, and what not—all that now sickens me. When I use an adjective I use it out of laziness, because it is too much trouble to try any longer to do without it.

I should like to write in the coldest shortest words, without emphasis or charm. I loathe and distrust charm in writing.

Yet how I envy the fluency of—and—. Those immense novels—poured out in the intervals of lecturing, reviewing, entertaining, and so forth. Where do they get the courage to write at such frightful length? Do they never feel uneasy as to the worth of so many words and words? No—clearly they find it easy to write thousands of words a day. If they began to think, this fluency would dry up. I should like for one day to change my slow, cold, awkward mind for a mind that is always at flood and finds pleasure in describing scenes and emotions which it has described a hundred times already.

Victoria was not reconciled to her daughter's marriage. Camilla had been married now for two years and she was still, to all appearances, pleased with her young, commonplace husband. But Victoria thought she could detect fresh signs of a change.

Camilla had herself to blame for this. With a shrewdness worthy of either of her parents she had been careful to mislead her mother. Victoria knew that Richard must have questioned Camilla on her friendship with Saint, but since Camilla never touched on the incident with her she supposed the girl had managed to soothe him in some lying way. Then—although she refused to drive with him again—Camilla was clearly pleased when she found Saint at her mother's house. From all this Victoria reasoned that she was almost in love and anxious to avoid present trouble.

The truth was simpler. Camilla did not care to lose the gifts of money and the treats Victoria gave her. She could not scold her mother about Richard and keep her temper. And a quarrel would mean an end of the parties, small cheques, and the casual gifts of hats, gloves, and frocks, without which she would be a great deal poorer. She always had an eye to the main chance, that girl. She kept her mother and Richard apart.

At the same time she had not, I am sure, any but the vaguest notion what was passing through her mother's head. She forgot her mother the moment Victoria left. Her life with Richard was her real life and to everything outside it she gave as much attention as you give to the other passengers in a 'bus. If Victoria had once understood this—but how could she have understood it?

One day Victoria took Camilla, Saint, and another young man down to the cottage she had bought in Essex. They were to stay a week. Camilla had been ill, with a bad sort of influenza, and Richard was anxious. He had begged her to go. He thought that Camilla and her mother were alone in the cottage.

They had been there three days when the servant Victoria took down with her was seized with pains. The cottage was ten miles from the nearest station. To get her to London, and also to fetch another, Victoria packed her into Saint's car. Taking the other young man with her, she drove herself up to London. They were to return in the afternoon.

I am certain that she had every intention to come back. But she was tired when she reached Chelsea and the thought of another long cold drive made her groan. The next moment a gross idea jumped into her mind. She would leave Camilla and young Saint alone in the cottage and before evening they would fall into each other's arms. It says everything for Victoria's stupidity that she supposed all she had to do in order to bring this about with any two persons, was to leave them together for a night. She sent the car to a garage and told the young man who came up with her that they would drive back in the morning. He looked at her with a fatuous smile. He supposed it had been arranged beforehand with the other two.

Camilla spent the morning tidying the cottage and the afternoon writing a long letter to Richard. At seven o'clock, it began to grow dark. From then until nine she and the young man spent their time between opening the front door to listen for sounds of a car in the lane and speculating on the causes of the delay. At half-past nine Camilla suggested to Saint that there had been an accident. She wanted him to set out at once to walk to the village, to telephone to London. If there had been an accident they would naturally take Victoria to her house, where no one would know how to get news of it to the cottage. Saint protested weakly. It was teeming with rain, cold icy showers blown by an autumnal gale. He did not relish the notion of tramping six miles to the village, in darkness, and through a frightful storm.

"They may be dining somewhere and coming on afterwards."

"On the other hand they may have had an accident," Camilla said. The thought had already crossed her mind that Victoria meant to leave them there alone. She was a little annoyed.

She went to the door again and opened it. The rain flung itself into the passage, drenching her in a moment. She forced the door to. "If you won't go I shall go myself."

"Don't be an ass, Camilla."

Her obstinate face vexed and alarmed him. In an extremely bad temper he wrapped himself up and set out. Just before he left Camilla said in a serious voice: "If everything is all right, don't come back. Make them give you a bed at *The Golden Lamb*."

"But suppose they don't come at all to-night?"

"I shall be perfectly happy," Camilla said. "I shall read until midnight and then go to bed. I'm not nervous."

"There are some of *my* books in the other room," Saint said with an encouraging smile. He was trying to atone for his bad temper.

"Oh, I can't read your novels," Camilla exclaimed. The simplicity with which she said it made the wound to his vanity all the crueller.

He reached the village at eleven o'clock in a state of utter exhaustion, his clothes plastered to him. After an exasperating argument with a sleepy postmaster he managed to telephone to London. Victoria's maid told him that Mrs. Whimple had dined out and would certainly be sleeping at home. He was not surprised. The idea that had lodged in Camilla's mind had occurred to him during his uncomfortable walk. Shivering outside the post-office he tried to make up his mind what to do next. He felt that his duty was to go back to Camilla, not to make love to her (he had scarcely ever felt so little like anything of the kind) but to protect her from the dangers of a solitary cottage. A pool had formed round his feet in less than a moment as he stood. The wind struck him on the cheek like a stone. Finally the memory of her parting words occurred to him. He decided that she was well able to look after herself and turned himself towards the inhospitable door of *The Golden Lamb*.

In the morning he walked another mile to hire a car from a cross-roads garage. He reached the cottage as Camilla was finishing her breakfast. She listened to him with a polite calm face. "Well, I'm glad you've brought a car," she said brusquely. "I've had a letter from Richard asking me to come back. His uncle is very ill."

Saint knew this to be a lie. He had called at the post-office for the letters and been told that there would be none for some hours, owing to the floods.

These floods took them several miles out of their way and in Bishops Stortford the wretched hired car broke down and they had to wait three hours for its repair. With

a tardy recognition of his sufferings Camilla tried to make
herself pleasant to him. He received her advances coldly
and they drove into London with feelings of mutual dislike
and boredom.

Camilla found Richard eating the supper Mrs. Rosenbaum had cooked for him. He was at first overjoyed and
then surprised to see her. She told him, with perfect truth,
that the cottage was damp.

Even now Victoria might have escaped the punishment
that fell on her if she had had the sense to hold her tongue.
Two days later she called for me and we drove to Stamford
Hill. We found Richard in alone. Camilla was in the downstairs flat learning to make *Salzburger Nockerl.* Irritated
beyond what she could bear (which was not a great deal)
by Richard's youth and want of admiration for her, Victoria
gave way to a very foolish impulse. I suppose she wanted
to see him redden and look sullen.

"I came to see how Camilla was after her little adventure."

Richard did not say, "What adventure?" He assumed
an air of cold understanding and had just answered that
Camilla was very well when the girl ran in. From pure
nervousness I made the mistake of frowning at her to
warn her. She looked from Richard to her mother. Victoria's widely-opened eyes told her more than Richard's
angry ones. She turned directly to Richard.

"I suppose mother has been telling you what happened
at the cottage."

"Dear me," Victoria said. "I thought from what Richard
said that he knew."

Camilla compressed her mouth to a thin line. She realised
that she had given away not herself alone but Richard's
childish pretence of knowledge. She said roughly: "I meant
to tell you in any case. I'll tell you now—exactly what
happened." She looked at him as if no one else were in the
room.

When she finished Richard, who had turned his back
on Victoria, said quietly: "You had better have told me

about it, Camilla. I'm not a fool." He gave her a long, clear look.

You could see she would have hard work to put herself right with him. He believed her, certainly, but he was cruelly hurt by her distrust of him. Why had she not told him the moment she came home? She still had that to explain to him.

He went out almost at once. Since his stroke his uncle rarely appeared at the works and Richard spent every Saturday from four o'clock with him, to answer questions. Camilla followed him into the hall. He was off in a moment, scarcely giving himself time to say good-bye to her. After he had gone she stood without moving for some time, then went into her bedroom and shut the door.

She came back in less than ten minutes. During this time Victoria had been considering her best move. She stood up when the girl came in and said gently:

"I must go now, Camilla. If Richard is tiresome come and spend a few days in Chelsea. I'm sorry if I made a mistake."

Camilla was completely self-possessed. "You did it on purpose," she said in a cold voice. "I don't blame you for trying to live up to your novels. But you don't seem to realise that you are nearly out of date. I haven't the slightest ambition to lead what you would call *a full life*. I'm quite satisfied with Richard. We have enough to live on and his uncle is going to lend us the money to buy a small house with a garden. I like gardening." She stopped, as if she had said more than she meant. "I think you had better keep away from us for a time."

Victoria had kept a calm face. "Do you mean you don't want to see me? I'm not to come here?"

"For the time being it would be better if you didn't," Camilla said. She looked at me. "You see, Fanny, Richard *must* have certainty. If he once begins to distrust me it will be all up with us. We shall never be happy again."

I looked at Victoria. I had never seen her too sharply stung to defend herself until this. She was almost plain, and she kept touching her mouth with a finger. She stood

up and looked at herself in the glass. Perhaps the sight
gave her energy. She smiled at Camilla and patted the
girl's arm. Then she turned round to me and said loudly,
"Come along, Fanny. We have to dress before dinner.
Camilla doesn't dress—they have a simple meal and call
it supper."

We drove to my flat. On the way Victoria had said
nothing, but as soon as we were in the flat she made herself
comfortable on my sofa and began to talk.

"Do you remember," she said, smiling, "the day when
Camilla was so naughty that I told her she would have to
go back to school for the rest of the holidays? She was just
six. I didn't mean it, of course. But she went calmly upstairs and told Clarke that she was going and came down
carrying her little coat. In the end I had to beg her to
stay with me." She arranged herself and went on speaking. "Of course she is behaving in a very foolish way now,
but we needn't take it too seriously. I shall treat her like
a child who is showing off, and not look at her. No—that
would be too much trouble. I shall write and invite her
to dinner and when she comes I shall talk to her as if
nothing had happened."

"But suppose she refuses?"

"I shall wait for her to come to her senses. ... After
all, Fanny, she and I have always been *friends*—we have
never been mother and daughter. She tells me everything
and I talk to her just as I should talk to you. We have
never had any of those silly lies and evasions that parents
indulge themselves in with their children. I brought her
up to be absolutely honest, and fearless." She gave a little
sigh. I did not say anything. I was afraid that in another
minute Victoria would begin to cry tears very different
from those she cried over young Long.

At this moment an ex-servicemen's band marched down
the street playing, badly and gaily. I walked over to the
window to watch it pass. I love to hear music played in
the street. It fills me with a freakish excitement for which
I cannot account. In the street bad music is as good as
the best. It reminds me of the street outside my mother's

house, with the long gardens, the double hawthorn tree, and the sand-stoned steps. It is romance in its least debatable form. (I see that I am becoming enthusiastic, which does not suit me.)

Victoria was still talking when I was able to hear her again. She had opened her handbag and was studying her face in the mirror fixed to the inside. "I have plenty to occupy me, without giving a thought to the rudeness of a silly girl—even if she is my daughter. I'm still young. How old should you say I was, Fanny?—if you didn't know."

"Thirty-three," I said drily, allowing her ten years.

"Oh, but I'm tired now. When I'm feeling well I look younger. I think I shall go to Biarritz for the winter. Next year I am going to write my autobiography. It will be the frankest book I have ever written. Don't look owlish, my dear. I'll let you down very lightly. Perhaps I shan't even put you in. That would be too cruel." She gave me a malicious glance. "You will be disappointed not to see your name in the index. So will Camilla. The silly young fool—you can see she's getting sick of her dear Richard. In a year's time she'll be running to me for help. Well, I'll be merciful. I won't even say I told you so."

She went into my bedroom to powder her face before driving home, where the three persons she had invited to dinner were already waiting for her. As she was going down the stairs she said:

"It seems you are all I have left, Fanny."

I looked at her without speaking. For a moment I wondered whether I cared for her at all. Can I be an egoist? I remembered—of all things—a hideous bead necklace she gave me when we were at school. (It has been lost many years.) I turned scarlet and mumbled something. It occurred to me that Camilla had been a little smug in her attitude.

I went back to my room. Victoria had scattered a trail of powder over my desk. I brushed it away, sat down, and began to write.

THE SINGLE HEART

CHAPTER I

PEOPLE who were born a little before 1900 belong to
no age. The old one had dried, and it split round them
before they could accustom themselves to it, and the new
one was not ready. They have to get along as best they
can, with the help of a few uncomfortable memories of
what was still considered decent in their childhood, and
an uncertain grasp of newer ideas.

When Emily Lambton was twelve years old she went with
her mother and father on the trial trip of the *Russian
King*. The *Russian King* was the newest and largest
of Sir John Lambton's ships. He owned, as well as the
King line, the directing share in another Newcastle firm
and in two older London firms, but the King Line was his
own child. For this and no better reason he chose to drag
his tired peevish wife on the boat's trial voyage from Newcastle to Antwerp. They had the captain's berth next the
chart house, and Emily slept below, in one of the narrow
berths opening off the saloon. On the opposite side of the
passage Captain Smith and his son shared a berth as small
and uncomfortable.

Lady Lambton came on board protesting that she would
be ill and was. She lay in bed—a genuine bed, with brass
rails and a curtain—groaning, in an atmosphere of Florida
water and weak brandy. Her husband walked about over-
head, pleased with everything and almost believing that
the sun shone on the water for him alone, and descended
to eat and drink lavishly in the saloon with Captain Smith
and his officers. After dinner he offered cigars to the
captain, the first mate and the chief engineer. At lunch
only to the captain. He smoked them himself all day and
smelled of them and of claret, good soap, and the fine salty
air. When he came in to see his wife he left the door open,
so that curtains and papers blew about and her querulous

voice rose thinly over the sudden inrush of sun, wind, and the noises of the ship.

Emily spent a great many hours sitting restlessly on the hard narrow couch facing the bed. The seat of the couch lifted up and inside she found Captain Smith's library—*The Home Doctor*, *Views of New Orleans*, and a paper-covered novel entitled *Dead Sea Fruit*. She had scarcely begun on the last when her mother caught sight of the cover and snatched it from her with a scream of horror. After this she studied each New Orleans *View* in turn and imagined herself walking along the streets, pausing at the windows of shops, and at last entering the house in which she lived with her lover, one of the heroes of the Indian Mutiny. The delights of this game soon vanished and she began a furtive study of *The Home Doctor*. Since she had been brought up in a decent ignorance this proved very exciting.

At lunch—the only meal for which she descended to the saloon—she sat opposite the captain's son. He took no notice of her. He was two years older than she was, no taller, with dark hair, thick arched eyebrows, and features of unusual fineness and delicacy. His name, she soon heard, was Evan. Since he looked at his plate throughout the meal she was able to admire fine curving eyelashes. On the second day out she managed to meet him in the passage dividing their berths. He was stiff and unfriendly and she thought he must have been told to keep away from the owner's daughter.

When the *Russian King* docked at Antwerp she confidently expected to be taken on shore. But her mother, though she sat up in bed and had her hair brushed by her maid, refused to leave the ship, and her father went off by himself, red and jovial, secretly pleased to be alone. Poor Emily spent all that day on board. From the top of the companion-way she watched Evan Smith and his father going on shore. The boy glanced back and saw her. Afraid that he would see her tears she turned and hurried behind the chart house. In the evening after dinner she went down to her berth. Evan was sitting in the saloon and ran after her into the half-lit passage.

"Aren't you going on shore to-morrow?"

"I don't know," Emily said. "I don't think my father will take me."

"It's a shame you're left all day," the boy said. "I'd take you myself if I could. Come outside and look."

They stood side by side looking at the darkened wharf. A long shed cut off the farther view. Emily was nervous. She glanced stealthily at Evan, waiting for him to speak or move.

"The Queen is dead," Evan whispered. "My father had a telegram. There's one for your father—it came when he had gone ashore."

"What will happen?"

"The end of everything, my father says. That's not my opinion. Would you like to walk to the end of the wharf?"

"Can we?" She followed him down the gangway, treading softly. No one had seen them. In the darkness she felt herself stepping on small hard objects. She stooped and picked one of them up—it was the dry husk of some fruit. She was thinking without much interest of the dead Queen. The darkness, the black mass of the shed, the ship, the strange dried husks underfoot, were part of the same thought. Evan grasped her hand. "If your mother asks, say I never speak to you, do you hear? I won't speak to you again unless you promise."

They left the wharf and began to walk down a wide road with tall old yellow houses on one side. In the feeble light of a street lamp Emily made out a doorway and a shabby wall. She stumbled and Evan put his arm round her. The road seemed empty. A man stepped suddenly out of one of the houses in the moment they reached it and the light from the passage fell full on them. The man jumped and seized Evan by the shoulder. "Where are you off?" Evan wriggled away and faced him. "No business of yours, Mr. Second Mate," he said furiously. But they were caught and had to turn and walk back to the ship. The young man meant well: he ran up the gangway ahead of them to see that the coast was clear and the watchman still absent and then beckoned them to follow. He had made both of them promise not to leave the ship again, and on that condition he would say nothing of their escapade. Emily promised willingly, relieved, but she could see that Evan was smarting under their humiliation. She tried to console him with an affectionate smile and he gripped her arm so hard that she almost screamed. For the rest of the trip he avoided her. She had fallen in love with him, and his indifference, which she put down to pride, made her shed tears at night in her uncomfortable bunk.

She thought of him every night for a few weeks and then forgot him. She went away to school, not sorry to be out of hearing of her mother's endless complaints. She had just realised that these all had to do with her father's fondness for another woman—or women—and she rather despised her mother for lying about in tears when she could go out, spend money, and enjoy herself in her own way. For her father she felt a guilty liking. He was kind to her when he remembered her, which was seldom enough.

She grew up without knowing that she was beautiful. She was like her mother, but some indefinable change— as if the sculptor's file had worked with more love and freedom over the copy—had turned prettiness to beauty. She was lazy, intelligent, and quite without knowing it, sensual. Some of her father's gross vitality had gone into her. She scarcely knew her parents, nor they her.

At home she was reserved and gruff. With her two chosen friends she plunged into all that *talk* which expressed the unashamed idealism of the young in the years just before the War. The exquisite irony of it would have been apparent to an invisible listener who could have gone straight from any gathering of intelligent young in England to the Ball-Platz in Vienna at the moment when the Chief of General Staff was explaining himself to Count Berchtold. How fortunate it would be if, when we die, we find ourselves reduced to the state of a freely-moving spirit, with eyes and ears, but without a nose. There are so many bad smells in a world run by international business, patriotism, and hunger.

Emily and her friends belonged to the Fabian Society:

they discussed free love, the relations of the sexes, birth
control, the anodyne effect of religion, Bernard Shaw's
plays, and the novels of H. G. Wells. Emily at least had
only the vaguest notion of what would happen to her when
she married or had a lover, but she was able to sustain
a long conversation on the intricacies of sexual life without
giving herself away. The other two young women were
both ardent suffragists, but Emily lacked courage to face
her father's coarse humour. There was a contradiction in
her somewhere. With all her intelligence, spirit, and stub-
bornness, she had a mortal horror of ridicule—which often
drove her to conceal her real thoughts. She could not bear
to be disapproved of.

When she was eighteen she met Evan Smith again. He
was now a clerk in the London office of Sir John Lambton's firm, and they met at the garden-party her mother
gave every year, in June, to the staff of Lambton and Grey,
inviting everyone from the managing director to the door
man. She saw him standing alone, with his back to a
game of croquet, and spoke to him. He pretended not to
remember her.

"Don't you remember the *Russian King* in Antwerp?
You told me that Queen Victoria was dead." As she spoke,
she felt under her feet the wooden beams of the wharf,
strewn with queer dried husks. Light falling on an old
yellow house flickered weakly against the sunshine. "We
walked down a wide street together. It was dark."

"Did we?"

He was offended by her frank interest. She had a way
of staring into your face that disconcerted some people
and attracted others. She did not know she did this. It
happened from her intense, unconscious curiosity to know
what was going on inside your mind.

"You don't remember me. Well, never mind," she
sighed. "I don't suppose you would. You must have a
great many other things to think of."

"I remember you perfectly," Evan said curtly.

He looked at her so fiercely that she was taken aback.
They were about the same height, but he managed to look

down at her. There was a deep line between his eyes, his nose was more beaked than she remembered and his mouth smaller. He had a look of fineness and sulkiness. He was, she saw, extraordinarily attractive.

He was very badly dressed—his brown serge suit hung anyhow on his slight body and the pockets gaped. He was wearing a pair of yellow-brown shoes.

She had reached the shoes in her survey when she caught sight of her brother and his friend William Holl skirting the lawn towards her. "Have you seen the rose garden? I'll show it to you," she exclaimed. She led the young man, now very silent, towards the terraced gardens that cost Sir John a mint of money. By making a double turn she thought she had thrown Eliot and William Holl off their mark.

"Why did you pretend not to know me?"

"It's no business of mine to remember Miss Emily Lambton," Evan said.

"Don't be silly." Emily smiled at him. The garden party, to which she had looked forward with a mixture of boredom and shame—she was ashamed of the voice her mother used in speaking to clerks—had suddenly become delightful. She was pleased and happy. "I didn't pretend not to know *you*. Do you like living in London?"

"No."

"Why not?"

"You can't live decently in London without money," Evan said. He spoke simply. His air of sulky ill-humour had vanished.

"I know that. I mean I can imagine it. Tell me something—why did you never speak to me again after that night? I hung about outside my berth hoping to see you. I was awfully miserable."

"Lady Lambton told my father at the first that she would not care for her daughter to become friendly with his son."

"Oh," Emily said. She put both hands on his arm. "And I liked you so much."

Evan looked at her with a smile that gave her an extraordinary sensation of weakness. She leaned towards him.

Their faces, his with the smile softening his beautiful mouth, almost touched. Her brother and William Holl appeared at the other end of the path, walking quickly. They had deliberately followed, she thought. She felt a momentary dismay, which her face showed. Evan drew back and waited with a calm face for the other young men to come up. Eliot Lambton called out before he reached them.

"What are you doing here, Emily? William and I have been hunting everywhere for you to have tea in the library." He took no notice of Evan.

"I was showing Mr. Smith the gardens," Emily said. She turned scarlet. "Have you met my brother, Mr. Smith? And this is"—she blundered—"William Holl—Lord Holl."

Evan put his hand out, which both young men ignored, Eliot deliberately and William because he was looking at Emily and did not see. This was the moment in which Emily should have said warmly, "Come along, Mr. Smith, we haven't looked at the roses." Taking his arm, she could have walked past her brother and William, leaving them to swallow their resentment. This was what she would have seen herself doing, if she had imagined the scene beforehand. Her courage failed her in face of her brother's smile. She could not help seeing Evan through his eyes, a slight sulky young man below middle height, obviously a clerk. His clothes, which had seemed pathetic, were now only ridiculous. She blushed and longed for him to vanish. She was ashamed of having been friendly with him. How she paid, later, for this moment of weakness, but without remembering it!

She made an attempt to carry the situation off without taking any responsibility for Evan. It failed because Eliot was quite brutal, as she knew he would be. Still, she tried.

"Very well. We'll all go and have tea in the library. You and I and William, and Mr. Smith."

"I don't think we want Mr.—Smith," Eliot said. "He'll be much more comfortable with his own friends."

Emily felt tears of mortification under her eyelids. There was a kind of masculine brutality that, in theory—as when

she read the arguments against giving women the vote—
made her rage. In practice, and directed against herself,
it made her cry. The effect was precisely that wrought on
the nervous system of a little girl by Sir John Lambton's
hard voice, raised in anger.

Even William was a little taken aback. He was completely under Eliot's thumb, being far too gentle, good-
tempered and lazy to stand up to him. Eliot Lambton
had managed to join his mother's petulance to his father's
crass will and vitality. When he chose to remember it he
had the appearance, only the appearance, of good manners—learned by rote at his first school. He was as handsome as a painting, well-built, tall, fine reddish hair, straight
nose and lips, eyes of a warm bright brown. He had no
gentleness, and the social sensibilities of a Cossack, or an
eighteenth-century Whig.

Evan lost his head and his temper in the same moment.
He jerked his chin back and said loudly: "Don't speak to
me like that, you fellow. I won't have it."

Eliot was walking away. He stood still, and half turned
his head. "Did you speak to me?"

"I did speak to you," Evan said.

"Then don't again."

He resumed his sauntering walk. Evan sprang forward
and seized him by the shoulder. The scene was over in a
moment—Eliot sent him sprawling among the flowers with
what looked like a lazy push, then walked on. William
held out his hand to help the shabby young man to his
feet, but Evan jumped up without touching it and stood
brushing leaves and earth from his jacket. "Aren't you
coming?" Eliot called. William looked helplessly at Emily.
"You'd better go," she said. He went, and she was left
with Evan, whose fingers were exploring a tear in the sleeve
of his jacket. It seemed the only thing that now interested
him. His best suit, I suppose, Emily thought. No concrete
image of genteel poverty was created in her mind. The
truth is that her notions of poverty were all very sentimental. She insisted that she was a Socialist—the brother-
hood of man and all that—but you know the sort of Socialism

conceived by an intelligent young woman of the upper middle classes. Her own clothes were divided into "new" and "bought a month ago." The Socialism of the well-off is an affair of the head (perceptions of injustice) or the heart (pity for children born to eat dirt). Never of the blood and bones.

"Are you hurt?" she asked, shamefaced and awkward.

"No," Evan said. The skin of his face had a stretched look, as if the effort he was making had expanded the muscles beneath it. Under his strongly arched eyebrows his gaze had become fixed. He walked in front of her along the terrace to the first lawn. She had time—and an eye—to notice that he held himself erect and walked as though he had springs in his shoes.

Evan stood still on the edge of the lawn. "Good afternoon," he said.

"I'm sorry," Emily stammered.

"What have you to be sorry for?" he said lightly, turning his back on her.

She felt a fool and very small. When she came into the library Eliot was pouring tea into three cups set on a desk between the windows. He looked at her without turning his head. "Got rid of your elegant friend?"

"I suppose you think you behaved well," she said hotly. "You behaved like a cad. What had he done to you?" Eliot only smiled.

"You were as bad," she said to William. "Is that the sort of thing you learn at Cambridge?"

"Never mind," William said soothingly. "He's gone and you won't see him again. You didn't really want him to have tea with us, did you?"

Emily did not answer.

She could not bear to remember the episode in which she had played so wretched a part. In a moment of exasperation with herself she begged her father to let her go to Oxford, but she stayed there only two years. During the summer vacation of 1910 she married William Holl. She was twenty and he twenty-six and the first time he had held her in his arms was on the day she was a month old. On that occasion she was sick over the front of his sailor blouse.

She was really attached to him and for nearly a year she had believed herself in love. William's mild adoration helped the illusion. Actually, she only wanted to be loved. The secret impulses of her young, scarcely rounded body, the nervous vitality she had inherited from her father, made her restless. She thought about love and love-making. When she was with William she alternated between stiffness and a passion which he respected because he could not doubt that it was innocent.

Everyone liked William Holl. He was the kindest of men, sober, honest, intelligent, almost a scholar. He loved France and the French, and he read the French of Chrestien de Troyes and du Bellay as easily and with more pleasure than that of Paul Fort. His friendship with Eliot Lambton is one of the mysteries of that complicated emotion. When a man falls in love with a woman very much his inferior in intelligence and breeding we say: "The attraction is obviously physical." Some emotion of the same kind, differing perhaps in degree, must have held him to Lambton. The two had no taste or character in common. What passion there was in their friendship was all on William's side—Lambton's passions were speed, women, and destruction. Probably it never occurred to either of them that William's love for Eliot at this time was his strongest passion—it might even have been his only one.

Did he love Emily? Very much, perhaps, as he loved to handle a La Fontaine of 1762, in green morocco. He would take as much care of one as of the other, to see that they were well housed, at the right temperature, with not too careless an exposure to the air.

They were married in the morning and left on the two o'clock train for France. When they reached Folkestone the sea was still running very high after a gale, and Emily felt ill at the mere sight of it. William engaged rooms at the Pier Hotel for the night. After dinner they walked along the cliffs, and when they came in Emily went directly to her room. She was half afraid and half excited—afraid that William would notice some defect in her which had escaped her own eye. In the bath she looked at herself carefully, at her knees and elbows, still sharp and a little rough from her schoolgirl habit of kneeling on the floor to read, with her elbows on a chair. She cupped her hands under her half-formed breasts and felt suddenly frightened. Suppose he disliked them as much as she had disliked them herself when they began to show? She used to go to sleep face downward, in the hope of flattening them away.

Sitting up in bed she brushed her hair and turned over the pages of a book. She heard William moving about his room. It seemed a long time while she was waiting and then, when he opened her door, she thought she had scarcely had time to breathe since she stepped into bed. William came over to her and sat on the edge of the bed. She looked at him with a weak smile. He put a hand out and stroked her face, then very carefully, drew her to rest against his shoulder.

"I had no idea how small a woman is without her clothes," he said.

Emily laughed, a choked little laugh. "Oh, William", she said.

He went on stroking her hair and the arm lying across her book. Emily was incapable of moving. She said nothing, afraid of breaking a spell.

"Would you rather I didn't stay with you to-night?" William said gently.

She had the physical sense of falling from a height. Involuntarily she stiffened. What could she answer to such a question? Without thinking about it she felt angry that it should have been put to her. How could she answer: "No. Stay with me"?—and if she said nothing, or said "Yes," he would go away—leave her. The notion of being left alone was intolerable, and humiliated her to the point of tears. William laid a finger on her closed eyelids. "Poor child," he said. "Perhaps I oughtn't to have married you yet. Try to feel used to me." He stood up. "Now I'll leave you and you shall sleep just as if you were still in your room at home."

He took her book and the hairbrush away from her and drew the clothes over her shoulders. Emily said nothing. Then he kissed her and turned the light off.

"How unselfish you are," Emily said bitterly. The door had already shut.

She was ashamed of herself and tried not to think that she had been more eager for William than he for her. When her marriage night did come she was awkward and constrained, unwilling to show any emotion. William was careful not to ask too much of her.

There were moments when she longed for him to take her, but she was ashamed to make any sign and the impulse died, leaving behind it a weak feeling of reproach and guilt. She wanted William to approve of her. Rather than offend him she would pretend to have no desires. When he advanced she responded. At all other times she refrained from making any movement that might be read as an invitation to love.

She liked William so much. When they went down to stay on the Yorkshire estate and she saw what he had done already in the way of housing and so forth she began to respect him. She found that he took immense trouble to see that his tenants were well treated. He looked into everything. On the other hand he evaded all personal contacts. Every improvement on which he decided, often at some cost to himself, had to go through his agent and seem this man's work. He would never meet his tenants. He avoided the frightful possibility of a welcome for his bride by arriving unexpectedly, at night. To her plans for visiting each farmer's wife in turn, beginning with the oldest tenant, he opposed a gentle and implacable discouragement. "They don't expect it." A little more strongly—"They wouldn't like it." When she doubted the last, he said: "*I* shouldn't like it." She gave up the idea at once.

With her plans all flattened out she found life in the country unexpectedly dull. There were calls at the neighbouring big houses and elaborate dinner parties, arranged by the housekeeper, in her own. She did not play tennis, bridge, or diabolo. When she confessed that although she liked to ride she was not looking forward breathlessly to the first day's hunting, she felt that her failings were a great deal more conspicuous than William's virtues.

Fortunately William, though more discreet, was as lukewarm as herself. When Eliot and the friends he brought down with him, or ordered her to invite, had shot as many birds as they thought proper William was quite prepared to take her back to town. He never stayed many weeks at a time for fear of being tricked into making one of those personal contacts he shuddered at. Also, there was a conspiracy among his neighbours to force him into Parliament. The division was half Conservative and half, in the narrow industrial section that bit off one corner, Liberal and Socialist. So far the Conservative candidate had held it at successive elections but it was no longer considered "safe." William was clearly the person to make it so, when the sitting member retired at the next election. William thought otherwise. The notion of politics was intensely distasteful to him. He had few ambitions—none of them public.

Back in London Emily read, attented Fabian lectures, and walked in a Suffrage procession. She had begun to feel ashamed of a Socialism that stopped short at theory. She had not even any money to give to it, since she could not spend William's money on a Cause of which, in his curiously unimpassioned way, he disapproved without reserve. When she married, Sir John Lambton gave her a pearl necklace but not a penny by way of dowry. He would have thought such a gift un-English and a waste of his money. He had been forced to support Emily Lambton, but why should he give money to Lady Holl?

She tried writing, but gave it up as soon as she discovered that it is easy to have interesting and delicate thoughts but not very easy to fit them with words.

She did not want a career. One of her friends had become a factory inspector and the other a Bond Street milliner. She admired their competence, but when she thought of imitating them her energy fell back. The mere notion of putting herself forward and of competing with other people paralysed her. She had boundless energy and no self-confidence. She would have been in her element in a society where women pull strings for their men. In pre-War London she was already out of date. She spent a great many hours in useless day-dreams. In one of these William came to her and explained that he was about to lead a crusade against the fatal determinism of the rich, who believe that an accident, the accident of birth, is evidence of an immutable law. He asked her to work with him. She lost herself in a delicious vision—"Gentlemen, I must consult my wife"—emerging from it suddenly, with a smile exactly like one of her father's. It was as sensible to dream of working with the Albert Memorial.

In the end she discovered a Settlement in Hoxton which was in need of workers. She went there four days a week. Her fellow-workers and the Warden himself knew her as a Miss Emily Holl with an address in Earl's Court. The address was that of her maid's aunt. She had an extravagant horror of finding herself the subject of a paragraph in the gossip columns.

PEER'S WIFE WORKS AMONG POOR

"Among those of our young Society matrons who give their time and energy to charitable work is Lady . . ."

The coat-and-skirt she wore as Miss Emily Holl was one she had worn in her last year at school. It hung loosely on her body, which had lost the abrupt vigour of the schoolgirl without acquiring any suppleness since she became a young, happily-married woman. She had to take two people into her confidence, her maid and William, and she had determined, if she were found out, to leave the Settlement at once and begin again at another, under another name. She found that the nights, on which she came back from Hoxton, physically exhausted, were the only ones when she slept. On other nights she was too restless to sleep, and after William had left her she lay awake for hours. Her life seemed futile. She would like to have seven children, but she and William had not managed one. After a time she allowed herself to have the silly feeling that they had missed their chance on the first night.

She met Evan again in 1912, when she had been married two years. There was a board fastened to the shabby wall of the Settlement dining-room, on which the Warden pinned notices of lectures, social evenings (refreshments 3d.) and articles for sale and wanted. Between offers of a second-hand accordion and a child's Sunday coat (trimmed swans-down) she read the announcement of a lecture by Evan Smith. Subject—The Future of Labour.

She persuaded one of the helpers to take her place in the evening gymnasium and went off to listen to the lecture. She sat at one side of the draughty lecture-hall. Evan's face, in profile, came exactly in the centre of one of the fake panels of this improvised room. She began by listening to his calm voice, uttering extravagant prophecies—in ten years, he said, a Labour Prime Minister would lead the House of Commons—but before long the sense of his words vanished. She watched his face, surprised to find how sharp and perfect an image of it existed in her mind, below the soft overlying matter of the last four years. He had a trick of jerking his head back, which she remembered. His lightly-arched nose, small mouth, the underlip too prominent, and boldly-rounded chin, were those of a Roman head on a coin. He looked small beside the bluff figure of the Warden. She noticed that his fingers were short and stubby, in contrast with the delicate lines of his face and erect slight body.

After the lecture she went up to him, nervous, but positively refusing to let him go. Before the Warden he showed no surprise. They left the building together, and he took her arm in the ill-lit street, stinking of drains, fried fish, and ordure. They walked easily together with no sense of the awkwardness that comes of badly-matched bodies.

"I saw you when I began my lecture," Evan said.

"I work here."

They went into a café at the end of the street. A few

tables, covered with cracked oilcloth, were arranged between the wall and a counter. Evan ordered coffee. While they waited for it his glance rested on her hands. "You married. Where is your ring?"

"I don't wear it in Hoxton," Emily said softly. "I'm Miss Holl. Don't tell them." They both laughed, as if she had said something witty. Evan put his arms on the table and leaned over them.

"Do you remember the garden-party? How ashamed you were of knowing me!"

"I shouldn't feel like that now," Emily said, quite calmly. She sipped her coffee, to conceal the excitement that made her want to laugh, run, cry out.

Evan smiled at her and she gripped her hands together on her knee. There is always some look, or gesture, of the person we love, which destroys our defences, no matter on what occasion it is used. Emily realised that she was in love with this young man. Drunk with joy, she lost all sense of responsibility and felt her body drawn taut to receive a touch. They left the café and climbed on to the bus that took Emily to the Mansion House, where she caught another to Berkeley Street. Evan was talking to her about himself but she no longer heard anything except the words spoken in her mind. "I love you. Take me . . ."

As soon as she was at home she realised that she did not know where he lived or anything about him except that he was still working in the London office of Lambton and Grey. It was eleven o'clock. She shut herself in the library and rang up her father. Fortunately, Sir John Lambton was not at home, and when William came into the room he found her putting down the receiver with a frown of indecision.

"What's the matter, my dear?"

"I wanted to ask father—" She bit her lip, suddenly aware of the dangers she was inviting. Suppose her father had answered the telephone! Forcing herself to speak calmly, she went on: "He wants me to ask Mr. Waley to dinner here next week." Mr. Waley was the managing director of the firm. She smiled at William. "I'm so sleepy." Emotion had released a warmth in her, a current of sensual force. It deepened her voice and made her movements seem ampler and slower. In a few hours she had lost the restless darting curiosity of the young girl and withdrawn into herself, guarding her secrets.

William was stirred. He followed her to the door and laid an arm on her shoulder. "Are you tired?"

She leaned away from him. "Too tired to lift a finger," she said, laughing. Her voice was full of vigour and her cheeks glowed. Disturbed, he let her go. His smooth kind face had a hurt look. He had suddenly become very young and bewildered. Emily did not notice it.

In the morning she had recovered, if not her senses, her wits. She had never consciously planned a line of conduct in her twenty-two years but now she lay in bed, weaving schemes. The first of these took her to lunch with her father. Sir John loved to talk about the firm he had started, with two second-hand tramp steamers, in 1875, the first of the bad years. At the end of the meal she had learned that Evan Smith was now chief clerk in his department. He was marked for promotion, a young man who at twenty-four had impressed himself not only on his immediate superiors but by an adroit action on Sir John Lambton himself. She was pleased to find him so remarkable.

That evening during dinner she brought the conversation round to Lambton and Grey, of which William had become a director.

"Do you remember the garden-party four years since, when you and Eliot were so brutal to the young clerk I was showing round? Father spoke of him at lunch to-day."

William made an effort to recover the memory and succeeded in seeing Emily in a yellow dress that did not suit her. "Eliot knocked him down," he said at last.

"Yes," Emily said. Her voice had flattened. She did not care to remember the ridiculous figure Evan cut sprawling among the lupins. "He's been on my conscience ever since." She looked directly at William. "I should like to do something for him."

"I don't see what you can do."

"I could ask him to dinner when Mr. Waley comes."

"Is that quite necessary?" William said mildly.

"Only to quiet my conscience. I let Eliot knock him down. I should like to give him a hand now."

"You may embarrass him in doing it," William said. "Very likely he has no dinner jacket."

I must see him and ask him, Emily thought, at once. Overjoyed to have an excuse for doing a rash thing she decided to wait for him outside Lambton and Grey's fine new quarters in Lombard Street. Before twelve o'clock the next morning she was walking up and down the narrow street, on the side opposite the new building. She wore a hat pulled down over her eyes to disguise her from the doorkeeper, who might recognize her across the street. The necessity for speaking to Evan had cleared every other thought out of her mind. There was no room in it for coquetry, and no room for the notion that Evan might think her wanting in discretion. At twelve o'clock the first batch of clerks hurried from the building, like rabbits rushing into the open air, among them a very few young women. Sir John Lambton did not approve of women in business. He was able to think of women only as the instruments of sex and as such they were obviously out of place in a shipping office.

As the half-hour struck Evan came out alone and walked quickly down the street. The fear that he might not be alone had only just crossed her mind and in her relief she ran after him, catching him as he hesitated before the streams of traffic washing the Bank. He was startled.

"You here? Where are you going?"

"I wanted to see you," Emily said gaily. "It's important. Where do you lunch?"

"At a place in Friday Street. But we can't go there."

"Why not?"

He looked at her without speaking. She felt a pang of mortification. When he took her arm she walked beside him in silence until he stopped before a door and a flight of stairs going down into a basement in Queen Victoria

Street. "We shall be all right here." She followed him without speaking.

The room was crowded with small tables hidden by plates, glasses, cigarette ends, and black-coated elbows. The smoke made her eyes smart. She felt that she had no right here, in a room consecrated to the day's market figures and projects.

Evan chose a table in a corner. He ordered their meal with an air of anxiety and turned quickly to her.

"What has happened?"

"Nothing," Emily said. She tried to choose her words. "Mr. Waley is coming to dinner with me next week. I wondered whether you would like to come the same evening." She hesitated. "I haven't your address."

"I'll give it to you." He tore a page from a notebook and wrote on it. She took it in confusion and slipped it into her glove without looking at it.

"Are you sure you want me to dine at your house?"

"Of course."

He smiled at her. "You're being very kind to me. Why?"

His smile had restored Emily's self-confidence. She gave him a demure look and said: "Have you dress clothes or a dinner jacket? Mr. Waley is very formal."

"I've been meaning to buy them," he said, with a slightly vexed air.

"You must at once. How did you think you could succeed without dining and meeting people!"

"But I'm succeeding so far." He frowned.

"Yes, but—" She leaned towards him, offering herself with her eyes while she spoke in a calm, matter-of-fact voice. "In any career the point comes when hard work and merit have to be supplemented by something more ornamental. You must be seen—outside the office—able to idle in company. That marks you off from all the other hard-working clever young men. Once you have dined with Mr. Waley he will never be able to think of you merely as a useful subordinate."

Evan listened to her with reluctant attention. He knew that she was talking sense and he did not want to admit it.

In his heart he despised all social accomplishments. A
dinner-party would bore him. He resented the social
conditions that made it necessary for an ambitious under-
ling to dance for his reward.

The notion that he was behaving ungratefully stung him.
He lowered his voice to say: "I can't thank you. You're
doing too much."

"I want to help you," Emily said.

As soon as she was at home she looked at his address
and wrote to him—to give him the name of William's tailor.
"He will charge you a great deal and you must not pay him
for at least a year. Use my husband's name when you call.
I have arranged everything." She felt ridiculously happy
in giving him these instructions. It was a little like the
happiness she would have found in teaching a child to speak.

Evan was successful at the dinner-party. He talked well
and not too much, and only Emily noticed that he watched
another guest before picking up his fork or spoon. She had
to remind herself not to keep looking at him. She felt
exactly as though she were seated opposite an object so
much more beautiful than anything else in the room that
it needed an effort to turn her eyes from it.

William had taken an immediate liking to the younger
man. He meant to tell Emily so as soon as they were alone.
As for Mr. Waley—when the managing director of Lambton
and Grey had recovered from the surprise of finding one
of his clerks at Lady Holl's dinner-table he came to the
romantic conclusion that Evan was the illegitimate son
of Sir John Lambton, and amused himself through the
meal by finding resemblances between the young man and
his supposed father.

During the evening Emily found the moment to say to
Evan: "Do you go regularly to the Settlement?"

"No," he answered. "I have only been once."

"I work there on Mondays, Tuesdays, Fridays and
Saturdays," Emily said, with a vague, bright glance. An
unsentimental reflection helped her to forget that she was
making all the advances—the knowledge that she could
be useful to him. He must, she thought, feel that.

She was not Sir John Lambton's daughter for nothing. Her love for Evan could make her indifferent to truth, dignity, and safety, it could persuade her calmly to the most outrageous indiscretions, but it could not make her lose sight of practical details.

Evan was at the settlement on Saturday night. She saw him as she passed through the common-room, his head bent over a magazine he had taken from the rack. For the first time, she thought that he might be falling in love. At least he had taken the trouble to come from Ealing to Hoxton, merely to see her.

She invited him to come and watch her dancing-class. He was startled by the extraordinary beauty of one girl, a button-maker, and when formal dancing began he made his way directly to her. Emily was still teaching the steps to a late-comer in a corner. Evan passed her, smiling at his partner. For a moment she felt that she would fall. The next, she had spoken to the girl at the piano. The music stopped. The etiquette of the class required that Evan should return his partner to her seat among the other young women. When the next dance started Emily was at his elbow and he had the courage to ask her to dance.

During this dance she suggested that instead of going straight home they should take a bus to the Embankment and walk there for a few minutes. At eleven o'clock they were leaning on the parapet opposite the tunnel leading to King's College, their elbows touching. Evan had told her about his father's death, which left him alone in the world, and about his three years' struggle to escape from the position of junior clerk to the one he now held. She listened to him as intently as if he were relating a life and death story of adventure in an African jungle. The world of business, of which she now caught flying glimpses through his eyes, seemed as intricate and menacing. Part of her mind was alive with schemes for furthering his ambitions.

Now she wanted to see the room in which he spent his evenings and Sundays. He lived with a distant relative, in one of those streets of neat hideous little houses, each with its finger-width of garden, which stand for the first triumph of the machine age. The second is in those superb and dignified blocks of flats which a ruined city like Vienna erects for its working-men. At the time of going to press the third has not yet revealed itself. She suggested to him that she should come to supper one evening. If he liked, she would bring the supper, and they would eat it together in his sitting-room, which she saw in her mind's eye as bare and clean, with photographs of Keir Hardie, George Bernard Shaw, and Kropotkin over the fireplace. The eye of Evan's mind, on the contrary, saw—all at once, like the fragments of a child's puzzle—the green plush tablecloth, the cottage piano, never touched, displaying a music album open at the *March of the Troubadour*, the print of *Stag at Bay*, the wicker plant table blocking up the window, and his cousin's peering face. He knew beforehand exactly what his cousin would think of Emily, and he almost disliked Emily for wanting to expose herself to the suspicions of a mean, unhappy, tired, vulgar-minded woman.

Emily was no more able to imagine a woman like Evan's cousin than she had been able to imagine his room. She wanted simply to sit with him in his home—instead of sitting in the impersonal intimacy of a restaurant. It was an exact opposite of the impulse which made him try to keep her at arm's length. He would have preferred her to remain apart from his everyday life. She, on the other hand, wanted to penetrate deeply into his, to take it by stealth, to become a part of it, of its common daily actions, eating, dressing and undressing, putting on one's slippers. She was simple enough to believe that in this way she would be bringing herself closer to him.

She was ashamed to arrive in a cab and walked a mile out of her way looking for Ethelfrede Road. Inside the house, her sentimental notions of quiet poverty received the rudest of shocks. She had never imagined anything like these stuffy, hideous, respectable little rooms. Nor had she ever thought that in a small house all that is going on in the kitchen can be smelled and heard in every part of the house. When Evan opened the front door to her she stepped into a passage filled with so many smells—cabbage water, dirty wallpaper, brass polish, and the indescribable frowstiness of a little house in which too many people are living and eating and wearing month after month without changing them the same tight-fitting dresses—that she could scarcely speak to him. She followed him into the sitting-room, laying on the table the bag of pears she had bought on her way. He had declined curtly to let her provide the meal.

The cousin served it, ignoring both Emily's soft-voiced apologies for giving trouble and Evan's frown. She knew what she thought of Emily and her heart burned under her inflexible corset. If she—and her mother, father, grand-father, and invalid sister—had not so badly needed the thirty-five shillings he handed to her every Friday she would have given him notice that evening.

Emily did her best to eat tough steak and overcooked cabbage. Afterwards, when they were alone, she tried to bring the conversation back to the point where they had left it two evenings before in the obscurity of the Em-bankment, standing between the river and a seat occupied at one end by a drunken woman and at the other by two lovers fastened tightly to each other. On the opposite bank a firm of whisky distillers had been so confident that vulgarity always pays that they had gone one better than any of their competitors and erected an enormous tippling Scotsman. Confronted by this spectacle and by the magical silhouette of the Houses of Parliament, and wrapped in a brown aqueous darkness, Emily and Evan had felt free and happy. They had discussed their childhood, their favourite puddings, and D. H. Lawrence's new novel. Nothing either said was of the lightest importance to the other. They talked for the sake of talking and of being close together. Sometimes Emily answered a question by beginning an entirely new topic or Evan broke in on her account of the opera in Vienna with the title of a new Fabian pamphlet which he pulled out of his pocket and gave her, all warm and creased, to take home.

But here in this room, with no chance of being disturbed or spied on—the cousin had gone up to the bedroom she shared with two other persons, clattering the door—alone in an intimacy broken only by the noises of a household going to bed, they had nothing to say. Emily's wits dried in her head. She looked round her with a fixed meaningless smile. When Evan began a conversation she could only follow him for a sentence or two. After that no more ideas crossed her mind and in despair he began another, which fell dead at the second breath.

The evening was a failure. At ten o'clock Emily said she must go. Evan rose silently and opened the door into his little bedroom, where she had laid her coat and hat. Looking at herself in the mirror fixed to the wall between the bamboo cupboard and the washstand she had to hold her breath to keep from crying with shame. Never had she been so stupid and unattractive.

Evan was waiting in the passage to take her to the bus. As they walked up the empty little street he took her arm suddenly.

"I should like to spend a whole day with you."

Emily stood still. "Why?"

"A day with no other people, no noise, no buses—just ourselves."

Her spirits rose with a violence that made her tremble. "We could take a train into the country, and walk," she said in a low voice.

"Can you manage that?"

"Of course."

They walked on, slowly. A feeling of peace and security had descended on them as soon as they were a few steps beyond the snug little house. Their constraint vanished. Moving as if they had only one heart and one set of limbs between them they reached the main road. Two buses passed them while they stood in a vague dream, reluctant to move, to make any gesture that would break through the diffused cloud of happiness surrounding them like an invisible sheath. As the third approached Emily said sadly:

"I must take this."

Evan signalled to it. It stopped beyond her. She ran. Leaning from the top, she waved her hand to him. Misery

and happiness struck her down instantly and together, so
that she could not find her pennies for tears and did not
know that she was smiling.

She waited several days for Evan to suggest definite
plans. But though she saw him at the Settlement he did
not speak to her again of a day spent alone, without other
people, noise, buses . . . she had so many of his remarks
by heart.

He was almost distant. When she tried to bring the
conversation round to themselves he evaded her with a
smile. She was in despair. She could not sleep. Day and
night, she imagined scenes between herself and Evan and
invented conversations which led inevitably to the words
she wanted him to speak.

In the end she wrote to him. She had looked up the
trains to Goring. They would take one at eleven o'clock,
climb the hill on that bank of the river and come down
to Pangbourne for tea. He wrote back agreeing to everything. His letter was friendly, amusing, and formal. She
read it a dozen times, trying to extract from its few words
the assurance she needed. She hoped that he was playing
a part. Then a frightful thought jumped into her mind.
What if he were interested only in Sir John Lambton's
daughter? He might really be indifferent to her—or in
love with a young woman of whom she had never heard,
another cousin, this time a young, pretty girl, who said
to him: "Well, did you see your Lady Holl to-day? Has
she done anything for you yet? When is she going to
speak to her father about helping you?"

He had too much sense to think that she could arrange
a promotion for him. But what if he still hoped for something, some advantage, from knowing her?

She read his letter again.

On Sunday morning she went to Paddington station to
tell him that she had changed her mind. He was at the
booking office. Hurrying towards her with a smile he took
her arm.

"Come along. I have the tickets."

She was moving mechanically towards a first-class car-

riage. When she looked round he had disappeared. In a
few moments he ran back, red in the face and half-laugh-
ing. "I forgot. I bought third-class tickets. I've changed
them."

"Oh, why did you?" Emily exclaimed. "I can travel
third-class."

He touched her hand lightly. "Please forgive me. I am
a clumsy fool."

The train had reached Goring when Emily found the
courage to ask the first of her leading questions. Absorbed
in an effort to open the door, which had stuck, Evan did
not hear. She was ashamed to repeat it.

They climbed up through beech trees and emerged on
a green ridge, chalk-strewn, and lifted high over the valley.
Evan had brought hard-boiled eggs and figs. He took off
his jacket for her to sit on and she saw that his shirt was
darned in several places. Who did his mending? His short
slender back was close to her hand. She looked at it as he
bent over the egg he was peeling for her. Would he dislike
it if she touched him?

"Are you happy, Emily?"

It was the first time he had used her name. "Are you?"

"I'm gloriously happy. I wish we need never go down
again."

"There must be people you'd miss if you never went
back."

"No one."

"No one?"

"You're the only companion I'd want. When I'm with
you I forget that there is anything else in the world."

Emily listened to this, trembling. If she had not been
in love with him she would have taken it as a declaration.
As it was—instead of thinking: He does love me, then, she
began turning over his words in search of a contradiction.
They must mean nothing—the polite flattery you offer to a
woman who is giving up her time to you. She sat silent.
Surely, if he loved her, he would say so now.

Evan jumped up. "Come along. We have six miles to
do before four o'clock."

"You're in a great hurry."

He frowned. "You said in your letter that you must catch the five train back."

Emily felt a spasm of anger. He had never asked her whether she found it difficult to get away for a day. She thought bitterly: He takes everything for granted, and me, too.

"I have a husband," she said brutally.

Evan looked at her with raised eyebrows. "Why are you here?"

She felt his anger like a blow on the chest. Tears of helpless misery sprang to her eyes. "I don't know."

There was a moment's silence. Then Evan said gently: "Come along."

She followed him down the side of the hill in silence. When they reached the path he began to talk to her about Antwerp. "I wanted to show you the cathedral in the little square. Perhaps one day I can."

"One day," Emily echoed. She did not know whether to smile, laugh, or cry.

They had tea in Pangbourne and caught the train. When they were nearing London Emily said: "Shall we come again next week?"

Evan did not return her smile. "Is it wise?"

Her heart checked. "Wise?"

"Suppose your father—or your husband—found out?" he said brusquely.

If he had now struck her suddenly she would not have felt it. She was not able to speak. The carriage was full of people who were taking no notice of them. She was concerned to keep from them the fact that she had been mortally hurt.

Evan looked at her and held his tongue. When they reached Paddington she let him put her into a cab. He stood below the window.

Leaning back in her corner she did not look round when the cab started. She was still numbed.

In the morning she telephoned to the Settlement that she was ill. She stayed away for a fortnight. When she returned the Warden came up to her with an inquisitive smile.

"Oh, Miss Holl. Your friend Mr. Evan Smith was enquiring for you."

"Has he been here?" she said calmly.

"He came twice. Last week he didn't come at all. Perhaps now—"

She passed the day in an alternation of excitement and suspense. If he came directly from the office he could arrive at six-thirty. At six o'clock she began to calculate his movements. Now he is walking past the doorkeeper. Now he reaches the end of the street, swerves left instead of right, taking the turning towards Hoxton. She found an excuse to work in the hall. At seven o'clock he had not come.

She went back into the lecture-room and began to look over the exercise books of a class in grammar. Evan stood in the doorway. He came over to her.

"Here, take these," she said, and thrust a pile of books into his hands. "Correct them for me." She was laughing. Her body felt light and weak, so that she had to catch the edge of her desk to keep from being blown away in the draught from the door. Evan touched her hand as he took the exercise books. She felt a thread of fire drawn from her throat to her eyes.

"Are you better?"

"Better?" She stared at him foolishly. She had forgotten everything.

"He said you were ill."

"Were you anxious?"

"A little." His face changed. "A great deal," he said in a hurried voice. Emily turned away to hide her eyes. She had given herself away too many times. Now she would be cautious.

For this reason—because she was still being careful—she did not suggest the Embankment when they came out into the squalid street. They walked slowly, passing stalls lit by flaring gas-jets, buses, narrow shops where fried eels were displayed in white enamelled dishes between double frills made of newspaper, women whose faces, in their flattened contours and bold lights and shadows, were like studies for a design of moving figures, starved cats, young men with brutal eyes, broad shoulders and waists too tightly defined by their clothes, stunted Gentile children and lovely little Jews, nourished on scraps cooked in oil. In a doorway of exquisite proportions an old man stood dangling a single pair of shoe-laces from a finger. He had the head of a corpse preserved in sand, brown and shrivelled, a few hairs adhering to the wrinkled scalp. Emily glanced at him, and glanced away. Socialist as she was, these sights, scarcely living witnesses to the savagery of society, offended her. She reflected that if she were Dictator she would forbid all persons earning less than five pounds a week to have children—so that there should be no surplus of broken and diseased.

Evan had followed her glance. "In a really civilised state," he said bitterly, "one such object would cause people to say: There has been a breakdown in the system, we have failed, we are creating hunger and misery from the ribs of plenty. In the State as it is, the only people who shudder at the contrast between an overfed dowager and that starved wretch are spoken of as enemies of civilisation. Enemies of what!"

"I believe in Socialism," Emily said.

"You!" Evan laughed.

"You don't believe me."

"I believe anything you say. Now listen to me. Last week I bought ten shares in a shipbuilding firm. The month before, five. I have a friend in Middlesbrough who can make these small purchases for me. Shipping shares are now worth nothing. In a few years—perhaps with the war your Tory relations are expecting—they will be worth a great deal. I shall buy as many as I can before it comes. Then—*then*—I shall have money and I shall stand for Parliament as a Socialist. I shall get in. You don't believe it. Never mind, it is a prophecy."

Emily watched him in the light escaping from a squalid restaurant, young, his cheekbones too prominent in sunken cheeks, his arched nose. She was nearly ashamed to hear him boasting of the impossible. How could he and his even worse-equipped friends accomplish anything against her father, against William, against the men to whom belonged all the ships, land, minerals under the earth and buildings above it, armies, guns, banks, bars of bullion and cargoes of wheat and steel rails? Like all social rebels who do not belong by birth to the working classes she was more conscious of the forces ranged against the rebels than of the faith that destroys without guns. Her practical common sense told her that Sir John Lambton could crush Evan without turning a hair. Her heart sank. She wanted to prepare him for an inevitable defeat.

Socialism has advanced by refusing to be prepared for an inevitable defeat.

"Let me lend you a hundred pounds," she said in a low voice.

Evan turned scarlet with anger. "What did you say?"

"To buy shares."

"I don't need any money," he said coldly. He added in an ungracious voice: "Thank you."

"Forgive me," Emily said. "I only wanted to help you."

They had turned into a narrow street between high lightless buildings. It was too dark to distinguish the edge of the pavement and Emily's foot slipped suddenly, throwing her against the wall. She seized Evan's arm. They walked on in silence, slowly. Another lighted street appeared at the end, sliced by the houses. Suddenly Evan stood still.

"I love you." He said it as though he were ashamed, with a loud indrawn breath.

Emily closed her eyes. "I love you, Evan."

They leaned on each other in the darkened street, their bodies touching, first at the breast, then their knees, then mouth on mouth, in an embrace that was half merely the relief after long suspense. Emily drew back in order to breathe.

"Not yet," Evan said. He held her again, this time with a conscious need. "Oh my love."

"My love," Emily sighed.

"What can we do?"

"Anything you like," Emily said. She put her arm round his neck and kissed him. She did not want him to begin to think yet. Her quick practical mind was already grappling with difficulties. At this moment she felt confident that she could arrange everything, but she was not ready to talk. Evan would lose his head the moment he began to think. He would want to leave her. To do the right thing—the right thing, in his illogical masculine view, being to plunge into despair and misery the woman you love better than anyone in the world. She stroked his face and thrust a hand under his jacket to feel his heart.

"You love me."

"I adore you," Evan said. "I should like to die—now."

"Stupid! We are just beginning to live. Oh my love, my love. Don't talk nonsense. Touch me."

"I want—" Evan began. He stopped, feeling himself as exhausted as a runner, his heart labouring to keep his lungs going for another moment. "Oh, Emily." He rested his arms on her shoulders, letting his body hang from them. She had to stiffen herself to support his weight.

"Don't worry, don't worry. It will be all right," she said in a soothing voice.

"Are you sure?"

"Quite sure."

Evan pulled himself together. She felt the muscles harden in his arms, under the thin cheap stuff of his jacket. His grip lasted until she was forced to cry out.

"Am I hurting you?"

"A little. . . . I must go."

"Not yet."

"I'm so tired, Evan."

"Very well, then." He released her. Smiling foolishly—unable to see each other's smiles except as deeper shadows under the cheekbones—they walked towards the buses. Evan walked lightly. He had forgotten realities. They would return in force as soon as he was alone, but at the moment he felt young and victorious. Emily looked at him through the window of the bus, trying by her smile to ward off the moment she was coming towards him.

It was midnight when she reached her home. The door of the library opened as she hurried upstairs. William stood in the doorway and looked at her. "Emily."

"What is it?" She scarcely saw him. She felt as though she were enclosed in an opaque, invisible envelope, formed of the emotional states through which she had passed. At one moment she saw him clearly, his face fallen into unaccustomed lines, at the next he was very small and far-off like a figure seen through a diminishing glass.

"You're an hour late. I don't like this Settlement affectation. I shall send the car for you to-morrow night."

"I don't want it."

She shut the door of her bedroom. Kneeling before the fire, she gave herself up to a delicious sensation. Word by word she re-lived the evening, closing her eyes in order to have a clearer image of Evan's face. She found that she could only recall it in flashes, at the moment, for instance, when he stood still in the dark narrow street. She lived through these moments again and again, to squeeze from them the last drops of pleasure and relief.

Sitting with closed eyes, she did not hear the door open. William's presence in the room came to her as a shock, driving the blood from her heart. She stared at him with widened eyes, her face open to his question.

"What are you thinking about, Emily?"

"About nothing. My hair. Look, it's coming out." She held up a long hair in the firelight for his inspection.

"Do you realise that for four days in the week I never see you between eleven o'clock in the morning and midnight?"

"If you had gone into Parliament, or if you were in business, you would be occupied during those hours yourself."

"I don't expect to have to occupy myself with either business or politics, Emily."

"I can't live an empty life."

William leaned against a table. In his dressing-gown

he looked so exactly like his great-grandfather, the friend
of George III., that Emily could imagine she was confronting a portrait by Reynolds. It gave her a sense of
freedom and cruelty—to make an impression on an oil
painting you must damage it.

"You can live the ordinary life of a woman of your class."
He meant "my class," and was too polite to say "our."

"We haven't a child," Emily said.

William met this in a way she did not expect. Taking
her by the arms he made her stand up. "Any child I gave
you would have been frozen to death. You have never
taken the trouble to accept me."

She was surprised by the distortion of his face, caused,
she felt, less by his emotion than by the pain of expressing
it. He is thinking that it is nearly impossible to say these
things, she reflected, and angry with me for making him
think them. As it happened, she was clean off the mark.

"William!"

"Emily!" He put his arms round her with less than
his usual kindness. She realised that he was no longer
vexed with her. The unexpectedness of this love-making
destroyed her self-protective calm and she flung herself
back. William's face became severe and haughty.

"You don't want me to stay with you?" he said.

"Not now. Not to night," Emily exclaimed.

"You're tired."

"Yes. Tired."

The door shut behind him and she sat down on the bed,
with her arms folded across her body. "Thank heaven we
are civilised people," she exclaimed. She was incapable of
realising the frightful cruelty of which she had just been
guilty. Love of one kind—the kind she felt for Evan—
sterilises all other emotions. A normal decent woman, who
is in love in this way, can endure the sight of the torture
she is inflicting on a third person with far greater ease than
she can endure the slightest suspicion of misunderstanding
between herself and her lover. She fell asleep thinking of
Evan. In the morning she rang him up at the office. The
hurried way in which he answered made her sick with dread.

She would not see him for thirty-six hours, when they met at the Settlement. During those hours, though she spoke to William, dined out with him and went with him to a private view, she was less directly aware of his existence than she was of a dozen immaterial things, the tablecloth, a woman's earring, the feel of her own dress under her hand.

When she saw Evan crossing the room to her the following evening she was like a person reprieved from the threat of a long illness. Her body came alive first, then her mind woke from the numbed state into which she had let it sink. She was afraid to move until he came up to her, then she directed his attention to the books in her hand, in order to be able to whisper: "I wanted to see you." She saw that she was going to have a bad time with him. For two days and nights he had been thinking over their situation and he wanted to put an end to it.

Far from worrying, she felt her spirits rise. She looked forward to persuading and comforting him. Her smile as she touched his arm was radiant. "Leave everything to me."

A week later she became his mistress—without any fuss or doubts. As soon as it had happened she felt calm and practical. She saw at once exactly how she must behave—to Evan and to William—in order to be able to help Evan and to keep him as her lover. Her life fell into clearly-defined lines. All the doubts and upheavals of the past weeks vanished—together with the dissatisfaction she had been feeling since her marriage. She was sure of herself and very happy.

To Evan she explained that William was as indifferent to her as she to him. This assuaged the jealousy he suffered when he thought of her returning to William's house. She was too deeply in love to feel any pleasure in his jealousy. She only wanted to remove it.

As for William's—she took steps to deal with it in precisely the spirit in which, if she had been married to Evan, she would have dealt with any situation likely to annoy him. She was not in the least shocked by the need for allowing William to have her on the very night of the Sunday she

spent with Evan at a small hotel in north London. Far
from seeming impossible to her now that she was Evan's,
it had just become possible—and for the simplest of reasons.
William was nothing. If by closing her eyes and surrender-
ing herself to him for a few moments she could buy another
week's safety for Evan she would do it without a sigh. She
was even sorry for William—not because she was deceiving
him but because he did not know what it was to lie on an
uncomfortable bed in a dingy room lost to everything but
an unimaginable happiness.

She arranged her life afresh. The restlessness which had
driven her to spend four days a week at the Settlement
had sunk to nothing, so that she found it easy to make a
show of pleasing William by giving up all but one day there.
She began to occupy her neglected place as Lady Holl, "one
of the youngest and most energetic of Society hostesses."
Luncheon parties were followed by dinners and these by
"small" dances and boxes at the theatres. She drew up a
plan of campaign, marking in advance the evening on which
she could safely introduce Evan into another dinner-party,
under cover of a vague charitable interest. Everything she
did had for its single aim his ultimate advancement. She
thought of him as "Evan," or as "my husband," without
any of the endearments in use among lovers. These she
kept for William, who had more need of them.

The notion of a romantic elopement never entered her
head. If it had she would have shown it the door without
an instant's hesitation. She had no impulse to ask Evan to
sacrifice his whole future to her. Perhaps without knowing
it she was afraid to test the weight of his love against
his ambitions. Certainly she had none of the vanity that
might have driven her to make the experiment. If she had
thought it out she would doubtless have decided that she
could perhaps be happy in a small house working and
cooking—she had learned to cook at the Settlement—for
Evan as he now was, but not for an Evan spoiled and
embittered by disappointment.

Her present life, crowded with schemes for the man she
loved, seemed to her as simple and right as her life before

she met him had been confused and all wrong. She asked for nothing better.

William was puzzled by the change in her. He was now a mature man of twenty-eight, with a ready-made scepticism which fitted him like an old shoe. He knew that a grown-up person does not change character overnight by a simple exercise of will, but he was too lazy, as well as too dignified, to probe her mind. That would have impressed him as a little like spying—a dirty job, which you pay people to do for you without looking closely at their hands.

Emily imagined that she was being too subtle for him. She had some excuse for thinking it, since she was becoming an adept in handling other people. Her mind had developed at the same time as it steadied itself. A great many of her father's unsentimental and masterful qualities were lying dormant in it when she fell in love. Under the influence of that passion which inspires great artists, musicians of the class of Schumann, politicians, and novelists like Miss — with equal ease—these came slowly to the top. And not only her mind but her voice deepened, becoming rich and caressing, a valuable medium for extracting confidences. She arranged Evan's admittance to a week-end party at her sister-in-law's house by drawing from her the complete story of an indiscreet act. Not only this, but her sister-in-law, the wife of an immensely rich Jew, a member of one of those four—or is it five?—Jewish families who select a Christian Governor for the Bank of England, had no suspicion that in inviting Mr. Evan Smith she was making it easy for Emily to spend the night with him under her impeccable roof.

During this week-end Evan met the general on whose staff he would afterwards serve, and two of the directors of Lambton and Grey, to whom Mr. Waley had confided his groundless suspicions as a fact. They were noticeably polite.

A month later she invited him to her house for the second time. To cover her tracks she made William telephone to him at the last moment, to fill the place of a guest who had cried off.

Evan came. She took scarcely any notice of him and made him sit at a corner of the table where three draughts met, the seat allotted to unimportant persons. William went out of his way to atone for the slight.

The next evening when she saw Evan he told her coldly that he could not go on. He had never noticed the draughts or his deaf partner but William's solicitude had touched his pride. He raged against her for being willing to bring him into the same house with her husband.

"Either let me go or give up everything else and live with me."

Emily's knees shook. She pressed her hands together. "Very well. When do you want me to come? And where? To-night? Now?" She saw that he was nervous and over-tired. Sooner than undertake the trouble of an elopement and a divorce he would give her up. Her cleverness was useless to her at this moment. It is only when you are not really in love that the notion of failing sharpens your wits.

All at once Evan gave himself into her hands. "Are you telling me the truth? You assured me that you and William live together like strangers. I saw him look at you and take your arm. Tell me the truth. I think I'm going mad."

Emily closed her eyes to hide an insane relief. "Like friends," she said quietly. "William and I are good friends —nothing else. You mustn't undervalue him. He is extremely intelligent, kind, upright, good company, and not very sincere. There are some things that I can discuss with him. He—"

"Don't tell me any more about him," Evan begged. "Is he your husband or not? That is all I want to know."

"You are my husband."

Unexpectedly he came across the room and knelt beside her, pressing his forehead against her knees. "Tell me the truth, Emily." Without lifting his face to look at her he put both arms round her waist.

"I have told you. I love you. William is nothing to me."

"You don't . . ."

"Never. Never since I fell in love with you."

Evan looked at her with the ghost of a young smile. "Say: I wish I may die if I am telling a lie."

She repeated the words, smiling.

"Oh my love," Evan said.

She slipped to the floor beside him, taking his head on her arm. He fell asleep there, from fatigue and a nervous exhaustion. While he slept she went over in her mind the various plans she had made, and altered them to guard against the repetition of such a scene. Evan must not be harmed. Unless she strengthened him she would have failed. When he awoke she was smiling at him, a mother and a wife in one.

She had realised that she would have to be extremely careful at present. If it occurred to him that he could not become anything without her help he would at once drop her to make certain. His pride was too easily upset. Unlike William's, it sprang from his belief in his own ability. William never troubled to think that he was intelligent. He took his intelligence for granted, together with his long, very narrow feet, an estate of twenty thousand acres, and two town houses. Later perhaps, when Evan had succeeded, she need not pretend that she was not working for him. She thought his scruples childish. She respected them only out of fear, the fear of losing him.

One day her father spoke to her about Evan. He had had his eye on the young man for nearly a year, since Evan's name came before him at the foot of a suggestion which he could not use only because the firm of Lambton and Grey was going through a financial crisis. The shipping world this year was one large crisis. Ships were laid up, yards idle, and the staffs of shipping offices cut down by half.

Sir John Lambton had not relaxed his grip of Lambton and Grey when it became a limited company. If he did not himself engage the junior clerks he was consulted when one was dismissed. Just now it was a question of economising by uniting two departments under a new manager.

He remembered Evan Smith. At the same time he remembered having been told that his daughter sometimes
invited the young man to dinner. He went to see Emily.

"You've been doing Settlement work in my office."

"You mean young Smith," Emily said, calmly. "I remembered him from the trial trip of the *Russian King*.
He was on board. Then four years ago Eliot quarrelled
with him at mamma's garden-party and knocked him
down."

"Eliot's a fool and you're another," Sir John said, in
very good humour with her. He disliked his son and was
very fond of his daughter. Privately, he thought William
a stick and regretted that she had married him.

"Do you disapprove of my inviting him here, daddy?"

"Not if William doesn't, ho, ho."

"William likes him."

She had been going to seat herself on his knee. She drew
back abruptly. Only that morning she had calculated that
her child—Evan's child—would be born in less than five
months. Perhaps she was already heavier?

She blushed. Her father, who had been watching her
without a thought in his head, suddenly had one that made
him creak with rage and swell with amusement. Suppose
she were Evan Smith's mistress—what a filthy trick, what
unheard-of impudence on the part of the young man, and
what a sell for William! He finished by clapping both hands
on her shoulders with a gross smile.

"Would you like me to do something for Smith?"

Emily felt herself scarlet with shame. Rallying, she
forced herself to look at him as one good fellow at another.
She felt that she was positively leering.

"Just as you like, daddy."

"I'll do it." He turned with his hand on the door, and
shook his fist at her. "Be careful, now. No nonsense, my
girl—you know what?"

As soon as he had gone Emily ran upstairs—she wanted
to be before him with her news, to write to Evan about
his first child before he could write to tell her that he had
been promoted.

Their child was born in June, 1913. She was weak for a long time afterwards—a physical idiosyncrasy made child-bearing more than usually painful and dangerous for her, and this time was not the worst. Because of her weakness she began to feel a slight remorse. She felt that it was hard on William to be succeeded by another man's child. From remorse she passed quickly to anger—why had she to let William pride himself on being the father of a son, and to send, hiding pencil and paper under her pillow, long letters to Evan filled with details of the child's progress and explanations of William's attitude? She had to persuade Evan that William was so indifferent that he did not care how many children she had by another man.

With returning strength her sane practical intellect reasserted itself. She turned out all thoughts of confessing to William and asking Evan to take her away. Her father's comments when he came to see the baby strengthened while they irked her. She realised that at the first breath of scandal the noisy, gross-living old shipowner would turn Evan out of the firm. Then, too, William's dignity must be saved. That, and Evan's happiness and success, were her task in life.

Before long, she was deeply, richly happy again. She felt her life unfolding itself with a new richness and a slow subtle beauty in her schemes for Evan's future. He would accept help from the mother of his child. She regretted nothing—she had no longer either regrets or doubts.

CHAPTER II

THE War breaking in on her plans made them seem even more innocent. What did her few easily excusable lies matter in a world which was shortly to turn rotten with lies, dead bodies, and the useless tears of women?

She was asleep when the telephone rang in her bedroom at two o'clock in the morning, and William's voice speaking from a room in the Foreign Office warned her that war was certain. Still half asleep as she listened she spoke to him as "Evan," but without noticing it. The mistake did not make any difference in William's manner to her when they met at luncheon. It had told him nothing that he had not known for six months.

When he discovered that she was Evan's mistress he had passed through a crisis of rage and mortification that emptied him for the time being of all emotion. But he was pre-eminently a sensible man, as well as a cool and well-bred one, and he took into account the fact that very few people knew of his misfortune. If he said nothing himself, there was little chance that it would ever become known. He had great faith in Emily's genius for management, which he had seen in practice and admired for two years. At the same time he discovered, in her choice of Evan as a lover, a reversion to type. It was the kind of thing he ought to have expected from the daughter of a milk-boy turned shipowner.

To his surprise he felt no less drawn towards Emily than before the discovery. He even felt a certain mischievous satisfaction in the reflection that he could have by merely strolling into his wife's bedroom a pleasure the other man had to plan for and achieve with difficulty and at long intervals. His desires, never at any time in his life strong, actually needed some such complicated mental stimulus.

He was now mildly interested to see how she would behave if the young man enlisted—and if he did not.

In fact Evan was the first employee of Lambton and Grey to enrol, on August 6th. He was moved by two conflicting instincts. The first, which was deliberate, warned him that he would further his ambitions better by going than by staying. If he stayed he would certainly rise in the firm, with the possibility of becoming rich. But this was only half his ambition. The other was to be rid of the shocking sense of inferiority which, in defiance of his will, seized him the instant he entered one of those brilliantly lit rooms whose hostess had invited him for no clearer reason than seeing him in Emily's drawing-room a week before. In a moment—the moment when he heard the word *War!* spoken breathlessly in his ear by Mr. Waley, his eyes popping in and out like a rubber toy—in that moment he saw the chance of putting a background of trenches, military tailors and Brigade Staff councils in place of his other drab, mortifying background of elementary school and the pencil of a junior clerk.

The other impulse at work in him was the sudden emergence, after ten years, of the boy who had hungered for excitement and adventure and taken in exchange the uncomfortable stool thrust upon newcomers in Lambton and Grey's office. He felt wildly happy.

Sir John Lambton saw to a commission for him. In December he spent three days with Emily before going to France. They arranged to meet at a small country hotel in Sussex. Emily was late, and very nervous. She did not at first see him in the badly-lit lounge. A young subaltern, exactly like every other young man she had seen that day in streets, trains, and cafés, threw down the magazine he was reading and hurried towards her. She suppressed a cry. At that moment she felt as old as the world and completely helpless. There was now nothing she could do for him.

On their last day she was in despair. She hid it as well as she could. Evan was excited and happy, eating and laughing like a schoolboy and making love to her with a passion in which already she detected the rough touch of experience. He was no longer a young single-minded lover. It was a soldier who took her in his arms, without any of the sensitive ardours which she had enjoyed. He was gay, hurried, and violent. She could imagine that their bed was a sinking ship, and only a few minutes were left them in which to make certain they were alive.

"You'll come back?" she said foolishly.

"Of course. You'll bring me back."

"I?"

"I shall come," Evan said, "for this. I have too much life in me to let it run away over there."

"Will you ever love anyone else?"

"I don't suppose so," he laughed.

"Aren't you sure?"

"I'm only sure of one thing. Please don't talk so much, my darling—I haven't the breath to answer you. Do you see?"

Emily closed her eyes, to shut out the sight of his young, charming mouth, less kind now that it had become familiar with shouted orders, oaths, and bawdy stories. He loved her as much as ever but he was no longer very much surprised at his good fortune. These things had happened before. What surprised him was that he had once thought of Emily as conferring a favour.

It was only when he said good-bye to her that she had again, for a few final moments, the earlier Evan. He took her hands and pressed them over his eyes. Then he kissed the palms and closed her fingers over them.

"Keep them until I come back."

"Until—oh Evan. *Evan.*"

She travelled back to London in the corner of a third-class carriage, her eyes empty, meeting the emptiness in the eyes of other women. Why do women tolerate war, which robs them of their identity? During a war the papers which women present in order to draw separation allowances and so on and so forth ought to bear only the words: "Female, one. Useful (according to age) for breeding, nursing, amusement, and work behind the lines."

William was expecting her. He had taken the trouble to find out, with the help of a school friend at the War Office, the movement orders given to Evan's battalion, and he knew exactly what train Evan would have to catch to present himself at the last possible moment. He saw her come in, exhausted by grief and the kind of love-making provoked by the threat of separation, and felt sorry for her. He felt, too, a serious repugnance at the thought of touching her hand.

During dinner he avoided any reference to the War. He talked instead of the country in winter. He had just come back from his Yorkshire estate, where he had spent the fortnight in which Emily was expecting every day a telegram from Evan with the news of his final leave. When he spoke of the rimed grass sparkling like a lake in the sunlight he saw the pupils of her eyes contract and her fingers close over her napkin. He realized that he was recalling to her some scene which she had admired the day before with Evan.

"I was rejected again to-day—for even the lightest of War office jobs."

"What did they say to you?" Emily asked. Her mind supplied her with the words, which she made use of without understanding them.

"Just what the other doctor said. My heart, which is sound enough for all ordinary purposes—such as riding and marriage—would collapse under any long-drawn-out strain. I can no doubt find some sort of civilian job, under the government, but they won't have me in the army or give me a uniform to cover my shame."

Emily felt an embarrassed pity. She saw that he was suffering and put it down to his disappointment.

"You can help at home," she said. "We must offer a hospital."

Her pity made William dislike her. "That can be your work," he answered in a light voice. "It will take your mind off your other anxiety."

"My other—?" Emily echoed.

"I mean your anxiety about Eliot. Who else have you at the front?"

She had forgotten everything to do with her brother, who had joined the Flying Corps and had already been decorated. From William's manner she understood that he knew, or suspected her. She felt an impulse to tell him everything. If it had no other effect it would at all events relieve her of a crushing burden. She need no longer lie and scheme in order to see Evan alone, and if William wanted a divorce that would release her for good.

In another moment she had rejected the impulse as weak and vulgar. Only hysterical or badly brought-up women confessed without being asked to do so. If William wanted information he would ask her for it openly. In the meantime she was not to be let off the task she had set herself when she began with Evan. She had to work for Evan, who needed her help, and at the same time to protect William's name and dignity. (She forgot that she had already given his name to Evan's child.) Now that it was too late, since he knew already, to save his dignity in his own eyes she could still, if he wished, save it for him in the eyes of other people, by putting up a show of being a devoted wife.

She waited to see whether he would ask her about Evan. He said nothing. Instead he began, with a friendly air, to talk about turning the big unwieldy house in Yorkshire into a hospital. She listened to him, putting Evan out of her mind and giving it wholly to her answers. Politeness and an appearance of interest were among the things she could still give him.

The hospital was offered in her name. William had managed to have himself put in part charge of the propaganda that was to be carried on in neutral countries, in explanation of England's attitude to such thorny questions as trading with the enemy. He began his work by preparing an immense campaign in the United States, where there were a great many Germans who had failed to repudiate their country, as well as a great many Americans who were happy in the belief that the hand of the Lord had smitten Europe and purposefully spared His Americans. He stayed in London, working ten or twelve hours a day—while Emily established herself as almoner and secretary of the hospital, which was soon filled with the bloody wreckage of Loos. The house was improved out of knowledge by being purged of the Edwardian decorations carried out by William's father. Painted walls and bare floors restored it to a decent dignity.

At the end of 1915, when Evan came on leave for the first time, she returned to London. Her earlier feeling of helplessness had vanished. She saw that there were a great many ways in which, as William's wife, she could help a young officer, intelligent enough to say only what was expected of him and to smile by way of disagreement. She gave a number of dinner-parties, where he met the

influential people of the moment, those who were really
influential as well as those who like Colonel Repington
were anxious to seem so. She was able to invite Evan to
these through her unspoken bargain with William—by
which she received a reasonable licence in return for the
appearance of order.

She had taken for him a small furnished flat, the entrance
to which was behind Selfridge's, so that she approached it
under cover of sacrificial dumps of silk stockings, umbrellas,
bargains of the day, and iced drinks. Here they spent every
afternoon together, and every night when she could leave
her house early enough to avoid surprising the servants.

Evan had changed—for the second time. He was a different being from the boisterous young soldier to whom she
had said good-bye, locking her fingers together to prevent
them from tearing at her flesh. He had not become again
that shy, serious, abominably touchy young man elbowed
aside by the soldier and now finished off for good by ten
months of war. The new Evan was sturdier in body and
steadier in mind. He did not try to dominate her. He
seemed glad to find that she had acquired a more definite
personality under the blows of doubt and circumstance.
Her hospital work had convinced her that nothing excuses
war, not even victory. Evan encouraged her to talk. It
was as though he wanted above all to be spared the effort
to be anything of himself. She spoke and he listened, she
made herself the staff on which he leaned. The efficient
soldier—the disguise in which he appeared before General
Staff Officers and friends of G. S. Officers in her drawing-
room—became, as soon as he was alone with her, a middle-
aged man of twenty-seven, silent, grateful for kindness,
taking his cue from her for everything he pretended to want.

"Did you think of me when you were in France?" she
asked.

"Yes."

"Often?"

"Not very often."

Emily's eyes filled with tears. He smiled lovingly at her,
and took her in his arms. "My dear little love. I don't

think of you because I can't live in two worlds at once. As soon as I stepped into the leave train I began to think of you. I thought of nothing else until the moment when I heard your voice at the other end of the telephone. Then for the first time I thought of a bath, clean sheets, and a bed. I wanted to have a bath before I touched you."

"You still love me better than anyone?"

"Better, a great deal better than anyone. I was a fool when I left you last December. I didn't want to promise. I imagined I didn't know myself well enough?"

"And now, Evan?"

"Now I know that I shall never love anyone as I love you. You are in my bones. I wish we could marry."

"We are married."

"Before everyone, I mean. I hate privacy. I should like everyone to know that last night you—"

"You are talking dreadful nonsense, my poor Evan."

"I should like to sleep like this all night."

In everything he did when they were alone together, even to the gesture with which he opened his suitcase to display his need of new socks and shirts, she detected a fresh surrender. He was deliberately re-vowing himself to her—no longer as a dazzled boy, but with the seriousness of a grown man who has fewer illusions and fewer, stronger desires. If she had nearly lost the boy she was re-capturing the man. Before he left, he brought her a copy of the will he had made in her favour. She laughed with tears dropping on to her hands at the care with which he had enumerated his few possessions, a gold repeater watch of his father's, a jet locket, two china figures of the Virtues, and a caseful of books on economics and political science.

When he went back, in December, he joined the staff of her friend, General R— S—, as a learner. At the same time she heard that he had been awarded the D.S.O. for his conduct in holding a redoubt for five days with a handful of men. She had no idea what this meant—the War had become incomprehensible to all civilians. Too many men were engaged, over areas in which an advance of a few feet represented so many hundreds dead and so many thousands maimed and tortured that the whole action entered the realm of nightmare, and could not be translated into terms of a sane world.

Four months later he wrote to her that he had been made a G.S.O.3. She wrote to congratulate him, taking care not to say: "I suppose this means that you are now comparatively safe." She was afraid even to think it, since the afternoon on which, when she was sitting with her school friend, Diana West, the telegram announcing Tom West's death was brought in to them. Diana had just said: "Now that Tom is comparatively safe I can go to sleep without dreaming that I hear his voice saying: *Diana, they're hurting me*. I used to hear it every night and wake crying. Since he was sent to Brigade headquarters I've been able to sleep." The door opened and a servant came in carrying the telegram as though it were nothing.

In June Evan wrote to her that he hoped to come on leave during the next few weeks. The same day William decided to visit America as a missionary from civilised Europe, and invited her to come with him.

It was a moment when she had to choose between two impossible duties. This was the first moment in which Evan's private happiness had come sharply into conflict with William's public dignity. She rejected without thinking about it the notion that William had a higher right to be considered. The promises she had made him, when she married, weighed as heavy but no heavier on her than her promise to Evan, made with an equal seriousness and assented to by her whole mind.

In fact, if William had known nothing about the other man she would have made some excuse to let him go to America alone. She could plead her work in the hospital, or the health of her son. But she saw that he would resent bitterly a refusal. The occasion was too important. There was no way in which she could manage to save his dignity and at the same time stay in England, to be there when Evan came on leave.

She told William that she would go with him. They sailed before she had had a reply to the letter she wrote to Evan, explaining—something he could not understand but would have resentfully to accept.

America was hot and over-simplified. It was the only country in which idealism was still paying thirty per cent. In England, as in the rest of Europe at war, ideals were being worked to death to keep up the supply of ammunitions and lies, or flickering quietly out in the brains of men tried beyond endurance or sliced in half by a shell. William's job was to persuade Americans to enlist their ideals more directly in the cause of civilisation—as expressed in the tears of women, the sighs of children condemned to death by the Allied blockade, and the growing piles of torn male flesh, severed limbs, and entrails hanging down like bunches of unwashed tripe in a butcher's shop—than they were doing already in sending only their manufactures to take part in the great struggle. Not content with these, Europe wanted the bodies of their young men to make certain of victory. Both parties to the struggle coveted the as yet untapped reservoir of blood on the other side of the Atlantic. Both were prepared for any lie, bribe, or special pleading, to prove the advantage of dying on one rather than on the other side of a line drawn from the Belgian coast to one of the cradle rivers, the Euphrates. The German emissaries were at a disadvantage. They were astonishingly tactless, and told lies only when the truth would have made a better impression.

William had overworked in England. In America he found himself called upon to make a double effort. He had not only to arrange and modify the information at his disposal, but to present it in such a form that it would not irritate the palates of Americans used only to a few simple violent flavours. He was not liked. The newspapers made fun of his voice and clothes. "Everything about our latest visitation, Lord Holl, was cool except his suit." Cartoons of him, a long blank face surmounting a stick of a body, began to appear in the Sunday supplements. Even his invariable politeness was an offence. People suspected that he was unable to see any difference between one American and another.

After the first month, when she nearly died of the heat, Emily revived sufficiently to see that William was a failure. She took him in hand. A vein of coarse good humour ran through her, not too deep. She managed to make use of this to establish William as a good fellow. She wrote his public speeches, told him what to say to reporters, and even succeeded in teaching him the social differences between a Senator from Oregon and a Boston banker. She herself became an adept in assisting at those purely American ceremonies which begin: "I come to you as one woman coming to other women, to talk together about the things we all know."

They stayed six months in America. As she stepped on board the boat for home a clerk from the Embassy rushed after her with a package of letters. Among them was one from Evan, to whom she had cabled the date of her return. He wrote that he had arranged to go on leave in January. He would be there to meet her.

In fact he was a day too late. She arrived in London at five o'clock on one of those afternoons when, with every light blazing, the West End looks like a fair. Impossible to believe that within a short walk of it women in coats too thin to keep out the cruel damp are fingering cheap pieces of meat exposed nastily on stalls and looking closely at rough badly-made shoes that are yet too dear for them to buy. Now, in the third year of war, all was darkened, and late shoppers hurried along with the air of persons engaged in some not very reputable business. When her car stopped in the traffic block before the Ritz Emily noticed the two occupants of a taxi drawn up on her left. They were half-lying, clasped together, the man's arm, in a khaki sleeve with two stars, holding the girl so that she seemed fitted into a groove formed by the curve of his body.

As soon as she was at home she hurried to dress for an important dinner-party. (Any dinner-party was important which included a member of the War Council, a military correspondent, and one or two elderly gentlemen known to be keeping diaries in which the conversation would be recorded between a word of praise for the *coq au vin* and an estimate of the numbers killed in a recent engagement.) She could scarcely keep her eyelids apart. Seated between a portrait painter and a diarist she tried to keep her thoughts from going in search of Evan. It was no use. After a time she gave herself up to a half-deliberate dream. Evan's physical presence, conjured by her imagination within the narrow walls of a taxi, became so real that she sank out of touch with the people on either side of her. She forgot to eat, and the smile left over from her last spoken words remained fixed.

She did not hear Evan's name spoken at the other side of the table except as a disturbance in the centre of her body, affecting her like noises heard at night, not identified, familiar and still frightening. Half roused now, she caught the name of Agnes Wilmott, her friend since their childhood. She looked up.

"Agnes? But I haven't heard from her for nearly five months. How is she? Does she still prefer a Russian uniform to any other?"

"My poor Emily, you've been lost in America too long. Agnes became a patriot in June last year, when she fell in love with a young man I met, if I am not mistaken, my dear, in your house. Evan Smith. . . ."

There was an arrest in her blood. It hesitated at the entrance to her heart and rushed forward madly. "Evan Smith?" She seemed to herself to have dropped the name into a deep shaft. It echoed back to her in fragments, broken by its descent. Ev-an. "And does he—did he seem flattered?"

"They were inseparable."

The heavier the blow the longer the interval of comparative insensibility. Emily's hands trembled and her throat closed against food, but her mind remained unmoved. "And Agnes's husband?"

"You don't expect Jack Wilmott to trouble himself about Agnes any more? Besides, he was in Mesopotamia."

Emily laughed.

One or two people at the table had an uneasy memory

of gossip, as stale now as last month's communiqués from the front, in which Emily had been credited with a serious weakness for the young man. Their silence was enough to spread a feeling of constraint and discomfort which froze round the conversation. Emily could feel the unspoken alarm in their minds but she could not deal with it. Her own mind was isolated, cut off from her body by the snapping of a cord. Frantic telephone messages ordering her to smile, to pick up her glass, to speak, to cease shaking, failed to reach the affected centres. She was speechless and quivering. William had been watching her with admiration. This now became pity, sharpened by a prick of alarm for himself. If Emily were to collapse here, in front of them all, it was he who would be stared at the closer, and his pride suffer a more lasting collapse than her courage. He came to her help with more adroitness than he had ever shown in playing off the German Ambassador in Washington against the President's advisers.

"Do you realise, Emily, that you are half a year behind all the really important war news? You will have to give up studying the front pages of newspapers and learn instead who has advanced or retreated at home." Then, with a gesture that drew the attention of everyone to himself, he exclaimed: "You don't know Emily over here. If you had seen her, as I have, standing between the President of the Anti-smoking League and the Chairman of the Tobacco Trust and smiling happily at both, you would never trust her again. Let me tell you that she is far too intelligent."

During the drive home he allowed his hand to drop accidentally on hers. She was very cold. She turned to him with a smile.

"I think I shall sleep well to-night. Shall you?"

"I daresay," William said.

In the morning Emily rang up Agnes Wilmott. During a sleepless night she had tried to balance Evan's unfaithfulness against her own. But it is impossible to feel that the sins one commits are as serious as those of other people. She reflected that Evan had deliberately chosen Agnes, where she had sacrificed herself to William simply in order to keep the peace. It was like her to try to strike a balance, in order to convince herself that she was still a little on the right side.

It did not comfort her. A frightful anguish took hold of her whenever she pictured Evan with the other woman. She wept bitter scalding tears. You, whoever you are, who have not yet had the experience, can say what you like—no crushing intellectual defeat, no loss of public prestige, is so hard to bear as the private torture of imagining a husband or a lover lying naked in the arms of another woman. It is part animal jealousy and part an extraordinary complication of emotions, hopeless childish grief, disappointment, shame, queer bitter pain. No one who has not yet had to endure it has more than a pallid notion of its cruelty. Emily felt a hundred years old.

"Now why," Agnes cried, "have you never written to me? Come to lunch and I'll tell you all I have been doing."

At lunch Emily explained that she had given up eating in the middle of the day. Banting had not yet become a craze and Agnes was amused to hear that in America fashionable beauties keep themselves in looks on a diet of black coffee, grape fruit, and spinach. She was a plump young woman with the sly beauty of a Flemish burgher's wife. Emily and she were the same age, twenty-six. Beside this laughing young woman, whose breasts pushed upwards against her dress, Emily saw herself peaked and old. She thought of Evan's brusque seeking hands and suffered frightfully. Fatigue had blacked in an ugly triangle below her eyes.

"Is it true that you are Evan Smith's mistress?" Emily asked. She could not wait to be tactful about it.

"Who told you?"

"Is it true? I ask because I am in love with him myself."

"Well, really, Emily, what an extraordinary creature you are. Why tell me? I might easily give you away."

"I should only deny it," Emily said calmly. "And you are such a liar that everyone would believe me."

"You're calling me a liar!"

"Why not? Do you remember stealing sixpence out of

my pocket when we were at school? You always said you
hadn't taken it."

"I never did."

"I saw you."

"What has all this to do with Evan? ... I daresay if
you had been at home he would never have looked at me,
but don't get it into your head that he was not so very
anxious to have me. He enjoyed it, too. We have a good
time."

"I don't want to quarrel with you," Emily answered.
Among other things she had made up her mind during the
night that no blame attached to Agnes. I am a modern
woman, she said to herself: I won't try to punish her for
poaching my land—jealousy is an inexcusable fault.

"What are you going to do?" Agnes asked, smiling.

"Nothing."

Evan was due to arrive in the evening. She went over
to his flat to wait for him, taking the opportunity to search
in every room for traces of Agnes. She found nothing
except a photograph, which Evan had thrown into a
drawer. She destroyed it, crouching in front of the fire in
order to burn it piece by piece.

She had not yet arranged with herself what to say to
Evan. The only thing she wanted to know was whether
he loved Agnes. At first she had taken it for granted, but
a few hours had been long enough for her to become familiar
with the notion that Evan was after all exactly like other
men. She even felt surprised that she had expected something better.

He arrived while she was still trying over questions and
answers. To touch him reassured her. At once she knew
that he had not altered. Agnes had not come off on him.
Their bodies came together as easily as if they were still
of one mind.

After a long time Evan said: "You are crying. What's
the matter?"

"Nothing."

"Tell me! Is it from happiness?"

"Are you happy?"

"It's nearly a year since we did this."

"Agnes," Emily said.

"What did you say?"

"Do you love her? Don't be angry with me. You can tell me—I only want to help you."

Evan had moved away from her. Emily watched him without being able to understand what was going on in his mind. She felt a moment of panic. What if she had made a mistake and he were about to leave her?

"You have explained to me about William," Evan said slowly. "How did you think that—"

Emily was ready to admit everything. Her reason issued a final warning to her. No man, it said, least of all Evan, will forgive you for all those lies: he half believes them still. Confess to him and he won't believe any longer that your child is his. She dragged herself up from the couch.

"William is nothing," she began. "Nothing at all. I have only—"

She felt the room slip its moorings and begin to move sideways. Her knees sagged. Exhaustion, emotional strain, and the fact that she had had no food for twenty-four hours were enough to account for a faint that lasted almost ten minutes. When she recovered consciousness she was stretched out on the floor and Evan was kneeling beside her. She forced herself to sit up, only to reassure him. "I'm all right," she said.

"What would you like? A glass of brandy? I have some in my flask."

"I'd like a good cup of tea," Emily said.

"I'll get you some. I used to make tea for my mother, when I was little."

He went into the tiny kitchen. In a few moments she followed him. He had remembered to warm the teapot. She held it while he poured in the water. When they were drinking it she said:

"Now tell me about Agnes."

Evan looked uncomfortable. "There's very little to tell," he answered. "I was bored without you. I thought I might be killed when I went back. That—and vanity. . . ."

"Vanity?" Emily said. She had begun to feel wretched again.

"You forget that I was nobody when you first picked me up."

"I don't understand. . . ."

"I couldn't make you," Evan said. "For pity's sake, Emily, try to believe me. I love you so much that I don't even think about it any more. You're—what's the use?—you're the woman I love, always have loved and always shall. Agnes is a nice creature. I like her, she amused me. I wouldn't care if I never saw her again."

"Then why did you—" Emily said.

"I don't know. On my honour I don't. I suppose I do. It just happened."

"Will it happen again?"

"I hope not."

"Aren't you sure?"

"I'm sure now. But I was sure before. Before it happened, I mean."

Emily folded her hands to help her to bear that. "You hate to miss anything, don't you, Evan?" she said quietly.

He looked at her, and came over to the couch. "Try to forgive me."

"I don't need to forgive you. I love you. I believe I could make myself give you Agnes if you needed her."

"Don't."

"Don't what, my dear?"

"Don't say things like that," Evan said, in a low voice. "I can't stand it. I don't love you in that way. If I weren't sure of you I should want to go away." He was kneeling in front of her and took her hands. "Just now I began to ask you about William. Promise me that when I ask you to leave him, you'll come at once."

"I promise." She knew that he would never ask her. It was only—he liked to think that one day he would carry her off. But it was not true. When it came to the point he would think of his career and his future and all that. She looked at him and saw that he knew what she was feeling about it. She pulled her hands free and took hold of him.

"If I try not to think about you with Agnes, will you promise me something?"

"Do you think about me with her? Oh my poor Emily."

"It doesn't matter."

"It does. I've hurt you horribly. ... What am I to promise?"

"Promise me to say this to yourself: Emily loves me so completely that she doesn't mind what I do. She doesn't care whether I'm successful or not. She doesn't want me to do or be anything except for myself."

"Is that true?"

"True as I see you, as the children say."

She was deathly tired. Tears sprang from her eyes before she could check them and she let them run over her face while she sat with crossed arms, rocking herself on the edge of the couch.

"I hate her. Do you know what she is? She's had half a dozen men since she married. You'll be able to replace her any time by taking a walk through Leicester Square at seven o'clock. They come out earlier now that there are no lights."

"Emily," Evan said. "Listen to me, I can't let you talk in this way about a woman I've ... liked."

Her tears stopped as suddenly as if she had been able to press a thumb down, hard, at their source. She looked so old. "Liked, Evan? What a word to use?"

"I do like her," Evan said. A nervous contraction of his face alarmed her. "For God's sake, Emily, don't put me in the position of having to defend her to you, or else to listen to your abusing her. I couldn't stand it."

"It's your first evening at home—I oughtn't to behave like this," Emily said. "I won't. I won't speak of it again. I was a fool. You see, it doesn't matter—when I love you so much. ... You haven't had any dinner."

"I dined on the train. I didn't want to waste any time to-night in eating."

"I've wasted it quarrelling with you instead."

"We don't quarrel," Evan said. "You don't quarrel with your blood. ... I'm tired, Emily."

"Let me rest you."

His forehead was covered with a film of sweat though his body was cold. She felt his hands move over her for a moment. Then she felt him falling asleep, lying heavier and heavier on her arm and side. After a time she was able to slip her arm out without rousing him.

When she reached home she went straight to her room, avoiding William. She fell asleep at once, waking in the early morning with a strange heavy sense of loss and for a moment her mind drifted whirled in undersea currents. Fully awake at last, she lay motionless, like a swimmer who has barely been able to reach the shore in safety.

She looked at her watch. Three hours before Hester came in with tea—a narrow ledge of time on which she had no duties except to herself and could take stock of her thoughts.

"The first thing I must realise is that it has happened." She was seized by a frightful despair. When did it happen? What had she been doing in the moment when Evan was taking Agnes for the first time? She pressed her fingers over her eyeballs, to blot out the picture.

"Whatever happens, I must do better than this," she thought. "These—images—are degrading and foolish. I must clear them out of my mind. I am a sensible woman." Her teeth chattered. "There—that's better. Silly Emily, you can get over it. You must. There are only two ways of dealing with these—incidents of a woman's life. One would be by getting rid of Evan. The other is to say nothing about it—if I speak of it I shall cry, and that's neither decent nor dignified. ... There ought to be rules for this sort of thing—it must be always happening to women everywhere. What To Do When your husband goes with another woman." She laughed a little angrily.

The idea of leaving Evan had only passed through her mind without entering.

In order to think more clearly she sat up in bed. For a fraction of a second she wondered who it was confronting her from the mirror—plain, haggard face. She must have been crying while she was asleep.

"I shall get over it," she thought calmly, "but if it were

to happen again—" She felt a momentary and intense conviction that it would happen again, and after her first pain she was surprised to find herself thinking that it was natural and reasonable. Naturally Evan, as a young, good-looking man, would want to enjoy everything that life offered. It was not reasonable to ask him to give up all curiosity. "If I were a young man I should want to try every kind of woman." She thought of her brother: Eliot had five German aeroplanes to his credit and talked instead of having had a different woman every two nights during his last leave. Her own father. . . . "It's not because I'm a woman that I want only Evan. It would be better if I were more like Eliot. Or like Agnes." Another surprising thought—"Evan and Agnes are a little like two graceful pretty little animals—playing together." This was a bit too thick for her. She calmed herself by looking in the glass at the tears trickling over her cheeks, and tasting one on the end of her tongue. There is no better way of checking a crying fit.

But if it were only natural, and even—given youth and spontaneity—charming and decent, what a shocking mistake to bring up the young to think of it as a sacrament. "My sentimental education was all wrong," she exclaimed. "Instead of bringing me up to expect that I should have a lover who would never want to look at another woman they should have begun at the earliest possible moment explaining that it is natural to want to enjoy as many different pleasures as possible while you are young. They ought to teach you that this is the right thing and nothing to be surprised at. And they ought to finish by telling you that it is only when you are old that it is ugly, and foolish!" The kind of teaching she had had, the kind that was always impressed on the plastic minds of boys and young girls, led to the most frightful unhappiness. It taught you to expect the impossible. And when the impossible failed to happen, when the person you were in love with yielded to an impulse, you tumbled from your ridiculous heights and landed flat on your face. And it hurt. It hurt ridiculously and made you feel so damned old and ill.

She grew red in the face and banged her fist on her knee as she used to when she lost her temper at school. "I should like to do something to make people realise what shocking unhappiness they cause by their ridiculous talk of sacraments and eternal love. Marriage is a sacrament"—she always argued as though it were Evan she had married—"but making love is not. It is a natural, irresistible impulse, which is just as pleasant without marriage. Evan had every right to Agnes." Her mind pulled her up with a severe jerk. "If only I could believe that!"

In all this she never thought once of William. She thought of a great many other things in a confused childish way, now that the excitement of making what she thought was a discovery had worn off. "I was thinking of Evan as belonging to me—a piece of my property. That's what hides at the bottom of all the poetry and the idealism. And that's really disgusting." The servants had begun moving about the house, and she thought of her tea, and with that she began to feel sorry for herself again. It is impossible to keep up an illusion of intellectual freedom when all you long for in the world is a cup of tea. For the moment she wished that she were the wife of a young working-man—Evan—getting up at six to cook his breakfast. They say that poor men are usually faithful to their wives—want of leisure, or over-crowding, perhaps.

"All that about the results of a bad sentimental education is true, but I didn't think of it in time. I shall always suffer horribly at the thought of Evan and Agnes together. . . . Next time will it be Agnes? I was brought up with foolish and romantic ideas and now I shall have to make my own re-adjustments."

Stirring her tea, she said to herself that the only re-adjustments she could make were on the outside. For show purposes only. She must act as though she were an enlightened being, who had dispensed with sexual jealousy; when she was old it would be true. She would not confide in anyone. No one must know when she was hurt, and Evan must not know.

During the rest of Evan's leave, they were happy. Al-

though it was winter and very cold they went to stay
together at a little seaport on the Norfolk coast. Evan
had learned to ride in France: they hired two decayed
hunters from the livery stables and spent their mornings
from ten o'clock learning that Norfolk is a county of serious
colours and lovely flattened lines. Evan did not ride well:
he managed not to fall off and that was all.

In the evening they went to bed immediately after
dinner. An enormous fireplace threw out enough heat to
warm a room that was twenty-five feet long, with three
doors, and windows facing the sea. They sat up in bed
and talked until they felt tired. Evan had to get out of
bed to turn out the oil lamp. Then he came back and took
her in his arms. They were very happy in the wide creaking
bed. It felt a little as though they were in their own home.
This was the first time they had had that feeling about any
place.

A week later Eliot Lambton was killed. He had enjoyed
his share of the War. Nervous, brutal, with a quick finely-
trained body, he had never known what it was to be really
happy until he joined the Flying Corps. He was an admirable pilot. His hands, which Emily had always disliked,
became part of the machine as soon as he laid them on
the controls. His friends said of him that he would fly
anything and stick at nothing. He liked killing. Above
all he liked killing in a particular way—in the air, in a duel
that could only end in the death of one or of both fighters.
He once said that no big game thrills could equal the thrill
of killing a man—but you had to *kill* him—with a bayonet
or by shooting him down in flames—and not merely to
murder him at long range.

The shock of his death unbalanced his mother's mind. So
far as her emotions were concerned she had never had more
than one child. She shut herself up in her room. When
Emily tried to force her way in she was pushed out again
by her mother's German-Swiss maid, a tall elderly woman
as strong as a man. Through the closed door Emily heard
her say: "There now, my lovely. Anna is with you. Shall
I rub your legs again?—that always sends you to sleep."

Her mother's groans rose to a climax and died slowly away, to the accompaniment of a gentle hissing noise from Anna, the sound a groom makes over a nervous horse.

For years after this—until the week before she died, when she said suddenly: "Emily, I don't like you in that hat"— her mother always spoke to her as "Lady Holl," and in the voice she used for a distant acquaintance. After a time, Emily became used to it. It seemed to her no crazier than most other things in a world which was seriously engaged in turning millions of men into rotting flesh, tearing the entrails and making pulp of the faces of millions more. At the same time, her father, a rich man in 1914, was now fabulously wealthy. This year he sold out of all his shipping interests except Lambton and Grey. Shares that had been changing hands at a few shillings before the War were now worth fifty pounds apiece. Even Evan would have six thousand pounds if he sold now. She wrote to tell him that her father advised selling and he sent her a power of attorney to act in his name. She sold everything and re-invested the money in bank shares. When her father wrote her a cheque for twenty thousand pounds for her hospital he gave her an extra five thousand. She invested it in Evan's name. She was ashamed to spend it on herself.

Ever since she came back from America she had been working in the hospital and she continued to work there until a week before her second child was born, in October. This time she had a girl, and at her first glimpse of the child she was startled by the likeness to Evan. It was more expression than any definite resemblance, and in an hour or so it wore off, but the child's eyes were Evan's.

Again she was very ill. During her convalescence she had time to think. She thought a great deal about Evan, now the G.S.O.2 of a division, a little about her children, and a little about William. For the first time it occurred to her that she had not treated him too well. When he came to see her in the evening before dinner she noticed that he had become thin and bent-shouldered. His hands were swollen.

He talked to her with a calm gentleness. When he was

going away one of the nurses came in bringing the child. He looked at her for a moment, and said to Emily: "She's not very like you."

She might have thought about him longer than she did at this time but for the fact that Evan had abruptly ceased to write to her. At the end of a fortnight she heard through her father that he had been shot in the neck and arm during a tour of inspection. He was badly but not seriously wounded. As soon as he was sent to England she got up and went to see him. A day or two later Agnes Wilmott rang her up to ask where he was. She gave her the name of the hospital in a matter-of-fact voice. Agnes went on speaking about him. Emily listened and answered: she had to bite into her hand so as not to lose control. . .

William was ill. He went about his work with a mind shut against everything else, except the necessity of concealing how ill he was. People who spoke to him were shadows until they stood directly in front of his desk, when they acquired definite outlines, a mouth and two eyes, sometimes a hand holding papers. When he answered them his own voice sounded unreal to him and as hollow as though he had been left to talk on in an empty room.

As the weeks passed his sense of his unimportance became complete. He no longer took the trouble to wonder which, if either, of Emily's children was his. It no longer interested him more than a little. One child would do as well as another to inherit a name and an estate that another generation might see parcelled out to Socialist co-operative farmers. And why trouble greatly about a succession that might be cut off by another Great War?

He could not feel that Emily was any more important. He was pleased that his son, or Evan's, was healthy and intelligent, and had nice manners. Perhaps he had been born late enough not to feel uncomfortable in an altered world. "So far as I am concerned I am no longer in the game. I have taken back my stake," he said to himself.

CHAPTER III

NEVERTHELESS, in spite of a severe nervous breakdown, and in spite of being willing to die, he lived for two years after the Armistice and died at the end of 1920. To her surprise Emily found that she missed him. She had come without knowing it to rely on his unfailing gentleness and sympathy. He had long ceased to make any demands on her but he was always at hand to be consulted and to listen. She took his advice about the education of the boy, and when the little girl became seriously ill it was to him she turned and not to the child's real father. He watched beside her during the hours that would decide whether the child was to live.

He comforted her—and Evan had to be comforted and upheld. When she was with Evan she was always listening. It was a relief to go home and to feel that William was interested in knowing what she felt about the Versailles Treaty, starving Austrian babies, and the poetry of T. S. Eliot. When he died she realised that he had been helping to sustain not only her but Evan and that henceforth she would have to carry on alone.

Evan was in America at the time. He sent her a long cable and followed it by a letter which reminded her of a much younger Emily and Evan. She was glad that he was so far away. For the moment she had lost courage and she wanted a few weeks in which to harden herself. She was now nearly thirty-one and she was afraid of seeming ridiculous.

At the end of the War Evan had returned to Lambton and Grey, but on a different footing. He was now secretary to the managing director and a personal friend of the Chairman. He said himself that he had managed to persuade the army authorities that he was intelligent and the Board that he was successful. When Lambton and Grey entered into negotiations with an American firm of shippers and bankers for mutual assistance during the lean days ahead he was sent to New York. He showed himself

quick, shrewd and stubborn. Emily was able, through
her many friends in financial and political circles, to give
him introductions that saved him days and weeks of
tortuous diplomacy. He was able to take short cuts. His
letters to her, asking for advice and information about
personalities, crossed hers warning him in advance of snags
arising from the American business temperament. "Always
remember," she wrote to him, "that the hardest-headed
business magnate is probably a crashing sentimentalist and
that he knows nothing of affairs outside his country and
is very likely to be proud of his ignorance. Do not talk
to anyone of international understanding. It will frighten
him, and make him think that he is being asked to
finance French greed, English opportunism, and German
enthusiasm. Stick to the moment. Americans are not
equipped for long-distance thinking. Above all, do not be
flippant. The kind of American who appreciates flippancy
on serious subjects is of no use to you at this or any stage."

He came back to England in May, and was rewarded
by the congratulations of the Board. William had been
dead for eight months, and he asked Emily to marry him
at once. She hesitated. It was not that she was afraid of
comment. Three of her friends, whose husbands had been
killed during the March 1918 retreat, had re-married before
the Armistice. People no longer waited for what used to
be called a decent interval before committing the indecency
of second or third marriage. It was becoming recognised
that the expectation of life has shortened by a decade or
two since 1914. You cannot be sure at what moment
another war will swoop down to destroy what is left from
the last.

She held back because she was still a little afraid of the
future. She knew that she would have to subordinate
herself to Evan for the rest of her life. In fact, she would
have no life of any kind outside his. His ambitions, his
needs and desires and failings, would become her responsibility, the only one she would be allowed to keep. Evan
was seriously determined to become a public figure. She
had always wanted to fight for him openly, as hitherto she

had fought for him behind cover of William, and yet she hesitated. Since the trouble with Agnes she had felt a great deal older. She knew it would not be the only trouble of that kind that she would have with him. Evan would always yield to a sensual impulse the moment it became less trouble to yield than to hold back. He would not feel that he was injuring her by what meant very little to him. In the end he would expect her to understand him.

One day her eight-year-old son asked her when she thought of getting married. He was not seriously interested. He had overheard his governess discussing it with a friend and he wanted to know more than they did. He was mildly attached to Evan.

She told Evan that he would have all the advantage of enjoying his son's liking for him without the trouble of having to behave like a father.

They were married in July. Evan had made friends among the Labour politicians in the House. He was still a Socialist, but his Socialism was less now a matter of personal bitterness and more a conviction—based on his reading of the world situation and his researches into the nervous system of industry, that is, into credit—that Socialism provided the only workable alternative to decay. He believed that the day of Capitalism was over. With markets shrinking through the spread of industrialism to the East, and the workers unsettled by education and the failure of orthodox religion, its usefulness had reached a limit. Within a measurable time the very forces that had worked for it would turn and rend it. At this point a reintegration of social energies would begin.

He forgot to reckon either with the incredible patience and greed of the French or with the stupidity of nine out of ten of our masters.

In September he fought a by-election in the Labour interest and was defeated by a decently narrow margin. A few weeks later he was invited to Vienna. A committee of investigation had gone out there in July and a prominent member had just succumbed to one of those mysterious diseases bred of hunger and misery, which attack

even the fortunate onlooker. Another member had known
Evan in America and the invitation, sent by him, was
written in the form of an appeal.

Evan jumped at the chance. He asked for leave from
the firm and left London in November, taking Emily with
him.

Vienna was under snow. The children of well-to-do
industrials and financial experts dragged sledges up and
down the main walks in the Prater and the Stadt Park.
Most of the shops were closed. Those that remained open
displayed riding saddles of Austrian leather, sledges, and
skis. It looked as though a country that was being starved
to death had lost interest in everything but winter sports.
As a matter of fact no one was buying either skis or saddles
but there were plenty of them in stock and they took the
place in the shop-windows in the Kärntner-Strasse of cakes
made with cream, sugar and eggs, model gowns, walking
suits in English tweed, and salami. The only other things
offered for sale were second-hand necklaces, watches, family
heirlooms, prints, oil-paintings, little-worn fur coats, minia-
tures, exquisitely bound books, spoons and wineglasses
engraved with a crest and the date, tapestries—the jettisoned
cargo of a sinking vessel.

The weather was intensely cold. The Jews on the Black
Bourse had icicles at the end of their noses as well as round
the edges of their greasy fur caps. Children were dying
quickly from cold instead of slowly from starvation. Each
death reduced by a unit the appalling total of suffering and
despair which the statesmen of Europe were trying to
balance. One morning Emily saw the maid who was sweeping her sitting-room scrape a few flakes of chocolate off
the table and stow them carefully in a screw of paper in
her pocket. Another day Evan told her that a professor
from the university, a scholar of international reputation,
had seized the chance when his back was turned to steal
a few coins from his desk. Another time it was a lump of
sugar and the thief was the wife of a well-known doctor.

They stayed in the Imperial Hotel. Food was plentiful:
it was delivered at a side door in the early morning, after

the waiters who slept out had gone home. Lavish meals of meat—the Viennese eat quantities of pork and beef during the hottest summers—not very good fish from the Danube, oysters, fresh caviare, fruit, ices, white bread. The waiters were carefully selected by the manager for their discretion. It was considered unwise to allow the starving mob outside to know that rolls of white bread and huge joints of fresh meat were devoured daily in the dining-room of the Imperial Hotel. By whom? By wealthy industrials, landowners who had escaped the general ruin, French, English, Italian and American investigators, members of the Danube Commission, and by Herr Castiglione.

One afternoon as Emily was hurrying along the Kärntner-Ring towards the hotel she noticed a young woman a few yards in front. Swaying from side to side as she walked, the young woman finally collapsed in the middle of the pavement at the moment when Emily drew level with her. Her head fell backwards, as if there were no stuffing in her neck.

Emily bent over her. At the same time a policeman stepped up and jerked the young woman to her feet. "Be off home," he said curtly. "You tried this yesterday." The girl looked at him, smiled, and began to walk away.

"Stop," Emily said.

The young woman stopped, looking over her shoulder. A short fur coat fitted tightly to her waist. Under it you caught glimpses of a light-coloured blouse and a tie like a schoolgirl's uniform. She wore shoes and thin black silk stockings.

"I warn you," the policeman said, "I have observed this person before. Yesterday she pretended to faint in front of a French general. The officer was wise. After one glance, he stepped over her and walked on."

"Please let me speak to her," Emily said, in a precise slow voice. She spoke German as though it were an exercise.

The man shrugged and turned away. His attitude suggested that he had done his duty and it was in any event too cold to stand talking to foreign lunatics. The Austrians

are an extremely charming race. They dislike trouble, and
if it were left to the ordinary Viennese bourgeois to arrange
it no war would ever be worse than a riot.

Emily took the girl into the hotel and up to her room.
In the corridor the manager hurried up to her and began
to remonstrate in rapid French against the introduction
into his hotel of a young female probably already infected
with influenza or the plague or merely with the instinct to
steal. Emily answered him coldly in English. She drew
the girl into her bedroom and shut the door. The central
heating had broken down the day before and fires had been
lit in the enormous baroque stoves in the best rooms. The
girl went directly over to the stove and laid her hands on it.

"He wasn't very polite, the manager," she said, yawning.
"All the same, you should have listened to him. How do
you know I shan't steal your rings?"

"Because I don't care if you do," Emily said. "You understood him, then—you speak French?"

"And English, and Italian. I am an honours student
at the university. We'll speak English now if you like."

"Won't you take your fur coat off?" Emily said.

Smiling, the girl unfastened its two buttons and drew
her arms out. She wore no blouse, and not even a vest.
A brown silk tie was knotted round her neck and hung
down between her tiny breasts. She wore a black skirt. It
was too wide for her and hung from her delicate hip bones.

"Have you really no blouse?" Emily asked.

"I have a very good one," the girl said calmly. "I took
it off this afternoon and washed it and hung it to dry.
Then I thought I would come out and try whether I had
the nerve to attract the attention of some fat Yugoslav
factory-owner or a Rumanian colonel."

"What did you hope he would do for you?"

"Invite me to have dinner with him first. Afterwards—
well, I suppose my having scarcely any clothes on would
have simplified matters." She lifted her arms, as yellow
and brittle as a famine child's.

Emily had opened her wardrobe trunk and taken out
a woven vest and a thick silk jumper. "Put these on."

"You're very kind," the girl said, without a trace of pleasure. She slipped both garments on, tucking the vest inside her skirt and fastening the jumper round her waist with her tie. This naturalised it at once, so much so that you would have sworn it had been bought at a little shop in the Mariahilfer-Strasse instead of in Bond Street.

"Were you doing all this because you are hungry?" Emily asked bluntly. She spoke English. It seemed better suited to the occasion and her questions. The English are very humane but they like to know everything about the person they are succouring and if possible to fit him into one of several prepared moulds. Emily was mentally labelling the young woman: Weak but not vicious: can usefully be assisted.

"Really, I'm ashamed to tell you."

"Do trust me. I don't want to pry, but. . ."

The girl was almost beautiful. She had black eyes, set under brows so fine they were like a silk thread. Her lips were pale from under-nourishment, delicately moulded, the lower one short and full. Her hair was dark brown and smooth, plastered to her head. She had pulled her hat off and was passing her fingers over the flat coils, looking at herself carefully in the glass. "My name is Sophie," she offered, over her shoulder.

"You haven't told me yet why you. . ."

Sophie forced open her eyes. The warmth of the room, after the cold outside, was making her sleepy. The tip of her tongue appeared between her teeth: she was like a kitten considering a strange room.

"I am tired of having only one blouse," she said calmly. "Then, too, my mother is dying of some illness or other—she is always shivering and she says her stomach has folded up like a gladstone bag, and sometimes we have nothing to put in it. To tell you the truth I have no objection to being hungry. I am used to it and it improves my figure. In the ordinary way I should be plump, perhaps fat, at my age."

"How old are you?"

"Nineteen. . . . How much would you say I weighed? Listen, I'll tell you. Under eighty-four pounds!" She patted herself triumphantly. When she seated herself on the bed her skirt fell into folds between her knees and you saw that she had long thin legs, like a pair of compasses.

Emily had ordered a meal of soup and *Backhuhn*. The girl ate delicately, with an air of indifference and boredom. When Emily's back was turned she slid the remains of the chicken into her handkerchief and thrust it out of sight under her coat. She chattered about her studies, about the War, about trotting-races in the Prater. As she was leaving Emily held out to her a large envelope into which she had put all the Austrian money she had in her purse.

"Thanks ever so much for the meal and the blouse," Sophie said. "They are things any young woman is allowed to take from another."

"Take the money, too, " Emily said.

"No thanks."

"Oh, why not?"

"Really, I don't know," Sophie said lightly. "I suppose I ought to take it and burst into tears. Perhaps even kiss your hand. ... 'Noble and charming Englishwoman, my thanks are those of my country. Long live England.' ... But, do you know, I find I can't. Isn't it strange? I like you frightfully, too. Come and see me sometimes."

"Where do you live?"

"10, Wipplinger-Strasse." She reflected, wrinkling her nose. "No, don't come there. To tell you the truth, mother would disgust you. She has running boils all over her body like Job, and the smell is enough to knock you down. Her doctor says she needs a great deal of cream and nourishing foods. The American Mission sent her a bottle of cod liver oil but she wouldn't drink it. I used it up on my hands."

"I must see you again," Emily exclaimed.

"Very well. Walk down the Neu-Gasse, off the Wiedner Hauptstrasse, and ask at the café at the corner for Herr Friedrich Laube. They will tell you where his room is. I am there every evening from eight o'clock onwards."

It was four or five days before Emily was able to go in search of the young girl. She had said nothing to Evan. For two reasons—because he had ordered her not to go out alone after dark, and because she did not want him to meet Sophie. The girl was too attractive.

She seized her chance when Evan had an official engagement for the evening. He was to dine with the heads of the American Mission, to discuss informally problems arising from the extraordinary apathy of the Viennese population. Instead of being up and doing, as the English and no doubt the Americans would in similar circumstances, they had sunk into a dreadful apathy. Even very young children were dying as quickly from disgust and hopelessness as from cold, hunger, influenza, and colitis. It began to look as though the Allies had gone too far at Paris in 1919.

Emily dressed herself in a dark knitted dress and long coat and slipped out of the hotel at half-past eight. The porter spoke to her and she gave him a forbidding smile. As she crossed the wide Karls-Platz a drunken man emerged from the Underground station wearing half of an immensely shaggy fur coat. The coat had been divided vertically down the back. Against his uncovered side he clutched a large canvas. He was singing, breaking off to laugh and stamp his feet like a ballet dancer. She hurried away from him and plunged towards the shadows of the Hauptstrasse. An icy wind rushed across the Platz from the east, charged with hatred and resentment.

In the half-lighted café in the Neu-Gasse the proprietor offered Emily a chair. "I will send someone with you to Herr Laube's." He was polite, but his dark eyes examined her from head to foot. She felt dreadfully uncomfortable.

Just as he turned away to summon a waiter the man in the half-coat lurched into the café. He dropped the canvas he was carrying and shouted for a glass of coffee. The proprietor and a waiter carrying a glass of muddy steaming water arrived together.

"This Lady is enquiring for you, Herr Laube."

Emily stood up. "I came to meet Sophie. . . . I don't know her name."

"Look at that," Herr Laube shouted. "Why do you call it coffee? Why not own up that it is nothing but infected Danube water. It tastes of a painful death."

"We have some drinkable *Gumpoldskirchner* ..." the proprietor began.

"I never drink. You know it. All the same, give me a bottle of your *Ersatz* Tokay, for the comrades."

He tucked the bottle under an arm and offered Emily the other. She was stiff with embarrassment. In the same moment as she realised that he was not drunk she remembered Evan's warnings against walking alone in the districts occupied mainly by the unemployed. She was ashamed to show any hesitation. As they left the café Herr Laube apologised for his coat. "The other half is covering the bed in which my friend Werndl sleeps with his wife and their infant, a week old. Perhaps you think I should have given the whole coat? You are wrong. What guarantee have I against another such request? ... Friedrich, lend me your coat. My wife's pains have begun and we have nothing to put on the bed.... Certainly, my dear fellow, take half. ... Would you believe, madam, that less than a year ago I was a family man? Now ἐγὼ δὲ μόνα καθεύδω, I sleep alone ... children die easily nowadays. As for my wife, she was always running after them in a fright.... Ludwig, Elizabeth, where are you? what are you doing? have you fallen? Mother's coming. ... So of course she must be after them. You never saw anyone in such a hurry to die. ... Here we are. Please be careful of your head."

Herr Laube's room was at the top of a shabby mansion. You crossed the courtyard, climbed four flights of unlit stairs, each flight marked by a different layer of stench, and passed under an archway into what had been a gallery overlooking the yard. The fourth side had been boarded in. There was a stove in the middle of the room with a little wood burning in it, and three people seated near it on the floor. Two of them, a young man and a very young woman, were sharing the same jacket. Sophie was not there.

The third of Herr Laube's guests, a young doctor, was waiting for her. He told Emily that he wanted to marry her, but she would not leave her mother, with whom she lived in one very small room.

"And the old lady has the bed, you understand," interrupted the young woman. "He even has to come here to be with Sophie. . . . Friedrich lends them his bed."

"When do you expect Sophie?" Emily asked. She had begun to shiver with cold, in spite of her warm frock. She was vexed with herself for coming. What good was it to get mixed up with these people? There was nothing you could do.

She remembered that she had some English cigarettes in her bag and shared them out. Sophie's lover took her share and put them away for her. Herr Laube did not smoke. He sat in a corner near the only candle, and read, breaking off every now and then to slap his thigh and laugh like a fool. The others talked among themselves. They took no notice of Emily, who sat preparing polite speeches to explain her departure. She rejected one after another as not friendly enough or too condescending. In the meantime she caught snatches of conversation.

"He wouldn't advance another cent on it. I threatened to give away his dirty thieving from the American Mission. . . . Would you believe?—Georg has a job now. He stands every evening in the vestibule of the *Jardin de Paris*, merely upright. He has no duties. Only to stand. . . . Sophie talks a great deal of nonsense, the silly girl. She said she would offer herself for what she could get. She would be afraid! Do you remember the New Year parties her father and mother gave when we were children? I was sick after one, from eating too much rich food. Think of it!"

If she had considered it at all, Emily would have supposed that the frightful insecurity of their lives would drive these young people, the children of cultivated middle-class parents, now penniless, to snatch desperately at such pleasures as were left them. On the contrary, they were languid and uninterested. The minds in their young bodies were already old and played-out: in their hold on things and on each other they had none of the fierceness of youth. They behaved as though so few years separated them from extinction that to attach themselves to anything or anyone would be useless and silly. She had noticed the same kind of indifference in very old women, who have survived husbands, friends, even their children, and to whom the sudden death of a grandchild is less shocking than a smashed vase or a badly-cooked meal.

The door opened suddenly and Sophie walked in. She came in with a smile and stood in the middle of the room, fumbling at the inside pocket of her coat. "Look!" She showed them five English ten-shilling notes, spreading them out with her thumb, like a hand of cards.

"All the same, he wasn't English. He was a Pressburg Jew. I made him give me the money first." She looked at them as though she were going to cry. "Not bad for a first attempt, eh?"

The other girl had pulled herself up and came across the room to finger the notes. "Beginner's luck," she said softly. "You won't pull it off again."

"Here, take one," Sophie said. She thrust a note in the girl's hand, which curved round it like a claw. Folding the others, she turned sharply to the young doctor. He was still leaning against the stove with his hands in his pockets. "You haven't said anything, Püppchen."

"What do you want me to say?"

"Aren't you interested?"

He turned his back on her and walked across to Herr Laube, who was reading aloud something that Emily took to be verse. Actually, it was a list of the trains to Wiener Neustadt for the summer of 1913. Half turning his head he answered: "I hope you enjoyed yourself."

Sophie's face changed quickly. Forcing back tears of fatigue and humiliation, she assumed the air of jaunty cynicism she had worn on first coming in. "Let's talk about something interesting. You wouldn't believe how little conversation those people have."

Emily stood up noisily and came forward. "I must go," she said in an awkward voice. She peered at her watch. "You've been so long coming. It's nearly eleven o'clock. My husband will be wondering where I am."

"Why, it's the Englishwoman," Sophie said.

"She came in with Friedrich."

"I think we might have done something to entertain her. She'll think we have no manners."

"Friedrich! Your guest is going."

Mortified by their complete indifference, Emily almost ran out. The young doctor followed her.

"Please mind the stairs. If you fell and were killed, the Allies would start another war on us." He took hold of her arm. "It's not a bad idea," he said, laughing. "We could surrender *en masse*, and they would have to feed us. They say the English are kind to their prisoners."

Arrived at the street door, Emily drew her arm back. "Good-bye."

"Allow me to see you to your hotel."

"No," Emily said.

In her confusion she ran off in the wrong direction. There was not a soul in the street. She ran to the end of it. The unfamiliar look of the street into which she emerged halted her. Making a blind choice she plunged to the right. If she were not hopelessly lost it would lead to the Karls-Platz. It did. She reached the hotel to find Evan walking nervously up and down between the doors. The porter saw her first, and called out: "Excellency! It's all right."

Evan had sent out search parties. He ordered them to be fetched back. Forgetting the nervous politeness he always showed, because they had lost the War, towards Austrians and Germans, he waved his arms and shouted, drawing down on himself a shower of friendly reassurances. The word "Excellency" pursued them to the door of Emily's bedroom.

The moment the door was closed he almost fell with her on to the couch. He held her closely, too angry with her to speak. Emily had begun to tremble. She expected to be roughly scolded. She felt extraordinarily happy.

"I'm sorry, Evan," she said with a hypocritical tremor.

"Where have you been?"

She told him a little about Sophie. She kept her account as brief as possible because she was anxious not to draw any of his attention from herself. He listened, frowning.

"Do you realise that you are lucky not to be lying with your throat cut, in some doorway?"

"You're really hurting my arms," Emily said.

Evan's face twitched with nervous exasperation. "I should like to give you a sound whipping. I've been off my head. When that fool told me you'd gone out at eight o'clock. . . . I believe he thought you were up to no good."

"It seems I wasn't," Emily said, smiling. She leaned against him with a delicious feeling of security and self-importance. "What would you have felt if I had been murdered?"

"Don't," Evan said, seizing her arm. He almost disliked her for asking the question.

Long after he fell asleep she lay thinking of Sophie. All that indifference, that casual vileness, horrified her. She wanted to forget it, but she could forget everything except the moment in which Sophie had folded the notes carefully into her pocket while the others looked on. For some reason that seemed to her the final horror. She began to shudder as when she was running down the stairs, away from them. Evan half awoke and flung an arm over her. "Emily!"

"Do you really love me so much?"

Still half asleep, he took her in his arms, and tried to reassure her.

CHAPTER IV

ENGLAND, with its new smart restaurants, its complacence, its vulgar ignorance of the rest of the world, its rising tide of unemployed, its pointless extravagance, was surprisingly unchanged. She could scarcely believe that two days' journey away people were dying of hunger. Respectable people. Evan plunged into Labour politics with renewed eagerness. His work in Vienna had given him a lift. He felt confident. The figure of a disgraced and badly-dressed young man retreated to an infinite distance.

Emily worked harder for him than ever. He did nothing without consulting her. To save him time she wrote many of his speeches, she entertained—their house in Queen Anne's Gate became a neutral corridor in which eminent politicians of all parties met and exchanged views before going into action. She saw to it that the leaders of the Labour Party turned naturally towards it when any business that required long, informal discussion was under way. She made friends with the women of the party, keeping one self for use with Mrs. Philip Snowden, another for Miss Wilkinson, and another for Mrs. Clynes, whom everybody likes without having to think about it.

When, in 1924, Evan became the member for Harleston, she had a division bell installed to ring in his room and in the hall.

She had two more children, one born in April, 1922, and the other in May of the following year. Evan was less fond of them than of the two who did not bear his name. He was especially fond of the boy, who was like him and would never have to blush either for his clothes or his accent.

It was not very long after he came back from Vienna that Agnes Wilmott got hold of him again. That was how Emily described it to herself. Actually, she knew quite well that Evan was to blame for this revival of their relationship. Why had he done it? Every reason she started circled back to the same place. It was just because Agnes meant everything to him for a few moments and then nothing at all that he found it easy to be with her. He did not love her but he enjoyed her, and she (Agnes) lent herself to this light-hearted indulgence in the sharpest of pleasures.

She was not the only one. There was a friend of hers with whom Evan had been in love for less than a month. And a young woman who had quickly lost him by asking for the loan of a hundred pounds—Evan hated to lend money: he was always a little afraid that he would wake up one morning to find himself penniless again.

None of these others gave Emily any trouble except

the pains she took to seem unaware of their existence. Agnes, on the other hand, almost lived in the house. She pretended to be very fond of Emily and often told Evan that what she admired most about him was his wife. She copied Emily's way of doing her hair, bought her little presents that Emily passed on to the children's governess, praised her extravagantly to other people, and went so far as to write a letter in which she implored Emily to tell her whether she objected to Evan's infatuation. Emily took no notice of the letter.

Next day Agnes called on her, wearing a dress of violet taffeta, and mittens. She had had herself made up to look like a schoolgirl—only her eyes remained those of an experienced and stupid woman. She swept aside Emily's attempt to treat her as an ordinary visitor and began at once to talk about Evan.

"I don't know which of you I love the more, you or Evan. I've always admired you. You don't rush crazily about in search of change and excitement. To look at you anyone would think we were still in the 1870's. No wonder Evan puts all his weight on you. You invite responsibility."

"Did you come to talk about me?" Emily asked.

"I came to say that if you want me to I'll order Evan to give me up."

"Don't trouble," Emily said. "You amuse him and you don't trouble me, I assure you."

"If I could only believe that!" Agnes sighed. Her eyes sparkled with annoyance.

"My dear Agnes, you're the last woman to expect consideration from other women. If I objected to you I should get rid of you at once. You don't suppose Evan would make any sacrifices for you!" She spoke in a light voice, with an air of innocence. She felt an atrocious and degrading happiness in being able to insult Agnes. If she could she would have made the other woman roll on the floor and beg for mercy. She smiled pleasantly.

Agnes stood up to go. Disappointment made the corners of her mouth droop. She had come expecting a new excitement in discussing Evan with his wife. Emily had been too much for her.

Fortune always rewards the stupid. Just as she was going she managed to do more damage by accident than a clever woman could have done by design.

"When Evan and I were in Norfolk..."

Emily had lost her air of assurance. "Norfolk?"

"Yes. We went down to —— and stayed in a wretched little hotel facing the sea. That was only a month ago, when you were in Yorkshire." Feeling that she had scored a bull's-eye and too stupid to leave it at that, Agnes talked herself out. She described the room, and the breakfasts, and supplied Emily with a hundred details for want of which she would have had to torture her imagination for a year. Long before she stopped, Emily had regained complete control of herself.

"Do you know," she said, in a pitying voice, "you're really very conventional. Fancy staying at the seaside. That's what Evan meant when he said to me the other day that you had the mind of a tripper." This was not true.

As soon as Agnes left her she began to take stock of the position. The memory of the days and nights she had spent with Evan in that same room poisoned her mind. He had disgraced her by taking Agnes there. An extraordinary grief took possession of her. Her body felt as though it had been drained of blood. She had not even the energy to cry.

"Another room that must not be opened again," she said to herself. "I thought I had prepared myself for everything but I had certainly overlooked this. How extraordinary men's minds are. I suppose Evan took her to that especial place because he had once been happy there. Only a very cruel or a very stupid woman would have done that." After a time she found a certain pleasure in thinking that the worst had happened. "I can walk now without holding," she thought. She meant that her love for Evan had dispensed with all those props, cut out of memory, which are necessary even to a good marriage. Hers was her life,

a single arch, of the height and breadth of her life. Within
it, Evan had complete liberty to behave as he liked. "I am
like Sophie," she thought. "Nothing now matters more
than a little. I am so old or so ruined that I realise the
futility of possession. I have let go my last confident hold
on Evan—my hands are the freer to work for him, only
for him."

She sat for a long time, looking at her hands. She felt
tired and weak, but she was happy.

CHAPTER V

EVAN lost his seat at the general election of 1924. He
had no liking for the place, in which the majority of his
supporters had been Liberals who for sentimental reasons
voted Labour at the previous election. With Emily's help
he managed to arrange for himself to nurse a Yorkshire
constituency where the chances of success were fairly even.

He was now irrevocably committed to politics as a career.
He resigned his position in the firm and allowed Emily
to settle five thousand a year on him so that his private
spending need not come under the eye of her accountant.
Her father died this year, leaving her a fortune little
depleted by the ruin of shipping. He had withdrawn in
plenty of time. She was able, without touching William's
money, to buy a slum estate in Evan's constituency and
build on it blocks of workers' flats with modern electrical
equipment and gardens. This gave her a deep impersonal
satisfaction. She detested the complacency with which
fat-minded people resign themselves to the economic
necessity of slums. If she could she would have condemned
a score of delicately-nurtured women to spend a year in
one of those loathsome places, less decent than a field
latrine. The effect on their skins alone would be a salutary
lesson. She was delighted to read in the *Yorkshire Evening
News* a letter in which the writer called her "an enemy of
her class."

She was astonished by the stupidity of her friends, the
young women with whom she had grown up, who now,

married to rich manufacturers, bankers, under-secretaries, and soldiers, talked only of defending themselves against the encroachments of the workers. Each of them, meeting Emily at a dinner-party or private view, would say: "Well, you Bolshevik, what are you doing here?" She answered honestly: "I am terrified of Bolshevism. That is precisely why I vote Labour and tear down slums." She was surprised when they refused to agree with her that the only way to prevent a class war is to destroy the divisions between classes. The English are the most patient people in the world. In the late War it was always English troops who held out the longest under shell fire. But though they are patient they are stubborn and the only idea for which they can be made to kill is the idea of justice.

Before going down to live for a year in the constituency they spent a month walking about Austria. This was the happiest time in her life. At night, except when they had reached a town or city, they slept in a small inn. They ate pork flavoured with rose-coloured pepper, onion, and caraway seeds, and drank the *heurigen Wein*, new wine of last year's pressing, unloaded, as clear as spring water. The beds were atrocious, a feather mattress below and another on top. Fleas hopped between the wooden boards of the walls. At an inn in the Wiener Wald Evan was taken for a Jew and refused even a half-litre flask of the thin sharp *Fasswein*. The scenery was a little like the Cairngorms but burnt-up and dusty, with the tops of the mountains sticking through the stretched skin like knuckle-bones. The sun fell direct on to the valleys, turning the soil to powder. In the dried grass on the Raxalpe Emily found flowers which had only German names.

One night they found a layer of garlic under the mattress in their room. Evan suggested going outside to sleep. They spread copies of the *Neue Freie Presse* on the grass and lay down in their clothes. It was so warm that the darkness seemed unnatural, a stage darkness.

Evan lay on his back and talked. By living sparsely and going without baths he had taken a short cut back to his youth. A little of his youthful passion for Emily triumphed over the immovable affection he felt for her, the almost romantic affection some Englishmen retain for their wives to the very day of their death. During the long days he looked forward to lying beside her in a detestable bed and using the curves of her body to make himself comfortable when sleep overcame them both in the same moment. When he talked it was usually about his youth or about the future. He avoided instinctively a period which was made up of so many events that had hurt and disappointed her.

"In those days I used to walk to Lombard Street from West Ealing, and spend the money on Fabian tracts. I propped them open on the mantelpiece and read while I dressed. During meals I folded them beside my plate. I bought books on banking instead of replacing my worn-out shirts and struggled to understand them. I knew nothing. Everything I read seemed profoundly unanswerable, and it was only from prejudice that I believed one set of ideas and rejected another. . . . Do you remember the first evening I kissed you, Emily? I thought I was going to faint. Falling in love with you made me horribly ill. . . ."

"You recovered quickly enough," Emily said.

"No. I never recovered from you. I hate being away from you. I hope to the Lord you'll see to it that we're buried together. I couldn't stand it without you."

"Then don't die at the other side of the world."

"Not if I know it . . . when I was in France I used to think sometimes: If I'm killed now they'll put up one of those ridiculous crosses with my name instead of *Here lies a body of Emily's*. . . . All the same I'm glad I didn't miss the War. It gave me a new vision. I never realized before how shockingly helpless ordinary people are. They have so little confidence. They submit to any will that is insensitive enough not to mind inflicting cruelty. Have you noticed that our leaders are always what nowadays one calls extroverts? They have very few ideas. They give orders without being afraid of the consequences. Above all, they are not paralysed by an authoritative voice.

Most of them have voices like files. The Tories score by having no sensitiveness. They really believe that the lower classes have smaller stomachs and thick skins, impervious to cold and wet. They identify themselves with their possessions and the moment they feel these threatened a shudder of real horror runs through them—as much as if you'd laid a hand on their flesh. I've known Tory canvassers who wore pearls and fur coats to ask for votes from out-of-work men—they did it without thinking, so certain do they feel of their right to jewels and warm coats. The surprising thing is that they came away with their lives and, as well, the promise of a few votes. . . . The War was the natural result of this insensitiveness. What else could you expect from a society which can think of nothing to do with its surplus grain but to let it rot? It is like a motor-car which has reached the point where it no longer pays to repair it. . . . Order is unnatural. The natural tendency of everything, including social systems, is to decay and disorder. I believe this is a physical law. Unless we reverse the process in time our civilisation will fly to pieces from internal pressure. The War was the first warning siren. Perhaps, after all, we did not stop it in time. Everywhere you look there are cracks in the surface—Austria, Germany, China, Italy kept quiet by castor oil and shootings, India in revolt—even in America. . . . The Russians have a plan. . . . Among us nothing is organised but fear—fear of the rich that they may become poor and of the poor that they will perhaps starve to death. . . . Neither of them has the courage to make a fresh start. . . ."

The sky had grown perceptibly lighter, as if one skin after another were peeling off: in the east the edges had curled over in readiness. Evan complained of cold. By lifting herself on her arm Emily could see his face clearly in the semi-lucent darkness. It had an air of delicacy and reserve. Her love for him became a painful and definite feeling, knotting together the nerves round her heart. It would be unbearable unless she touched him.

"Lie against me and let me warm you."

The newspapers creaked with the sound of the dry grass

by the wall. Evan lay as relaxed as a child. In a drowsy voice he asked her whether she regretted marrying him.

"How could I?" Emily said, with a sigh. "I adore you."

"I make you unhappy."

"I'd rather be unhappy with you than happy with anyone else."

"Are you sure?"

"Sure as death."

"I hope we shall live an awfully long time," Evan said. "I should like to live for a hundred years—to see what is going to happen. Are you certain you like being married to me, Emily?"

"What did I have before I had you?" Emily asked. "Nothing. I hope you will never get everything you want. I think of our marriage as a defence unit—Evan and Emily against the rest of the world."

"I want so much."

"All the better. We shall be able to go on until we're very old."

"Emily—love—don't you want anything for yourself?"

"Why should I? . . . I love you."

A tongue of flame darted above the horizon, licking at the loose edges, which caught fire from it. Burning fragments of cloud floated above the uprush of flame. Life began again in the inn in a grumbling undertone. In her sleep Emily was aware of the growing light and of the weight of Evan's body on her arm. Her mind spoke to itself in pictures on a level below thought. "I am a tree bent down with fruit," she said. "All my branches are heavy with their burden of leaf and fruit." The sun strove to rouse her, falling through the dense layers of her consciousness, light refracted in deep water. Slowly, reluctant to wake, to lose in waking her exquisite sense of completion and satisfaction, she came back to life, the light blinding her as she came nearer and nearer to the surface. Images dissolved round her in a shattering brightness. Evan was still asleep. She let him lie for a time longer before she woke him by drawing her finger lightly across his eyes.

CHAPTER VI

EVAN's chief supporter in Brallington was a well-to-do wool buyer. Actually a Liberal, he had joined the Labour Party to annoy his wife's relatives and nothing short of the death of every one of them would allow him to change his mind. So long as a single one of her family remained alive, to be infuriated by his attitude, he would remain grimly Socialist—against every one of his deepest convictions. None of them went so deep in him as his perverse obstinacy, a peculiarly Yorkshire affliction of the will.

He and Emily understood each other at sight. She had been brought up, though at the other side of the county, among just such men, shrewd, stubborn, devoted to their wives—to whom they rarely addressed an affectionate word—hard, incapable of a new idea, capable only of forcing the old ideas to work even against the facts. She had a great deal of his spirit, subdued in her to her love for Evan as in John Gill it was subdued to nothing except his passion for buying modern pictures. He would pay any price and go to any lengths, of cajolery, trickery, and bluff, to secure a Van Gogh or a Manet on which he had set his heart.

No one understands these people who is not one of them. To strangers they appear to be either deliberately clowning or else so self-centered as to be unworkable. Evan did not understand John Gill, though he responded to the older man's obvious liking for him. He got on better with Mrs. Gill. Emily, who was present at their first meeting, noticed without surprise that in less than half an hour he and Margaret Gill were glancing at each other like old friends.

Mrs. Gill was twelve years younger than her husband. At the age of thirty-six she had just learned how to control her deep rich voice and how to make the best of herself in looks and conversation. She was very intelligent, with a touch of something better in her, which had never been developed. Marriage at the age of twenty, to a possessive domineering man, had slowed down her mental growth. She was only now feeling her strength, and what had been mere physical energy was turning into something more dangerous and disturbing. It was at this precise moment that she met Evan Smith, and for want of anything more definite to absorb her new energies fell in love with him. It happened so quickly that she forgot to be ashamed. Instead, she bent all her forces, hitherto unsuspected, to attach Evan to herself. It did not take very long.

To say that Emily did not know what was going on would be strictly untrue. She hooded her mind to avoid having to notice it. This was made all the more difficult for her because she really liked Margaret Gill. She wanted to know her, to make advances to the other woman's strong subtle mind. To avoid stumbling on certain proof of her relations with Evan she had to give up all this. In a curious way she felt that it would be ungenerous to Mrs. Gill to put her in the position of having to snub his wife's advances. She hung back, uncertain and almost lonely.

At one time she became afraid that Evan was deeply in love with Mrs. Gill. She felt very tired. Though she was only a year older than the other woman she began to think of her as young and of herself as nearly an old woman. Her doctor, to whom she went at this time for a persistent headache, told her that her heart muscles and blood pressure were those of a woman of sixty. "You have been living like a fool, or like your father," he said, "using up reserves that ought to have lasted you for another twenty years. Do you want to die at forty? Go away and rest." As soon as she was at home she sat down in front of her glass and added up the lines round her mouth and eyes. Their sum equalled the total of all the tears, the heart-burnings, and the jealousy, that Evan had made her feel.

They stayed in Brallington, with intervals of not more than a month at a time, until the election of 1929. Evan was triumphantly sure of getting in. His popularity had grown steadily from the day it was discovered that although not born a Yorkshireman he had been brought up in Middlesborough during the years when his father was one of Lambton and Grey's shipmasters. Then, too, the country was ready for a Labour experiment. The nullity of the past five years had given people a taste for adventure. As far as Brallington was concerned, all that remained to be settled was the size of Evan's majority over his Liberal opponent.

At the last moment Margaret Gill's brother had arranged to fight the seat as a Liberal. Gill's secret contempt for the Labour Party vanished in a flurry of rage and he prepared to work all the harder for Evan, swallowing his distrust of Evan's political associates, his hatred of Trades Unions, and his anger at finding himself, at a political meeting, sharing the platform with shop stewards and shabby women wearing immense home-made rosettes of red ribbon. He winced when *The Red Flag* was sung, but catching sight of his mother-in-law in the audience he opened his mouth and bawled it out as he did *The Church's One Foundation* from his pew in the Congregational chapel.

A week before polling day he found his wife writing a letter to Evan. He took it from her and read it—and realised that she had been Evan's mistress for nearly four years.

An extraordinary scene followed. It lasted for an hour —during which time not more than a dozen words were spoken. Gill tramped up and down the room, pausing now and then to look steadily at his wife, who sat with her hands folded in her lap and answered Yes or No to his questions. Husband and wife were both paralysed by the disaster. For the first time in eighteen years they were conscious of a profound sympathy—as if this landslide had laid bare the existence of a subterranean tunnel uniting their separate lives.

As soon as he left her, at the end of a silence that had lasted twenty minutes, Margaret Gill ran out of the house to see Emily. She had no idea why she was doing it. She acted on instinct—the instincts of a mind now fully awake. She was determined to defend herself.

Emily listened without interruption. She was curiously

moved and excited, her heart beating quickly in response
to the other woman's repressed fear. She felt a little as
though she might faint, and held the sides of her chair.

"Tell me one thing," she said gently. "Does my husband
—does Evan want to marry you?"

"He isn't even in love with me," Margaret said curtly.

"Don't answer me if you don't want to. Are you in love
with him?"

"Yes. I am. He's very attractive. . . . I don't love my
husband."

"Yet you want to keep him," Emily exclaimed.

"I've behaved like a fool," Mrs. Gill said. "The life I
live here in Brallington, with John, is the only life I could
ever live. Perhaps if I hadn't married when I did I could
have made myself another kind of life—with people who
read, and write books and so on—but now it's too late.
If John turns me off I shall become one of those back-
groundless women you meet in south-coast hotels—always
reading the latest novel, malicious, discontented, lonely.
I'm too old to begin another life."

"If your husband lets you stay with him, you will have
to give Evan up," Emily said. "Could you bear that?" She
passed her hand over her face, in a vague gesture. "This
is a difficult conversation to carry on in English, isn't it?"
she said. "It sounds unlikely."

"You haven't reproached me," Margaret Gill said.

"I don't think I shall . . . it's too late . . . this isn't the
first time," Emily said in a hurried voice. She felt suddenly
sorry for herself. Evan has really hurt me too much, she
thought, I can't bear it. Half crying, she saw that Mrs.
Gill had risen from her chair and was looking irresolutely
for her gloves.

"Do forgive me. I ought not to have come."

"But I'm glad you came," Emily said. Her perverse
humour revived, along with her common sense. "I think
I shall order us some tea. It's only three o'clock, but our
lives aren't wrecked every day. Don't you feel—a cup of
good tea . . .?"

"I've been a *mean* fool," Mrs. Gill said vehemently. "I had no idea."

"Tell me what you think your husband will do," Emily said. She had experienced a distinct feeling of superiority when Mrs. Gill said that she did not love her husband. How dull for her, Emily thought, aware all at once of the peculiar richness of her own life. "Poor things," was the phrase that sprang into her mind. Now that she need no longer pretend anything about the other woman she was free to like her. She smiled at Mrs. Gill with genuine affection. Her fine practical mind was already busy with the possible effects on Evan of John Gill's bitter resentment. "Did he say anything about the election?"

"Not a word." Margaret Gill was astonished that Emily could think of politics at this moment. She was still suffering from the shock of being found out and her mind saw nothing but herself, in an attitude unromantic enough to make her groan with embarrassment.

"After all—this may make a difference."

"Yes. I see," Margaret said. She jumped up, hot and flurried. "Oh, what can we do? Evan will never forgive me if . . ."

"Well. Shall I go and see John?"

"You couldn't do that."

"Why not?"

"You can't imagine what John is like when he's angry."

"That's where you're wrong," Emily said triumphantly. "I know exactly what he's like. Good gracious—I had your John for a father." She felt a familiar quickening of her mind, the feeling that she would be able to force her will on the other person. She had no fear of John Gill. By the inexorable logic of emotion, the only person she had never been able to work on was Evan.

"But don't you mind seeing him?"

"Why should I?" Emily asked surprised.

Mrs. Gill looked at her. "It's not any use my saying I'm sorry, is it?"

"I don't think so," Emily said, laughing. "Besides, you're not sorry."

"I'm sorry I did it to *you*," Mrs. Gill said.

"Do you want to make me cry?"

They looked at each other until Mrs. Gill turned her eyes away. From another angle than Emily's she was learning the anguish of the thing done, not to be undone.

"I wonder why you came here," Emily said quickly.

"I wanted to warn you. And I wanted help."

"You were sure I should help you, then?"

"I didn't think about it," Mrs. Gill said. She turned very red. "I've only been thinking about myself."

"I know," Emily said, with a wry face. "I can't help you through that. I couldn't help myself. You'll just have to remember—*nothing* goes on hurting. You'll come to an end of it. . . . Don't tremble . . . I think I'd better go and see Mr. Gill now, before anything can happen."

They went together. It was raining, and icy squalls blew against the Gill house. It was a monstrous stone pile, placed exactly in the centre of a pattern of soot-blackened lilac trees and shrubs in cemetery colours. The pavement, when they stepped out of the car, seemed to pitch like a ship, running with dark water. Emily kept Mrs. Gill talking on the stairs, for the benefit of the servants, before she opened the door of John Gill's library on the first floor.

He looked up as she came in, and seemed astonished to see her. In the first moment, before he had time to cover himself, Emily saw that he was suffering something worse than the soreness of a Yorkshireman wounded in his tenderest sense—sense of property. He had aged ten years.

He stood up. "What do you want? Is there anything I can do for you?"

Emily came slowly forward. He had made her feel that she was intruding, but she still felt certain of herself. After all, he liked her. "Your wife . . ."

John Gill frowned. "Did Mrs. Gill send you?"

"She has been to see me," Emily said. She gave him a clear look. "I thought I'd better come to you. I didn't know where else to go."

"Did you know what was going on?"

"No." Emily lied.

His face changed slightly. "It's been a shock for you, then."

It *has* been a shock, Emily thought. She was surprised to feel herself shaking. "I must be getting old," she said aloud.

Gill's eyebrows twitched. "I had the same notion about myself," he said drily. He stared at her. "Nice pair, aren't we? They've made rare fools on us, the two of them. I won't tell you what I've been thinking."

"I expect Evan was to blame," Emily said. She did not think this, but she knew that in his present mood Gill would contradict anything she said.

"Don't you believe it, Mrs. Smith. I don't. Mrs. Gill has always known her own mind and she's old enough to look after herself."

Emily closed her eyes. For a moment, as though his mind had infected hers, she felt a stab of physical jealousy. An image of Evan and Margaret, as they had been together, blocked up her mind. She made a sickening effort and it vanished.

"I'm not going to argue with you," she said hurriedly. "I shall need your help. What are you going to do?"

"You tell me that," Gill shouted. The veins in his face and neck swelled out. His hands, big and mottled, gripped the edges of his chair. "What *can* I do? I could thrash her black and blue but it wouldn't make a decent woman of her again. Nowt'll do that. As for yon husband of yours, Mrs. Smith, if I took and broke him across me knee it won't alter the fact that he's had her. *My wife.* The damned cheek of him!"

Emily waited a moment to give him time to cool down. "I thought you would be able to help me," she sighed.

Gill looked at her. "Oh you did, did you?" he said soberly.

"Perhaps you think that's damned cheek, too!"

He chuckled suddenly. "You've your own way of going about things," he said.

Emily relaxed, certain of him, unless he fell into one

of those flurries of masculine rage which destroy in a moment what has cost tortures to build. "Do you want to keep your wife, Mr. Gill?"

"Eh? I don't know."

Emily smiled at him, friendly and reserved. "I rather wanted to keep my husband."

"Keep him out of my sight!"

"You can't punish him without punishing me," Emily said.

"Do you know what?" Gill said. "A wife always has to suffer for her husband's misdoings. You can't alter that."

"Could you forgive Margaret, Mr. Gill?"

"Eh? Do you want me to?"

"Do you want to know what I think? I think you've been putting too much on her. Five years I've lived in Brallington and each year you and Margaret have gone to Scarborough for August and stayed in the same hotel and done the same things. ... If you did business on that principle you wouldn't be where you are."

"You know a lot about me," Gill said, staring at her. He struggled with himself for a moment, scowling, and brought out his question. "Perhaps you know what Margaret wants?"

"What would she be likely to want?" Emily said boldly. "She wants to be given another chance. ... If all the years you've been married are not to count for anything. ... You have Margaret's life in your hands. You can save her or finish her off. What's going to happen to her if you don't want her? She'll drift off somewhere ... trying to hold her head up ... getting old. ... You've had her since she was twenty—she can't make a fresh start by herself. No one knows about this. Can't you and Margaret work it out together—without bringing the whole of Brallington in to stare at you?"

"And you'll come in for your share of looks," Gill said swiftly.

"Not Brallington's looks. I can always go back to London."

Gill stood up. "God help us," he burst out. "How am I

going to keep my hands off him—let alone sit on his platforms? I can't do it. I tell you straight out—if I have to shake his hand on polling day I'll tear it off his body. The damned Socialist!"

"Will you listen to me?" Emily said. "Let your wife go away—now, to-night. Let her wire you to-morrow morning that she's ill, she's had an accident, anything. You'll hurry to her at once and stay away at least a month. You needn't see Evan again for two or three years." I'm done, she thought, stopping suddenly. A dreadful certainty of failure seized her. She stiffened in her chair, waiting for him to speak. If he refuses—I shall get up and go away. I shall go directly to Evan and warn him. I shall see his dismay and then his resentment and impatience with her written across his face. He will stand, frowning, and then he will turn to me, with the question: What is to be done? I must be prepared with my answer.

"Very well," Gill said. "I'll do it."

Emily stood up. She was trembling and her tongue felt swollen. She wanted to say something, to say the right thing, to make sure of him, but her voice came out in a rough squeak.

"I hope you've done right."

"That's my business," Gill said heavily.

Emily held out her hand. "Good-bye, then."

"You've pluck," Gill said. "Are they worth all this? . . . Damned if I know. Better not know too much. . . . I know one thing, though. You're a sight too good for him, Mrs. Smith."

"You can't strike a balance in things of that kind," Emily said wearily. "I used to think you could—but you can't. Margaret's goodness is different from yours, and mine different from his. Good-bye."

He let her go downstairs alone. The drawing-room door had opened a finger's-breadth at the sound of their voices. He could imagine his wife's face, but he did not want to see her through the mind of the other woman. He would wait until they were alone in their house. He went back into the library.

As Emily passed the door it opened widely and Mrs. Gill came out holding a letter. She looked at Emily with an unspoken question, ashamed to speak. Her face showed that she had been crying, perhaps over her letter. "It's all right," Emily said, scarcely moving her lips. She did not want John Gill to hear her talking to his wife. Women against men. . . .

"Will you give Evan this?" Mrs. Gill said. "It's only to finish things off—but without telling him that John knows. If you'd rather I did nothing at all I'll tear it up."

"You ought to have posted it," Emily said loudly. She took the letter. On the way home she stopped at the Post Office, bought a stamp, and dropped the letter in the box. She thought: If I take it home with me I shall read it, and I know already enough. I know too much.

She shrank from the people on the pavement, shrinking into herself, small, solitary, old. I go on, she thought. I still have Evan and I go on. I care nothing for anyone else. My children are nice, well-behaved, affectionate children. I love them, but not as I love Evan, not with this last squeeze of my strength, the last sigh, the last look. What is John Gill saying to his Margaret. I don't care. I don't care about either of them. Let me get home. Only get home.

On the day of the poll she was too tired to get up and go the round of the committee-rooms with Evan. She stayed in bed, and towards midnight, when Evan should have been telephoning the result to her from the Town Hall, she fell asleep. She was asleep when he came in, flushed with victory. He woke her. She started up.

"Oh, Evan. How much?"

"Majority nearly eleven thousand. I'm sorry you missed the count. Everybody asked for you. And they cheered you in the committee-room." He drew a telegram out of his pocket. "Look. Gill sent this from Dover. We've had it pinned up in the Fletcher Street committee-room all day."

She glanced at it. "All the luck you deserve to-day. Gill."

CHAPTER VII

EMILY considered herself to be under sentence of death. Like so many pure-bred Yorkshire women she had a deep vein of eccentricity and superstition running clean through her nature. It never appeared, in recognisable shape, but it dictated many of her actions. She took no notice of her doctor's advice except to say to herself: So I am going to die. The words made no commotion in her mind. Instead, it was as though a tide of water flowed in over it, silently, deeply, bearing on its surface forgotten images, a doll with a kid body she had once liked, a dress, an evening cape of her mother's, yellow buds shaken from a spring-flowering tree. She felt no stir of protest.

They did not go down to Brallington again until just before the election of '31. Many things were changed—in Brallington, in the country. John Gill sat solidly on the platforms of Evan's National opponent, never opening his mouth, glad to have found an excuse to leave his uncomfortable friends in the lurch. In his heart of hearts he despised all politicians, not least the rather querulous retired colonel who was opposing Evan. When Evan and John Gill met in the crowded High Street, their cars held up side by side, Gill ignored the younger man, looking sourly past his outstretched hand.

In the country, workless disappointed men faced the prospect of winter without hope. They snatched from one side and then from the other, accepting and rejecting promises. Promises had been made to them before, and in the end they were poorer, their wives poorer and more hopeless, their children fettered. Outside the country, in other countries, the same tale—grit choking up the wheels, absence of hope, of vision. In every country many who lived from day to day, ignoring the future.

Evan worked hard. The Labour Party was facing certain defeat, brought on itself by its failures. The men who had led it to failure now separated themselves from it. The savagery of Snowden, the charm of Macdonald,

were turned pitilessly against their late followers and
friends. To Evan the break with Macdonald was a personal bitterness. Not alone in the party, he had given
more than his mind to the man. He really loved Macdonald. He would cheerfully have faced a firing party
with him. The break gave him the same sense of fathom-
less treachery a child suffers who has been laughed at in
public. Only for Snowden's whirling blows he could feel
an honest contempt, pricked by surprise.

He worked Emily off her feet. She had been learning
to make political speeches and she addressed meetings
in her low, clear voice, trembling with nervousness. Her
earnestness and simplicity caught at the sympathies of
an audience. Evan praised her and told her that she was
saving votes. Night after night she woke, damp with
terror, from a dream that she was standing in the Market
Square in Brallington, before an audience that stretched
out of sight, unable to utter a word. The day after she
faced another meeting. She spoke, she trembled, she went
through the new tricks she had taught herself, and afterwards, when the applause started, she felt nothing. Her
mind went dead for a few moments.

She visited committee-rooms daily, and canvassed.
Once, waiting on a doorstep to be admitted, she saw Margaret Gill on the other side of the street. A smiling look
passed between them. Mrs. Gill's said: You know less
about me than I know about you. I am grateful to you,
too, but I don't want to talk to you again. Emily's: You
poor woman, I hope you are happy. Of course you have
lost Evan and so cannot be as rich and happy as I am.
All the same, you know too much about me because you
know my husband—so let us pass on, liking and respecting
each other, without meeting.

If the day was a nightmare, the nights themselves, except when she dreamed, were islands of refuge. She began
to think of her bed as the one place where she would be
safe. On polling day she thought of it all the time. When
she was driving the car, when she was talking to tired
women in the committee-rooms and when she was tying

up the cut finger of their agent, John Barrett, she could
see a phantom bed a few feet off in the air. Its turned-
down sheets invited her tired limbs.

Counting began in the Town Hall after the poll. She
drove there about ten o'clock, showed her papers, and
was admitted. Inside the Council-room the black shiny
ballot boxes were stacked against one wall. The tellers
were working in groups of three, smoothing out the
papers and tying them into neat bundles of fifty. A clerk
walked about in the square formed by the tables, gathering the bundles and dropping them into a wastepaper
basket. The long tables grew emptier. Emily looked over
the shoulders of the tellers, counting the number of times
Evan's name came in a fifty. When the box came from
a ward she knew, she leaned forward eagerly. After a
time it became certain that the wards she had thought
solid for Labour were nothing of the kind—not this time.

She crossed to the other side of the room and took
Evan's arm. He smiled at her. "We've lost, but don't mind
too much," he whispered. She felt his arm round her
shoulders for a moment, holding her. He went away and
she turned to speak to their agent. Jack Barrett's round
comical face was grey. He had been working nineteen
hours a day and he had a wound that hurt him at night.
Sometimes she missed a word when he dropped his voice
to a vehement whisper. He had been a weaver before the
War and the missing nails on his hands were ripped off
when he first went to work, at the age of thirteen. He had
not understood very clearly what he was working at and
he had been thinking of something else, of the game of foot-
ball he had been playing the evening before, with Tom and
the other boys and Tom played badly. Then the machine
did something suddenly and tore his fingernails off.

The votes were being sorted out now, and the doubtful
papers put aside for another scrutiny. Evan's papers went
to the right and were fastened up with a red card. Now
and then a checker said "No!" softly, as a vote got pushed
over on to the wrong pile. The tellers worked fast and
competently, with very few mistakes.

Emily watched the bundles being stacked into red and blue boxes and tried to guess the numbers. Two of the unemployed were checking for their side. One of them, she remembered with an effort, was called Arthur Pearce, a youngish man with a neat, delicate wife and three children. He had been out of work for two years. He had been excited and very happy all through the fight. His lips moved as he watched the tellers. Emily wondered what he was thinking and how Mrs. Pearce would manage through the winter, with the cuts, and that heavy baby dragging at her shoulders. She felt angry and helpless. No change would come in time to save Mr. and Mrs. Pearce. They would go on hoping and hoping, until the day when it was too much trouble to hope.

Evan was looking at her and she went over to him and touched his arm. "If you weren't here I couldn't bear it," she whispered to him.

The Conservative candidate came in now, with two ladies, his wife and another woman. Emily saw Arthur Pearce look at them angrily. Both the women were in evening dress, with cloaks just parted a little to show a sliver of polished skin and necklace. Rosettes of red, white and blue had been pinned on the shoulders of the cloaks. How extraordinary that they should be so insensitive, Emily thought. Both women walked past her without speaking, but the candidate himself stopped and shook hands with Evan. She saw Jack Barrett avoid having to shake hands.

Now news began to come in from the other Brallington divisions. Both the Labour seats had been lost. Between eleven and midnight the results kept coming in, whispered across from the door. A trail of defeats. Lost. Lost. Lost. Then—"Henderson's out!" "I don't believe it," Emily whispered. "It's reet enough," Joe Lodge said. He looked tired to death. He had worked as hard as any of them, coming straight from the factory and working until eleven.

Now the counting was finished. Papers were being handed about between the Town Clerk and his assistants.

Emily stood close to Arthur Pearce, waiting for the figures. She wanted to speak to him, but nothing seemed worth saying at the moment. When the figures were read out Evan had been defeated by nearly eight thousand votes.

In his speech the new Conservative member said that the results up to the moment showed the Labour Party to have been wiped out all over the country. His wife and her friends clapped excitedly at this. He added something about the eyes of the world on Brallington and a clean fight. In the group of people round him Emily caught sight of John Gill, unmoved, except for the twinkle of triumph in his brown eyes.

She felt done with depression and tiredness. Jack Barrett said bitterly: "They'll mess up foreign relations. If only they don't bring another war on us. I've a boy of sixteen."

"They can't do that," Emily exclaimed.

She dragged her mind back from the darkest forebodings to think of Evan. She began to long to be alone with him. Then this cloud of fear and depression would lift from her brain and she would think of some phrase with which to comfort him. He had his back to her, talking to Joe Lodge and Barrett. She shook hands with Arthur Pearce. He managed a quick smile and said: "Better luck next time." Then Evan turned back to look for her and took her arm. Outside, in the Square, the crowd swayed and roared and hooted at them. A woman with a crimson face leaned out to snatch the rosette Emily wore. "We've showed you," she screamed. "Thieves. Dirty thieves and liars. *Soshies*."

"Let them be now," a man said to her.

Another man said: "Never mind, missus. I voted for you. We'st *not* done."

"It's the women as 'as let us down," said another.

Evan was smiling. In the car he put his arm round her and kissed her. His voice had a warm excited sound.

"Not feeling wretched, are you? It's all right. I know it's all right, Emily. We're certain to win in the end. You

see, these others are only defending themselves. *We're* the
army with banners, the future."

He helped her out of the car and stood a moment talking to the man. She went on into the house and up the
stairs. At the top she stood still to gather strength 'for
the journey across the landing. Endless dark tracts of
floor separated her from her room. She stumbled across
them, blindly, her hand gripping her dress.

Evan caught up with her as she was feeling for the
handle of the door. He leaned across her and opened it.
She saw the firelight and a chair in the broad wedge of
the firelight. She sat down. Evan sat on the floor beside
her and rested his head against her knees. In the firelight
she could see the deep lines round his eyes, and round
his mouth. Her hand felt the shape of the bone under
his hair. He was saying that they would have to work to
recover the ground lost. His voice rose, still warm and
excited. It echoed in the darkness behind her eyes. All
the time she was thinking: I shall get into bed and I
shall sleep. I shall close my eyes and let sleep take me.
My hands will lie still by my sides. My body will lie perfectly still. I shan't know that I am asleep.

"So it begins again," Evan said. "You and I, Emily . . .
again together . . . again another fight . . . another . . ."

Her silence and her exhaustion at last alarmed him.
Breaking off in the rush of his words he said urgently:
"I'm ghastly sorry about Agnes and the rest. . . . That's
finished with, Emily."

Emily looked at him. She roused herself to make an
effort. Which was a final effort. "They were pin-pricks,"
she said.

A DAY OFF

SLEEP drifted across her mind, tattered edges of fog
vanishing in the strong light. She stirred, trying to escape,
pursuing anxiously the shapes of her dream. Voices died
away. The substantial dream became insubstantial. She
grew confused, afraid, as the uncertainty touched one
and then another of her friends. Let me stay, she said,
with doubt and growing fear. But now she was conscious
of the room and of a half-seen whiteness on its wall.
Slowly, with a heavy sour reluctance, she awoke to herself lying between coarse sheets in the tumbled bed. The
whiteness resolved itself into a shape of sunlight on a
level with her eyes. It had entered the room under the
blind, and she raised herself to lean out of the bed and
drag angrily at the cord. The brightness gone, she tried
to fall asleep again, turning her back to the window and
drawing the quilt up behind her head.

It was no use. After a time she opened her eyes and
lay over on her back, staring at the ceiling. Its cracks
formed crazily the plan of a house, and unnumbered
times she had tried to arrange its rooms in an order she
knew. The biggest room was the kitchen with her
mother's sewing-machine under the window and the sofa
pushed against the wall behind the round table. She
crouched under the table, hidden by its dark red cloth,
hand pressed on her mouth. In another moment her
mother's voice, light with its pretence of fear: Where
has the child gone? Running along the narrow dark passage she pushed at the door of the front room. The walls
were papered in glistening white and blue stripes, satin-
paper that was; she felt carefully the rough-smooth of
the pattern. A palm-leaf fan, dry and brittle, rested
against the mirror. Through the window she saw the

streets of small houses falling steeply into the valley, the blackened factory: the hill beyond them was scarred with houses built closely across and across, to the dense sprawl of trees full on the sky-line. A woman holding her shawl close flitted across the street, calling to her neighbour in an urgent voice like the strong whir of a spring. Lovely the pure bend of the sky over trees, hill, and spoiled valley. It filled her with happiness, not knowing, thinking it without words.

The woman in the bed gazed at the cracked ceiling. That oblong mark was—but the game had ceased to interest her. She gave it up and began to think about getting out of bed. After some minutes she sat up and put back the bedclothes. Her nightgown had worked up, uncovering a thick veined leg. She sat on the side of the bed, curling damp fingers over her knee. I'm growing heavier, she thought. She felt herself settling into her body, not caring; then setting her feet apart awkwardly, stood. Always now in the morning she was a minute or two before she could get herself going. Her body stiffened during the night. Walking heavily, with groans she need not silence, since she was alone, she reached the washstand. A long glass, bought in the second-hand shop in Judd Street, leaned against the wall. Must hang it, she thought, for the hundredth time. One day, in a burst of energy, she would borrow nails and a hammer from Mrs. Purefoy downstairs and fasten it to the wall. Meanwhile it leaned, and behind it there was an oblong patch of less-faded wallpaper.

The room was warm because of the June sun outside, filling the narrow street to the neck. She looked quickly and uncomfortably at herself in the glass, then reached across the bed for her chemise. That made her look thinner, coming down nearly to her knees. It was the middle part of her that had thickened so in the last years. She bent down and felt under her feet the wrinkled yellow skin. It wouldn't surprise me if the arches gave. I ought to get supports now. Another thought jumping into her mind she straightened herself with a sudden effort and went over to the window. Just before she slept she had been saying to herself: If it's fine I'll have a day off. Go to Richmond or somewhere. She jerked at the blind cord. The blind flew up and at once the street entered the room.

A row of geraniums in the opposite window blazed all the hotter for the strong light. Beyond them the potboy at The Swan was sweeping last night's sawdust out over the doorstep. Dust thickened the sunlight. On the edge of the pavement a thin dirty child scraped the gutter with his fingers to make a ring of dust round two slivers of wood. Some game he's playing. At what? A woman bent her head in the window, doing something to a garment she squeezed between her hands. With the heat and the fierce light, noise flowed into the room, the squeak of wheels on asphalt, voices, a girl's shrill with anger, rough male laughter.

She drew back, shrinking from the impact of the street on her unprepared body. Her clothes lay in a heap at the foot of the bed. Fumbling among them she brought out her purse from the toe of her stocking and emptied it into her hand. Eleven and fourpence. She slumped against the end of the bed, trying to think. Thursday. If George came on Saturday as usual, or sent the usual—if he failed—A curious blankness succeeded this thought. She groped with her hands in the sheet, feeling the bed end cold and slippery against her knees. No use thinking. She let herself down carefully and drew a stocking over her foot. Grit, from the carpet, stuck to it. Fastening her corset she drew the suspenders tight and stood to see the effect. She felt better now that she was held up. Safer. She gave herself an encouraging slap behind, and high-kicked warily before she pulled on her knickers. Artificial silk. Laddered before you could turn round. Shall I wear my real? Better not. Save them for Saturday—to show, as my dressing-gown opens. Who's my luxurious little girl?

Wetting a corner of the towel she wiped round her eyes, then spread the cream over her face and throat. She was used to the coarse look of her skin, puckered under the jaw. It pulled at the corners of her mouth. I ought to wear something at night now. The powder lay in thick dabs, waiting to be worked in. Mechanically, with wetted finger, she smoothed her eyebrows and laid the red on her lip. She scarcely glanced at herself as she turned away from the glass. It was a daily rite, nearly without meaning. The notion that she took all these pains to attract belonged now to the past.

The smell of stale scent came out of the cupboard when she opened it. She looked doubtfully at the navy silk and finally hung it back, taking out that knitted thing instead. The skirt sagged a trifle at the seams, but she freshened up the front of the jacket with the damp towel and pulled the belt tight.

I ought to tidy up a bit first, she thought, looking round. The rumpled bed was the centre of disorder but everywhere there were clothes tossed down on chairs, bits of paper, a banana skin, used cups, the cover of a magazine sticking out from the bed, an empty powder-box with a dead puff inside, cigarette ends, a paper bag of something, and a towel-rail-ful of limp damp stockings. Dust, too, everywhere, on the walls, on the shabby paint, on the floor. A film of dust on the water in the hand-basin.

I'll do it this evening when it's cool, she decided. She pulled the door to after her, locked it, and stood hesitating on the unswept landing. I could do with a cup of tea now. Her mouth was dry and sour.

Picking her way, she sauntered briskly along the street. The manager of The Swan was warming himself in his doorway. He spoke to her and she answered amiably, with a smile.

"Fine warm day, missus."

"Indeed it is."

His gaze followed her to the end of the street. Showing her age, he thought, not unkindly: queer, too, how they all walk in the same way—as if they had an extra joint behind, jerking it. He went in and spoke about it to his wife. "Who's that you've seen? That woman?" she asked drily.

That woman had reached Tottenham Court Road and marched across in to the bright side. She almost strutted along by the shops, enjoying the heat, the glare, the press of traffic. Proud like a peacock she felt. In the hinterland of her mind the gaunt Yorkshire valley where she lived out her first seventeen years was immovable, a closed pass. That way she could go no further. But she could turn her back on it, and she did that, preferring the endless coloured dusty circus of London, the scarlet dragons of buses, the drays drawn by smoking horses, the neat bustling taxis, and the nippy cycle-vans that cheeky boys bestride. She swung along by all this as happy as a child —as happy as the pinafored child who ran whooping along The Bottoms when the circus came to Staveley. But she had forgotten the child.

There were sunblinds out across the street, throwing blue shadows on the pavement. She felt pleasantly warm. A fair scorcher by the afternoon, she thought. I like it. Makes you feel young. A boy in a white coat was placing boxes of strawberries in the windows of Shearn's. Morning gathered. Mn. Do you believe it? Must be at dawn then. The word spread a brief silence round her, as if she had walked clean out of Tottenham Court Road into another state of mind. But in a moment she was nearly knocked over by a girl rushing out of the restaurant next door and not looking where she was going but charging straight across the street into the traffic and how she escaped death Heaven and the driver of that 24 alone knew, the clumsy fool, jolting the breath out of people's poor bodies.

She stood a moment getting her breath. I'm as empty as that bucket. Now she quickened her pace, thinking what she would treat herself to for breakfast. A pot of tea and two poached eggs, please Miss. No—have you any kidneys? Crossing Oxford Street—and what a crossing— she cut delicately into a richly-browned kidney. A thin trickle of red gravy ran out under the knife. Her tongue felt gritty with longing.

She could not walk down Charing Cross Road without wondering whoever thought it worth while to write, let alone to buy and read so many books. Some shops that were not book shops placed paper-back novels in their windows. *A Bed of Roses*. She had tried to read that, and found it dull. Now here was a pile of music, rather dusty and dog-eared. Someone had been turning it over: she stood still to have a proper look. I know that, she thought quickly. A silly joy seized her. *I feel so silly when the moon comes out*. Moving away, she began to hum the tune. Her feet kept step in sudden gay rhythm. La-la, la *la* la.

Rude old ape. Actually pointing. She swung round to stare angrily after two elderly ladies. What if I was singing. There's no law is there? She wanted to shout a word or two after them. Give them a few they won't have heard. Tightening her lips, she stalked on, but now she was all on edge and bothered. The disagreeable impression faded slowly. The bright warm lightly-moving air, distraction of faces and colours sliding past the edge of her eye into vacancy, ripples of sound from a street band splitting the other noises of the street, flowed over it, pressing it down, out of sight. A dress shop in Shaftesbury Avenue caught her eye. She pressed close to the window. Black satin and of course too narrow, but they've pinned it over behind—perhaps wider than it looks. Nothing to let out, I suppose. No, I didn't, think you. Can we copy it for you, madam? Reluctantly she turned away from the window. No use even asking about it, she hadn't the money, nor would unless George—But the thought of George was definitely unpleasant. As always, she tried instinctively to close her mind. What shall you do if?—thoughts that began in this way terrified her. No, no, her mind cried. Not now, not yet. Think of something. I am thinking. Think. I'm not old yet, I'll look that chart out and exercise every morning. She felt a vague comfort, sprung from all the other moments in which she had made an identical resolution.

The sun hurled splinters of light across the Circus.
They met and crossed, glancing off polished cars and the
watery surface of windows. Coloured jumpers and straw
hats trimmed with flowers floated close up to the surface,
like the exotic fishes in tanks, in the Aquarium. Her eyes,
a little weak, dazzled. She turned along Coventry Street
to the Corner House, passing two flower women outside
the Pavilion. One of them, the thinner, older, and shabbier
of the two was trying the effect of a new ribbon round her
hat. Her face had a grave innocence, but she was rigid
with excitement, watched half in pity half in scorn by her
friend. The flowers in the baskets had lately been sprinkled
and large drops of water trembled on the leaves.

She stepped into tepid light and air in the Corner House.
The Open All Night café was nearly empty. Behind the
counter a man with a fresh pink face yawned and yawned,
putting his hand up to cover the gaping cavern. It made
her feel sleepy. She sat down close to the wall and read
the menu. The insides of her cheeks puckered with the
foretaste of happiness. She glanced up at the waiter with
a haughty air.

"Bring me a grilled kidney, and bacon."

"No kidneys this morning, madam."

Really, she could slap him in her disappointment. Her
voice was sharp.

"It *says* kidneys. Look here."

"I'm sorry. Not here yet, madam."

"Bring me some bacon, then. With roll and butter and
a cup o' tea."

She drew her gloves off, folded them, and looked about
her. That woman over there now. Looks like a school-
teacher. What's she doing here then, this time in the
morning. Perhaps out of work. Like me. No not like me.
I'm all right, I'm safe. Safe enough. If I could manage
a new coat, now, that would be a grand thing for me.
She began turning over in her mind ways in which she
might come by a new light coat. She might go to work
again at the cinema. But she hated the uniform and
standing for hours to show people their places in the

dark and she had an uncomfortable notion that she was
too old for them now. I don't care to be made a fool of,
she thought uneasily.

She imagined the coat accurately, a loose silk garment,
in black or biscuit, with pleats under the arms to give
fullness. They suit even a stout woman, she thought, and
I'm not that.

No, I'm not that, she repeated, stirring the sugar into
her tea with the handle of her fork, since the waiter had
forgotten to bring a spoon. "Here," she called loudly.
"You haven't given me a spoon." She stared, dissatisfied,
at his departing back. No respect, she thought, vexed.
For two pins I'd complain, report him.

Her glance wandered round the room, resting with
momentary interest on a woman in a shabby coat, hunched
over her cup. She reminds me of someone, now who is it?
Her mind cast about, like an old gossipy woman peering through a blind into the street. Yes, yes, she looks like
one of the Willises, Polly Willis it could be. Polly went
to Australia that year, Coronation year—I believe it's her,
why not? She could come back, I suppose. She felt quite
excited. I'll walk past her as I go out and take a good
look, and if it's her I'll say, Why Polly it *is* Polly Willis
isn't it? She'll be that surprised. She'll want to know what
I'm doing now—Here her thoughts swung round quickly,
looking for some cover from the other woman's sharp
eyes. Ask too many questions, I shouldn't wonder, she
thought moodily, and began to wish again for a new
smart coat to cover up all deficiencies, moral as well as
physical.

There was that buyer she knew slightly—wasn't he for
one of the big shops, now? If she asked him he might pick
her something good, cheap. Trade prices. She tried to
forget the hateful fact that any price at all was beyond
her now.

A man coming in knocked against her table and made
her start. She glanced up, and got another and worse
start. He was the living image of that one who was killed
in the War. Eyes, colour, wide comical mouth—even the

way he looked round him with a faint grin was the same.
It's given me a turn, she thought. Cold entered her
veins. What was left of a young man fifteen years after
they buried him in the earth? Her mind went blank and
she gave a little whimper of fear.

She came back quickly to the dim noisy room, staring
greedily round her over the edge of the cup. The last of
the tea. It had gone cold, and she half beckoned the
waiter over to order another, then changed her mind.
Better keep the money. Points of light started wherever
she looked, from the knife in a man's hand, from his
bald head, from the chandelier, the marble facings, then
from the glasses and the metal fittings on the counter.
The shabbily dressed woman stood up to go, fumbling
in her purse, and she saw that it was not Polly Willis, not
even very like her. Oh well.

I must go, she thought, but she sat on, while her
thoughts went busily hither thither, birds pulling at
straws. The only other way she could manage the coat
would be to get friendly with a new fellow and try to
touch him for something before he got too bored. That
could happen.

She would be swaggering into the Café to-night, looking her best, and a well-dressed man seated there alone,
after a good look, up and down, I must remember to
change into those Spanish kid slippers, would say casually, Like a whiskey? and sucking in her cheeks to bring
the dimples out she would answer, No thanks I prefer a
Martini. That made a good impression at the start. Later,
perhaps, when they were going along nicely she might
say laughing merrily, Well perhaps a small whiskey then.
As if it were a great joke her drinking whiskey and only
doing it to please him.

It might be wiser to get a cloth coat, though. After all
—June. September would be on them in no time and
then long mist-blown evenings, the air heavy and the
wind chill and harsh. Wine colour, with fox at the neck
and cuffs, is smart and becoming to a full figure, she
thought, sighing. The waiter strolled past the table and

glanced at her. Anxious to get rid of me. When I'm ready and not before, mister—. You can't sit a minute in these places until they're at you. She lolled in her chair, affecting indifference. The next time he passed she took up her knife and began tapping a tune out on the marble. He stopped. "Can I get you anything more?"

"No. When I want something I'll tell you." She made her voice as overbearing as she could.

He put the bill down in front of her and went away. Suddenly she felt miserable. I might as well go. It was no use staying, it was no use doing anything. She felt inclined to go back and see whether any letter had come for her by the post. But no, I won't, I said I'd go to Richmond this morning and I'll go, she thought, obstinate since it was of no importance. The letter won't run away. Half consciously she knew that if she went back and again there was no letter laid, that would be the worst of all.

She looked round her for her gloves and walked out.

In the street the air was dry and hot and the fumes of oil, petrol and gaspers were almost visible. As she crossed Leicester Square Garden a child ran sharply against her knees and fell over. She picked it up, dusted it, and was trying to find a cachou in her bag when the mother snatched it up. "Oh, keep your brat," she muttered, but she felt mildly sorry that the child had missed its treat. She popped the cachou in her mouth.

The train was nearly empty. Leaning back in one of the cross-seats she pretended that she was going down to Richmond on the invitation of a friend. What friend? Well, it could be a man of about forty, like the man in that book, she couldn't recall the name, whose wife never understood him, though he was well-off and had married her when he was too young to know his own mind. She half closed her eyes against the sun (they were in the open now) and to imagine it better. At first he was reserved, pleased to be with her but not yielding himself to the strong fascination. Then one day she called at his city office to ask his advice about her investments (naturally he had told her how to make money by buying something that was going up and selling it again in the nick of time), and when she had thanked him he looked at her with a strange smile and said quietly, You know I love you of course. And she said, Yes, just as quietly, because she would never make the mistake of raising her voice at a man with his disposition and refinement, Yes I know. He closed his eyes. I suppose you don't feel anything for me. She was tense and composed. I made excuses to come and see you because I—love you. He came round his desk to her and took her in his arms. When he kissed her it was like the first time, only better, because she knew what to do. He let her go quickly and stepped back. His face was very stern and what was it, distorted. (She distorted her own, acting the word.) He looked at her and folded his arms. What is going to become of us, he sighed. That was a thing to ask her. I don't know, she said, I'll go. Quickly, before he could speak, she had gone. Well, she was travelling down now to his house, because of course she knew his wife, who was civil to her though of course not liking her, afraid of her looks and her strange power over men. After dinner another guest in the house would suggest a moonlight drive. Off they go, he, she, and the other (featureless) woman. The hedges flow past like pale water. They have driven a long way when the car breaks down and leaving it they walk through the forest to a small inn. She saw it with great clearness: it was The Three Pigeons from past Staveley. Their rooms were small and bare. She noticed at once that the washstand in her room only half concealed the door leading to his. He saw it too. We didn't plan this, it happened. Very well. When she left the stuffy parlour to go up to her room his hand brushed the side of hers.

Here a woman stumbled in and sat down facing her in the narrow place formed by their two seats. She carried a bag bursting with packages. A strong smell of onions came from the bag and flowed through the carriage.

Where was I? She closed her eyes and settled back easily into the familiar excitement. She was waiting all ready for him when he came (having nipped out to the village general store and post-office and bought a jar of cold cream and the only bottle of *Quelques Fleurs* they had) and they were together all that night. The train lurched, the train stopped, and went on again with a cripple who got in at Baron's Court and three unemployed men who had heard that there were jobs to be had in the motor works at Gunnersbury. The oniony woman got out but the smell of onions stayed.

None of these events were as real to the woman as her thoughts. An imbecile smile crossed her face. She knew nothing about it, given up to the sensual pleasure she was enacting. When it was over, when her mind, limp and spent like an animal after a hard chase, turned to stare at the other people in the carriage, she did not know which station they were approaching. It might be Richmond. Smoothing back her hair and giving a set to the front of her jacket she looked nervously through the window. A middle-aged gentleman had moved into the seat left empty by the onion woman. She spoke to him, and such is the idiot simplicity of our bodies, she could not help giving her words the form of a smiling invitation, though all she said was: "Where are we?"

"Kew," he replied.

She leaned back again, relieved, and then thought that a woman at the other side of the carriage was looking at her disdainfully. She sat up, adjusted her belt, pointed her right shoe (the left had a dark stain across the top), and assumed the glassy stare proper to an attractive woman whose butler held the door open for her to step out into Portland Place, leaving behind her the black and white paved hall, the plants, the stags' heads—she had seen it all, that day trudging past in the cold, in the bitter rain, when the door opened and she saw. Through the warmth in the carriage she felt that cold, that rain. It was as if she carried about with her everywhere the horror of some winter when, for all anybody cared, for all the women who lived warm and snug in houses in Portland Place cared, she might perish of cold in her lonely room. But she must not think such things. She tilted her hat back cleverly and smiled in an amused absent way, looking directly at the woman opposite, but as though she were, as a woman, scarcely worth the trouble of noticing.

The middle-aged gentleman had glanced at her when she smiled. She now began to watch him from the corner of her eye and to play carelessly with her beads. The tips of her gloves were all screwed and wrinkled. Still, he's not looking at them, she thought. He's looking at me, wondering which part of Richmond I live in and whether we shall ever meet. There's no doubt he's keen. I can always tell. Something in the eyes. The train slowed into Richmond, stopped, and she got out, followed by the middle-aged gentleman. She was aware of him walking a few yards behind her in the sunny street. She hesitated, half turned as if meaning to cross the road, walked on, with a smile and a swift glance behind her, the ends of her scarf blowing out as she walked, like an invitation, like beckoning arms. She felt young and gay. "The handsome reckless young woman drew all eyes." All at once, as she was passing the shop where they sell the maids of honour, she felt certain that he had gone; and she swung completely round to look. He was nowhere in sight. Some side street had swallowed him and he had gone without a word or a sign. Her eyelids sank slowly once. She turned; thinking, Oh well. Her foot dragged a little scraping the pavement as she turned. There's as good fish in the sea, isn't there? This sort of thing had happened to her before. She went on, slowly, a little confused now by the heat and the morning brightness. Still, it was very nice, and reminded her a little of some seaside town—Ramsgate?—the tea-shops, and the young rosy women in thin dresses, and then the air, too, filled, wherever she looked, with points of light that might have been flung off, flung high in the air, by the many-waved sea.

Farther up the hill the street was less crowded and the pavement narrower. Two women, walking together,

came towards her. They filled the breadth of the pavement. At once she was on the defensive, thinking that
they would expect her to give way to them—and I won't,
she said, I won't step off the flags into the gutter for anyone, man or woman, I'm as good as anyone. She adopted
a harsh expression, prepared to return rudeness by rudeness, and when she came close to the women she looked
them full in the face with an insolent smile. The one
walking on the outside fell back, to make room. She
stood plump in the path of the other, who was compelled
to walk round her. This little triumph put her in a good
humour with herself and when she reached the top of the
hill and could sink, thankfully, on a wooden bench, she
felt that she had adjusted the score against her by at
least one heavy stroke on the right side.

It was a picture up here, really—but she had made out
to see the Park that morning, and see it she would, so in
a few minutes she started up: and stepped through the
wide gates and onto the turf feeling that she could do
almost anything since she had, without encouragement,
without even a friend to walk with her and sustain her,
reached Richmond Park from a bed-sittingroom off the
Tottenham Court Road, on the warmest day of the year,
and with less than ten shillings between her and—nothing.

At first, when she had found a good place—she could
see the road and the cars gliding along, and lean back
against the roots of the elms—she felt a vague discomfort.
As if it were somehow quite wrong that she should be
sitting here, her legs stretched out wide apart, for the
sake of coolness, her suede bag with the initial lying between them where she could keep her hand on it supposing she dropped off for a minute—the wild idea crossed
her mind that she ought to undress and hide her clothes,
gloves, bag, high-heeled shoes and all, in the bracken and
let the sun do its worst. A sight I should look sitting up
here in my skin, she thought, abashed. I'm too fleshy—
and gone—here and *here*—and my feet swelled the way
they are, I suppose with the heat and this walking, and
of course I'm not a child, not a girl, I was thin enough

once but you can't stay looking like that all your life, can you? Regret moved in her, gentle, inescapable, but for what she scarcely now knew.

The sun fell through the leaves in heavy yellow drops, splashing the mould, the grey roots of the trees, her legs and arms. Everything was quiet, not even a car hummed along the road far below her. In this stillness she could hear after a time the creaking of stems when an insect scuttled through them, and the cries, thin and far-off, of children on the farther edge of the trees. She dozed a little, and woke in a few minutes with a heavy start, saying to herself: "I can't think."

For a moment she stared vacantly, trying to remember what it was she could not think. But at once she knew. She made an effort to thrust it from her but it came on, hovering between her and the bright scene like a cloud, like the shadow of a cloud moving swiftly, inexorably, across the side of a hill. Warmth and the light were both diminished by it.

If George—she picked up her gloves and began to smooth the fingers—if George did not come on Saturday, or write, sending money; she was done for. Nothing for it then but to try for a job, and that failing her—not acknowledged by her yet the notion of failure had grown into a conviction, which was only waiting its moment to pounce on her from some dark alley of her mind. She was forty-six and getting stout.

A squirrel leaping up the tree behind her made her jump. She pressed her hand to her heart.

"Well! What next, I wonder?"

She did not know that she had said anything. She went on thinking, her poor head, never to be relied on since the days when she could not remember the capitals of Northern Europe (as if their names were going to make any difference or be of the least use to her then or ever) as helpless and baffled as a calf at a gate. In some place older, bleaker than the known places of her mind, dark, and washed by a dark tide, she knew more than she said. Knew indeed everything that could happen to women,

in this world—and it was not much help to think about
the next, not now. It's a fact I'm getting too old, she
cried in the darkness. And as if the tide moving sluggishly about her had flung them up she saw clearly a coat
trimmed with fur, and a child's shoe. But she had never
had a child. I've always been respectable, she thought
angrily. Not one man here and another there, like a
common woman: I've kept myself to myself. Many an
evening when she was alone, no chance of *him* coming,
she could have had company and men had spoken to her
in the streets, one man in particular she remembered,
four years ago in the empty street at the back of Regent
Street, because he had seemed a well-spoken merry
fellow, and she had been feeling low that evening, too—
but no, she had walked on, disregarding him and his
quiet friendly voice and gone home and cried, and thought
of telling George and then not told him. You never knew
with men.

Her anger against George increased. Five years it was
he had come regularly, once a week, usually on Saturday,
except during the time when he was working in Manchester
and even from there he had never forgotten to post on
her weekly money, though for all he knew she might
have been having men on all that time. But he did know.
He knows he can trust me, she thought bitterly; he
knows I won't go back on a friend. I'll stick to one man
just as long as he sticks to me and give others the go-
by, now and forever amen.

(The lean stooping figure of George's predecessor
darkened her mind, as a man walking past a window
darkens with his shadow the unentered room.)

Her fingers pressed on the dry earth, reckoning the
time since he had written. Three, no. Four weeks. He
had come, earlier than usual, and seated himself on the
bed while she dressed, elbow on his knee, a familiar gesture.
She felt his glance on her as she moved between glass
and cupboard, doing up her hair, her shoes, whatever
it was. When she asked him to hook her skirt over he
did it silently, bending under her lifted arm, afterwards

without the friendly smack she expected, and then when she was ready and took his arm, he stood stock still in the door, looking at the room as if he had forgotten something. She asked him, What's the matter with you? and Nothing, he said, nothing, I was just thinking. He walked in front of her down the unlighted stairs, so familiar to her that they were only an extension of her room. As she pulled the hall door to after her he said that the whole house smelled of dust and females. But it was not what he said, it was his face. She felt anger squeezing her across her throat.

But she had nothing to reproach herself with. Provoked as she was she had kept her temper and taken his arm again, and coaxed him. And before long he was joking and pinching her thigh as if nothing had happened. But something had happened that evening—though for the life of her she couldn't tell what it was. But instead of coming back with her as usual, he made an excuse, something she didn't catch, and left her gaping after him in Tottenham Court Road long after he'd ducked like that into the Underground. She couldn't take it in.

Since then, nothing. Not a sign.

Her hand moved blindly, feeling for something, some support. There was nothing. But a door flew open in her mind, letting through the rough noise of a gramophone. *He left her behind before*. She stared at the road, at the lightly waving trees, at her hand clasping the suede bag, and said angrily, Nothing's going to happen, not to you, not this time, dearie. Fear moved horribly in her, fold gliding over dry cold fold. But for what had happened, and might happen to her, she had no more tragic expression than the idiot stuttering of the gramophone.

E-e-e ee-yi eeyor

It seemed to her that she had never been left by herself like this in her life. Even when she was alone in it she did not feel that her room was empty. Perpetually there were sounds in the street, children, dogs quarrelling, a

sudden taxi, people shouting to each other outside The
Swan after closing time—their loud friendly voices died
away with the shuffle of their feet on the flags. *See you
Monday. He didn't 'alf cut up rough he didn't. Well goonight. Goonight ol' girl. Goonight*. In the mornings she
padded about the room in a kimono that it was all right
to wear when she was alone, and did odd jobs or cooked
herself something over the gas ring with the fullness of
her nightgown tucked safely between her legs. It was
a chance, too, to let that cream soak into her face. There
were a dozen things that needed doing, if she had the
time and the patience to do them. Last Friday she had
emptied out the contents of a drawer onto the bed, looking for the little bottle of brown cascara tablets, and she
was folding the things back into it when she saw the
time and it was just time to tear her clothes on and round
to May's, not to be late for the funeral—she'd given to the
wreath when she was asked, a waste—so everything had
to be jumbled back anyhow. The bottle was there all
right.

Suddenly the surface of her life split across and its
days poured out in an untidy crumpled heap, like clothes
emptied from a drawer. She could not tell one from the
other. All she knew was that something terrible had
happened, something she couldn't have prevented—(she
thought confusedly, I might have done something, kept
the room cleaner and tidier, I could have taken a course in
book-keeping at that college, they say they guarantee a
good post, nothing grand I daresay but better than nothing)—and now the walls of her room were giving way,
dissolving, before her eyes. She pulled at her skirt. It
was like an earthquake, like the scene at the cinema, with
the woman's arm sticking from a pile of bricks. They
saw a man run up and tug at the fingers. "He's pulling
her wedding ring off," her friend said. That was awful,
awful. If the rings were tight and stuck, they sliced them,
sliced the fingers off, he meant.

Panic swept through her, one wave meeting the next
in a fume of spray, of fear, but without forcing her to

cry out. She sat still clasping both hands over her bag,
dumb, as though she had grown to the earth. But all the
time she felt herself falling, falling, and the other things
fell cruelly on top of her, the trees, the walls of houses,
people, the manager of The Swan, waiters, broken plates.
She was caught, squeezed—but she could not die. She
would live a long time, because she was strong and had
never been ill. And then she was afraid of dying. So that
unless she could be instantly painlessly done away with
she was bound to go on trying to live.

She saw the street differently. To step out into it from
her over-habited room had been an adventure, a release
(she could not explain it) of all her senses. The room now
was her refuge. It was to it she belonged; to the faded
wall-paper; the cupboard; the cracks in the ceiling; the
smells, of old rotten wood, clothes, the worn mats. In
silence she rocked and quivered, mad with terror at the
thought of leaving it. And to go where?

"But it's all his fault," she cried.

Still, she was alive. She was sitting, warmed and comfortable (but for the hardness of the ground), in Richmond Park. The awful fear drew back, slowly, leaving
behind it small pools over which she could skip. She was
like that, hated to think of disagreeable things, to be upset and moody. So little contented her. I've been a fool
really, she thought. Resentment flowed smoothly over
her mind, hardening into a crust on which she could
move in safety.

I've been too soft, she repeated, surprised, now that
her eyes were opened, by her forbearing conduct for so
many years, too many, her whole life. Mending over old
petticoats to save their money, she cried—even if they
were grateful for it which they never will be as like as
not they only spend it on some other woman not you—
and then begging him to get cheap seats at the cinema
always, and that day when he wanted me to answer
should he get me a dress at Marshall's and I said No, I
said no they'll shake your waistcoat to find your last
shilling, I know two of that I laughed, I'll go to a woman

I know in one room (you can call it a room) in Herbrand
Street and she'll run me up one up for a quarter their
figure. Of course I ought to have stung him for the money
for the other place and put the half of it by. I'm too
honourable.

Some women would have skinned him properly, and
serve him right. They deserve to be skinned for the way
they treat us, married to them or not married, it's all the
same. If there's a meaner creature on God's earth than
a man I only hope I never meet it.

Upright, she looked about her with a bold unheeding
stare. Her eyes were gipsy brown and hard. They had
seen everything and nothing, so that behind them were
stored innumerable copies of the same object, of no further
use, collecting dust.

The warmth pressed in on her through the mesh of the
leaves. Looking up, she could see the edges of leaves
drawn with a hard line on the blue. The intense burning
colour poured round them like molten lava. Flies hovered,
falling and rising, in the sunlight below the shaggy pent
of the trees.

For some reason she felt less angry with George. Her
mind had been bumbling round like a bee in a clover-
field, now it knocked clumsily against something—against
the hot, draughty shop in Tottenham Court Road and
her meeting George. People came and went, the door
swung, opened, shut; each time she moved forward to
serve she felt a knife through her feet. She tried pressing
her hands on the counter to take the weight. But it was
no use, they throbbed worse every moment, and the only
thing she could do was to stand and pray for closing time.
"Crawl home on me hands and knees," she whispered to
Miss Lewis, who knew what she was going through. She
nodded and said Thuh! that was sympathy and a fat lot
of good it was. Oh they were chronic.

The door opened again and a man came in. He looked,
fingering them, at a pile of gloves. "I want some gloves,
please." He had a low, easy voice.

She pulled the box nearer. "These are slightly marked. See?" Glancing over his shoulder she could see his back reflected in the glass. Holds himself badly, she thought. She felt an immediate interest in him when he opened the door and now, watching him furtively, she saw that he had a white romantic face, dark eyes, dark hair brushed back with oil. It lay in thick glossy ridges raked by the comb. He took up gloves and laid them down again, anxious and doubtful.

"What is it you want?" she asked, speaking to him in a low confidential voice. You're not used to this, I can see. Wife died lately, perhaps, you miss her. "Kid or suède? Brown?"

"I don't know," he said petulantly.

"See, here's a pair hardly touched. One yellow stain. See? Like them?"

He looked at her. "You choose me something."

She glanced round her. Miss Lewis had gone with a customer to the far end of the shop. "Very well," she said quietly, looking into his face, quietly smiling. "You'll have to tell me your size, though."

"But I don't know that, either." He was half laughing himself and held his hand out for her to measure.

She turned it over gently. "Double your fingers." He did nothing, letting his hand stay limpy on the counter. With another swift glance to see that Miss Lewis was still occupied she took hold of it and doubled the fingers under. "Now," she said, giving him a light pat. She tried the glove over his knuckles. Long lovely fingers he had, with two lines of fine black hairs on the back of his hand. "These go right the way up?" she asked, smiling into his face.

"Like to see?"

"Like to show me?" It was all easy, and the usual thing. She had nearly forgotten how bad her feet were until they reminded her. But the gloves fitted. She eased them onto his hands, buttoned one, and gripped the edge of the counter.

"What time d'you close, eh?"

My feet, she thought quickly. I'll have to bear it, I—
"Why, about seven," she said in a low voice.

"Not before then, eh?"

"We stay back an hour to clear the shop," she lied.

He pulled his lip. "All right. Where'll I see you?"

She asked him to wait for her near the tube station.
When the old ape came through the shop at six, to lock
the door, she had her hat on, ready. She had a pair of new
fawn stockings in her pocket. "I haven't seen you waiting
outside to start in the mornings," he said, looking at her
as nasty as you'd want. If he could hear what I think of
him, the nasty old ape; for two pins I'd tell him would
I—here Miss Lewis came up to her with a sickly smile
and offered to help her home. No thanks, I said. The
other woman looked at her queerly.

Lips pressed to keep back the groans she walked down
the street to the tube station and asked the woman there
in the lavatory if she could soak her feet. The woman
knew her from a year ago. "I've been on them all day,"
she said, letting out a groan. "That's something cruel,
isn't it?" the woman agreed.

"Cruel. It is that." They were twice their size, with
veins like twisted bits of string. The feel of the cold water
on them was heaven for the first minute, and then no
good, but she dried them and rubbed soap over the worst
places and then in the new stockings first standing then
walking cautiously she could about manage.

He was waiting, and she saw the quick look he gave
her, from waist to toe. Of course he had to take the
lower half of her on trust as it were. Hope I suit. A sick
doubt ran through her underneath her surface boldness.

The heat had been terrible that day, and now a leaden
sky boxed London in on all sides. A single clap of thun-
der exploded suddenly, like a hand clapped against the
hollow box. "Don't let's go far," she said, really afraid.

They went to the new Corner House in Oxford Street.
Sitting there, in the big glittering room, an orchestra in
one corner playing *I Love My Baby and My Baby Loves
Me*, people talking, laughing, reading evening papers,

she felt happier than she had felt for months. I knew this
morning something would happen. Now I remember
the spoons were crossed, and "That's for you," Miss Lewis
said, giggling. And the Sunday before, in bed turning
the cards, the same dark man came out again and again.
It meant something.

"What are you laughing at?"

"Nothing," she said. "It's lovely here, isn't it?"

"If you're happy it is."

"Well, I hope you aren't unhappy. Never conk out till
you're. You don't have to."

"Who told you?"

"No one. Go on, men can always have a good time,"
she said, with a softened glance at him. She saw that he
didn't want her to be gay, not yet. He wants a little pity
first, that's it. An emotion less definite than contempt
crossed her mind; a sudden recognition, vague and familiar.
They're all alike, she thought swiftly; as soft as butter if
they're respectable. I'm in a terrible way. I get these
moods, and y'know my wife doesn't care a thing about
me since we married. They think we get our pleasure
listening to their lies. Old as the hills. Older. More fools
us always to do it, then.

"My wife's left me," he said slowly. He stared away
from her.

Go on! You don't say so. "That must be terrible for
you," she answered, in a quiet voice.

"Waiter. Bring us two more Guinesses." He sighed
deeply, with resignation. "Yes. It's more than a month
since, but somehow I haven't got used to it."

"You must be lonely."

His fine, dark eyes clouded up. "Yes, I'm lonely all
right," he answered. He began eagerly to tell her about
his wife, describing her and her ways so that she could
see the other woman, lifting her arms, walking about
her house, and then one day walking out of it for good.
She telephoned from her sister's. Tired. That was all.
Just tired.

He pushed his plate aside and rested an arm on the table. Peering, she caught the light on a gold cuff link. While he talked she ran a practised eye over his face and clothes. A little over forty, well-covered, turning a bit soft round the chin and neck. Good clothes, too, collar fastened by a gold safety pin. Or is it rolled? He had broad shoulders, long full red mouth, dark moustache, strong black-haired nostrils. She clasped her hands between her knees, alert, and let him talk himself out: easy with money; no patience; brags about himself—I expected that, the man hasn't been born yet who couldn't wouldn't.

"One thing about my wife, she couldn't laugh."

"No!"

"No."

"How d'you mean?"

"She couldn't laugh," he repeated.

"Ttt! Well—it's always something."

"And she didn't understand me, you know."

"Didn't she?"

"No."

"That must have been terribly bad for you."

He nodded. "You're dead right."

"How was it she, I mean, didn't she ever—you know?"

"She always seemed as if she hadn't any interest in me, don't you see? She didn't respond—see?"

"It beats me how a woman couldn't be interested in you," she said firmly.

Their eyes met in a long glance. The waiter, clearing away the used plates, was in their way. When he had gone George said in a full, hearty voice: "Not married yourself, I see. Always earned your own living?"

She began with energy and growing confidence an involved story of her life. It came back to the friend with whom she had been living, it would be until eight months back. For eight months she had worked in that shop. A real emotion seized her; she told him with rising anger about the long hours, the miserable pay, the fines. He yawned, and said with his hand halfway up to his face:

"As I was telling a friend of mine in the train a man like me, anxious to be in business for himself, can't look for any help from bankers. It kills enterprise."

"It must do," she said quickly.

"This friend of yours, now. Did he die, or what?"

With the briefest pause she said: "Yes. Yes, he died." He didn't believe her, of course: she saw that. "We were going to be married if he'd lived," she said.

"And now you're alone, eh? That's hard for a woman like you. I can see you've got temperament. I can always tell when a woman has temperament."

"I can laugh at myself," she said quickly. "You're not dead till you die. I learned once that you can laugh everything off and I still do." For a moment she forgot that everything depended on the success of the evening. She looked round her and felt alone.

"Listen," George said solemnly.

She listened with covert eagerness, her eyes, bold, seeking his.

"I'm none of your undomestic men. I like to feel that I've got a home, and someone waiting, even if I can't be there that often." Saturday to Monday. The rest of the week he was here there and everywhere, one of the old brigade, one of the lads; he travelled in fact for a firm of stocking-makers. Well. Life was like that. You wanted to do one thing and you did another. And one Friday you came home as usual and your wife had left you, gone, saying she was tired. Tired! You needed courage to face a blow like that. For it was a blow. It destroyed confidence. Habits of a lifetime. You had habits. You suffered.

She stirred thoughtfully her coffee. The good food, the rest, the lights, the music, had roused in her a familiar rough excitement. If I can't bring this off I'm finished, she said to herself; I'm cats-meat. She felt her face straining, and tried to give it a look of indifference. He had been talking now for at least ten minutes and without coming to the point. I wonder is he serious about it, or is it wind? All in his tongue. Would I better say something? lead him on—what? to say what?—anything, I'll say anything, the first thing comes into my head, and see whether I'm wasting hopes or not.

He said suddenly: "Would two pounds a week mean anything to you?"

Outside, a yellow dusk spread sluggishly to the street-lamps. "London's grand, isn't it?" she said. She wanted to sing, shout. In the cab he pushed his hat to the back of his head and smiled at her sheepishly. Satisfied with himself I see. She rested a hand on him, but she was scarcely thinking. Actually she was thinking a little about the room and that she would buy some stuff for new curtains, run them up herself, and perhaps pick up a good rug second-hand, fix the glass then and try what a coat of paint would do for the chairs and the other things—make a different room of it. He could bring her his mending, and she would do it during the week and give it him Saturdays. He'll soon realise what he has in me, she thought. Who knows, in time he might come to want marriage.

When she opened the door of her room she thought that it looked different already; it was warm and darkly friendly. She lit the gas and turned to smile at him. "Here's luck," she said. Her voice had an excited sound. She noticed it with a little surprise.

Moving swiftly about the room, she felt that she was beginning a new life.

In the morning, waking, it was like other mornings. She lay and stared at the ceiling, too tired to move.

You can't have everything, can you? Dragging her hands through the mould and dry leaves, she comforted herself awkwardly. It had not been a bad five years. Though she never got round to buying those new curtains and one week's mending had been more than enough for both of them. Still—that's how it is, she thought—but suddenly the memory of the evening split its husk, and something infinitely weak and young showed through, trembling in the light.

She was in the kitchen of her mother's house; she watched the parcel being made of her flannel nightgown and the slippers. Then the parcel was lying on the table, and the edge of the table was the same height exactly as her chin, so that she had a curious view of it; it looked nearly like a blue and brown pie, worked over by her mother's thin seamed hands. She noticed that her mother's wedding-ring was surprisingly loose, only kept on its finger by the shiny knuckle.

She grew afraid that they would be late, but the last slow knot was made in the string and then she was seated high up, it felt dangerous, in the butcher's cart, with the parcel clutched to her, whirling and bumping along a lane. The hedge was full of convolvulus and as soon as the cart stopped for a few moments she leaned out to pull one. It lay in her hand. She had barely admired it when it died suddenly. The pale delicate cup went limp and flat and hung down as if it had breathed its last. She let it fall and pulled another and the same thing happened. "Convolvulus won't live in your hand, child." She pretended to laugh, but she pulled flower after flower, hoping secretly that one of them would decide to live. A curious excitement filled her when the frail white flowers lay across her palm. It made her light and blown-out.

The butcher, John Alfred Cratus, had a full small-eyed face, more like one of his own pigs. He drove in style and at last drew up quickly, pointed with his whip and said: "There's t'farm, Missus." Her mother thanked him and lifted her down and together they opened the gate into the field and walked along by the hedge in silence. Somehow she knew that her mother was afraid they ought not to be walking in this field. They kept close to the hedge, away from the young corn. After the streets and after the chimneys the air in the country was intensely clear and glittering, so that each ear of corn stood up nakedly in a ring of light.

They were in the farm kitchen. She must have had a meal, because her small stomach had stretched against

the band of her knickers and she clasped her hands over
it and stretched her legs to the warmth of the fire. The
flames squeaked like mice running between the hot coals.
She fell asleep and woke to find herself alone, except
for a large ginger cat. The kitchen was full of sunlight,
striped and blurred with shadows like a tiger's back.
After a time she managed to lift the wooden sneck. She
stepped out into a yard. Moss grew between the stones
and a tree with thick creamy flowers sprang close to the
door. The yard was empty, with high walls from which a
few bricks had crumbled. She stood in the centre of it
and felt as though she were in a well of clear, yellowed
water. When she touched the flowers with her finger they
were cool and slippery. Very high above her head she
saw then an immense dazzling white cloud and a bird
pinned quivering to the cloud. Her white pinafore floated
straight out in front of her, lifted by the current.

Now she was with her mother and her aunt in the
bedroom. The window was small and shut, and covered
with a lace blind. A plate made of glossy pink china lay
on the dressing-table, filled with pins. Thou God Seest
Me was written on the plate under the pins. On the bed
a white quilt with a thickly-raised pattern like nothing
she had ever seen: she stood tracing the pattern with her
finger and half hearing the voices of the women. The
room was sleepily warm, thick yellow sunshine filled it
from floor to ceiling. "And see what he's left me, the
mean fool. He's been here less than a week, then off,
then gone—but what he's done stays."

"You should have made him leave you alone," her aunt
said.

"*Him!*" answered her mother. Her face changed in an
extraordinary way as she spoke, so that the little girl
scarcely knew it.

She made a pretence of reading the plate. Because her
father, who was a sailor, had been home, her mother was
going to have a baby—but she had no idea how she knew
it. She had felt it when her mother was whispering in
the other woman's ear. She tried to put the ugly thought

out of her mind. She did not want such a thing to happen, it would be a nuisance and a misfortune. She felt ashamed, as she had been ashamed when her mother forgot to take off her old skirt and went down the street with it showing and flapping under the other.

The days were immensely long, mornings that winked and glittered through a complete roll of the slow earth, afternoons let slackly down across a warm sleeping valley. The stream in the narrow wood was deep and still, with spicy woodruff on its brown banks. Beyond it the meadow was sheeted with a bright burning yellow. Bees mumbled in the pinks and hollyhocks in the garden. The cool of the yard flowed into the kitchen, clear dusk-brown water mounting slowly to the ceiling.

They stood waiting in the lane for the cart. It came slowly, bumping over the ruts, driven by the butcher in Sunday black. I'm sure I'm obliged, her mother repeated; it's kind of you to fetch us, isn't it kind of Mr. Cratus? She nodded, hating her mother's put-on voice, and felt in her mind for words she was punished for using. The sky burned out and the green waters flooded over it; these darkened.

They came to the turn of the road: there were houses below them and houses on the opposite hill: the darkness was spattered with seeds of light. It was lovelier than the farm, lovelier than the meadows, the woods, the stream. A strange feeling in her breast, as though feathers were moving up and down, up and down. She could not help the sob. "Tired?" No, no; she had nothing to say. "She didn't at all want to come home," her mother said in a whisper. But the strangest part was that now she did not mind it in the least.

In the morning she went straight to the window. Nothing had changed: the houses with their soot-blackened walls were the same, a lean cat scraped its ribs on the street-lamp, and dirty torn paper blew round the railings. A stale smell rose from the street, smells of beer and closets.

She heard her mother raking the fire in the kitchen, and slowly, crossly, she began to do up buttons and drag a comb through her hair. She felt that she had been tricked.

The first thing she noticed was her hand. It lay on her thigh, a big, fleshy hand, with veins like welts and thick swollen knuckles. For a moment, she could not imagine whose hand it was.

The other the child's hand had been crushing dead, sodden leaves. She gave her skirt a little jerk to rid it of them. The Park, the sky, sprang round her, a water-clear globe of blue and green.

"I haven't done so badly," she said out loud, stretching her legs out to ease them.

That year she was fifteen she began in the mill. She was awakened very early, in the dark, by her mother knocking on the wall between their beds. The cold, when she put back the bedclothes, welled over her, a flood indistinguishable from the darkness. She felt for her candle and lit it. The room struggled to come alive in the faint light.

As soon as she had dressed, fumbling with cold fingers, she went downstairs, raked the fire and made herself a pot of tea. She poured a cup for her mother and took it up. The stairs creaked in the darkness. Her mother had lit her candle and then dropped asleep again, lying on her side with a hand under her cheek. When she opened her eyes they were dilated with terror. "You did give me a start," she said.

"I brought you a cup up," the girl mumbled.

"I must have been dreaming." She called out as the door closed: "I put your piece ready on the dresser. Don't forget it."

The girl went downstairs, and drank her tea standing by the table. The kitchen was warm and lived-in. She cut a good thick slice off the loaf, spread the dripping and ate it in large mouthfuls. She was afraid of being late on her first morning. As soon as she had swallowed the last bite she took her piece from the dresser and went.

It was still dark outside, the sky, when she looked up, invisible. Her foot slipped from under her and she saved herself by catching at the door frame. The road and pavements were covered with a film of black ice.

She saw and heard no one moving in the streets. There were lights in several houses, and her first shocked fear that she was the last dropped quickly as she realised that in fact she was very early. A single door opened and shut farther down the street. It made a noise like a shot in the brittle air. Then silence, not even foot-steps.

She walked slowly, sideways, facing the wall of the houses, both arms stretched out hands flat against the walls to keep her from falling. After she had gone some yards like this her shawl slipped back off her head. She made a grab at it and fell, hurting her knees and grazing the side of one hand. Still she seemed to be alone in the street, the only creature moving at this hour. She got up, feeling the wall, and now the fear of being late sprang at her again. At this rate she would be hours reaching the mill. A feeling of helplessness invaded her, as though she were really alone. It was like the first day at school when she was given a slate and told to write, write down this, write; the same feeling of weakness and emptiness, not knowing what to do.

A hand touched her shoulder. She had not heard a sound. Her heart seemed to drop through her body and she stood still. In a moment, as soon as the woman spoke, she knew her. "You did give us a start," she said, drawing confidence from the words, used so often that they were like the known sound of feet or water dripping.

The older girl was wearing a pair of man's socks over her boots. "It's either that or your hands and knees," she laughed. Doors opened and shut the length of the street, and the women threw their voices across from one to the other, until the darkness was filled with voices. At the end of the street she came on two girls crawling along on hands and knees. Suddenly one backed and gave the

other a great punch with her hinderparts, like a cow.
A screech of laughter went off, and a man's voice.

With some hesitation she got down then herself and
crawled along, quickly and clumsily. She felt ashamed
to be seen in such a posture.

A grey light had seeped through the darkness. There
were people moving in all the streets and a cackle of talk.
One voice flew above the others, coming down in a sputter
of laughter. The faces of men and women had a grey
shiny look in the sour light.

The girl straightened up to walk into the mill and as
she crossed the last yard of pavement she fell smack on
her face. The shock brought tears in her eyes. She
scrambled up, red with shame because of the good-
humoured advice and the sniggers, and hurried through
the door. Behind her the street clattered with people.
The six o'clock whistles jumped up and began to slit
the air.

She put her coat and shawl with the other women's.
Her hands felt very cold. She found herself working with
a big noisy woman called Kate, who showed her what to
do. She was able to do it all right, though she was still
uncertain of herself when the foreman walked past. He
watched her for a moment, then big Kate spoke to him—
"How's your poor feet?"—and he went on. At eight o'clock
they crowded into a sort of lean-to shed at the back of
the mill, dark and very draughty, where there were benches
and a dusty trestle table. She seated herself at a corner
of the table and unwrapped her piece, two slices of bread
and dripping and an apple. Big Kate had a bottleful of
cold tea and offered her a drink. She refused, out of a
feeling of awkwardness.

"Here we go," Kate said, tipping the bottle so that
the tea poured down her throat. She held it there until
the bottle was empty. This was a daily rite and she was
excessively proud of her accomplishment.

"In at one end and out the other," a girl shouted.

Kate wiped her mouth and said: "If you'd let nothing
worse in you wouldn't be laying off next month."

"Let be," another woman called out. "Poor lass, she's had a misfortune—she's none the worse for it."

"Did I say she was?" Kate said loudly. She turned to the new-comer and laid a huge mottled hand on her. "If anyone tells you old Kate's a liar and a —, don't you believe them. I'm not. And if there's owt you want telling ask me right off and I'll tell you. See?"

The girl thanked her and finished eating her piece, and tried not to yawn. She felt drowsy with the pressure of a new experience. The day before at this hour she was just getting up. She looked from face to face among the women, trying to find one she knew. But she had been forced to start at a mill a long way from her home and they were all strange.

Back at her machine she began to feel very uncomfortable. It was the excitement. She bore it as long as she could and finally asked Kate where the women's closet was.

"Downstairs and along the passage. Turn to your left," Kate said. "You'd better look sharp, though."

She walked out of the room and then ran, holding her long clumsy skirt, down the stairs and along the passage. She found the place—it was no better than part of the passage walled off: there was no window and a little light and air came over the top of the door through a gap the breadth of a hand. When she came out the foreman from her room was waiting for her close to the door. He had his watch in his hand and he said sharply: "You've been in there four and a half minutes. I was timing you. Don't do it again. I'm up to those tricks, see?"

She looked at him and rushed back to the room.

Big Kate saw that something was wrong. After a moment she came and stood by the girl, watching her movements. "You c'n do that without moving your arm. See? Saves trouble—you don't want to kill yourself working for the —s." Her voice, warm and not loud—it slid itself through some crack in the deafening noise—poured an amazing relief through the girl's mind. She said nothing but she felt less disgraced.

By noon the ice had thawed in the streets. It took her only twenty minutes to get home, against the hour and more she was coming. She found her mother and the three younger children half way through their dinner. This made her feel at once that she was a wage-earner; she sat in to the table and let her mother fetch her dinner from the side of the stove.

"Did you get on all right?"

This question, which she had dreaded, was after all easy to answer. "I got on fine," she said, loudly. "A woman showed me what to do and right off I did it. It's as easy as touch me. You on'y have to look sharp. Can I have a sup of tea with my piece in the morning, mother?"

She finished her dinner and sat on, elbows over the table. Her mother had to remind her of the time. Folding her shawl across, she stared foolishly round the room; the clock, the gleaming steel fender, the strip of rag carpet of many colours. She felt weak and little, though she knew she was a great girl, as big and strong and plump as a tub of butter.

"Do you wish you was back at school?" her sister asked.

"No I don't." That much at least was certain. She hurried off.

It was black dark at six when she left the mill. The stream of men and shawled girls and women swept her along the streets. At the corner where she turned up the hill—as steep nearly as the side of a house—she fell in with some girls she knew. It was icy cold, with a cold noisy wind tearing at the houses. Her cheeks smarted and all the blood in her body seemed pressed against the back of her head. She was very tired.

(Sitting in Richmond Park, she felt the cold of that winter in her body. It got between her and the sun. She saw, as though it were something hard, indestructible, behind the flimsy screen of grass and trees and blue sky, the night, the street of squalid houses, the unseen noisy wind, and then inside the house her mother bent over the low fire, and the yellow circle of the lamp.)

In a few months she was a changed creature. She held

her own with the foreman and even invented a name for him that sent the others into paroxysms of rude laughter. They caught their hands to their sides and screeched. When she ate her piece, she yelled to her new friends across the voices of the others: one day she stood up on the table and danced, lifting her skirts. The men standing round in the yard crowded to the window and bawled their interest in the performance. She didn't care, not she. She cake-walked the length of the table, head back, her behind well out, elbows sawing the air in time to the steps.

The noise and the constant throbbing of the looms played on her nerves. There were days when every vibration of the machines repeated itself in her body, until she was nearly crazy with excitement. The other young girls felt it the same way. In the evenings when they left work they could not go tamely home. They screamed and shouted to each other across the road. As soon as they had swallowed a meal they tidied themselves and rushed out into the streets again. Here until bedtime they paraded between the street-lamps, talking and giggling, five or six abreast with linked arms. Now one of them would start a song and the others snatched it and flung it back on their strong piercing voices.

Good-bye, my Bluebell, farewell to you

The older girls who had young men with whom they were "going"—there was a table of affinities on every derelict door and wall: Clara Lamb goes with J. T.— and the married women, looked angrily at these young fly-by-nights. But that was no use.

Her mother said nothing. She was so tired that she did not seem to care if her daughter paraded the town the whole night. Besides, she expected her to settle—as if youth were a jelly.

I was young and fond, the woman admitted. She opened her bag and held the small glass up to her face. It showed her the yellowed skin starting through the powder and the deep lines of her mouth. She tried to

imagine the smoothness of her face those many years
since, but it was no good, it was like struggling to recall
her mother's face after she died. Eyes, hair, a fold of
loose skin—the rest a blur like a bad painting.

A fond fool, she said. Yes, you were that. Still I'd do
it again—every turn and moment. You don't know till
you've tried, you don't know anything, anything. She
shut the glass angrily away into her bag and smiled, a sly,
childish smile. Girls—what did girls know? They talked
rubbish, nasty rubbish some of it, and thought they
knew more than their mothers. A lie. It was only living
it taught you. It was—a vague gesture swept up her life
to this moment and thrust it in the eye of the world.
See? What I did I did. If you don't like it don't look.

Her hand strayed pulling at the short delicate grass
near the trees. She felt confused. Little currents of
feeling ran under the surface of her thoughts, darkening
it, as in a spent wave the undertow darkens the surface
of the water. She was suddenly certain—but the certainty
was inexpressible, too remote from anything she knew
to be fixed in words—that the young do know more.
Some moment of her childhood came close to her, time
doubling back on itself; not so close that she saw either
shape or colour of the objects that peopled it, but close
enough for its light to fall round her. Blinding, that
light. Her eyes no longer accustomed to it were able to
endure its peculiar intensity for less than a minute. In
that minute she saw nothing, understood nothing, but
she felt that for which she had no words, the irrecoverable
sharpness of young senses.

When she was a child, the whiteness of marguerites in
the long grass, the pale fawn of buds thrust between her
and the sky, absorbed her whole being through her eyes.
Too early she lost this gift of complete response. Her
mind saw no further than the surface of her eyes. What
she could have been (if the writ of the kingdom of
heaven ran on earth) fell away quickly into what she
was. She began to die when she was still very young: as
we all do.

The mill did worse to her than bring her to be familiar with lewdness. She was not innocent when she began there. You wouldn't expect it had you lived where she did. (To be innocent one must be a little private.) But the mill, with the curious disintegrating assault it made on her mind, on the fibres of her body, subtly hurt and confused her. The yelling, the cheap songs, the jokes, the swaggering about the town at night, were defensive. Within, she was expectant, lost.

She lived two years in this way. Then—she was seventeen—she let herself be seduced, her mind (which was the readier for it) first, and then her body.

She was with the other girls outside the mill, waiting for the horse buses that were taking them to Staveley Forest for their Bank Holiday. A young man, but older and better dressed than the rest, came over to speak to them. He knew one of the girls. He talked to them all, made jokes, and was very obliging and pleasant. When the bus started she was the last in and he climbed in with her, squeezing himself into a corner where, since he was the only man in that bus, he came in for a great deal of notice. He was not abashed; he had a ready tongue and sat smiling, with his long legs stretched out.

They played Up Jenkins, in which a button is passed frenziedly from hand to hand, and even in the excitement of it she felt that his hand stayed in hers. Before the day was out she was *gone on him*. She was so *gone* that she saw nothing except his long body and his face: she could not help looking at them and she had lost the use of her tongue. When he spoke to her she turned red and mumbled an answer. He saw that she was put out, and had no doubt that he was the cause. He was not much surprised.

The next evening he was strolling along the street where she and her friends paraded. He took off his cap and spoke. Obeying a strict code, the other girls walked on, leaving her with him. They talked. She had flamed up at seeing him and had almost nothing to say. They strolled together to the end of the street. He invited her to walk by the canal but she was crazy to be seen with him and kept him standing where four streets meet until everyone had noticed them. The following day he waited for her at six o'clock and saw her home. It was a declaration.

She did not join her friends that evening. They did not expect her. The streets are all very well when what you want is noise and light and company but for serious walkers the lanes and the canal bank. There was a walk that led round the brow of the hill and down, by dusty narrow lanes, to a valley of green fields. The fields led to a wood and the wood to a slender hillock known locally as King Arthur's Seat.

The Seat itself was a rock, worn away in the centre by much plebeian sitting. It must have been visited by generations of lovers, since the story about it ran that no young woman who sat there with a young man would die a maid. Very few of them did, but there may have been less virtue in the stone than in the deep dark wood.

She was willing for anything. Her body, possessed by an energy which the machines wearied without satisfying, so that it was renewed each morning, asked to be used. Her mind was full of imaginings. All the tales she had been told, the jokes, the chafing of her imagination since childhood by scenes enacted almost under her eyes, increased her excitement. She wanted what she could think of only as an act of the body. The curious thing is—it would have been curious to an onlooker who could see into her mind—that her thoughts and her desires were not simple. They were muddied and confused by the thinking of other people, her mother, the young women who as she was had been debauched by the machines, the men and women and children, street on narrow street of them, heaped together in rooms much too small for them, scarcely separated by walls too thin to keep back a sound, forced to abandon privacy, to deny the decencies, like animals penned together, and their souls a burden to them. No, no, she was not simple. She was sly, coarse, pliant, fanciful (in a useless way), slatternly, undisciplined, timid, ignorant, experienced—and still malleable, still, in spite of herself, fresh and warm, still young. If nothing was to be made of her—or if what was made of her is nothing—why go to all that trouble? The answer may be that there is no answer. Life is meaningless.

Her young man had scruples—perhaps they were fears. He did not want to find himself in trouble, or with a wife and a child. He was mortally afraid of ridicule. The accident that he had had a year's better education than the rest (he was a clerk in the counting room) and had an uncle in London who was doing well, gave him a troublesome opinion of himself. It made a difference to him. He came of strict, Baptist parents who had taught him a great deal about sin.

One evening towards the end of August or the beginning of September they walked slowly through the wood. He was talking—she paid scant attention to it and followed her own thoughts.

"You know my uncle has a big house in London— Streatham it is. He's had luck. He's always telling me London's the right place for a man like me, and with his connections and so on I daresay I'd do well; I'm going to learn French this winter and I've been reading Ruskin— you ought to read more, you know."

"Aren't we going to sit down soon?" she asked. Her shoes, new and high-heeled, pinched.

"Very well." He left the path and they chose a ring of hawthorns and lay down in it. The day had been hot; its warmth lingered in the humid air of the wood and the breeze lifting the leaves was warm. After a few minutes during which they lay still, breathing deeply, she unfastened the front of her blouse. It was part of the ritual; this evening he varied it by saying: "I should like to touch you nearer." It took him a little time to remove collar and tie—he wrenched at them and broke the button-hole —then they lay closer than before, drowsy with feeling.

It came on to rain, heavy summer drops slapping the leaves. Still he did not move. "You'll get your death," she whispered. She raised herself up and lay across him, trying to keep him dry. He had grown very pale and she, to her surprise, began to tremble. Her lips trembled when she was trying to smile, and the little joke she made, a line from a song, sounded wretched. But she had to say something—to let off steam, she said, thinking about it afterwards. So many and strange occasions in a lifetime and so few words.

The rain fell thicker and faster. Reluctantly they stood up, arranged their clothes and walked quickly home. He had caught a chill, of course. He went about very miserable, sorry for himself, as long as it lasted. It was a lesson, he said.

A lesson, the woman in the Park thought sardonically. If that was what it was, I learned mine.

But what had she learned?

She remembered the path along the canal, the mist-thickened darkness, and the feel of earth under her hands. They lay near enough the water to see by lifting their heads the lantern on a barge moored for the night. The ditch and a bank of earth (in spring yellow flowers started there in the rank grass) hid them from the passers-by. It was uncomfortable, but there you are, the poor can't choose—and nothing, if she lived to be a hundred, would warm her as did the hurried clumsy touches of that boy. Nothing.

He had said his uncle would help them. He must take one of those night excursion trains to London, see his uncle, insist on a good safe job being found for him (easy enough, when you knew the ropes), then he would send for her. They would be married. Was there, he asked anxiously, any hurry about it, about their marriage? No, there was no hurry, she answered; except—it would be easier when they were married. He said little in response, weakly greedy for her.

I might have known he wouldn't come back, she thought. Seeing him off, the raw breath of the fog whipped her cheeks. She watched his train disappear, his face fading to a blur on the lit window. She never

saw him again. After a few weeks she went at night to
his parents' house and asked for his address. But that
was no use—they sent her off sharply, without a trace of
surprise or pity.

But pity is for who needs it, she thought. I don't. I
never needed it. I'm not downed by things. I found then
you can put up with anything.

She smoothed the skirt over her knees. He knew he
wasn't coming back, she thought; all those months he
was meaning to shake me some day. A tremor ran
through her life, so far below the surface that she scarcely
felt it.

I feel hungry again, she thought. I shan't go anywhere
yet, though. I'll wait and go to that place I went with
Mr. Cohn three or four times, that time he, I thought he
was getting serious. He wasn't. The waiter might remember me coming with him and he'd serve me as though I—
she broke off, not anxious to finish her thought. It didn't
do you any good to go thinking about your troubles. I
ought to move, smarten myself, look for work. Her hands
lay slackly folded in her lap. I'm too old, she thought,
terrified. Once, but it was so long ago that she could not
feel it, she had had spirit enough to leave Staveley, leave
her home, leave everything. She gave out that she was
going up to London to be married. Some believed her.
When she reached London—in the early morning it was,
the sky grey and feathery, a wind blowing grit through
the streets—she had no idea where to go. She wandered
round until night and then seeing a card outside some
bed and breakfast hotel in the Euston Road—Wanted, it
said, a strong girl—she went in, offered herself, and was
taken at once. That was a bad place. After a year she
left it and took a place as bedroom maid in the Dorset
in Bloomsbury. She was on the fourth floor and she slept
with the other girls, upstairs over the seventh, in an
attic to which they climbed through a dark shaft up
worn creaking stairs.

She stayed five years, descending by stages to the first
floor, where were the best bedroom and "the suite". She

did not like the work but there were hours, in the afternoon, when she had little to do and could idle time away
in the dark service room. The floor waiter was a German,
almost a boy, thin and excitable.

She went out so seldom that the hotel became like an
island from which she gazed over the dun tossing sea of
London. Buses rocked up and down the streets and on
her evening out it was like going on the sea, not that she
went far, and was relieved when the German boy offered
to come with her. He changed his night in order to do
it. They went to the Empire twice, and to cafés where
he spoke to the waiters and they accepted him at once as
one of themselves. But he had very little money to spend.
From his wages he sent part to the wife in Hamburg
whom he wanted never to see again ("What did you
marry her for if you feel like that?" But he seemed not
to know the answer) and the rest he was hoarding—he
meant to save enough to rent a café and he talked to
her about it hour after hour, until she yawned in his
face.

She felt a meagre interest in the Dorset's guests. They
came in at dusk, demanded hot water, fires, the bathroom, papers, early tea, strewed the room with their
clothes; in the morning, gathering their possessions, left.
The room, which easily defeated all their attempts to
change it, had then to be pushed and smoothed into
blankness before the approach of the next visitor. A tear
in the eiderdown was infinitely more interesting than
the people who slept under it. They slept and went. It
remained and bred endless chatter, runnings to and fro,
visits from the management, locking and unlocking of
doors, and only after hours of indecision was it removed
and an identical quilt provided from store.

How on earth did I stick it so long? she wondered.
Sheets; hot water cans; those stairs, too (she was not allowed to use the lift). But it was safe—and she, as always,
planning one thing and doing an easier. She might be
there still; but for what happened in the suite—and Ernst
begging her again that very day to come with him, and

she felt I can't stay here, I should be seeing them. It gave her the horrors only to pass the door afterwards.

She was not on duty when Mr. and Mrs. Schlegel came in, and her first sight of them was in the evening of that day. They had gone out to dine, and returning sauntered along the corridor and stood side by side at the door of the suite. He had an arm round her as they stood there. In the half-lit corridor they looked somehow strange—the long shadowy walls, the dark figures, backs turned to her—she could not explain what, for a moment, as she walked towards them, she had seen. Afterwards she imagined a tremor in her flesh—a cold turn, she told Ernst.

Mr. Schlegel turned round when she reached them and said in a friendly voice: "I say, I can't make this key fit."

If you took both hands to it, she thought. "Yes, sir." She unlocked the door, and held it open for them to pass her. Mr. Schlegel was fumbling for the light switch—she reached out and pressed it for him. The room sprang out in the yellow light, everything in place, not even a newspaper on the red tablecloth. Tidy, she thought, a little surprised. Most people laid things about, dropped them, spoiling the room. As she turned to go she looked in their faces for the first time—the husband tall, slender, with dark hair and bright dark eyes. Young, startlingly young; smiling. His wife had unpinned her hat; she was running the pin through folds of thick shining hair to loosen it. She was not older than her husband but she had an older look, a faint shadow lying over round cheeks and dimples. Ignoring the maid, she waited for her to go. She moved as the door shut.

A little time later their bell rang. She found Mr. Schlegel with a foot on the fender peering down at the grate.

"Will this fire light?" he said.

The things they asked! hadn't he a match? "Certainly, sir. I'll light it for you at once." The night was warm, no need, she thought, vexed, for them to have a fire.

Kneeling, to see better the wood and paper, she watched Mr. Schlegel cross the room to the bedroom. He pulled the door behind him but the catch, she knew its tricks but visitors did not, slipped, leaving the door ajar. There was a silence. Then the wife's voice:

"Must I?" Too ordinary a phrase for the way it sounded. Affected, thought the kneeling woman. They're all alike. She felt a resentment against rich leisured women that centred itself in the muscles of her knees. They ached and she rubbed them angrily through her dress.

Mr. Schlegel let down the blind in the other room. "Did you put this up, dear?" he said.

"Henry!"

"You remember what we agreed, darling."

There was silence again, then a weak sound as though he had touched her.

Her voice had changed. "Oh very well."

Light quick steps crossed the bedroom and the sitting-room. They stopped so close to the girl bent over the fire that she heard silk rustle itself into silence. Unexpectedly Mrs. Schlegel knelt beside her. "Has the wood caught?"

"It's young wood, I think, madam."

Flowers of smoke rose through the coals. Mrs. Schlegel poked with her fingers at the flattened paper. "Don't soil yourself, madam."

"Oh, I shan't do that," Mrs. Schlegel said, laughing. She jumped up—no twinges in *her* knees—and walked to the window. Parting the dark curtains she looked into the farther darkness.

"What's through here?"

"What, madam?"

"Where am I looking?"

"Over the gardens, madam."

"Do they belong to the hotel?" Mrs. Schlegel asked, trying to see, her hand on the curtain.

"No, madam. You come into them from the street at the side. They say a great many Jews walk there."

"Why shouldn't they?" Mrs. Schlegel said lightly. She drew back. "I can't see anything but the reflection of the room. Isn't it a pity!"

"Yes, madam."

"Are there trees?"

"Yes. And grass. Trees and grass. I don't think you would care for it, madam." She wouldn't go there herself, because of being spied on from the hotel.

"Well." Mrs. Schlegel sighed: she let the curtain fall across the window. It swung and settled. "The fire's going nicely now."

"I think it will be all right, madam." She stooped to it again. Now if I put more coal on, she thought. The charred sticks glowed in the centre.

When she straightened herself Mrs. Schlegel was standing so near that their shoulders touched. Vexed, because she was being hindered, she gathered up brush, shovel, and duster, and moved to go.

"Ah, wait," Mrs. Schlegel said.

She waited, indifferently. Mrs. Schlegel felt in her pocket and brought out two half-crowns. "This is all I have, I'm afraid." She pressed them in the other woman's free hand with an eager quickness.

"Thank you, madam." Surprised, she took the coins and was trying to open the door with them in her hand when Mrs. Schlegel came past her and opened it.

"Good-night," she said, smiling.

"Good-night, madam."

She hurried along the corridor, feeling the money in her hand. It was late now and the lights had been turned out on the staircase. She banged into the service room: the German boy was waiting for her; he took her shovel and the other things from her and took her in his arms. She returned his kisses with real warmth—a thought brushed her mind that brought Mrs. Schlegel into it. She forgot the resentment she had been feeling. There was not much to choose between kissed, whether Ernst did it to her or Mr. Schlegel kissed his young wife. She felt suddenly friendly towards the other woman.

"I think always how I can be to you," Ernst said tragically. He meant that he wanted her to live with him. She smiled into his arm.

At one o'clock the following day the door of the suite had to be opened. No answer to loud repeated knocks had come from those inside. The door, which had been bolted, gaped from burst hinges. Ernst went in first and looked in the sitting-room. It was empty. The manager had gone into the bedroom. He came out in a moment and spoke to the three women. "Clear off, all of you." Then he said angrily to Ernst. "You. Come in here and help me."

Ernst obeyed him. They bent over the Schlegels, who were dead, and covered them with the sheet, after composing Mrs. Schlegel's dress.

Ernst had brought a letter in from the sitting-room. In Mr. Schlegel's neat writing it gave the address of a brother with instructions for reaching him, and another address—Mrs. Schlegel's solicitor. Nothing but that, except a quite perfunctory regret for giving trouble.

When Ernst told her about Mrs. Schlegel's mouth, and her clenched hand, she began to cry. She cried into her apron behind the service room door and went with reddened eyes when she was summoned. The housekeeper came upstairs and spoke to her sharply. On no account must other guests be upset.

She could not say why she was crying. Not for Mrs. Schlegel, who had been forced to leave with her the last words anyone would ever hear her speak. No knowing what she had said when there was only her husband to hear her. No—it was something else that made her cry. It had to do with herself and made her frightened and giddy. She clutched the handles of doors and once, when she was laying the fire in another room, she thought she was going to faint. Her youth—was it?—had been given a severe shock. She would never feel safe now.

So she thought. At night Ernst told her to shut herself and the other maid in the service room while the Schlegels were taken away, down the service stairs, to the police van. The brother had never come.

She went out afterwards and waited for Ernst to come back. They stood together on the back stairs, flattened against the wall. She roused herself to ask: "Was her hair fair or dark?"

"Whose?"

"Mrs. Schlegel's, of course, stupid."

"I do not know," Ernst said wearily.

"I can't just remember," she said with a feeling of anger and dissatisfaction. "It's vexing. I ought to—seeing I saw her touch it."

Afterwards Ernst asked her again, for the hundredth time, to come with him. He had now taken his café—it was in Greek Street. If she came with him it would be *ein Stück vom Himmel:* in any case he was leaving the hotel. He repeated this over and over, until the foolish foreign phrase began to ring in her ears like a churchyard bell. She would be alone with the Schlegels. "A café'll be downright hard work," she grumbled. There were ways, made holy by use, of evading it in the hotel, but foreigners are cruel to work. She felt in her bones that there would be no evading Ernst.

"Here you have also hard work," Ernst said eagerly.

Her mind was made up, but she would keep him waiting a little. Not to seem anxious. "What's it like, your café? I mean—where would we sleep?"

"Behind the kitchen is two rooms—"

"Dark, I daresay."

One of them had no window, Ernst said humbly. Light entered it through a skylight, but—his voice grew husky—there was nothing to be ashamed of in the other room. It could be their bedroom.

She squeezed his arm. "Right ho," she said kindly.

Ernst went crimson. "Right ho, my dearest," he said.

After all—she sighed—he had been kind. He worked her to death, of course (but she had expected it), getting her out of bed at cockcrow and on her feet until close on midnight. He worked himself harder. They bought second-hand furniture in Wardour Street, ugly strong chairs and tables, and a bedstead with green hangings. A good easy bed and she would have spent a great deal more time in it if Ernst—but the night when he stayed five hours with her was a miracle. She hated the very smell of coffee first thing; and to please her he made tea and fetched it to her in bed. His mind was already on the day's work. "What time is it?" (but she knew—summer or winter, he had her up at six). Once when she was furious at being wakened he simply turned and left her. She heard him talking German to the other man and her fury passed off in a fit of sobbing. She felt cruelly abandoned.

Of course, she wore a ring and called herself Mrs. Groener. Every month the same sum of money went to the real Mrs. Groener in Hamburg. After one outburst—why, she shouted, must she slave to earn money for the other woman?—she had to give in, as she gave in to the incessant work and the long hours. There was an extra-ordinary passion in Ernst—she felt it ready to spring on her when she crossed him. She had to give way.

There were other reasons—not only the real Frau Groener—for his leaving Hamburg. He told her about them in one of his rare moments of sadness. She did not take it in very well, but gathered that he had had trouble with the police—but not in any way disgraceful. A meeting. He was a Socialist, he said. She knew nothing about it and thought him a fool to care.

Those years, she thought—then stopped. She felt faintly that they had been easy (in spite of the work), the sun was warmer and brighter, people different—she did not know how, but they had been different, younger, perhaps that was all. We were young enough, she said, and stared. Twenty-four. Then one day someone asked her and she had to think a minute before she knew. "We've been here four years about." Twenty-eight—but she felt the same.

That day she and Ernst went down to Brighton to look at a small hotel he thought of buying. It was in a back street, narrow and shabby. Ernst saw something in it. He said she would have an easier life of it—that made her laugh, and ask him whether he was tired of her. They roamed about Brighton all the afternoon, Ernst deep in calculations, and she exclaiming at everything, the shops, the gay people, the houses with green sunblinds over the steps, the glittering sea. "Look, Ernst." She pulled at his arm. He smiled, his lips moving—he was considering the risk and balancing it against the tiny hoard in the bank.

At last he made up his mind. They went back for a last look at the place, then had a meal, the first for four years she had eaten outside her own house. She wanted Ernst to note the fact. "I say, old boy, don't you think we might go out oftener?"

He did not answer.

"What ho!" she said impatiently. "Wake up, old boy!"

Without looking at her he laid a hand on her knee. He was listening to two men who had come in and taken the table next theirs. One of the men had a foreign newspaper sticking from his jacket. She listened too.

"But I say there's going to be war. And well time. Haven't the Germans been asking for it since 1911? Of course they have."

"But—" his friend began.

"Nothing of the kind. I know what you're going to say and that's all stuff. We're going to fight them and we shall give them the licking of their lives—don't you make any mistake about it."

"I must say I don't like Germans," the other man said.

Ernst leaned forward. "I beg your pardon." She looked at him, frightened. What was he going to say? All at once she saw that he did not look like an Englishman.

"I beg your pardon," he repeated. "Would you tell me—I have been away—is there a question of war?"

"I should jolly well hope so," the first man said. He sounded excited. "Here—I suppose this is no use to you?"

He offered his newspaper to Ernst who drew back, smiling slightly. "We have to go," he said.

She dragged her scarf together and hurried from the place. On the station he bought a paper of his own and read it, taking not the least notice of her questions. At Horsham a man and a woman came into their carriage and began at once to talk like the two men. Only they spoke about Germany as if it were a country of devils, never guessing that the thin young man in the corner was a German. She grew frantic. Ernst would not speak to her, but the woman did. "Don't you feel it's time we settled with those people?"

"I don't know," she said insolently. She hoped she had given the impression of a woman who did not choose to be spoken to by strangers.

At home Ernst still said nothing. She rushed at him and shook his arm. "What is it all about? Why don't you explain to me? Show me the paper." He gave it to her but she made nothing of it. "Tell me one thing," she said. "What happens if you are still a German?"

"I am still a German," he answered.

She went to bed, unable to hold her eyes open any longer though her brain was jumping. All this excitement was not unpleasant. So few things happened to break up the days—she quite hoped for a war. The consequences, to Ernst and herself, were still outside her grasp.

In the morning she understood from the Sunday newspapers what had been hidden from her. England was not yet at war with Germany but already someone was writing: Watch the Germans in this country. She showed the place to Ernst.

"Leave me alone," he said.

"I'm not touching you," she protested. "I only want us to know."

When she could she watched him furtively. He was very quiet all that day, and the next. The other man, their waiter, did not turn up and she asked Ernst whether

she should go round to the man's lodgings. He shook
his head.

She began to worry. The day after that, when they
were at war, a man, a customer with whom she had been
friendly, asked Ernst if he were a German. Ernst smiled
and spread out his fingers (watching, she spread hers),
but he went very red.

"It is true I am of no country," he said apologetically.
She saw the man look at him and notice.

When the café shut at eleven he went directly to their
bedroom and began to change his clothes to his outdoor
suit. She followed him. He had bolted the door but he
opened it to her frenzied knocking.

"What are you up to?"

"I must get away." He looked at her from the corners
of his eyes, ashamed.

"You're leaving me?"

He turned to gather a few things into a parcel. "Don't
you know what's happening?" he said bitterly.

"No, I don't. Ernst!" She stood close to him. "You
can't leave me. What am I to do?" Her mind could
not grasp what was going on in the room, only she felt
frightened. All at once he had become a foreigner. He
might do anything, murder her—they did these things.

Her head cleared and she saw that he was only Ernst,
tired and worried. She snatched his hand from the parcel.
"Ernst, will you take notice! I want to know where
you're going and what I'm to do, about the work and
the customers."

Ernst suddenly lost his temper with her. He freed his
hand and struck the table with it so that the things
gathered there flew a dozen ways, the comb into the fire,
where it flared up. "Do as you please," he shouted. "Do
you want that I stay here for the police, eh? Prison, eh?
You would like that, I guess." He swept his arms round
the scattered clothes, half sobbing with rage and impatience. The paper tore when he dragged at it.

"Here. Let me," she said.

She smoothed and folded, fetched more paper, string,

her own comb. The neat parcel lay on the table between them.

By the time she finished the simple task she was convinced that everything was all right. Ernst was calmer, too. He stood biting his fingers, watching her as she pulled the knots.

"If I do not go at once I shall be caught and held," he said in his usual manner. "The police may be coming now, this minute. I am an enemy."

"I suppose you are. It's funny, isn't it?"

"I think so indeed!" Ernst, mimicking her voice.

Her own anger was rising. "I say. You haven't said what's to become of me."

This reasonable demand roused Ernst to fury. "I see what will become of you," he said, looking at her with loathing. "You will get up every morning later. Nothing is done at the right time, the customers complain, then they do not come, the business dies, my work, my brain, my heart, all spoiled, ended. All because this miserable, fat, soft country is afraid of the Germans. Do you hear? England is a miserable fat soft rotten country. So are you soft and rotten. Soft—and—rotten. You think I couldn't see it? Why have we no children?"

"Search me," she said angrily. "You got me to come here and I've done my best, slaved—four years it's been—and now you—"

Ernst sat down slackly in a chair and burst into tears, shivering. At first she was satisfied. She did not stop scolding him. She let him cry, and moved about straightening things for the next day. Something happened in her in a moment. She rushed across the room and put her arms round him. "Here," she said, soothing him, drying his face. His poor head fell against her. "You come to bed," she said, "you'll feel better in bed."

He let her half pull half coax him into the bedroom. She took off his jacket, his shoes, and left him to do the rest himself while she hurriedly removed her own clothes. He seemed dazed. She wanted to comfort him but she did not know what to say. She said: "What ho, old boy!"

in a soft voice and stroked him clumsily with her free
hand. In the end he slipped off into sleep so suddenly
that she did not know he had gone.

A light noise woke her. The room was barely light yet.
Ernst was standing by the table, dressed, going through
the money he had in his pockets. When he saw her eyes
open he said: "Go to sleep, dear."

"Are you going?" she asked, stupid with sleep.

"Yes, just. I am going."

"Good luck, Ernst. Good-bye."

"Good-bye."

Hours passed, while she slept. When she woke, punc-
tually at six, she was still frightened by a dream she had
had. Half turning, she remembered the truth, no dream:
the door was open between the rooms and the silence
took all the strength from her. She lay, feeling her heart
thud. Slowly, with an extraordinary feeling of being
warmed and soothed, she remembered that she need not
get up: there was no cup of tea, no Ernst; she could lie
in as late as she liked. Her body relaxed into the hollow
it had made and warmed during the night: half asleep,
she listened to the tap dripping in the next room, her
thoughts circled slowly, lazily, seeking the level at which
she would enter her mother's house and hear without
hearing the drip, drip of water into an enamel bowl.

During the next few days she tried half-heartedly to
carry on. She engaged a man and his wife to help her but
they were dirty and incompetent. She had told them that
her name was Green; but the woman found out the other
name and addressed her by it, with an impudent smile.
The next day they did not turn up. She could not cook;
Ernst had always done that. To give herself time she drew
the blinds of the café, locked the door, and stayed in the
back room all day. A very few people tried the door.
After dark she packed all she could carry and went away.
If Ernst wrote to her she would not get the letter—but
for some reason she felt sure that it was all over. He had
gone: she never even knew whether he had got away or
not.

She felt strange, heavy. The light was now dazzling, as though the grass and trees had absorbed so much that they could only reject what came to them. A quiver of light ran in the air above the road; it came from the bonnet of a motor-car that droned slowly out of sight. Nothing else moved. The trees, the clouds, the stooping deer, were as still as stones. It was very hot.

She felt as though something in her had broken. There was no way back for her to the young woman who comforted Ernst, tied his parcel up for him, spoke to him. She had forgotten too much. She could not recall the clothes he had worn when he left, and this vexed her—it was like forgetting the colour of that poor woman's hair. "Ee, my memory," she murmured, hurt. She felt that she had remembered what was of no use, the last day or two but not any of the other days when she was wholly Mrs. Groener and without thought of any other life. She could not remember a single dress she had worn as Mrs. Groener, nor where the wardrobe stood in their room, nor their dinner service—all, all had gone.

Something in her cried that these endings were vile, cruel. To have finished with Mrs. Groener like that. It was horrible; it made out that you were nothing—she struck her breast—you, you here, nothing. She felt a deep —not grief exactly—confusion, a dull misery, as though all she did had been useless. You worked, cried, made plans, got up morning after morning in the dark, scrubbed the shelves—but it was nothing, it tailed off. "Oh my God, oh my God," she gabbled. She did not feel that she had spoken. Fear had overcome her again, the fear of finding herself without money, without a home. Her fingers dug, quivering, into her flesh, seeking assurance.

It came at the last moment. Something not courage, but it was not mere recklessness either, took hold of and steadied her. It had to use words she would know. "What ho she bumps!" it said, and—"You can't keep a good girl down."

She laughed out, and swallowed with a dry mouth. A square meal is what I want, she thought. Nature abhors

a vacuum. Holding the mirror to her face she tucked in
stray hairs and dabbed carelessly with the greasy red at
her mouth. Ups-a-daisy. Oh Lord. Oh I'm broken. I s'd
think I'm marked for life.

Swaying, she stood, and then walked painfully down
the slope to the road. Easy does it, you don't want to
spoil yourself. What time is it, I wonder. Ask. Why not?

An elderly gentleman approached, glossy hat, gloves,
stick, like something, in a play. He strolled past her with
his eyes turned to the distant wood, and jumped at her
question.

"About two o'clock, my good woman."

She took offence at his voice and raised her own. "You
could have looked at your watch, couldn't you? What's
in a civil question if I may ask?" She stared after him,
her good humour restored by the sight of his dismay.
A happier gibe occurred to her when he was some distance
away but she left it unsaid and walked on with more
energy. The gates came in sight. She saw them with
relief. I can't go much longer. I ought to stand myself
a glass of something. Port and lemon. No I can't afford it.

She stood rigid, struck. Here, you know—nine shillings
won't last forever. Might as well spend it now. Always
throw away the last penny when you come to it—brings
luck. Who told me that? The thought of food pricked
her mind and she began to imagine herself—supplied by
a miracle with a pile of money—taking a cab to the Café
Royal. Her favourite waiter came forward, chairs were
drawn, her favourite chair, a blind carefully adjusted—
"And what to-day, madam. I can recommend the *Plat du
jour*—pigeon and oyster pie."—Now what would that be
like? She ordered it to see. Leaning back in an easy
manner, she caught the mournful glances of a gentleman
near at hand. Recognition came slowly. "George!" No, no,
let him make the first advances. "Let me see—your face
is rather familiar—I'm afraid I—Why, of course. How silly
of me—George, isn't it? I'd almost forgotten—" Clumsy
explanations. His gaze devoured her face, her eyes,
sparkling with happiness and that girlish laugh she had

never lost, girlish eyes, figure, eyes. A rich fur lay
flung down carelessly across the seat. He said hoarsely:
"You're well, I see?" "Oh yes, I—but don't talk of me—
how are you, my poor boy?" He winced at the well-
remembered affection in her voice. His face was marked
by his sorrows, and whatever he had done he had been
well punished for it. A warm gentle excitement sprang
in her. My lost darling. In the end, after a suitable
period of suspense and delay, she forgave him. Their
reconciliation took place in her room, which she had had
done up to please herself, everything in the best taste,
and of course spotless, with a fleeting fragrance of *Puits
d'Amour*. With a deep sob he.

Had she come to the right place? She hesitated, full
of doubts, in the doorway of what had once been a private
house and now with the most grudging effort had become
a restaurant offering 3-course luncheons at 3/6. She advanced along the passage. It was six years since she used
to come here with Mr. Cohn. Six—a door opened to the
left of the passage, and two young women in flowery
dresses came out; thin and pretty, all smiles: they came
towards her without looking. Throwing back her head
she pushed between them roughly and into the room. It
was all but empty: trembling with resentment she made
for a table prominent in the window. A waiter stood in
her way. "For one, madam? This way." He led her to
the back of the room: the table had a curtain at one
side and the serving door was directly behind it. She
wanted to protest, but exhausted by the effort in the
passage her spirit failed and she sat heavily down. If I'd
had a man with me they wouldn't dare treat me like this.
Her throat hardened. Feeling for it under the table she
drew out a soiled powder-puff from her bag and passed
it across her face. The injustice of it sickened her.

She waited. "Here. Who's the waiter for this table?"
she said at last.

"I'll tell him."

Yes, tell him, tell him. Go on. Tell him he needn't
hurry himself for a woman.

Her waiter came in from the service room, his jaws working. Daresay he's hungry, too, she thought. She looked at him with an air of insolence. Well it's the one used to serve us but I suppose he won't—

"A long time since we saw you here, madam!"

Oh you do, do you? Her dejection vanished but she spoke to him in a morose voice. "I'm a bit late."

"If you'd come any earlier I couldn't have found a table for you. Every place was full."

"Indeed!"

He twitched the cloth cleverly to bring the worst stains out of sight. "And how's the gentleman, madam?"

"Quite well, thank you," she said frigidly. A try on, of course. He knew she wasn't—or why was she alone? "I'll take the lunch." She wanted to say: And be quick about it. Hunger gripped her at the smell of food.

"No need to ask you what you'll drink," the waiter said in a quiet friendly tone. "Port and lemon, I *remember*."

She had meant to do without anything but she agreed weakly. I need it to keep me going, she said to comfort herself. Leaning back, she gazed round the tables, all, except one in the corner, unoccupied. A man and woman lingered at it, hated by a weary dissatisfied waiter. The sense of her own unfriended days returned, a sour heavy feeling at the roots of her thought.

Other belated customers wandered in and her waiter went off to attend them. He kept coming back to her between courses; when he spoke to her his face and voice changed to the easy looks of a friend. She saw that the people at the other tables noticed it.

His behaviour vexed her. She did not want to be treated with familiarity but she felt helpless to stop him. She could be rude, of course, but then he might ignore her and that would be even worse. It had been a mistake to come to this place. Her annoyance brought the heat out all over her. Her face grew crimson.

"Let me see now," the waiter said, "it'll be five—no, seven years since you were here. Time flies. We had a bad season last year."

"How was that?"

"Oh, weather. The election. Why not hold them in winter, keep warm inside listening to the speeches? What d'you think?"

"What election?" she asked indifferently.

The waiter drew back a step. "That's good," he said with an idiot smile. "I'd like to have handed that to some of them came in here—" he lowered his voice to mimic an elderly well-fed woman—"*I hope you'll do your duty by your country on Tuesday*. G-r-r-r. If she had only known it waiters are all Socialists—if they're good waiters. On your feet all day makes you think. One of them comes to see my wife; fur coat, rings, twelve stone if she was an ounce. *Your country's in danger*, she says. *We're all in the same boat*, she says, *rich and poor*. Quick as drop, my wife says, *I hope you'll keep to the middle of it or we're sunk*. Laugh!"

"I'd forgotten about it," she said, more disgusted than ever with his way of speaking to her as though she were his friend and his wife's friend. A low lot they must be.

"What—with your country in danger?"

She nodded sourly. It was true that she had forgotten. She never read the newspapers, only glancing over the pictures on Sunday morning—and she could not feel that any danger was or had been so deadly and pressing as her own.

More at ease now that the other customers had gone she listened, amiable, to his stories. She was in no hurry to go. The room had taken on the air of a friend's house, in which if only for a little time she was at home. But she would outstay her welcome soon. She asked for the bill and gave the waiter the odd sixpence of change, leaving herself three shillings and some coppers in the suede bag. They stood for a moment in the passage, the woman large-bodied and impassive, leaning towards the agile little waiter. In an affectionate voice he directed her upstairs and lingered until she passed out of sight round the turn. When she came down, clutching the hand-rail, he had gone to his delayed lunch.

She had thought of going down to the river which gleamed, the colour of light, of the bleached sky, between trees and shining meadows—but the park was nearer and thither she returned.

The morning clearness had vanished. Over all, over trees, grass, deer, and clouds, a hand had passed smearing the edges. She trudged over the grass, peering through half-shut eyes. The quilted green round her flickered moving as she lowered and raised her eyelids. She was sleepy and walked to find a place not too far from the road back, in which she could stretch herself comfortably and sleep. At last she chose the compact round shadow of a hawthorn. The tree was still thick with tarnished blossom under the young green. It gave out the dregs of its scent, reminding her of something, pleasant. Fanning herself with her bag, she tried for a few moments to think what it could be, but she was too sleepy to care.

She felt very happy. A sense of ease and contentment spread from her body over her thoughts. She took off her hat and shoes and lay down among the young stems of bracken, first hiding her bag with its few coins inside her blouse.

A cloud, shaped like a camel, held her attention for a time, until it moved off slowly and majestically. It lost its shape as it moved. There was nothing then between her and the intense brightness of the sky, neither blue nor white, a diffuse bland radiance that hurt her eyes. She turned her head and stared at the bracken. Seen in this way it was like a forest of strange trees. She watched a tiny spider clinging to the tip of a frond before it hurled itself off into the air, clinging, at the end of an invisible thread. She wished quickly that she were small, strong, and free, like a child or a spider.

The sun, penetrating the deep shadow in which she lay, warmed her all through. She felt its warmth flowing in her limbs, through veins, nerves, muscles, and washing the bones of her body. She scarcely existed now as a body, her fingers lying along the ground touched without feeling them the hairy stems of bracken, smooth stems of grass, and warm earth. She was for the time outside herself. She was not stout, not middle-aged, not poor, not afraid. There was no poverty or fear. She was born in ecstasy into a life that made no calls on body or mind; it was enough that she existed.

After a time she slept.

She had a dream—but perhaps it was not a dream, in the sense that it recalled and summed up an experience she had lived through not very long since. She was walking along Oxford Street when a cry and the screech of brakes made her start round. A girl had been knocked down and as she was half dragged half lifted from the wheels her hat fell back showing smooth bands of hair. There were no marks on her. Thus far the day. In the dream, the hat falling off dragged off the long fair hair. The dreamer with horror saw a head like a large smooth pale egg lolling over the rescuers' arms. The victim was carried to her feet. There laid at the side of the pavement its clothes broke apart and the body shone through. But no longer the body of a girl, its folds and creases, the discoloured flesh, were dreadfully familiar. She knew before she looked at the face that it was her own, and for reassurance clapped her hands to her sides. At once the pain of the wheels overcame her, the houses and shops menaced, the sky over Oxford Street thickened its colours, and she felt a moment's pure terror. Knowing that the ground was about to open and receive her, its weight pressing out blood, breath, and sense, but before death the agony of death, before nothing everything, before the end the Whole.

The sleeper moved uneasily, one hand, flung out, seized a growing stem and bent it to the earth. As she sank into deeper sleep her body ceased to twitch and at last lay perfectly still. She lay on her back and her mouth hung open. Her face, purple with heat and the effort of walking, was puffed and old.

A car drew up at the side of the road, and the picnic party, exploring, came close past the sleeping woman.

One girl beckoned the others to look at her. They glanced aside with distaste: "She's not lovely."

"Poor thing," the girl said aloud.

The sleeper had descended to her mother's house. At first she was aware only of the room, familiar, darkened by the yard. It was outside her, part of the dream. Then she was *in* the dream, so that she saw the room on another level, not as something remembered but as lived. During the time it took her mind to describe an arc not measured in space, she thought and saw as a child. The part of her that went on while she slept, was actually and only a child.

She was by herself in the dark kitchen. Her mother was shut in the next room, preparing it for Aunt Ada. Soon the child heard the carriage and she drew back, placing the sofa between herself and the door. Her mother came hurrying in to open it for the men. They came in awkwardly, carrying the long coffin, and with some trouble—because of the little room and sharpness of the turn—they got it into the parlour. At once, with a subdued "Good-night, missus," they tramped out of the house again, feeling their hands, into which the edge of the wood had bitten. Involuntarily the child rubbed her own.

She felt bursting with excitement. The feeling had grown in her since she knew that this Aunt Ada, whom she had never seen and never until she died there in London heard of, was coming to lie a night in her sister's house. She knew that there were children watching shivering in the cold dark outside the house. Some of her pleasure vanished after she was forbidden to lift the corner of the blind to sign to them. Her mother was still in the front room. Growing impatient, the child opened the door of the kitchen.

She meant to call, but she saw her mother at the end of the passage, her hand on the door. She did not say anything and the child was struck silent by the way she stood there, as if tired to her death, resting all her weight on the handle of the door. She did not look merely sorry

about the death. It was something heavier than grief she
felt, something that was in herself, not put there by the
coffin. The child never forgot it.

The outer door opened at that moment and a woman's
voice called out softly: "Are y'there, missus?"

The child started. "Run in by the fire at once," her
mother said sharply, "you'll get your death."

She obeyed, and sat down near the range. The two
women who had come in were both neighbours. Since their
call was in a sense made on the dead woman, it was more
formal than just dropping-in on a friend, and one of them
had discarded her shawl in favour of a cap which belonged
to her husband. A jet hat-pin held it flat to her hair.

Her mother made tea, and she was given a saucerful,
with an end of a loaf. She loved the taste of crusts soaked
in tea. No one took any more notice of her. She sat
quietly eating the sopped bread and listening.

"Did you hear from her, then?"

Her mother shook her head, slowly, to herself. "Never
a word."

"She was maybe ashamed."

"I don't think so," her mother said drily. The child
felt that she was vexed by the suggestion. "If she'd
wanted anything she would have sent. She minded no
one in Staveley."

"I never blamed her," the other woman said.

"Why should you?"

"Nay now, don't take me up wrong," the woman said
mildly. "Ada and me was friends all our lives until then.
I haven't forgot her."

Her mother was softened. "I see you haven't," she said.

"When our Will came in yesterday a' said, A friend o'
yours has died. You can tell me, I said. Ay, I can *tell*
you, he said; it's Ada Martin. You could have knocked
me down." It was the formula for any unexpected news,
an accident, a joke, a meeting, a death. It covered everything in their lives from birth to death.

"Yes, it *was* a shock," her mother admitted.

The other woman could no longer repress her curiosity. "How did you hear?" she asked, leaning forward.

"She sent a letter—"

"Oh she did that, did she!"

"Not until the day before she went," her mother said quietly. "She got the woman she was living with to write it for her."

"And what did a' say?"

"Told me she was very bad, dying, and would I let her come to my house the night to be buried. She'd always wanted to come, the letter said, and now it was too late— but if I wanted her I was to write and make arrangements."

"It must have cost a pretty penny," the other ventured.

"She left the money for it!"

Her mother had spoken sharply and the child, who was half asleep, started to the edge of her chair. She drew back again at once, afraid to be noticed and sent off. And her mother did look at her, but said nothing. For a moment the child had the strange tense feeling of Sunday night chapel, the preacher's loud voice starting a shudder in her body—World without end. AMEN. She hated that, and yet longed for it, for the fear and the strange strung-up emotion. It was as though she were light and heavy at once, her head light and the rest of her as cold and heavy as lead. Her mother and the two women seemed to have been talking round the fire for a long time—years, centuries. She settled into her chair, not sleepy and yet not truly awake. The room was so dark, except for the fire, that she was sure to fall asleep before long.

"Was he good to her, d'y'think?"

"How should I know whether he was good or not?" her mother said quickly.

The woman in the man's cap had been pouring herself another cup of tea and had missed the question. "Who —who? Good? Was that man who? I didn't hear that."

"It's no use asking me," her mother said. "Ada went keeping her mouth shut and she's kept it tight shut since. But if you want to know what I think—I think it's much the same life for a woman whatever she does, she has to

eat humble pie. Either to her husband or her children,
it's all the same. They do as they like, and she waits on
them—mending their clothes, on her knees cleaning after
them. Nobody asks her if she wants to go to bed or to
get up or to have children. I daresay Ada was no worse
off than if she was married, nor no better. There's bad
days and good, and what else? Nothing—if you ask me."

No one had asked her, but she seemed satisfied. So did
the neighbour women. She shifted the big iron kettle
over onto the coals and added a spoonful of fresh tea to
that in the pot. The water poured in a strong hissing
curve when she tilted the kettle. With an effort she lifted
it away again to the side. It stood there at the side of
the stove all day, ready in a moment to boil up when it
was needed. Like all the other women, her mother believed
in the virtue of stewed tea and usually the tea-pot stood
close to the kettle, half full of a nearly black drink.

She filled their cups and poured milk with grudged
hospitality from the half-emptied jug. Their thoughts
had wandered a little from the dead woman. They sipped
the tea, gripping the thick cups in their work-reddened
hands, eyes glazed with staring at the fire. How much
longer are they going to stay, the child wondered. She
began to feel faintly anxious and to want to be alone in
the warm kitchen with her mother.

"First thing mine does after he starts work is to fetch
me up a drink of tea in the mornings. Here, mother, he
says, see what I've fetched you. Looking at me round the
cup. Fourteen last week. You could have knocked me
down."

"Does he work in Hart's?" her mother asked.

"There weren't room for him anywheres else."

"They say it's not so bad now," she said kindly.

"They say owt."

"They do that," the capped woman said.

There was a silence. Reluctant to go, to leave the
warmth and go into the black winter night outside, their
minds turned them again towards the dead woman, the
cause for which they were there.

"How many years is it since Ada....."

"Ten. It'll be ten."

"It was when our Will lost his three fingers. He was at home that day feeling sorry for himself as I can tell you. I was down then with our Rose, and Fred's Kate coming in to do for me she said Ada's gone. Gone! I said. Where gone?"

"Yes, yes. I know all that."

"A ten years—our Rose is that. And she wanted to come back, did she? Did she so?"

"The letter says she wanted." Her mother moved slightly to work it from under the chair seat. "Yes—here. *I meant coming back to see you but have left it until too long, so now can you*—and then she says, or the woman says, about sending."

"No word for any of her old friends?"

"Well. She didn't write it herself." An awkward regret sounded in her voice. "Reach me your cup now. A drop's left."

"I can't think why she didn't come—she's come now, of course, I'm not saying she hasn't. Ttt. Never see her. What a do! It is."

"Poor thing."

Which of them said that? Starting awake now, the child looked at each of them in turn. Which? It must be that one, she thought. But uncertainty had entered her mind—and immediately after she knew that she would have to leave. This was not her real home, she had another life and another home—somewhere—where? The room became shapeless, and she struggled frenziedly to keep it. To keep herself in it. She went over to her mother and took hold of her. "You must keep me," she said, filled with the most terrible grief; "I'll do everything you tell me, I'll work for you, do the step, wash up—I promise I'll be good, if you'll keep me." Her mother said nothing, sitting still in her chair, vaguely smiling still but without a word to say. She did not seem to understand what was happening, nor to care very much. In terror the child appealed to the other women, offering to work for them, to run errands, if they would exert themselves for her. "Keep me," she implored them, turning their unresponding faces to her mother. Who had gone. "Keep me."

But it was no use. The room no longer held together. For a moment she seemed to be in the street. It was less substantial than the room, a faint tracing on the air. For another as brief instant she saw the Park through the outlines of the street. Shadows floated past her eyes. She lay staring at the branches, at leaves moving lightly in the bright air, dazzling: her eyes smarted.

Nothing remained of her dream except its sadness, and that too vanished.

Her hand went quickly to her blouse, feeling for the bag she had hidden there. Satisfied, she sat up, and looked gapingly round her. The Park seemed changed, widened, as though the sun, throwing in his descent longer and longer shadows, had drawn the round midday earth out to either side.

She wanted to resolve something definite for her future. What, if George really had left her, must she do? Go back to Staveley and ask help from her married sister? That I'll never come to, she cried. Unless I'm carried there in me coffin—like m'aunt Ada. A shiver, starting in the recesses of her life, broke at the surface into small bright bubbles. She saw a blind over a window; her mother who stood in the dark passage, leaning against the door; hands; rough, work-swollen, the wedding-ring sunk into the flesh, hands folded over the edges of saucers; the faces of women, not known, not remembered, yet not, not yet to be, forgotten.

What did I do? she cried. What made me this? Her body, its weight on her newly felt, became a burden she strove with uselessly. Everything she had done was foolish and a mistake, because she had never seen (until it was too late) what the next step must be. The steam of her acts rose all round her.

For a moment she thought with passion of her mother's life—which had been hard, narrow, settled for good in the first moment of her marriage. Never, since that moment, had she depended for her safety on the kindness of any creature. She had her house, her way of living, her place from which she could not be put. Kindness might have sweetened her life but she could and did live nearly without it. Trembling with pride and anger she had said: "Thank heaven I'm not beholden to a soul." Nor was she.

But *I'm* beholden, she thought, startled and disgusted. I've been beholden to some man or other for years. And for a brief flash she did really see that to expect kindness is a grave crime. *No one ha*s the right to depend on the kindness of another for his life. The exaction is too great. There must be rules, duties, to make life with another person tolerable. Because there was nothing between them but this thin, racking nerve of kindness men tumbled her off, went away to women to whom they owed a duty, not kindness.

It was too much. She understood nothing, nothing. The effort of understanding was too severe. The very centre and core of her life was rotten—but it was too late to cure it or to alter anything. She was finished.

She looked round her, at the grass, darkened by a passing cloud, at the trees. Her hat, which had apparently fainted, was lying near her on the grass; she seized it and with a despairing gesture began to pull and tweak the limp ribbon. And now what? she thought angrily. Now that I have snatched a dress, a few pairs of shoes, hats, I suppose I must give them up, go naked, starve, live in streets like a dog.

Her anger restored her. She began to think soberly about her room. It was the last thing to which she clung. Without it, without its chairs, curtains, bed, the rug from which she stepped into bed and onto which again she stepped in the morning, she was lost. None of these things, except the looking-glass and a chair, belonged to her and yet she clung to them, as dying men to the light.

She decided to be a servant. There were always cries in the newspapers for servants—wanted, working housekeeper for gentleman; wanted, strong daily woman;

apply here, there, everywhere. Half London was gaping
for servants. She would go out daily to work and come
back to her own place at night. Thus she would be fed,
keep her room, her freedom—and then (supposing George
some day to repent) she would be where he would look
for her.

"It's a gift," she said out loud, red and sweating with
pleasure. I shall want a letter or something—Mrs. Thingski
recommends—sober, honest, good cook, reliable, what's
all that they write? A testimonial I mean that. I'll get
Lily to help me with it. Was in good houses before the
war, she said, and got out of patience then with it. I
had some good times then. It's no use thinking about it,
no use. I was young then and all those men, the streets and
places full of them, everywhere you looked; say what you
like it livened things. That girl I saw crying—she's lost
someone, I suppose: well, she's not crying now, is she?
Got over it by now. *Tick, tock, wind up the clock, I'll
start my day over again.* "Tra-la, tra-la-la!"

A little abashed by the shrill loudness of her voice,
she began hurriedly to imagine her new life. At the first
go off her mistress saw that it would be foolish to ask the
usual questions; she hardly so much as looked at the
letter. Instead she asked nervously whether what wages
she was offering were enough. Yes—carelessly—for the
time. She had her own room, the other servants came to
her for their orders. Actually, she was a kind of superior
housekeeper, since the woman—but a single gentleman
would be easier, she thought swiftly: I could manage his
house for him and then if he wanted anything, a woman's
love and guidance, I'll give him that too. He'll soon know
what he has in me, and then—it's not too late, I'm not
old yet—I could be a good wife to some man. But what's
the use, she thought, with sudden passion. Men haven't the
gumption to marry a woman with my experience and go.
I daresay they know enough to know that a woman like
me sees through them—to their mean dirty bones I see.

She felt an inexplicable joy and satisfaction—as though
for a moment she had been folded in a familiar clasp.

There was a knowledge she had forgotten, a body of which
she was a member, a connection not yet broken between
her and the grass she pressed, the clouds, big and tumbling,
the moist earth. She felt this, but only in her blood, and
when the momentary thrill faded she was more than ever
aware of her thickened body and the pain of now.

"Oh God," she said quietly.

She began to destroy the bracken in reach of her hand,
pulling off the green curled ends. Her mind turned with
the movement of water, drawn aside in an eddy under
a stone. Soothed by the savagery of her hand it settled,
lapsing into stillness, reflecting the grass, the maimed
stems. She felt thirsty and began to think about tea.
Emptying her purse, she fingered the money spread in
her lap and tried to realize that it was every penny she
possessed. The only end of her effort was to make her
thirstier than ever. It won't last long, why try to make
it last longer? This thought had been so long at home in
her mind that it convinced without trouble. Under one
form or another it decided her lot and portion in life.
Rooms only get dusty again, why dust them? Cloth wears,
iron rusts, why mend, why polish. She tumbled the coins
back into the bag and shook out her creased skirt.

A reluctance to move seized her. It was partly the
serenity of the place fingering her senses and partly the
knowledge, unrealised except as a pressure on her mind,
that never again would she feel the impulse or courage to
break a day off from the rest. After this she would go on,
doing what seemed the easiest or next thing, but with a
deepening disbelief. Her life would become too humiliating.
It would wither her emotions, until a moment enclosed all
she felt.

The picnic party was hidden from her by a rise in the
ground. At this moment the girl who had pitied her
touched a knob and released the organist of a London
cinema to the unastonished air—which was helpless to
reject him.

The prancing heavy-footed noise he made cheered her

at once: she was so used to this kind of music (the only
kind she knew) that it had its own way of sounding in
her ears. She did not so much hear it as feel it, and with
it the over-warm air of cafés and picture houses, the softness of plush seats, abundant company, and the relief of
not needing to think. Something young and merry-hearted
woke in her—no doubt the very same young mill-hardened
female who walked all evening between the street-lamps.
She beat time with her hands and swayed, nodding her
head.

She stopped abruptly. What a fool she must look,
perched there, wagging her neck! Her hair was in a state.
She tried to arrange it, but she had lost the comb from
her bag and the result was doubtful.

A stub of pencil had fallen out when she emptied the
bag. As she put it back, she thought, why not write to
George? She had no address where to write—he had been
careful never to give it to her. She did not know even
the name of his firm. But the thought of writing pleased
her. If she wrote the letter an address might turn up.
She might see his name in a paper or meet someone who
knew him. There was magic attaching to the written
word: she almost believed the letter would make its own
opportunity.

In her pocket she found the sale bill for a pair of
stockings. It would do to make a rough draft. She
smoothed it over her knee and wrote "Dear George, why
haven't you been?" Stopped. Something less simple and
straight-out seemed needed. She wanted to reproach him
and at the same time to seem quite casual and light-
hearted—but then to *know*. She must know. She must
finish quickly with this torture of not knowing what he
intended, or what was going to happen to her. Somehow
the letter had to end all this and yet to sound as though
she did not give a curse whether he came back or didn't.

There were no words in her head for what she felt.
The very cruelty of her fears (when she thought that
George might not come) flung them away—and to begin
with they were so few and poor that they were no use.

She made a terrible effort and wrote: "am cut to the core by your treatment of me." But that told him too much. She crossed out everything except "Dear George" and began with more assurance, as though the words had been given to her—as indeed they had. "Have you forgotten the one who has been all in all to you for five years? I never thought you were that kind, I thought you would be true as steel. I pity you from my heart for your cowardly crime against our love. It is you who will suffer worst not the woman, I have learned to laugh at knocks. Some day you will regret the loss of a woman's love." She sat still for a few minutes and then wrote with convulsive haste, "You've done me down proper I haven't a bean—what are you going to do about it?"

Her mouth worked. She read through what she had written, her mind jumping with the excitement of it. But she felt too cruelly to be satisfied. The letter was no good at all. In her mind the letter and her fear and anger were the same thing but the words she had written down —and no others came to her—were a world away from all she felt. When she thought of herself, penniless, left, her heart thumped, the walls of her mouth dried up, and she felt empty. But she had no words at hand to describe her state. So far as she was concerned no words for it had ever existed.

She tore the paper into small pieces and pushed them into the ground. For a moment she felt as though the earth moved under her hand.

She was desperate for a cup of tea. Picking up her hat— which had only partly revived—she clapped it onto her head and got up. Now she could see the wireless, and the picnic party grouped round it. Two young girls, not more than seventeen, with their young men, three sitting and one lying on the short grass. Their car was not far off in the road, and they had cups, a thermos, and packets of food in white paper. The afternoon sun lay over them like a glaze, so that they blended into their blue and green background. She walked towards them, lurching from the stiffness of her knees and ankles, her hat fallen back, her face red. Just as she reached them she fell. Her toe caught in some unevenness of the ground and down she came, on both knees, with a groan.

One of the girls jumped up to give her a hand. The young man holding the thermos called out: "I say, bad luck. Have some tea, won't you?"

She was about to thank him and take it when she saw that they were all struggling not to laugh. At once her manner altered.

"Here," she said aggressively, "what d'you mean by planting yourselves just where people can fall over you? Who d'y'think you are? The Prince of Wales?"

"You didn't fall over us," one of the young men began.

A girl interrupted. "Don't take any notice of her."

She set her arms. "So—that's it, is it?" she said with bitter slowness. "I'm to be knocked down—a nice business —and then you'll take no notice. You—dressed-up young— monkeys!"

The boy tried quelling her. "Clear off now," he said in a loud authoritative voice. She had begun to enjoy the scene, and rocking from side to side she told them what she thought of them. For this she had words enough.

They had turned very red but they ignored her. One of them, altering a knob, increased the volume of organ music until it all but drowned her voice. She raised her voice against it but she was defeated: she had to go. She made a twitching movement with her hands. The sun fell across the back of her neck like a whip and a quiver ran through her. Dropping her head suddenly, she went.

I'm going to have a cup of good strong tea, she thought. Lurching along the road, she thought of nothing else. A cup of good strong tea, and a cake (she swallowed, thinking of mouthfuls of cake and the sweetened tea soaking into them, washing them down, gently)—what d'you call those cakes they sell at that shop?—maids of honour. Oh but that shop's at the pit bottom of the hill, she groaned. I can't walk that far, my feet are like burning fiery furnaces.

But she walked on, since there was nothing else to do. By the time she reached the gate her feet were hurting so cruelly that she was forced to sit down and rest them. She sat on the grass, just inside the Park. Some large dock leaves were growing near and remembering from her childhood that docks were good for nettle-stings she drew off her shoes, wrapped a leaf round each foot and laid another in the bottom of her shoe. When she stood up again she walked easier, but that may have been faith.

She was sorely tempted to go into a café on the hill, but had set her heart on an Original Maid of Honour. The shop where they were sold was as she remembered, at the bottom of the hill. She went in and asked for the tea-room; it was upstairs and she dragged herself up. At first sight she thought there was no room anywhere, and then she made out a table for two. One of its chairs was occupied by an elderly lady who looked up and smiled at her when she put her hand on the second chair. She had not expected to be smiled at and the deliberate rudeness of her glance was wasted. She felt annoyed. She put her bag down in the middle of the tea things, to assert herself and to give as much trouble as possible to the other woman. Again she was disappointed. The lady moved her belongings with a cheerful friendly air. Old fool, she thought angrily. When the waitress came she told her to bring tea and maids of honour and look sharp with them.

The girl was only too delighted to be able to say: "There aren't any maids of honour left."

"Ho, aren't there!" she exclaimed. She meant to give it to her straight for speaking like that but the disappointment was too much for her. After I came all this way. She felt fit to cry.

The elderly lady smiled at them both. "But I have two here I don't want," she said. "Do have them."

Raised so quickly from the depths, she could scarcely speak. The lady held out to her the plate with the maids of honour: she took one hurriedly and mumbled: "I'm sure I'm obliged."

"But the pleasure is mine," the lady said.

Looking at her more attentively she saw a round wrinkled face and a hat covered with ribbons of varied colours, red, green, yellow, blue, a blue dress with yellow lace and a red and green scarf over it. The only dark thing about her was her bag, of black leather with a thick heavy gold clasp. She had never seen so many colours on one woman in all her born days.

"I don't see my glasses and I can only just make out your face," the lady said. "I'm very short-sighted."

"Here they are," she said. They were behind the jug she had pushed out of its place. The lady thanked her, but for some reason—perhaps because she forgot—did not wear them. Instead she opened her bag, took out a little roll of pound notes, and laid the glasses at the bottom of it. She threw the notes in after them, with her handkerchief and a bottle of coffee mints. An envelope with a foreign stamp fell out of the handkerchief. "Where is it? Oh thank you. But you've finished your maid of honour. You must have the other now. They don't bring your tea, do they?"

"Lazy. That's what these English girls are," she said carelessly. She took the second cake onto her plate. The foreign envelope had put into her head to pretend that she was a visiting foreigner. Then she thought that perhaps the other woman was a foreigner—she looked queer enough—and it might turn out very awkwardly if she said she was a Frenchwoman and the old lady was French and began talking to her in the language. She asked cautiously: "Perhaps you're a stranger yourself?"

"Not exactly a stranger. But how odd that you should ask me," the other cried. "I was a German until I married and then of course I became English, since my husband was an Englishman." She said this with a sort of timid bravado, opening her eyes, which were pale and weak-looking, to their widest.

"How interesting," she answered languidly. "My husband was a German, a Mr. Groener. He was a very wealthy business man. Hotels he owned. He died not long ago. I expect I shall travel, but at present I'm resting."

The elderly lady blushed up to her hat. "I felt certain you were unusual," she said excitedly. "I felt it when you came in. Do you know, my dear, something always happens to me when I come out alone." The words got in each other's way to be out first. "I with I say live with my sister-in-law and her girls. I lived with them during the War, though it wasn't pleasant for either of us, then when my husband was killed my money wasn't coming, from Berlin you understand and I stayed on. But they watched me. Have you ever been the one watched? I was then a watched." Her face changed, and became startlingly vindictive and unpleasant. "They were eyeing me when the German aeroplanes came and one evening my sister-in-law said—no doubt she meant me to hear her— "She won't signal to them to drop bombs on the street she's living in." As if I wasn't to be trusted—they not to trust, with my little boy was buried in an English churchyard and my husband fighting. He never came home. I missed him very much and at night much. You won't mind my saying it—the minute you sat down I knew at once you were not like other women."

She had scarcely listened to these confidences. She was too busy pouring her tea, sweetening it, and enjoying the first heartening mouthfuls to trouble with all that. A few flakes from the second maid of honour had fallen on the cloth. She pressed a finger on one and put it absently in her mouth. I could do with another of them, she thought. Then remembering who she was she leaned back, washed the tea round in her cup, and said in a careful voice:

"My husband was going to take me to Germany this year. I haven't met his relatives yet, but I suppose I shall have to."

"Forgive me—but did your dear husband leave you his money?"

"Of course he did. Who else could he leave it to?" she

said tartly. "He never looked at another woman. He simply relied on me at every turn."

"Then keep away from them," the other woman said slyly. "They are almost certain to have lost everything in the troubles."

"Indeed!"

The other did not see that she was being put in her place. "I lost nearly all mine," she sighed, "and what little I still have my sister-in-law takes from me the day it comes. I owe it to her for the miserable home she gives me. I know they're waiting for me to die, but I've been too much for them. I've left the money away from her."

There was nothing unusual about her, apart from her parrot clothes, and they—their terrible colours—would be accounted for by her short sight. Her wrinkles, pale eyes, and thin stooping figure, were all commonplace. Yet she made her listener uneasy. She looked round for the waitress.

"I got to go now," she said loudly.

The elderly lady blinked as though she had been slapped. Her face crumpled up with disappointment. Even the look in her eyes altered and a film of moisture welled over them. "But we're just getting to know each other," she pleaded. "And I'm so happy to-day. Do you know— for the first time since the end of the War I have some little money of my own? The cheque was for eight pounds more than ever before. I didn't tell her, I drew the money and handed her what I always hand her, with no word about the eight pounds. And now—" she stroked the sides of the bag, as though it were alive—"I can buy myself some little things without asking her. "Why d'you want to buy stockings? Here, I'll darn up a pair of Ella's for you." Oh my dear, to put on new stockings again— the price of a concert—I came here now to plan it all. I've spent only a few shillings—and now you must let me pay for your tea. I insist. You've given me so much pleasure. It's many years since I had a friend."

Soft—that's what she is, she thought. An impulse of dislike and suspicion started in her, with the thought that she might touch her for a few shillings. Pretend I left my purse in the house. But her impudence faltered when it came to asking—"Pay if you want," she said brutally and turned her back on the other's vexed face.

Upstairs in the ladies' toilet she saw herself in the glass, hot, creased, the powder sweated off except in the creases. A feeling of dismay shook her. I don't look so old as that. She was alone in the small stuffy room. The curtained window was open. She banged it shut and feeling her legs weak sat down hurriedly. The first thing was to cover up the look of her skin. She wiped it with the towel she found there, and looked earnestly at the stains, then at her greasy flattened puff. At this moment the puff felt to her as a friend—she had had it before she had George and it never vexed her. There was a common glass bowl of powder on the dressing-table. She helped herself lavishly and rubbed her face until a smooth livid surface rewarded her. She wetted her eyebrows and spread a coarse bluish-red on her lips. This ritual soothed her. The room soothed her—she felt at home in it after the immense sunlit Park. Here was no mystery, no overwhelming sky. She felt safe. She took up the comb lying on the table and tidied her hair. It was a reasonably good comb and she had lost her own, so she put it in her bag.

She was rearranging her skirt and smoothing the jacket over it when the elderly lady came in, blundering against the chair, dropping her bag, stooping for it with the gestures of one half blind, finally laid it down on the dressing-table and vanished into the closet.

The bag lay at her elbow. With less than a second's hesitation she took it up, thrust it under her jacket, and went out.

Her heart shook in deep heavy strokes. When she came out of the shop she saw a 33 bus starting for Piccadilly. Pressing her arm to her side, she ran, climbed on and stood grasping the rail. The bus lumbered across the road. A lorry held it up for a moment and she shut her teeth to keep her heart in.

The top of the bus was open—it was a survival from
the days when people were simpler and did not mind
getting wet occasionally if they could gallop along in full
air. She lurched up the stairs, glancing back over her arm
at the shop. She saw it only for a moment before the bus
turned the corner. There was no one on the step, no
frenzied elderly lady transfixed in the doorway. Only
Shop for the Original Maids of Honour. Oh thank God
that's done with, she thought. Knocking against the seats
she reached the front of the bus and sat down.

The clasp of the bag hurt her arm. She pressed it less
firmly and it fell down against her breast. She had never
stolen before. Helped herself to things, yes—soap from
public lavatories, and umbrellas; in restaurants she would
take lumps of sugar and pennies left there for the waitress:
she chose a table that had not been cleared, and ran
her fingers under the plate. She was often tempted to
snatch things in the big shops, but she had been afraid.

The bus swung along a road between high walls. Looking over one she saw a garden, with young trees, a tea-
table, a girl in a white dress, and a laburnum tree in full
flame. It was like a fountain of yellow fire. She felt calmed
by it. When she was a child at home there was a laburnum
sprang over the wall from the next yard: it had made
her think of the cloven tongues as of fire that sat on the
apostles. She could see it now if she closed her eyes. She
closed them. When she opened them again the bus had
stopped near a public house and the laburnum was out
of sight.

There was no one near her on the top. She drew the
bag from her jacket and felt inside. The notes were there,
together with some loose silver and the other things
she had seen, and the return half of a ticket to St. James's
Park Underground. She wondered what the old lady was
doing now. If she had come out of the closet she might
still be looking short-sightedly about the room. I put it
down here. No, here.

A tremor passed through her body, as though a ripple
from the other woman's uneasiness had touched her. She

felt momently terrified. Hearing the conductor behind her, she pushed the bag under her blouse and sat upright. I needed the money, she thought; that talking old ape can do without her new stockings and what was all that? Oh my God, forget it. Nasty-minded, I call her, she wasn't English was she? you never know what they're thinking, I suppose she was a spy—what was she doing here during the War if she wasn't? I'm still sweating from it. If this bus hadn't been waiting I was done for certain, she'd have been screeching behind me Stop, stop—like a—parrot. They should of put all of them out, ran them on board a leaky boat in the North Sea and let them find their way home. I would of. There was a man wrote to the *Daily Mail* why not shoot a few Germans in England every time the Huns sink one of our ships, a good idea, they might of shot her. I've served her out taking the money from her.

She felt easier now that she had found an excuse for the thing done. Her feet hurt less—she pulled her skirt up quickly and loosed a suspender that was cutting the flesh—for what we have received, she murmured, with a bold smile. She daresn't tell anyone what she's lost—the dirty cat, she was keeping the money back. Perhaps it'll teach her to be honest.

The bus was crossing Barnes Common. Clouds gathering in the zenith sent flying columns to the four quarters. In the west, where the sun rallied his forces, the columns fell back, except for a few ragged companies that kept on into the heart of fire and now, cut off from their base, held out sullenly for the oncoming night. She looked up at these clouds and drew a vague comfort from the thought of darkness. In London, in streets lighted at night, there is nothing higher than the street-lamps or the tops of lighted buildings. A fish gliding under a bank from the brightness of wide water may feel as she felt. She thought with quiet relief that she now had money enough for three or four weeks. I shall sell the bag to Mr. Gapalous, she thought, and with that she drew it out again and examined the gold clasp. It was very thick and heavy.

She opened the bag. The lining was as worn as the leather and when she pulled at it she felt a card underneath. She found the rent in the silk and dragged the card out roughly. There was nothing on it but "With love. 1909", written there in a neat firm hand. Husband gave it to her, I suppose. For what, for a birthday? She tore the card into small pieces and dropped them over the side of the bus. For some reason she hated the other woman more after reading it. Why didn't she sell the rotten bag if she wanted money, she thought angrily: I've no patience with keeping their bally presents.

She examined the handkerchief for a name and slipped it with the glasses and the bottle of coffee mints into her pocket. Someone came into the seat behind her and she pushed the bag hurriedly out of sight. For a moment a chill of fear touched her, but nothing happened, no hand came round her shoulder. She drew a ragged breath.

The bus stopped in Piccadilly. She got down and hurried towards the Underground.

In the lavatory she got rid of the letter and transferred the money to her own bag. Then with the stolen bag over her heart she started out to call on Mr. Gapalous in Gerrard Street.

She strolled along in great happiness and content, in spite of her feet, which had begun to ache again as soon as she put her weight on them. The day's warmth had thickened into an almost palpable veil of dust and smells, the fumes from engines and the sour smell of clothes and bodies. A rich yellow light, the brightness gone from it, spilled everywhere, to the tops of the buildings. Piccadilly was a mere conduit for this light, which was like tepid water against the eyes after the day's glare.

As she turned into Gerrard Street she saw a woman signalling to her from the other street. Who's that it is? Her hand flew up to her mouth in the fraction of time before she recognised a friend. Oh. She doesn't mind the show she makes of herself, like a windmill, she thought angrily. But think now. I wanted her for something—what—oh the letter. I shan't need that. The promise to herself to begin a new life departed as vaguely as it had come. The other woman joined her on the pavement. "Where are you off, dearie?"

"I'm not," she said, with a loud laugh. The clasp of the bag, pressed by her arm, touched bare flesh. Get rid of her before I—"You're starting early," she said grudgingly. The younger woman's smooth face cruelly irritated her.

"First come first serve," Lily said. She looked at her friend's dress and feet. "Your shoes don't want dusting, do they? Where you been then?"

"Richmond Park," she said shortly.

Lily's smile broadened. "Whatever for? Oh keep it to yourself if you want to. I'm going into West's for a drink."

I might as well, she thought. Following Lily into the bar parlour she saw herself in a long glass, hat askew, skirt stained with green. I oughtn't to have told her that, she thought anxiously. Suppose they advertise for it—stolen, in Richmond. "Where d'you think? I've been in Brixton seeing a friend, and walked back."

"Did y'see Grace?" Lily asked.

"Who's Grace?"

"You remember her, don't you? She was that black-haired girl, married an Italian fellow and went to live, in Brixton. You were thick enough with her in the War, before she married."

"I remember," she said. But actually she remembered nothing except a rich laugh and the deep colour of an arm laid along a table. The woman herself had disappeared. It's too long ago, I wouldn't have known if she was dead; God, how old I'm getting, it's awful, awful.

"Here," Lily said, jerking her elbow. "Who's crossed you in love? You do look a sight nowadays. Why don't you buck up?" She stared with professional, not unkindly, interest. "You're letting yourself go. That fellow of yours has dropped off, hasn't he? Someone said as much."

"He's coming Saturday. I've had a letter from him."

"Smarten yourself up, then," Lily said. She finished her stout and sat twirling the empty tumbler. "I'll tell you

what I'll do. Come round to my room to-morrow and I'll
lend you a dress. You can give it back to me afterwards.
I can't bear the sight of you in that one, I tell you, it's
going so under the arms."

She raised her left arm slightly and peered at the
stain. That's right, it's going. I've had the wear out of it,
though—"How long've I had this skirt and jacket?" she
demanded.

"Years. Since the year dot," Lily giggled.

"I don't want your—lendings," she said, without any
feeling of bitterness. But her friend's next words vexed
her.

"Why be proud?" Lily said. "We've all got to come to
it. You're older than you were and it shows. What you've
got to do is to marry, before you're past it and before
you know. I mean t'say what else can you do, what's
going to come of you? Hold him off, you must, I know
what I'm talking about."

"Ho, you do, do you?" She stared angrily at the younger
woman. Her pride was sorely hurt by Lily's blunt speech
—she thought it mean and indecent. Without knowing
exactly why, she felt that she had been damaged by this
baring of her own fears. It was one thing to be feeling
old, and another to be spoken to about it like that. Through
this hole Lily had made, much would run out. "Ho, you
do!" she repeated, at a loss.

"Don't mind me, dearie," Lily said. "Have another
Guiness and see life. Here!" She called the potboy over
and paid him for what they had had. Her quick, pale
eyes saw through her friend as easily as they saw through
men. She had no illusions and no generosity—though she
would lend out her frocks and buy food and liquor for a
friend. She had no patience with softness or with calling
things by other than their right names, but she hated
waste, and that was why she was interfering now, to prevent what she saw was going to be an untidy end to a
life. She said good-bye, shook out her skirt, and went,
walking with a professional swagger.

Alone, the other looked sourly at her drink. She felt that she had been injured. She could not find a word for what had been done to her, but she was angry and dispirited. Her back ached, too, with all the walking she had done. She sat and brooded. She hated Lily and hoped that soon she would have a misfortune.

After that drink she ordered another. Her hatred of Lily changed into pity for herself. She was old, friendless. The more she thought about it the more piteous she seemed to herself. But it was not in the least like the horrible fear that came in spite of her and made her sweat and turn cold. This feeling sorry for herself soothed her in the same way that things she imagined before she slept soothed her. She began to think of a proud dignified woman, alone in the world, reserved for a mysterious fate. Perhaps she was fated to save the life of some wealthy man and marry him. Or she would discover a fabulously valuable painting. Would that picture in my room be worth anything? It was brown and very dirty and she had scarcely looked at it during the years she had lived in the room. She made up her mind to examine it that night.

Slowly the sting of Lily's words wore out. She finished her drink and remembered that she had been on her way to get rid of the bag. That, and the thought of the money, restored her confidence. She gave up resenting Lily: the fears that had made her sweat and groan in the quietness of the Park drew off—she thought for good. Before she went out she fingered her money.

Mr. Gapalous lived at the end of Gerrard Street, in the basement of a house he owned and let out in bedrooms. His wife served breakfasts to the tenants and advised them to get their other meals at Mr. Gapalous's brother's restaurant in Frith Street. They had one child.

When she knocked at the door of the house it was opened by this child, a boy with a large head and large pale eyes. He was studying his lessons for the morning and he never took his eyes off the book, reading it as he walked in front of her down the dark stairs to the basement. Still reading, he opened a door and spoke to his mother.

She was pleased to see that Mrs. Gapalous was alone. She had known her for a great many years—since the War—and she was as near fond of her as she would ever be of a woman. Yet it was not liking she felt for this particular woman, so much as strong likeness with her. When she felt cruelly down she would sometimes call on Mrs. Gapalous, and then it was as though she were talking to herself. Things came into her head and she said them, and a moment later she could not feel certain whether she had asked the question or answered it. It was not of the slightest importance and she was comfortable and happy in the underground room. Light came into it from a slab of glass over the narrow area; and it was as warm and as quiet as the grave. This Mrs. Gapalous was not easy like Lily, she never lent a dress, and if you were poor or in trouble she avoided helping you.

She knew that when she came to her last penny, Lily would help her once or twice (even if she then tired of it) but Mrs. Gapalous would let her starve in her room. Yet she disliked Lily and thought of Mrs. Gapalous as her only friend.

She went in and sat down.

Mrs. Gapalous was kneading bread. She was a small pale woman, brown-eyed, with hands that no amount of hard work cracked or spoiled. No one knew where she came from, except that it was somewhere in the Levant, but she and her husband who was a Greek had been living obscurely in England before the War. During the War they prospered by letting their rooms to officers on leave and it was in the company of a young officer that she had first met Mrs. Gapalous. They took to each other at sight. Later she discovered that her friend's husband had another trade beside his ostensible one of landlord.

It was in his second capacity that she had brought him the stolen bag. She asked after him and laid the bag on the table. Mrs. Gapalous dusted her hands and looked at it curiously. "You have had it some time?"

"A friend gave it to me in 1909," she said. "I haven't had any use of it lately. It's too shabby but the clasp is gold."

"He'll be in soon," Mrs. Gapalous answered.

She shaped the dough into cakes, drew a cross on each with her knife, and set them down at the side of the fire. Then she drew two chairs close to the window and sent her son into the back kitchen to finish his lessons.

When he had gone the room was quite still. A delicious yeasty smell came from the rising bread-cakes. What with that and her long day in the sun she felt pleasantly sleepy. Her friend's voice roused her.

"Have you been busy lately?"

She knew what that meant. Her friend had heard that she was alone and might need money—and she meant to defend herself against appeals. She felt slyly in her bag. The faintly oily surface of the new notes gave her fresh confidence. A fat lot you care what comes of me, I'd know better than to ask you for money if I was starving for it, she thought, but without resentment.

"I've had worries," she said easily. "George has been laid up, in what d'you call that place, Stockport—he's written and sent the money, though—bless'm."

Mrs. Gapalous did not believe it. She nodded.

"You can rely on some men as long as they want you," she said, crouching to turn a loaf that had swelled too quickly at one side. "After that God help you. An old woman's better dead, unless she has money. And then you may be sure that at least one person wants to see her out of the way."

As often happened when Mrs. Gapalous spoke to her she felt comforted by what were actually uneasy words. She might never grow old. There were women—if you could believe what you read—who scarcely changed. Looking at her friend carefully, she saw few marks of age on her. She must know of something. Excitement

made her squeeze Mrs. Gapalous in the thigh. A mistake
—the other woman did not like to be touched.

"Isn't there anything you can take—to keep you going?
You know what I mean."

"To keep young, you mean."

"Something of that."

"I know of nothing," Mrs. Gapalous said, after a pause.

"But I've read about it, I tell you. You can have something done." She rubbed the back of her leg, where it
ached. "I got a chemist to give me some stuff once—he
guaranteed that it would put breath back in a dead body.
I don't know it did much for me."

"Gapalous says you're young as long as you're moist,"
the other said quietly. "After that, after drying—"

"I don't see that helps much," she said, disappointed.
Her friend smiled. She was on her knees to her bread
again. The loaves that were risen enough she pushed in
the oven and moved the others nearer the warmth. "I've
often thought that women make a mistake in being so
what you might call separate," she said. "If I had my
way I'd have all the women registered—with what they
could do written opposite their names, and those that were
too old to do anything themselves might train the others.
Perhaps there's nothing in it, but it's an idea."

"What would you do yourself?" The smell of the fresh
bread made her feel hungry. She would have given a
shilling to break off and pop in her mouth the crust that
had run over one side of a loaf, like hard curdled cream
—kissing-crust, some people call it. She imagined the
savour of it in her cheeks.

"Teach 'em to make bread and enjoy their husbands,"
Mrs. Gapalous said quickly.

"Why, is there a living in it?" she laughed.

"Gapalous only eats my bread, and he says if he lives
to be a hundred he'll be satisfied with what I can do for
him. If you ask me, half the loving pairs that come here
wanting a room for their work don't know what to do
there with themselves when they get it. I could teach
them a few old things." She put the last loaf in the oven

and drew out the first. The kitchen was now almost dark, and as warm as pie. Mrs. Gapalous opened the cupboard where she kept her groceries, and other smells mingled with the smell of warm bread.

"What's that?"

"That's thyme," Mrs. Gapalous said.

"Will Gapalous be long?"

"I heard him shut the front door ten minutes ago. I daresay he's gone upstairs, seeing a tenant." She said something about the child and went out of the room, leaving her alone.

She looked for a moment eagerly at the still-warm crust. Her mouth dribbled at the thought of it, and if it had been any other place she would have torn it off and had it. But she was afraid of offending in this house. She rubbed her legs, groaned, and sank herself as low as possible in her chair.

A familiar feeling came over her. Though she could remember nothing that had been said she was as satisfied as if someone had made her a good offer. What she doesn't know isn't worth knowing, she thought, with a lewd smile. She felt at one with Mrs. Gapalous in the possession of a secret unspeakable experience, and warm and rested. I could live here. It was the only place, except her own room, in which she felt at home. It reminded her of her mother's kitchen, though the two rooms had nothing in common except an old-fashioned bread oven and a drying shelf, and both were dark.

Now another feeling took possession of her. She began to wish that she was in a man's arms, on the floor. She moved her heavy body gently to ease it. Her thoughts— if you can call that thinking which is only the twitching of old instincts—had sunk her so completely that she did not hear the door open. Mr. Gapalous touched her on the shoulder. She jumped.

"Gow, you did give me a start," she grumbled.

Mr. Gapalous was taller than his wife, but short for a man. He was fat. He had a round dark face, a greedy mouth, and eyes without much expression. She was a little afraid of him, and tried to cover it up with an impudent manner.

"You don't half take your time," she said. "I've run past m'self waiting for you."

Mr. Gapalous took the bag from the table and examined its clasp. There was a gas bracket over the mantel-shelf and he lit that and stood near it, turning the bag round in his hand. She wondered vaguely what the woman to whom it belonged would think, if she could see it being pulled about by those fingers. With love—1909.

"Where d'you get it?"

"A friend of mine gave me it," she babbled. "He was killed in the War, poor fellow, and the evening before he went we had supper at Scott's, oh I could tell you something about that. I kept it all this time in memory of him, I'm always like that, I can't bear to get rid of anything, photos, old furs, six or seven I have, and now with the gala novelties—"

"Ten shillings."

"It's worth a lot more than that," she exclaimed. "That thing's pure gold, I tell you."

"Take it anywhere you fancy."

He held it out to her. She wanted to tell him what a mean lousy bastard he was but kept it back. The very quietness of his manner frightened her. Something was in, yes in, the quietness, some rag of her fears flew out in it; she felt terror. It was nothing actual that she feared; she did not think that he would get her into trouble—or do anything to her. In a way, her fears had nothing to do with Mr. Gapalous. She felt that she was flat down, with her face in the dirt, and these safe people were treading on her. It was an animal terror—the fear without mitigation of thought that shows in the eyes of animals, no wordy veil comes between them and the menace of *things*—but the spasm tore her inwardly. It lasted in her only the fraction of a second and then the ordinary sense of resentment and annoyance flowed back. He had done her, mean wretch. She had expected it, and yet hoped for miracles. It's because I'm a woman and I haven't a man behind me protecting me, she thought bitterly. They're all alike, I'll say that for him, they all take advantage of us—how would they like it, I wonder, if we robbed them right and left—

"All right, give me the money," sne said.

She felt really dejected. She had almost persuaded herself that she was telling the truth about the bag. Mrs. Gapalous came back now, and the execution being over, she was very affable and less friendly. On rare occasions she would actually give her friend something, but today she had not been able to lay hands on anything so small and valueless that it was only fit to be given away. Instead she asked her to supper.

"Thanks, I'm meeting a friend."

"What a pity!" Mrs. Gapalous said, in a low voice. She called her son from the back room.

Still gabbling verses under his breath, he took her to the front door, opened it, and locked it again after her. Standing outside, she put the ten-shilling note in her bag with the others. Her spirits rose. She made up her mind to celebrate, never mind that she was alone. It was after half-past eight, time if she went at once, for a seat at the Holborn. The idea excited her. The pictures were well enough in their way but they hadn't the go of the real thing. She began to hurry.

Whether it was feeling tired, or her feet, or the asinine carryings-on of the two in front of her, but she scarcely enjoyed it until Ella Retford came on. Then it was like old times. She hummed under her breath, swaying, and helped to bawl the chorus. It's doing me good, she thought. She forgot the turns of the day. A rich, confused world opened in her and people she had forgotten tweaked her arm. "What ho!" she said to a young man in a serge suit and to another in khaki, several in khaki. Those were the times—why can't they have good times without their bloody wars, she thought quickly, killing all the good-looking happy young men, they ought to kill off old goats like Lloyd George. It's them do the dirty on the world. Who wants them? Coo, that's good, that is. How old is she, she must be getting on. My age. I daresay she's older. Well if I could kick like that I wouldn't be here.

The exhilaration lasted until she was in the street. She looked up and down, not willing to go home, to open the door feeling inside it with her foot for a letter—to admit then there was no letter. She strolled along Oxford Street, looking boldly into the faces of other strollers. I could do with a bite of something.

She turned into darker streets through which, looking at nothing, she hurried. It seemed that the older you got the more food and drink meant to you. She would miss anything for a good meal these days.

The Open All Night place was crowded. She saw a woman she knew slightly sitting at a table alone and went across to her. "What ho!"

"What ho!" the other said listlessly.

"Expecting anyone? Mind if I sit here?"

"Sit where you like."

A man at the next table was lifting a strip of red under-done beef to his mouth. Her own moistened pleasantly. An exhausted-looking waiter stopped at her table. Now what?

"Bring me a grilled chop and—lemme see—can I have a drink?"

"Up to midnight."

"A double whiskey, then, and look sharp will you? I don't want to choke." She glanced at the other woman. "You having something?"

"I've had all I want, thanks."

In trouble. She leaned back in her chair and gazed with easy smiles round the room. Her tongue quivered a little in anticipation. This morning I sat here, not here. She felt now different. Hours, an infinite period, lay between her and her morning self. The room itself had changed and where in the daylight it had seemed ex-posed, the street barely held off by frail walls, now it

was as separate as light and dark. Light in here and dark
outside, she murmured. She felt that she had made an
important remark. Whatever it was, she was happy. She
drank her whiskey.

"Can you lend me half-a-crown?"

She felt a shock of annoyance. "What's up?"

"I haven't a penny after I've paid for this. What am
I going to do?"

Her throat hardened. Give her any of my money? Not
likely. "I haven't anything to lend," she said shortly.

"Oh, all right," the other woman said. After a minute
or two she got up and trailed out of the room, knocking
against the tables.

She watched her at the desk laying down a coin. No
change. A half impulse started her in her chair but she
sat back again. I can't afford it. A sour rage against
the woman filled her. What right has she to ask for money,
I'm not made of money am I? Lend me half-a-crown.
Of all the cheek.

She ate with vexed haste. If she asks me again I'll
fettle her. Here of all places. Find your own half-crowns,
what d'you come here for if you haven't any money?
Let's see, she's the married one of them two. He went off
with some woman, that's right; he did and I don't blame
him. Well thank God it's not my business if she can't
look after herself.

A genial warmth flowed through her. She felt excited
and able to look after herself. An almost kindly contempt
for the woman who had gone out filled her. Sucking her
teeth, she felt mildly sorry that she had refused. A few
coppers would have been better than nothing. After all,
you never knew—it might break the luck. You gave a
penny to a beggar and somehow it did you good, like a
charm. God bless you, lady. He did.

An easy regret, the undertow of excitement, disturbed
her. It vanished quickly.

She glanced up, and saw the woman standing in the
doorway. She sent a vacant glance over the tables, spoke
to the uniformed doorman, who bent his head to listen,

and came in. The man's uninterested face turned towards her as she blundered across the room.

What's she coming back for? "Lost something?"

"I thought I'd left a parcel."

"You hadn't a parcel when I saw you," she answered, with contempt. The excuse was too obvious.

The woman sank to a chair. "What shall I do now?"

"What's the matter?" Uncertain curiosity moved her. She might hear something, a fat story worth carrying off to tell again.

"I told you. I haven't a penny," the woman said softly. "Not a God's penny. What can I do?"

"Where's Alfred, then?"

"Gone. Didn't you hear?"

"Something I heard."

"He went off a month Tuesday—with that Mrs. Boody she was making up to him the year we married. He said I could get something. Dear knows I've tried every way. You can't get anything how can you? The times are too hard."

"They are that," she said warmly.

The woman looked at her. "Can you lend me a shilling? I'll go in the river, I swear I will, if I spend another night like last."

"I might manage a few coppers," she was beginning. Not to break the luck. She felt, keeping it under the table, in her bag.

"I wanted a bed," the other woman exclaimed. Her face twitched. "I know you've enough." She looked meaningly at the plate with its brown meat-stains. "You'll be where I am one day and you'll know what it feels like."

She felt a chill, and quick rage flowing in over it. The coins slid from her fingers to the bottom of the bag. "You take yourself off," she said loudly. "Hop it. If you don't I'll complain to the management. See?"

With scarcely a change in her looks the woman got up. She stared for a moment, frowning vacantly, and passed her hand downwards over her mouth. The doorman was deep in talk: he broke off and asked her a question. Satisfied, he let her pass. She hesitated, turned blindly, went.

Of all the brazen ways. She ought to be ashamed of herself. Pestering people in cafés. Encourage her if I had. I'm thankful I didn't, I was on the point of going to, though. She must have thought I. First go off I. Well I didn't and that's enough.

When she stood up, the wall nearest her chair wavered and advanced. The woman at the cash desk looked at her, and she restrained an impulse to say something cutting and final.

In the street she walked quickly and unsteadily, humming under her breath, across Shaftesbury Avenue and turned into the narrower darkened streets that would lead her familiarly to Tottenham Court Road. She was walking along Carlisle Street when she noticed a young woman leaning against the wall of the second or third house. Her head hung forward and she was either ill or tipsy. After she had walked by she halted and turned about. She was still uneasy about spoiling her luck.

"Is there anything the matter?" she asked, speaking with a refined accent.

The young woman raised her head with awkward slowness. "I feel bad," she whispered. With a glance taking in the other woman's face and clothes, she added: "Help us home, will you? It's only three doors off, but I can't—" a spasm drew her mouth gaping sideways. She lowered her head.

"Come on then. Three doors is it?" She put her arm under the young woman's, gripping her with her free hand, and took short swaying steps. They reached the house. The young woman slid down on the step with a cry.

"Here. Buck up, you're there. Got your key?"

"In here."

She felt quickly in the pocket, drew a key from among coins, and fitted it in the door. It swung open, creaking, on darkness. The young woman staggered up and stag-

gered into the unlit passage. "Lights off at eleven," she
said, with a groaning laugh. "Did you ever? I can't get
up those stairs, though."

The two of them stood in the passage, their arms touching, in silence. They were both out of breath. The house,
too, was dead quiet. She listened and heard nothing,
neither up nor down. Standing beside the other woman
in the darkness she was oppressed against her sense by
a feeling that something important was taking place. She
was quite sober again.

She moved, trying to shift the weight on her feet.
"I can't stand here all night," she said in growing
impatience. "Where d'you want to be? Come on, I'll
help you up the stairs."

A sigh from the girl scarcely gave notice of her second
collapse. She sagged over on her knees, arms stretched
out over the floor. At the same moment a door at the far
end of the passage opened quietly, letting down a shaft
of yellow feeble light.

"Who's there?" a soft scraping voice asked—nervous, an
old man's voice, like a thin key turning loosely in the
lock. She moved towards it, exasperated by the turn
things were taking. Serve me right for interfering, she
thought. None of my damned business.

"Do you know who this is?" she snapped. "I brought
her in. My God, I am tired, too."

The old man came along the passage, peering. He held
the front of his shirt together with one hand, the other
scratched the back of his neck absently, to reassure himself. He looked down at the young woman.

"Yes," he said, with a quick half-laugh, "I know her. She
lives upstairs. I don't know her name, though."

The girl opened her eyes and said: "Hullo, Uncle," in
a friendly voice.

"Hullo," Uncle said shyly.

What's all this? Time to finish off. Sleep. I must, I
need. She yawned noisily. "What's the matter with you?"
she demanded. "I can't stop here all night. Come on now

for pity's sake until I can get off home. I didn't bargain for this."

The grip of the young woman's hands on her arm was again an extraordinary sensation. They dragged her down. She was so tired and vexed that she did not try to save her anything, pulling her from stair to stair until they reached the room. Here she tumbled her across the bed and turned on the light. As she did so she saw that the girl was smiling. It gave her a very unpleasant turn. She helped her to straighten herself on the bed, drawing off her shoes, high-heeled, thin-soled, the doubles of her own, and pulling the hat with more care but not with much over the cropped head.

Uncle waited to be given the money before he went out to fetch a doctor. He took it for certain that the doctor would decline to turn out at this time of night without the money. She obeyed the girl's pointing finger and pulling her skirt up sought and found the folded notes, a one and a ten, inside her stocking. She gave the old man the ten.

Left alone with the young woman she sat down and stretched her feet out, toes pointing upwards—that was to draw the blood away from them. The room was like enough her own to answer any questions she might have asked if the girl on the bed had been in a state to talk. As it was she lay there in silence, and when the old man's footsteps died away in the street the silence covered everywhere.

She had made up her mind to push off before the doctor came—if he came, they didn't always—but once down she felt the full weight of her body. She was dragged, fastened by her hips, into the chair. She wondered for a moment about spending the night there, but immediately the other thought jumped into her mind. He might have written, the letter might at this moment be lying half underneath the rug, pushed under the door. Once she had found a letter weeks after it came—it had slid well beneath the rug and it was when she lifted the rug to find something else that she saw the letter, a white

square webbed with dust. The white square blotted out
everything in her mind. She saw it flat, then tilted, then
sliding jerkily from sight. Her mind was blank for a
moment. The edge of a square white envelope showed
again at one side, under a door.

She roused herself to look at the young woman.

Her eyes and her mouth were both partly opened.
Leaning forward, she laid a hand on her hand. Not dead.

In the same instant as she thought first that the young
woman had snuffed out and then that she had only fainted
again she remembered the pound note folded in her stocking. It would be the simplest job in the world to lift
back the skirt and take the note. She could be gone
when the others came. A trickle of excitement started in
her. She moved her arm.

It was more the thought of tampering with unknown
and blindly-striking powers than anything. Money off a
dying woman might bring bad luck. She drew her hand
back, uneasy in the silence.

Disgust and disappointment struggled coldly in her.
She half stood up, to go, then with a stifled "Ouch!" she
slumped back in the chair. Oh for goodness sake what
possessed me to walk far in these shoes. She felt gingerly
between the back of the shoe and her ankle. I thought as
much. Where the skin had broken a patch of stocking
the size of a shilling stuck to it. A nice time I shall have
getting that off me, she thought. She passed her finger
gently round the edge.

Confused images moved behind her eyes, the green
curve of a hill, clouds, a hand holding a cup, the flash
from plates tilted to the window of a café. She felt over-
full of sun and air.

The electric light dimmed, glowed red for a moment,
and went out, leaving her in blackness. She felt first in
her bag, then remembering the loose money in the pocket
of the young woman's coat she groped for it, felt the pocket
and the coins and shook them out. Her hand recoiled in
the darkness from the other hand. She had seen the slot
meter near the door when they came in. Feeling her way

to the door she opened it and stood straining her eyes to make out the top of the stairs. In the silence she heard a bed creak in the room across the landing as the sleeper moved in it. The darkness rose in a thick shaft, like a jet of dark water, through the house from the lowest floor. On each side of the deepest shadow, spreading from it, a diffuse greyness clung to walls and doors. She listened.

The thought of going became a clear imperative. What use to wait here for the doctor and all that trouble? George's letter slid, tilted over, vanished. She transferred the coins in her hand to her jacket pocket and took a heavy-soft step forward. In the room behind her the girl made one short sound. A word?

It was not a loud sound, it was more like a sigh. Only in the darkness it sounded heavy and terrified. As if she now knew that she had been left. She turned and looked back into the room. The silence and the darkness were both absolute.

Gliding her foot from stair to stair, she reached the passage. Ought I to have shut her door? Too late now. She pulled the front door quickly shut behind her and walked, limping, along the street. Half across Soho Square she paused and looked back. Two men were turning into the street at the farther end. The doctor? no. They walked past the house, coming directly towards her.

She hurried, forgetting weariness. In Tottenham Court Road she remembered the before-breakfast look of the street. It was now empty, except for a policeman trying the shop doors, and a few night-stragglers. A car, moving quickly, had the polished road to itself. She trudged on, not strutted—drawing with her hours of memories freshly re-lived, and new events fast becoming memories, dead shells sunk in the sand.

She was purposely not thinking of the young woman. An obscure fear clung to the whole incident, the fear of having offended something or someone by reason of a few coins taken from the young woman's pocket. Under its skin her mind was busy with the impalpable connections joining her life to the girl's. Nothing of this showed, except in words and phrases that broke off and floated to the surface. You too. Blindly in darkness. Not yet, not here. Her mind wandered, turned by a deep current. She was walking in this street with Ernst. Shadows without colour or features looked at them in passing; Ernst himself was only a smudged ghost, his face hardly to be made out at this distance. She had expected nothing unless to end her life in that café or that hotel. An old woman I should have been, old Mrs. Groener, she thought, half laughing in half derision. It was the most extraordinary thing that could have happened.

But nothing joins, she thought confusedly, nothing meets any other thing. God knows I never *done* anything, knowing it. It's nature, I suppose. You'd wonder any living soul could be such a soft fool. I'm sure I laugh when I think of myself leaving home that time and then that nasty place in Euston Road I don't want to think about that and then Ernst and then the War we don't want to lose you—oh Great strike above, there's no end to it or only one. But there's life in the old dog yet. I'm not coming to an end yet, thank you.

I could of taken that money from her stocking as easy as winking, she thought swiftly. I wouldn't do a thing like that, it wouldn't be right.

The house was as quiet as that other. Climbing the stairs, the worn canvas catching her heels, it was like every other night.

When she lit the gas the letter was the first thing she saw, thrown a little to one side, so that she had missed it with her foot as she stepped in. Her heart seemed to stop and her blood rushed through her body. She bent down with difficulty. Laying the letter on the bed, un-opened, she began to get herself ready for bed. This was a shorter ritual than the morning's. Sighing with relief she tossed each garment across the chair and reached over for her nightgown. The loosening and falling of her body gave her an exquisite feeling of release. She

stood with her legs apart to enjoy the new coolness. Her
stained rumpled stockings were flung down with other
unwashed garments in a corner between the wall and the
cupboard.

The hand-basin was half full of dirty water. She padded
across the landing with it to the sink, but that was to
save herself trouble in the morning. She did not wash.

All this time she was thinking about the letter. She had
put off opening it because of some instinct urging her to
prolong uncertainty to the last possible moment. Standing
to the mirror to spread cream over her face she thought:
I don't look at all excited. I wish I knew without looking
what was in it. If it's to say he's coming on Saturday I
shan't half laugh. It must be that. If he wasn't coming
why write? I'll be off-hand at first, then joking with him:
where've you been? in jail? Or would I better seem different
somehow, start when he speaks to me, as if I had something on my mind? He'll have to coax it out of me.

If it's to say he's done with me. For a second she felt
horribly ill, but her fingers continued to rub in the cream
without a pause.

She settled herself in bed and took up the white envelope. Fingermarks on it. Looking inside she drew out a
pound note, then quickly the letter. It was very short.
It said that for private reasons (that was a favourite saying
with him) he couldn't see her again. He enclosed a pound
and would be sending the same every Friday, until she
could get settled with something. No claim on him to do
it, of course. Just generosity and. Take this in the spirit.
Hoped she. With all friendly feelings, George H.

It was the end. She knew that at once. He might send
once more but that would finish it. A frightful spasm of
rage shook her. "Generosity," she said, out loud.

She pushed note and letter under the pillow and lay
down. Her body found and settled into last night's hollow.
She had left the gas burning, and with a reluctant effort
she got up, trailed across the room to the bracket and
returned to the bed. In the darkness she felt herself pressed

heavily by the bedclothes and threw part off. She had a
strange feeling, as though she were whirling through blackness. That was because she was tired. She closed her eyes
and opened them again at once. But on nothing—the street-
lamp had gone off some minutes since and there was now
no light of any kind in the room. She sighed deeply.

Because I can't give up, she thought. I've got to live,
haven't I? Tell me that you with your generosity and
your no claims. I might have known how it was without
all this time waiting and wondering. Oh God it's over and
this time last year we were where, in Ramsgate, I shan't
ever forget it, if I live to be a hundred, the heat and the
dust and the sea smooth like milk, and then afterwards,
no I shan't forget. All he said then to me and his look.
It was like the canal at Stavelly when we lay out there,
that other, that boy he was: I was young too then I didn't
know, but I remember the water shining and sucking in
the darkness and that one lovely light, yes lovely. I ought
to have stopped up there instead of rushing off to London
like I did. Like a young fool.

She gave a passing thought to her mother, whom she
had not seen since that day. A letter came for her to the
Dorset (to inform her shortly and brutally that if she
wanted to see her mother alive etc), but she had left the
place tnen and it was a month before the waiter who knew
where she was with Ernst brought it. Then it was too late.
Poor mother! She was hard, though. She scalded her arm
that night and never called out or woke anyone. I'm not
like that. But I'm not done for yet. I'm alive still.

Half asleep she entered a colourless world peopled only
by the dead, those who had died in the flesh and been
forgotten and those who like Ernst were neither alive nor
dead. She was aware now of two different scenes, in both
of which and in the same moment she lived. It did not
occur to her that there was anything strange in being at
the same time in the dark passage of her mother's house
and in a crowded street. The two existed simultaneously
in her mind. At last she was deeply asleep, her tired uneasy
mind loosed to all the several circles of being.

She lies there in the darkness, her mind a meeting-place for every kind of event. A multitude of the quick and the dead exist in it. It is exquisitely poised to make her laugh, cry, speak, exult, suffer, and dream. Exactly as the separate parts of her body are held fast in equilibrium until an instant in a not unguessable future. Turning on her back, she makes a loud strangled noise as she breathes. The pulse in her arm lying on the dirty sheet is one of the stages of a mystery. Look once more and you can see how beautiful she is.

Poor woman, let her sleep.

THE END

The first Virago Modern Classic was published in London in 1978, launching a list dedicated to the celebration of women writers and to the rediscovery and reprinting of their works. While the series is called "Modern Classics," it is not true that these works of fiction are universally and equally considered "great," although that is often the case. Published with new critical and biographical introductions, books appear in the series for different reasons: sometimes for their importance in literary history; sometimes because they illuminate particular aspects of women's lives, both personal and public. They may be classics of comedy or storytelling; their interest can be historical, feminist, political, or literary. In any case, in their variety and richness they promise to confuse forever the question of what women's fiction is about, while at the same time affirming a true female tradition in literature.

Initially, the Virago Modern Classics concentrated on English novels and short stories published in the early decades of the century. As the series has grown, it has broadened to include works of fiction from different centuries and from different countries, cultures, and literary traditions; there are books written by black women, by Catholic and Jewish women, by women of almost every English-speaking country, and there are several relevant novels by men.

Nearly 200 Virago Modern Classics will have been published in England by the end of 1985. During that same year, Penguin Books began to publish Virago Modern Classics in the United States, with the expectation of having some forty titles from the series available by the end of 1986. Some of the earlier books in the series were published in the United States by The Dial Press.